GREAT LIVES

Nature and the Environment

Nature and the Environment

GREAT LIVES

*Doris Faber
and Harold Faber*

Charles Scribner's Sons · New York
Collier Macmillan Canada · Toronto
Maxwell Macmillan International Publishing Group
New York · Oxford · Singapore · Sydney

Charles Scribner's Sons Books for Young Readers
Macmillan Publishing Company • 866 Third Avenue, New York, NY 10022

Collier Macmillan Canada, Inc.
1200 Eglinton Avenue East, Suite 200, Don Mills, Ontario M3C 3N1

First edition   1 2 3 4 5 6 7 8 9 10
Printed in the United States of America
Cover illustration copyright © 1991 by Stephen Marchesi. All rights reserved.

Library of Congress Cataloging-in-Publication Data
Faber, Doris, date
   Nature and the environment / Doris Faber and Harold Faber.
   —1st ed.   p.   cm.—(Great lives)
(Charles Scribner's Sons books for young readers)
   Includes bibliographical references (p.   ) and index.
   Summary: Examines the life stories of twenty-six individuals from around the world
who made notable contributions as naturalists, conservationists, or environmentalists.
   ISBN 0-684-19047-8
1. Naturalists—Biography—Juvenile literature.
2. Conservationists—Biography—Juvenile literature.
3. Environmentalists—Biography—Juvenile literature.
4. Nature conservation—Juvenile literature.   [1. Naturalists.
2. Conservationists.   3. Environmentalists.]
I. Faber, Harold.   II. Title.   III. Series.   IV. Series: Great lives (Charles Scribner's Sons)
QH26.F33 1991 508'.092'2—dc20 [B] [920] 90-8847 CIP AC

Contents

Foreword

First, there were naturalists. Back when science was much less specialized than it is today, anybody who studied plants and animals was called a naturalist. Also, in that simpler era, no one imagined that people could ever seriously interfere with the world of nature.

Then—toward the end of the 1800s—lovers of the outdoors began banding together under a new banner. Worried because the march of progress threatened to destroy some of America's most spectacular wilderness areas and to kill off many species of wildlife, they demanded new laws aimed at conserving the country's natural resources. They were labeled conservationists.

Not until the 1960s did the word "environment" come into common usage. During that decade, warnings about air and water pollution stirred widespread alarm. All over the world, concerned citizens discussed the possibility that advanced technology might upset the entire balance of nature. As a result, environmental protection agencies sprang up everywhere, led by men and women identified as environmentalists.

Naturalists, conservationists, and environmentalists—these are the heroes of this book. Each chapter relates the life story of an individual who made notable contributions within a very broad field. How, though, did we select the twenty-six whose names are listed in our table of contents?

Taking our cue from the balance of nature, we have tried to achieve a balance among several different factors.

Rather than choosing only Americans as the subjects of our chapters, we wanted an international roster because people all around the earth should be included in this kind of book. Sadly, though, we were not able to find information about outstanding figures from Africa or Asia, South America or Australia. Since the cultural history of the United States has been so closely allied with that of England, most of our overseas contingent turned out to be English, with just a sprinkling from the rest of Europe.

Still, achievement rather than national origin was our main consideration. Apart from a giant like England's Charles Darwin, however, world-shaking achievers should not be looked for in the general area of the natural sciences. Yet there are hundreds of naturalists, conservationists, and environmentalists whose somewhat lesser contributions might be deemed worthy of remembrance—if we were compiling a whole encyclopedia.

Limited by the amount of space we had available, we aimed instead for a representative sampling over the past two centuries. Besides familiar names like Audubon and Thoreau, readers of this book will find less familiar ones, like Bailey and Olmsted. But all of our subjects had a significant impact in their own day, despite the fact that some of them have since been almost forgotten.

With the recent blossoming of environmental awareness, though, the careers of even those less celebrated figures have gained a new pertinence. So we hope that readers will relish making their acquaintance—along with that of other more familiar nature lovers—in the pages that follow.

D. F. and H. F.

Louis Agassiz

1807–1873   Swiss-American professor of natural history and explorer

Louis Agassiz (pronounced AG-a-see) led two lives. In the first, he emerged from a rural area of Europe to become a famous naturalist, known for his pioneering work on fish. Then, at the age of thirty-nine, he went to the United States and became even more eminent as a scientist and teacher.

His life in science began in the mountain village of Môtier-en-Vuly—in the French-speaking section of Switzerland—where he was born on May 28, 1807. His parents were Rodolphe Agassiz, a Protestant minister, and Rose Mayor Agassiz, the daughter of a physician. Although he was given the imposing name of Jean Louis Rodolphe Agassiz, everybody called him Louis.

From his earliest boyhood, Louis was fascinated by fish. Around the age of

seven, he started going fishing with his younger brother, Auguste, and Louis soon discovered that he had an unusual talent. If he stood very still at the water's edge, he was able to catch fish just by suddenly reaching out with his bare hands—an all but impossible feat for most people.

Louis captured so many fish from nearby lakes and streams that he converted a stone catch basin behind his home into a miniature aquarium. Also, he collected a variety of other creatures and made his own room into what he described as his "little menagerie." Along with birds, field mice, rabbits, and guinea pigs, he kept caterpillars, too, patiently waiting for them to turn into butterflies.

Until he was ten, Louis received lessons at home from his parents. Then he was sent to a boarding school in the village of Bienne, about twenty miles away, where he learned several new languages—German, Italian, Latin, and some Greek—besides his native French. A good student, he particularly liked the subject of geography.

Most of all, though, Louis enjoyed studying nature rather than books. Looking back many years later, he would recall: "I spent most of the time I could spare . . . in hunting the neighboring woods and meadows for birds, insects, and land and fresh water shells."

From the age of eleven onward, Louis wrote detailed accounts of his natural history observations in a series of notebooks. These descriptions were carefully divided into separate categories, showing an early tendency toward orderly classification of facts. When he was fifteen, he had already made up his mind that he would not go into business with an uncle, as his parents intended.

"I wish to advance in the sciences," Louis wrote in his notebook. He had his future all mapped out: He would attend one of Germany's leading universities, take further training in Paris, and then—by the time he was twenty-five—he would begin to make his own mark as a scientific writer.

It was a most ambitious program, but Agassiz, even at fifteen, possessed some basic requirements for the career he had outlined. Besides his curiosity about nature, he knew the languages that scientists of his day used to communicate with each other, and he also had an intense desire to succeed.

With the help of a teacher, Agassiz persuaded his parents to give him at least two more years of school—in the nearby city of Lausanne. There, he found a natural history museum displaying many plants and animals he had never heard of before. By the end of those two years, even his parents were ready to admit that a career as a businessman was out of the question for him.

But how would he ever support himself? An uncle who was a doctor recommended that Louis be permitted to study medicine, the profession closest to his interests. So it happened that, at the age of seventeen, Agassiz entered the university in the Swiss city of Zurich as a medical student.

His less ambitious brother Auguste accompanied him. Auguste cheerfully helped Louis turn their boarding-house room into a small zoo, with about forty birds flying about or roosting on the branches of a pine tree they managed to set up there. Still, Louis did not neglect his studies. His motto, he liked to say, was "first at work and first at play."

Sturdy and handsome, Louis had chestnut-colored hair that reached to his shoulders, as was the custom among students then. At Zurich, he gained the reputation of being a good companion who loved to eat well and attend beer-drinking parties. But after two years there, he seized an opportunity to move to a more highly regarded learning center.

When his brother Auguste went home to begin a business career, Louis convinced his parents to let him pursue his medical studies in Germany. Almost immediately on arriving at the outstanding university in Heidelberg, the nineteen-year-old Agassiz made a new friend—a German student named Alexander Braun.

Braun wrote to his parents describing Agassiz as "a young naturalist who has appeared like a rare comet on the Heidelberg horizon." He explained that, although the Swiss newcomer was preparing to be a doctor, he already was familiar with almost every known animal, "recognizes the birds from far off by their sound, and can give a name to every fish in the water."

Since Braun had similarly broad scientific interests, he and Agassiz decided to room together and work together, too. A third student, Karl Schimper,

soon joined them. This trio held long discussions at night about their daily lectures, they went on frequent field trips, and they read many specialized books.

Even so, Agassiz showed, as he had back in Zurich, that he could always find time for less scholarly occupations. When his fellow students from Switzerland elected him president of the Swiss club at the university, which sponsored regular fencing matches, he became such an accomplished fencer that a German expert challenged him to a duel. Agassiz won this match, then also defeated three other German challengers.

But within a few months Braun made a suggestion that changed the trio's lives. He proposed that all three roommates should transfer to the new university in the German city of Munich—where the eminent Professor Ignaz von Döllinger had consented to accept serious students of natural history.

How, though, could Agassiz secure his parents' consent? Once more, he used his powers of persuasion. He assured them that, after only two years at Munich, he could get his medical degree and then return home to start a medical practice.

In Munich, Agassiz took clinical instruction at the hospital every morning from seven to nine, but he devoted the rest of the day to his natural history studies. He, Braun, and Schimper had connecting rooms in Professor Döllinger's home, using them jointly as the group's apartment. They stacked books on the chairs and floor, they drew diagrams on the white-painted walls, and Agassiz continued his habit of collecting. Fish, animals, birds, shells, and plants filled the rooms.

The three students gave each other nicknames, two of them in the Latin language of science. Braun became Molluscus, the word for the family of creatures commonly known as shellfish, because of his interest in shells. Schimper, who concentrated on studying plants, was simply called Rhubarb. However, Agassiz had to endure being referred to as Cyprinus—the Latin term for carp, a fish noted for its rapid growth and great appetite.

At the university in Munich, Agassiz made another friend, an artist. Joseph Dinkel soon was spending four or five hours almost every day making accurate paintings of freshwater fish, an essential service for a naturalist in those days before photography.

Dinkel later described Agassiz as an exceptional young man. "He never lost his temper, though often under great trial," the painter wrote. "He remained self-possessed and did everything calmly, having a friendly smile for those who were in need. He was at that time scarcely twenty years old, and was al-

ready the most prominent among the students at Munich."

Agassiz himself, in a letter to his father, defined his own high ambition: "I wish it may be said of Louis Agassiz that he was the first naturalist of his time, a good citizen, and a good son, beloved of those who knew him." Furthermore, he expected to achieve his goal by means of his favorite subject—fish. Already he had started to work on a complete history of the freshwater fish of Central Europe.

But another project soon took precedence. One of the university's professors who had made a scientific expedition to Brazil asked Agassiz to put together a book describing the fish discovered there. Although the professor expected this task to take about four years, Agassiz worked with such diligence that he completed it much more quickly.

In May of 1829, just before Agassiz turned twenty-two, the book *Fishes of Brazil* appeared in print. Not only was his name listed as one of the authors, but he was also described as Dr. Louis Agassiz. The professor had thought that the title would bring more distinction to the book, so Agassiz had hurried to take his examinations for the degree of Doctor of Philosophy and passed immediately.

The following year Agassiz also received his medical degree, fulfilling the aim of his parents. Nevertheless, fish studies remained his major interest. Instead of returning to Switzerland to set up a medical practice, he continued working on European fish and fish fossils.

Agassiz was assisted by Cecile Braun, a skilled artist and the younger sister of his first German friend. As she made one drawing after another under his direction, warm personal feelings developed. Soon Louis and Cecile reached an understanding that they would marry as soon as he could earn a living.

First, though, Agassiz carried out his long-cherished plan of traveling to Paris, at that time the world center of natural history studies. When he arrived in the French capital, he requested an interview with Baron Georges Cuvier. This nobleman, who was an internationally known scientist, greeted his twenty-four-year-old visitor kindly.

When Agassiz showed Cuvier his manuscript and drawings of fossil fish, Cuvier seemed very favorably impressed. He, too, had been working on fossil fish. As a result of this meeting, Agassiz was given permission to work with the great collection of fossils at the French Museum of Natural History—and Cuvier invited him to dine frequently at his home.

One evening Cuvier asked his secretary to bring in a portfolio of drawings that he had made in the British Museum. Spreading them out on a table, Cuvier turned to his new young friend. As Agassiz related in a letter home:

"He said he had seen with satisfaction the manner in which I treated this subject; that I had indeed anticipated him, since he had intended at some future time to do the same thing; but that since I had given it so much attention, and had done my work so well, he had decided to renounce the project and to place at my disposition all the materials he had collected and all the preliminary notes he had taken."

It was a stunning display of confidence in the young man. Agassiz responded by working sometimes as much as fifteen hours a day on the fossil fish and other natural history projects. He made the acquaintance of Alexander von Humboldt, the famous German scientist who was in Paris then, and went to lectures with him. But the nagging problem of how to make a living remained.

The solution came in a letter from his mother. She wrote that the Swiss town of Neuchâtel would soon establish a new college and museum of natural history. What could be a more suitable site for his own collection of natural history objects? In addition, the town offered him the position of professor of natural history—and he accepted.

So Agassiz, in 1832, at the age of

twenty-five, returned to Switzerland. With two university degrees, a book already published, and another in preparation, he embarked on his career as a writer, researcher, and teacher, just as he had hopefully planned ten years earlier.

During his fifteen years at Neuchâtel, Agassiz married his Cecile, and they had three children. He lectured to students, he received prizes from scientific societies in several countries, and he was invited to deliver addresses at scientific gatherings in London and Paris. His books on fossil fish were described by one critic as "the work of a great master."

His home became his laboratory. He often invited young scientists to stay for weeks at a time. Their talk and the smoke from their pipes filled the house, sometimes to the distress of Mrs. Agassiz.

In 1838, he founded a lithographic printing establishment in Neuchâtel because he was not satisfied with the work done elsewhere. It proved to be a mistake. Agassiz was a poor money manager, and his expenses turned out to be greater than he had expected. The business collapsed.

Always enthusiastic, Agassiz took up a new venture—the study of glaciers amid the peaks and valleys of the Alps that surrounded his home. With his scientific collaborator Edouard Desor and the artist Joseph Dinkel, he explored the mountains. Everywhere he went he found grooved and polished rocks, often lying below the glaciers' edges, and erratic blocks of stone that had obviously been transported far from their place of origin.

In an address before the Swiss Society of Natural History, Agassiz announced his theory that during a prehistoric era ice had covered the world from the North Pole south to the Mediterranean Sea. He used the phrase "Ice Age" to describe this period, and it gradually became accepted by other scientists and the general public.

His epic work *Studies on Glaciers* came out in 1840. The book widely identified Agassiz in the public mind with the high adventure of scaling Alpine peaks to make personal observations, sometimes at great risk. But it also had great scientific importance— providing a key to understanding patterns of the geographic distribution of animal and plant life, as well as the structure of lakes, valleys, and rock formations.

Famous as he had become, though, Agassiz was a poor man. He had been made almost penniless by his imprudent venture into publishing. His rescue came through his friend Humboldt, who convinced the king of Prussia to offer Agassiz a grant to visit the United States.

And so, in 1846, Agassiz left his wife and three children and his native Switzerland. After stops in Paris and London, he arrived in Boston late the same year—and became an instant celebrity. Five thousand people turned out to hear his first lecture there.

Speaking with a continental accent, Agassiz charmed his audience with references to "God's leetle joke" in creating odd-looking crabs. Always the scientist, however, he gave careful descriptions of his research on fossil fish and his theories on glaciers. Not only did he establish himself firmly as one of the world's leading scientists, but he also raised money by more lectures to pay off some of his debts in Neuchâtel.

American scientists received Agassiz with open arms. Botanist Asa Gray thought he was a "capital fellow." Chemist Benjamin Silliman, Jr., said that "he is full of knowledge on all subjects of science and imparts it in the most graceful and modest manner."

What's more, Harvard University, which had recently received a gift of $50,000 for the purpose of establishing a school of science, offered Agassiz the position of professor of zoology and botany. He accepted.

So the winter of 1847–1848 became a most happy period in his life. Agassiz lectured in New York, where the *Tribune* printed his remarks in full, something very unusual for a scientific report. He lectured in Charleston, South Carolina, and in Boston again.

Agassiz even organized a geological museum at Harvard. First, he collected American specimens and stored them in an unused bathhouse along the Charles River. Then he rented a house on Oxford Street, which became a combination museum, aquarium, and botanic garden. Among his exhibits were a tame bear from Maine, snakes from Florida, fishes from Lake Superior, and snapping turtles sent to him by the American naturalist Henry David Thoreau.

That summer Agassiz, accompanied by some Harvard students, explored the Lake Superior region to collect freshwater fish for shipment back to Massachusetts. When he returned, he attended the first annual meeting of the American Association for the Advancement of Science in Philadelphia and delivered twelve separate addresses about his findings involving rocks, fish, and plants.

But Agassiz's triumphant success in America was marred by the tragic news that his wife Cecile had died in Switzerland. Soon his three children—Alexander, Pauline, and Ida, ranging in age from fourteen down to nine—arrived to make their home with him. Two years later, in 1850, Agassiz married Elizabeth Cabot Cary, an extremely bright and capable young woman related to several of Boston's leading families.

The new Mrs. Agassiz, who was usually called Lizzie, soon discovered the perils of being the wife of a naturalist. One day as she rummaged in her closet for a pair of shoes, she caught sight of a snake among them.

"I screamed in horror to Agassiz, who was still asleep," Lizzie wrote to her sister. Waking up, he said, "Oh yes, I brought several home last night—probably they escaped." When all the snakes were finally captured, Lizzie added, "He had the audacity to call upon me to admire their beauty."

Still, Lizzie Agassiz managed to bring order to her husband's household while also giving him much assistance in his work. During the golden years of his second marriage, students flocked to his courses, he continued his lectures in many parts of the country, conducted research, collected fish from all over the United States, and began a ten-volume natural history of his adopted land.

Agassiz also enjoyed himself in the company of intellectual men and women, just as he had in Europe. He became a leading member of Boston's Saturday Club, along with Henry Wadsworth Longfellow, James Russell Lowell, and Ralph Waldo Emerson. At one of its meetings, Agassiz told this anecdote:

"Many years ago, when I was a young man, I was introduced to an estimable lady in Paris, who said to me she wondered how a man of sense could spend his days in dissecting a fish. I replied, 'Madam, if I could live by a brook which had plenty of gudgeons, I should ask nothing better than to spend my life there.'"

That attitude reflected Agassiz's lack of concern about money. Once more he went into debt because of the costs of maintaining his home and laboratories and paying assistants from his own pocket.

To ease the financial burden, Lizzie Agassiz had the idea of starting a girls' school in the upper floors of their house. It opened in 1855 and proved to be so popular with the young women of Boston and Cambridge that Mrs. Agassiz soon was contributing as much as her husband to the family finances. (She later became one of the founders and the first president of Radcliffe College.)

Yet one of Agassiz's early ambitions still remained to be achieved. Ever since his student days he had wanted to be the director of a great museum of natural history. In 1858, he was offered the directorship of the Jardin des

Louis Agassiz stands by a blackboard covered with his chalk drawings, 1872. *The Library of Congress.*

Louis Agassiz's wife, Elizabeth Cabot Cary Agassiz, sits reading. *Schlesinger Library, Radcliffe College.*

Plantes in Paris, one of the world's leading botanical gardens. But Agassiz decided that he would remain in America and build an even greater museum in his adopted country.

It took time to accomplish this goal. First came a bequest of $50,000 from Francis Calley Gray, a pioneer shoe manufacturer in nearby Lynn, Massachusetts. Then the state legislature appropriated $100,000, and other donors contributed an additional $70,000 be-

cause of Agassiz's own money-raising efforts. Harvard donated a tract of land—and the Museum of Comparative Zoology came into being in 1859, with Agassiz as its director as well as its chief scientist.

That summer Agassiz returned to Europe for the first time since he had left, accompanied by his wife. In Paris, he received one of the French government's highest awards, the Cross of the Legion of Honor. In London, his reception was almost royal. In Switzerland, he had a joyous reunion with his mother. He was also able to buy some valuable collections of fossils for his new museum.

Back in Cambridge, Agassiz reported that 91,000 new specimens had been added to the museum. This was "a grand result," he said, noting that a century earlier when Linnaeus had published his historic natural history "the whole number of animals known to him from all over the world did not amount to 8,000."

Agassiz supervised a group of graduate students in identifying, labeling, and arranging the material. Sometimes he would help them with a cigar clenched in his teeth, a fish held out in each hand. One student recalled later: "In my room my master would become divinely young again . . . he would lie on the sofa, drink what I had

An illustration plate of young turtles from Louis Agassiz's *Contributions to the Natural History of the United States. Museum of Comparative Zoology, Harvard University.*

to offer, take a pipe and return in mind to his student days or to his plans for work."

But things were not so peaceful in the scientific world of 1859, the year that Charles Darwin published his new theory of the origin of species based on natural selection. Agassiz rejected the Darwin theory. He believed that species had been created by divine will and that there was no evidence to demonstrate the transformation of one species into another.

According to Agassiz, animals and plants had been created wherever they were found, and there had been several successive creations. For him, the geographic distribution of plants and animals was the result of God's action, not of natural forces.

The dispute about Darwin's theory divided scientists into two camps. Agassiz defended traditional religious views despite the growing sentiment among his colleagues in favor of Darwin. So Agassiz, who had been lionized as a leader of science ever since coming to America, found himself increasingly being criticized by other scientists and even by many of his own students.

"I am falling behind in my influence among scientific men," he wrote to a friend. His health began to fail, too. But his spirits were revived in 1865 when a Boston businessman offered to finance an expedition to Brazil to be led by Agassiz. He eagerly accepted and spent sixteen months in Brazil exploring the Amazon River, collecting specimens of South American fish.

Agassiz was sixty years old when he returned, but instead of slowing down he embarked on a new series of travels. He went to the Rocky Mountains to study glaciers there, and then he took a scientific journey by ship along the whole length of South America. He also helped to found the new Cornell University in New York and organized a summer school for teachers of science.

Despite increasing weakness, he remained active until the very end. Agassiz died in Cambridge on December 14, 1873, at the age of sixty-six. Then his friend, the poet James Russell Lowell, wrote a long tribute printed by the *Atlantic* magazine, including these lines:

He was a Teacher; why be grieved
    for him
Whose living word still stimulates
    the air?

Roy Chapman Andrews

1884–1960   American naturalist and explorer

On a hot summer morning in July 1906, Roy Andrews entered the marble halls of the American Museum of Natural History in New York City for the first time. He was twenty-two years old, and he had graduated from Beloit College in his native Wisconsin just a few days earlier. In his pocket he had thirty dollars, earned during the previous few months by stuffing and mounting birds.

He made his way to the office of Dr. Hermon C. Bumpus, the director of the museum. Some months before, Roy had written asking for a job. A note from Dr. Bumpus had come back, saying that if Roy were in New York on other business he would be glad to see him, but there were no positions available.

That did not discourage Roy. He turned down an opportunity to go on a fishing trip to northern Wisconsin that his parents had arranged as a graduation present. Seizing the very slight opening in Dr. Bumpus's letter, he determined to go to New York to fulfill his ambition.

"I wanted to be an explorer and naturalist so passionately that anything else as a life work just never entered my mind," he wrote later in his autobiography.

That ambition grew from his earliest days in rural Wisconsin. Roy Chapman Andrews had been born in Beloit on January 26, 1884—the son of Charles Ezra Andrews, a wholesale druggist, and Cora Chapman Andrews. Throughout his boyhood, staying in a house seemed like torture to Roy.

Whatever the weather, rain or shine,

13

night or day, Roy played outdoors in the fields and woods near his home. "I was like a rabbit, happy only when I could run out of doors," he once said.

On his ninth birthday, his father gave him a single-barrel shotgun. Not only did Roy love to hunt, but he also taught himself how to mount birds and animals to preserve them. As he grew up, he became the only taxidermist in Beloit. "Every bird and deer shot within a radius of fifty miles came to me if a sportsman wanted it mounted," he recalled later.

His ambition crystallized in his senior year in college, when a curator from the American Museum of Natural History came to speak at Beloit. Roy took him down to Moran's Saloon, where he showed his collection of mounted deer heads. That led to his correspondence with Dr. Bumpus and his visit to New York.

After a few minutes of friendly conversation, Dr. Bumpus said, "I wish it were possible to offer you a position of some kind, young man, but I'm afraid I have to tell you that there just isn't one open."

"I'm not asking for a position," Roy answered. "I just want to work here. You have to have someone to clean the floors. Couldn't I do that?"

"But a man with a college education doesn't want to clean floors."

"No, not just any floors," Roy persisted. "But [the] Museum floors are different. I'll clean them and love it, if you'll let me."

Dr. Bumpus smiled. "If that's the way you feel about it, I'll give you a chance," he said. "You'll get forty dollars a month and you can start in the department of taxidermy."

Because Dr. Bumpus was so impressed by the young man's determination, he took him out to lunch afterward. Andrews always remembered that lunch. He had cold salmon and peas in a nearby restaurant.

The same day, Andrews found a place to live with some former Beloit neighbors. He paid $2.50 a week—in those days everything cost much less than it does today—for a room on the third floor of their house.

The following Monday morning, Andrews reported for work. His eyes glowed when he saw a lion not yet completely stuffed in the center of the taxidermy department. At one end of the room, a polar bear and a kind of wild goat called an ibex awaited stuffing and mounting.

For the time being, though, Andrews had to mop the floors, clean up the room, and act as a general handyman. But soon he was allowed to mix clay for molding specimens and to help prepare animal and bird skins for mounting. In his spare time, he studied the animals in the museum, learned photography, and read books on natural history.

His immediate boss was James L. Clark, a young man his own age but with several years of experience at the museum. Andrews and Clark made a congenial pair, both being ambitious and dedicated to their work. They came into the museum on Sundays and holidays to finish various projects and frequently stayed far into the night. Dr. Bumpus noticed.

One day he inspected the floors of the taxidermy department to make sure that Andrews had mopped them clean. Satisfied, he called Andrews to his office and gave him a special additional job: to arrange a series of caribou antlers on the walls of a stairway. After just eight weeks, Andrews received a raise that increased his salary to forty-five dollars a month.

But he still could not afford any luxuries. For breakfast he had just cereal and coffee. A bottle of milk and a box of plain crackers made two lunches. For dinner he often went to a little restaurant where they served a meat-and-potato meal and coffee, too, all for twenty cents. He, Clark, and two other museum employees took a small apartment together, with each paying about twelve-dollars-a-month rent.

Andrews's big chance at the museum came a few months after he started to work there. He became the assistant to a man named Richardson, who was building a life-size model of a whale—seventy-six feet long—to be hung from the ceiling of a museum gallery.

Together, they built a framework of angle iron and basswood strips as the whale's skeleton. But when Richardson tried to cover the skeleton with an artificial skin of paper, it buckled and sank, giving the whale a starved appearance.

"That whale is getting on my nerves," Dr. Bumpus said to Andrews and Clark one day. "What shall we do?"

Andrews and Clark looked at each other. They had been talking about the problem and had a solution.

"Sir," said Clark, "let us finish it with wire netting and papier-mâché."

With a crew of twelve assistants, the two young men went to work using strips of paper soaked in flour paste, then left to dry on the whale's skeleton. "It was amazing what a well-regulated diet of papier-mâché did for the beast," Andrews said. "He lost that pitiful, starved, lost-on-dry-land appearance; his sides filled out and became as smooth as a rubber boot."

After eight months, the job was done. They suspended the whale from the ceiling, and it became one of the major attractions of the museum.

That led to a grisly opportunity for Andrews—handling a dead whale that had washed ashore on Long Island.

When Dr. Bumpus sent Andrews and Clark out to the beach, he told them: "Get the whole thing, photographs, measurements, and skeleton—every bone."

The two young men from the museum found the whale's carcass beached at the edge of the water, its skeleton imbedded in fifty tons of flesh. It was cold, the wind blew fiercely, and the tide lapped against the dead beast. They persuaded a few men to help cut the whale's flesh away, dragging it off using hooks and ropes pulled by horses.

Before they could finish, a storm blew up from the east, with high waves pounding the beach for three days. On the fourth day, Andrews and Clark returned to the beach and found a smooth bed of sand, with no sign of the whale's skeleton. It had been buried.

Frantically, they began to dig. They were lucky enough to find the skeleton, but it took a week of furious digging in the icy sand to recover all the bones and catalog them before returning to the museum.

Their work pleased Dr. Bumpus, so he permitted Andrews to write a scientific paper about the whale. In his research, Andrews found that little was really known about the habits of whales. When his report was finished, he convinced Dr. Bumpus to let him go to Vancouver Island off the Pacific Coast to study whales.

There, Andrews went to sea on a whaling ship, accompanying a crew that killed whales for their oil. With field glasses, he watched the men at work, observed whales, took pictures, and even drank whale's milk, which he didn't like. He became the first naturalist to watch a whale giving birth—the calf was twenty-two feet long and weighed about fifteen tons.

When he returned to New York in 1908, Andrews found himself a minor celebrity. His pictures of whales, printed in newspapers around the country, had aroused a widespread curiosity about the huge mammals of the sea. At the age of just twenty-four, he began lecturing about them to the public as well as learned societies. At the museum, he received a promotion and enrolled part-time at Columbia University to study for a doctorate.

Most of all, though, Andrews relished the life of an explorer, despite its dangers—and the museum gave him many opportunities to go to faraway places to collect animals for it. Once he was shipwrecked on a Pacific island and had to eat monkeys to survive. Another time he escaped death by inches when the carcass of a whale slipped from a ship's crane, crushing the man standing next to him.

Sailors draw up a gray whale during one of Roy Chapman Andrews's expeditions. *Courtesy Department Library Services, American Museum of Natural History.*

Before the age of thirty, Andrews became the nation's leading expert on whales. He sailed on expeditions to the Dutch East Indies, to Korea, and to Japan observing whales, recording their behavior, and sending back specimens to the museum. One of his greatest coups was rediscovering the California gray whale, which had been believed to be extinct.

Ever restless, Andrews changed the direction of his life in 1916, when he was thirty-two. He abandoned the study of whales to conduct land exploration in central Asia, then a largely unknown region. Impressed by the theory of one of his professors that Asia was the home of primitive man and the source of much of the animal life of Europe as well as Asia itself, he decided to go there.

First, though, there was the question of money. The museum could not afford to pay all the costs of an expedition, so Andrews raised half from rich friends of the museum. A pattern for his future expeditions thus emerged: Before departing on any trip, he had to convince wealthy patrons of the museum to contribute to the trip's expenses.

With his new wife—Yvette Borup, the sister of another explorer—Andrews set out in 1916 on the first of his many trips to Asia. Mrs. Andrews became the expedition's official photographer.

Arriving in China, Andrews found the country torn by battles between rival warlords. Chinese officials welcomed him but asked him to delay his exploring until things settled down. "If I wait until things quiet down, I'll have to wait forever," Andrews replied.

With a thirty-mule caravan carrying supplies, he, his wife, and their assistants marched into Yunnan Province, climbing mountain roads while avoiding armed bandits near the borders of Tibet. He searched for and collected animals—big mammals, small mammals, rats, mice, shrews, birds, reptiles, frogs, and fish.

After nine months in the beautiful but dangerous mountains of China, Andrews had collected 2,100 animals, 800 birds, 200 reptiles, and 75 animal skeletons, preserving them in salt and arsenic, sealed in large tin cans. But a big surprise awaited him when he came

out of the wilderness—the United States had gone to war with Germany in 1917.

The American consul in Rangoon issued Andrews a special wartime passport to take his cargo back to New York. It described him as six feet tall, with a high forehead, blue eyes, brown hair, round chin, oval face, and "normal" nose and mouth. Andrews himself said a more accurate description would have added "hair brown (bald)."

After returning to the museum with his precious cargo, Andrews enlisted in the United States Navy. He didn't go to sea but was sent back to China by the navy's intelligence service to work in Manchuria and Mongolia, up to the borders of Siberia. In his autobiography years later, Andrews said he was still not permitted to say what he did there.

However, his trips into the Gobi Desert and Mongolia convinced Andrews that those remote areas could be explored using cars rather than the traditional mules, camels, and horses, even though there were no roads there. It was a new idea. No one before had thought of using motor vehicles with their greater speed than that of the old reliable, plodding beasts of burden.

Back in New York, Andrews persuaded the director of the museum to back a series of motorized expeditions to China—to last five years at a cost of more than a quarter of a million dollars, a huge sum for that time.

But there was one major obstacle—the museum did not have the money. Andrews would have to raise funds himself, and he thought he knew how. First he went to see J. P. Morgan, the famous financier.

"How are you going to get there?" Morgan asked. "Why do you think there is anything there?"

Andrews explained the theory of the distribution of animals and possibly humans from a central Asian point of origin. He said a camel caravan carrying food and gasoline would be sent in advance during winter months to various parts of the desert, to be followed by motorcars with scientists in the spring.

"All right," Morgan said. "I'll give you fifty thousand."

Still, it took a year of endless appeals, discussions, and dinner parties before Andrews raised enough money to depart for Peking (now called Beijing) in March of 1921. There, it took a year more to make preparations: to arrange with Chinese authorities for necessary documents, to hire a native staff, buy camels, and get food and equipment packed.

That winter, a caravan of seventy-five camels laden with food, gasoline, and equipment left to establish supply dumps in the desert ahead. On April 17, 1922, Andrews jumped into a car, and the world's first motorized scientific expedition got underway—eight cars piled high with baggage covered with brown waterproof cloth. Accompanying him were forty men—scientists, camel drivers, porters—and one woman, his wife Yvette, the expedition's photographer.

Driving slowly through mud at times, but mostly through sand and gravel into the outer reaches of Mongolia, Andrews showed his abilities as a leader. Not only had he brought along good food from New York, but he also had equipped his aides with the best sunglasses and helmets available, sturdy tents, and sheepskin-lined sleeping bags.

He also insisted on something most unusual for an expedition into the wilderness—clean white tablecloths for dinner.

"I don't believe in hardship," Andrews explained. "Eat well, dress well, sleep well whenever possible is a pretty good rule. If a bit of hardship does come along, why you're ready to take it in your stride and laugh while it's going on."

There were hardships aplenty in the desert—sandstorms, bandits, poor maps. But the expedition moved forward steadily. Weeks later, at a camp

Roy Chapman Andrews in 1920 when he was making plans for the world's first motorized scientific expedition. *Culver Pictures*.

in the desert, Andrews relaxed by watching the sun set.

Two cars roared into the camp. In them were a team of geologists who had stayed behind a bit to look into a rock formation.

"Well, Roy, we've done it," one of the geologists said quietly.

They had found bones of the titanotheres, an ancient rhinoceros never before discovered outside of America.

The very next morning, another geologist excitedly called to Andrews. "Come with me," he said. "Look at that."

Andrews saw a beautiful bone perfectly preserved in the rock. There was no doubt—it was a dinosaur bone, the first sign of a dinosaur ever discovered in Asia north of the Himalaya Mountains. Together with the titanotheres bones, it was clear evidence to prove their theory that Asia might be the mother of life in Europe and America.

Driving farther into Mongolia, the expedition kept making discoveries. At one stop, they found the bones of the largest mammal known to ever have lived on the earth—a hornless rhinoceros standing seventeen feet high at the shoulders and measuring twenty-four feet in length—dating back probably forty million years. They even found the skull of this mammoth, which bore the scientific name *Baluchitherium*.

Returning to Peking, Andrews cabled a report to the museum in New York. Besides discovering the remains of the dinosaurs and rhinoceros, the expedition had also collected bones of other ancient animals as well as specimens of present-day mammals—along with mapping hitherto unknown areas of Mongolia and taking pictures of every phase of Mongol life.

The director of the museum cabled back: "You have written a new chapter in the history of life on earth."

But these discoveries paled in significance with a finding made on Andrews's second expedition the following year. He returned to an area of the Gobi Desert called the Flaming Cliffs because of the color of the sandstone hills in the brilliant sunshine. There they found some dinosaur skulls, as they had hoped they would. What they found next, though, was truly amazing.

"I think I've found some kind of fossil eggs," one of the scientists, George Olsen, reported at lunch one day.

The others said this was impossible and joked about Olsen's claim. Even so, after lunch they accompanied him back to the site of his discovery and saw what clearly were the remains of eggs, about nine inches long, some of them crushed. But the pebbled surface of some shells seemed as perfect as they had been some eight million years ago.

On their hands and knees now, all the scientists started digging. They uncovered the skeleton of a small dinosaur only about four inches long from one of the shells, and many more whole eggs. In five weeks' time, they found thirty eggs and seventy-five skulls and skeletons. Two of the eggs showed the white bones of unhatched baby dinosaurs.

There was no doubt. These were dinosaur eggs, never before seen by any person.

"As a matter of fact," Andrews said, "we didn't even know that dinosaurs laid eggs. We supposed they did, for dinosaurs are reptiles, and most reptiles lay eggs, but in the whole history of paleontology no evidence of how dinosaurs produced their young ever had been found."

The news electrified the world. Newspapers clamored for pictures of the eggs after Andrews returned to New York. On a rainy night there, four thousand people tried to fit into a hall with seats for less than half that number—to hear Andrews give his first report to the public about the discoveries of his recent expedition.

During the next several months, Andrews lectured all over the country about dinosaur eggs to an eager public. He thoroughly enjoyed delivering these lectures. Not only did they give him an opportunity for talking about the exploring he loved, but the talks also helped to raise money for more trips.

In the next several years, Andrews became a sort of commuter between the United States and China, leading several more expeditions and bringing back large new collections. His last expedition, in 1930, helped prove conclusively that Mongolia had been a major center of animal life during the Age of Reptiles and the Age of Mammals.

But for Andrews personally, the life of an explorer had its down side, too. His family life collapsed during his long absences and he scarcely knew his two sons, George and Kevin. His wife Yvette divorced him in 1931.

Still, his superiors at the museum recognized his many contributions by making him its associate director. He received numerous medals and honorary degrees, and large fees for lecturing. He had to give up plans for further exploring, though, when the director of the museum took sick.

In 1935, Andrews himself reluctantly assumed the top administrative post at the country's leading natural history museum. That same year, at the age of fifty-one, he married Wilhelmina Christmas. Until 1941, he remained in charge of the institution and lived with his second wife in nearby Connecticut.

Then, giving up administrative responsibilities, he moved with his wife to California. Living in the pretty town of Carmel, he wrote many books about his explorations, including his own story of his life, *Under a Lucky Star*.

Andrews died in California on March 11, 1960, at the age of seventy-six. Summing up his career then, *The New York Times* wrote:

"Roy Chapman Andrews was one of those supremely fortunate men who know exactly what they want to do in the world. He wanted to be a naturalist—and he was one—one of the best and one of the last whose range of knowledge spanned the earth."

John James Audubon

1785–1851   French-American painter of America's birds

It happened during his first spring in America. Near the entrance to a small cave he had discovered, he found an empty birds' nest left over from some other year. Then one day he saw a pair of peewees arriving with dried bits of pine needles to fix up the nest, and suddenly an idea struck him. Could these be the very birds who had lived here previously?

Back in France, the young Audubon had already become well acquainted with peewees—more formally called phoebes—so he knew they were friendly birds. He found it easy to win the confidence of this pair, even to catch them in his hands, and he decided to try a new sort of experiment.

As he later wrote: "I fixed a light silver thread on the leg of each, loose enough not to hurt the part, but so fas-tened that no exertion of theirs could remove it." Summer passed, the birds flew southward, and then the following spring he caught several peewees in the same area—and felt a great surge of excitement. For two of them still wore his "little ring" on their legs!

This is now believed to have been the first banding of a wild American bird, a practice widely adopted after Audubon's time to help scientists trace migrating patterns. He was only nine-teen years old in 1804 when he thought of his experiment, and he was supposed to be studying English instead of explor-ing along a creek's banks carrying pen-cils and paper. But as far back as he could remember, his favorite occupa-tion had been drawing pictures of birds—a hobby that eventually would bring him great fame.

That fame came only after he had repeatedly failed in various business ventures. Audubon once wrote to his wife marveling at what an extraordinary story his own life might make. He was right, for he had certainly had many remarkable experiences. Even the circumstances surrounding his birth were unusual.

Some of the truth did not come to light, however, until a professor from Cleveland went to France half a century after Audubon's death and pored over old records that definitely established the identity of the famous artist's parents. This research at last disposed of many romantic rumors. The most incredible of the tales described Audubon as the lost son of France's Queen Marie Antoinette and King Louis XVI, both executed during the terrible early days of the French Revolution. Although Audubon himself had never claimed such exalted forebears, he surely had often hinted at mysterious secrets in his background.

But Professor Francis H. Herrick proved that the artist's father really was Jean Audubon, a ship's captain and merchant who became moderately wealthy running a sugar plantation in the West Indies. As for his mother, she was a French woman referred to in surviving records merely as Mademoiselle Rabin, who met Jean Audubon during the six years he spent on Santo Domingo.

In that French colony on the island now called Haiti, shortly before her death from some unnamed ailment, Mademoiselle Rabin gave birth to a son on April 26, 1785—the date now accepted as the birthday of John James Audubon.

In his later years, when Audubon did a lot of writing about his adventures, he tried to disguise the fact that his parents had not been married. He told some people that his mother had been a rich and beautiful French woman his father wed during a visit to Louisiana and that this shadowy lady had died in his infancy. But Captain Jean Audubon already had a wife in France before he went to the West Indies and visited the United States. Indeed this warm-hearted woman, whom the artist affectionately spoke of as his stepmother, played an important part in his life.

For the boy's father brought him from Santo Domingo to France when he was four years old. At the captain's home near the seaport of Nantes, the childless Mrs. Anne Audubon warmly welcomed this child. Many years afterward, the artist confided about her: "She hid my faults, boasted to everyone of my youthful merits, and, worse than all, said frequently in my presence, that I was the handsomest boy in France."

As a result, he grew into a charming but spoiled youth. Because Captain Audubon was often away at sea, his wife took charge of the boy's education very indulgently. He spent far more time happily roaming the outdoors than in studying any books. Once when his father returned to find his son out hunting birds instead of taking a mathematics test, he swooped him off to a strict military school. But within a year the lad wangled his way home again to resume his old habits under the fond eye of his stepmother.

Although future generations of bird lovers would often think of Audubon as an extremely high-minded figure who never could harm any sort of wildlife, in reality he was an expert hunter. Like most people of his era, he saw nothing wrong with shooting game for food or even shooting for the pure sport of it—in fact, it was his skill as a marksman that enabled him to become an artist because he always made his drawings of birds that he himself had shot.

Following his brief stint at military school, he put so much effort into this hobby of his that even his father was impressed. Since drawing birds seemed to be the only pursuit his son would work hard at, the captain sent him to study art in the Paris studio of the noted painter Jacques Louis David. Yet the lessons lasted just a few months because Audubon showed no special talent for depicting human models.

Also, this was a period of severe unrest in France, and it seemed likely that young Jean, as he was then called, would soon be forced to serve in the French army. But his father much preferred another sort of training for him. Still hoping that Jean would help him in his own business, Captain Audubon decided to send him to America. There, under the supervision of the captain's American agent, he wanted Jean to learn to speak English and finally to show some interest in the world of trade.

The eighteen-year-old Jean, with his lively spirit of adventure, felt "intense and indescribable pleasure" as he embarked in the autumn of 1803 on a ship bound for the new land across the Atlantic. Since his father owned a farm not far from Philadelphia, the young Frenchman would live with the family renting it until he knew English well enough to start his business career. That was how he came to be excitedly observing a pair of peewees in a Pennsylvania cave the following year.

But even though he changed his name from Jean Jacques to John James soon after landing in America, he could not change his habits nearly as easily. He continued to behave like a rich young gentleman with a gift for enjoying nature, no matter that his father's comfortable income practically melted away in the heat of France's political struggles.

With his long dark hair curling onto

An 1884 drawing of Mill Grove, John James Audubon's home on the Schuylkill River, Pennsylvania. *North Wind Picture Archives.*

his shoulders, John wore satin breeches when he went out with his rifle and pencils, and he treated the family he was living with in a lordly manner. What's more, he displayed poor judgment about money matters when he brashly undertook a risky scheme for reopening an abandoned lead mine. During the next few years, he lost several thousand dollars on this project.

His father then tried to avoid any further losses by assigning him a level-headed business partner—the son of one of his friends, a young man named Ferdinand Rozier. Despite Rozier's preference for city life, he agreed with his adventurous new associate that their best chance for making money lay in the West. So they purchased a supply of cloth and other goods likely to appeal to pioneering settlers and, during the summer of 1807, started westward.

As their trip through the mountains of Pennsylvania grew increasingly rugged, the differences between Rozier's and Audubon's outlooks grew increasingly clear. Audubon rejoiced whenever horrible road conditions obliged them to climb down from their coach and walk beside it while the horses drawing it labored uphill with their heavy load. On foot, he had a much better chance to spy birds he had never seen before or peer at remarkable features of the landscape. Rozier, on the other hand, found the hardship almost unbearable, enduring it only because it might lead to a good profit when they finally opened their store in Kentucky.

Many years later, Audubon explained that they had chosen Louisville "as a spot designed by nature to become a place of great importance." If they had merely invested a few hundred dollars in buying land there, in another few years they would have reaped a fortune when land values around this settlement skyrocketed. "But it was not to be, and who cares," Audubon blithely added.

Instead, Rozier tried to run their Louisville store successfully while Audubon spent most of his time searching the nearby woods for birds. Yet even Rozier could not make the business prosper because President Thomas Jefferson's policies aimed at avoiding a foreign war were severely hurting trade all over the country. Nevertheless, Audubon's spirits rose with every passing month.

In the spring of 1808, he returned to Pennsylvania on horseback to seek more goods for their store—and to attend his own wedding. For soon after his arrival in America, he had fallen in love with Lucy Bakewell, the daugh-

ter of an English gentleman living near the farm where he had seen the peewees. Although both sets of parents insisted that John must have an income before undertaking to support a wife, they had finally given their consent. So John married Lucy at the Bakewells' home on April 8, 1808, when he was almost twenty-three and she just slightly younger.

Their difficult yet exciting journey all the way back to Louisville was their honeymoon—and it proved to be a good forecast of the ups and downs of their life together. In the next several years they joyously welcomed the birth of two healthy sons but suffered grievously when two infant daughters died. Similarly, Audubon kept embarking on new money-making schemes with vast enthusiasm and then being defeated by bad luck or his own poor business judgment.

After he and Rozier had to close their Louisville store, they thought they might do better further west in Missouri. When their store there failed, too, at least partly because Audubon spent most of his days out looking for birds, the partnership between these two very different individuals was dissolved. While Rozier went on by himself to become a rich merchant, Audubon sank deeper and deeper into financial trouble.

Audubon's "Cardinal" and "Great Horned Owl." *The New-York Historical Society.*

For a while it appeared that he might finally prosper as a storekeeper in the Kentucky town of Henderson, but again he took a chance on an unsound scheme. He borrowed money to build a steam-powered sawmill capable of producing more wooden boards than the area could possibly use. As a result, in 1819, Audubon could not pay his debts. At the age of thirty-four, he was arrested and put into jail.

Then Audubon had himself declared bankrupt in a legal proceeding that erased his debts and freed him from prison. But how was he to feed his wife and children? Because he still had a box filled with his drawings of birds, the idea of turning his hobby into a source of income at last struck him.

Audubon was thirty-five when he conceived his grand plan, in 1820, of issuing a series of books containing several hundred large illustrations—the series to be called *Birds of America*. But it took seven more years until his first book appeared, and during this period a man who had never been able to stick to any other work persevered tirelessly in his new goal despite all sorts of obstacles and discouragements. Once he almost gave up when he discovered that a family of rats had gnawed many of his pictures into shreds, but the next day he doggedly started to duplicate every drawing he had lost.

Since his first priority had to be earning enough to live on until he found a way to put out his books, he took up making crayon sketches of anybody who would pay him five dollars for a portrait. He also gave drawing lessons to the children of well-off families. Yet at the same time he managed to raise himself from being merely an amateur with a flair for drawing birds into a superb painter in his chosen field. Today, he is still regarded as perhaps the most skillful artist ever to concentrate on painting birds and their surroundings.

Part of Audubon's eventual success has been credited to his diligence, for he often spent fourteen hours at a stretch—from dawn to dusk—uninterruptedly at his easel. Also, it seems likely that he had exceptionally keen eyesight, making it possible for him to achieve a rare accuracy on minute details. Some experts think, though, that the most important factor was the unique method for painting birds that he himself developed.

While he used dead birds as his models, just as every other artist in this field did, Audubon built a device with which he could make his dead specimens seem alive. He accomplished this feat by using wires to hold the bird's body in any position he wished to show in his painting. Also, the bird was placed against a background ruled with lines corresponding to similar lines on Audubon's paper, so the size of its beak, for instance, could be reproduced exactly in the correct proportion to the rest of the bird's body.

But besides the awesome reality his system insured, by means of his wires Audubon was able to show his birds in many varied attitudes—in flight or at rest, craning their necks or fluffing their feathers. Further distinguishing his work from any previous efforts, he also depicted his birds in natural settings featuring trees, rocks, flowers, clouds, so that he produced real paintings rather than mere painstaking illustrations.

In 1824, Audubon brought a portfolio of his completed paintings to Philadelphia, where he hoped to find assistance in getting his series published. As he was already aware, it would be extremely expensive to reproduce his work for publication. The best process then available required the etching of exact replicas of each painting onto sheets of copper from which separate imprints could be made, and then each of the resulting engravings would have to be hand-colored.

Because of the expense involved, Audubon planned to issue his book in stages, offering new sets of etchings at regular intervals to about two hundred subscribers willing to pay part of the cost in advance. But in Philadelphia he was told that the books he had in mind would cost so much to produce that each subscriber would end up paying $1,000. How could he possibly imagine anybody spending such an immense sum for any series of bird books?

Nevertheless, one amateur ornithologist—ornithology is the branch of science devoted to the study of birds—gave him his first real encouragement.

As Audubon later wrote: "Young Harris, God bless him, looked at the drawings and . . . squeezed a hundred-dollar bill into my hand, saying, 'Mr. Audubon, accept this from me; men like you ought not to want for money.'" This generous gift convinced the artist that he should go to Europe, where sponsors would surely be easier to find.

First, though, Audubon had to increase his stock of paintings by tramping the northern countryside in quest of more specimens to draw. Then another long trip through the mountains and down the Ohio and Mississippi rivers

was necessary, not just to add to his collection but also to see his family.

In this period Lucy Audubon had, of necessity, become quite self-reliant. Believing strongly in her husband's eventual success, she had tried conducting a school in New Orleans to supplement the limited amounts of money he was able to send her. Now she was employed as a governess on a Louisiana plantation whose proprietor allowed her sons to live there with her.

But any brief account of the Audubons' wanderings in the 1820s can give only a few bare facts about the varied predicaments they managed to survive. While Lucy and the boys frequently had to depend on the kindness of strangers, Audubon himself traveled many thousands of miles, often on foot and looking like an unkempt tramp, painting birds in swamps, in forests, along the seashore. Alone, he faced raging blizzards and scorching heat, even a major earthquake once.

After Audubon made his way from Philadelphia down to Louisiana in 1825 for a reunion with his family, he spent several months there. He gave art and even dancing lessons so he could afford to buy some decent clothes. Then, in May of 1826, he boarded a ship in New Orleans bound for the English port of Liverpool—where, at the age of forty-one, Audubon finally tasted fame.

An engraving of John James Audubon with hunting dog and rifle. *Brown Brothers*.

By that time his long hair was gray but he still wore it curling onto his shoulders. With his fringed leather suit that he had bought as his European costume, his mere appearance attracted attention in sedate England. Wherever he went, people turned to stare at "The American Woodsman," as newspaper writers called him.

Perhaps Audubon had purposely aimed to present a romantic impression in order to arouse extra interest when he opened an exhibit of his bird paintings in Liverpool. If so, the scheme accomplished its goal, because his exhibit drew large crowds—and the money he made from admission fees enabled him to proceed to Edinburgh, noted then as a center for the engraving trade.

In Edinburgh, Audubon took his portfolio to the shop of a leading engraver. When he had held up just two or three paintings for this man's inspection, William Lizars jumped from his chair and exclaimed: "My God! I never saw anything like this before." Quickly Lizars agreed to make large engravings of about four hundred paintings and publish four books containing these life-sized depictions of American birds.

Yet even this triumph by no means ended Audubon's struggles. Although he was soon being invited to dine with dukes, a tremendous amount of effort still had to be expended before his *Birds of America* was completed in 1838—eleven years after the issuance of the first volume in 1827.

During these years, Audubon traveled back and forth across the Atlantic several times because he had to attend to so many different details himself. In Europe, he kept seeking new subscribers among the wealthy men he met. Also, problems over the engravings arose, and he felt he had to supervise the process personally even after a gifted London engraver, Robert Havell, Jr., took over when his Edinburgh arrangement became unsatisfactory.

But Audubon found it necessary, too, to keep making new paintings. With the project turning into reality, he ambitiously expanded his goal—aiming to include pictures of every known American bird. Thus, in the same period when he was working so hard on selling and actually producing his great series in Europe, he also undertook his most extensive and adventurous bird-hunting expeditions in America.

He went to Florida, and then he followed the Gulf Coast all the way to Texas. On another trip, he sailed the entire coast of Maine. Then the next summer he sailed to Labrador. Because he was also planning to publish a companion series of volumes he called his *Ornithological Biography*, telling where he had found every species he painted, he kept detailed journals of these trips.

For instance, one day during his Labrador expedition he wrote:

On the morning of the 14th of June 1833 . . . about ten o'clock we discerned at a distance a white speck, which our pilot assured us was the celebrated rock. After a while I could distinctly see its top from the deck, and thought that it was still covered with snow several feet deep. As we approached it, I imagined that the atmosphere around was filled with flakes, but on my turning to the pilot, who smiled at my simplicity, I was assured that nothing was in sight but the Gannets [white sea birds they were seeking] . . .

By the time the fourth volume of *Birds of America* appeared in 1838, Audubon was fifty-three years old. Even his amazing stamina was beginning to desert him, and his wife hoped he would now take life easier, enjoying the celebrity his great work had earned for him.

At least partly heeding her wishes, Audubon built a comfortable home on about forty wooded acres overlooking the Hudson River. His rural estate is now mostly apartment houses between 155 Street and 158 Street in upper Manhattan. There Audubon kept on painting, preparing for a new series of books picturing small four-footed creatures such as mice and moles. Yet he also managed to fulfill a dream by taking one more glorious wilderness expedition westward to the Yellowstone River.

Then in 1847, when he was sixty-two years old, Audubon felt a sort of film over his eyes one day, and he could not see clearly enough to finish a painting he was working on. The failure of his eyesight depressed him so deeply that, even though his general health remained sound, his mind failed, too. His wife cared for him patiently until he died on January 27, 1851, at the age of sixty-five.

Audubon's two sons had become a major help to him during the latter part of his career, Victor assuming many business responsibilities while John, with some of his father's artistic talent, assisted him on his paintings. Thanks partly to these sons' efforts to promote his work, his fame continued to grow after his death.

Still, the main reason that Audubon has become probably the most popular figure among all of the naturalists throughout American history is that in the 1880s a group of bird lovers decided to name their new organization after him. Today the National Audubon Society is one of the major forces in the United States working toward the preservation of the country's natural heritage.

But Audubon's drawings themselves continue to delight ordinary people as well as experts. Every year countless new calendars adorned with copies of his prints are widely distributed, and many other framed copies hang on the walls of the nation's homes. As for the superb etchings contained in the original edition of his *Birds of America,* most of these are now owned by museums. The value of a complete set has been estimated to be at least $2 million.

Liberty Hyde Bailey

1858–1954   American plant scientist and educator

Liberty—it was a most unusual name for a child. After Liberty Hyde Bailey became famous, a lot of people wondered about his name. The story went back to the days of his grandparents, before the Civil War.

Then Dana and Betsey Bailey, living on a Vermont farm, had been strong opponents of slavery. They both took an active part in operating the underground railroad that helped black men and women fleeing from a life of slavery in the South to seek freedom in Canada.

When their first son was born, neighbors asked Dana Bailey what to call the boy. He replied, "Call him Liberty, for all men shall be free."

Unfortunately, that baby died in infancy. But when the couple's second son was born a few years later, they named him Liberty, too, Liberty Hyde Bailey.

At the age of twenty-one, this young man left the rocky soil of Vermont to establish a farm on the more fertile lands of Michigan. He bought a tract near South Haven on the eastern shore of Lake Michigan. With his wife, Sarah Harrison Bailey, he began to clear the densely wooded area so that they could plant apple trees.

Sarah and Liberty had three children: first Dana, then Marcus, and finally on March 15, 1858, a third son. They named him Liberty Hyde Bailey, Jr.—and he grew up to become one of America's most widely known plant scientists.

But growing up was not easy in those pioneer days in Michigan. When Lib was just three years old, all the Bailey boys came down with scarlet fever, and Dana, the eldest, died from the disease. While the other two, fortunately, were less severely stricken, it still took many months for them to recover.

Not long afterward their mother fell seriously ill with diphtheria, an incurable disease in those days. Although Lib was not quite five when she died, he had already learned to be her main assistant in tending her flower garden. He kept her garden going for many years, besides planting one of his own with his father's help.

In addition, Lib worked with his father in the apple orchard and did his share of other farm chores throughout his boyhood. Yet he still found time for exploring nearby woods and stream banks. Also, he formed the habit of collecting all sorts of wildlife.

Taking over an abandoned toolshed in back of their house, Lib used it as his own private museum. Amid a jumble of unused odds and ends, he kept snakes, lizards, turtles, and frogs. Then one day his father found what he thought was merely rubbish in the shed and cleaned it out.

When Lib protested that he had been studying out there, his father said that school was the proper place for study. But Lib's new stepmother, Maria Bridges Bailey, proved more sympathetic to the boy's fondness for collect-

ing animal specimens. Even so, she drew the line at letting his milk snakes hatch in her kitchen.

Lib walked a mile to school every day. He studied reading, spelling, grammar, and arithmetic, sitting on a high bench without any back. It was so high that the younger children could not reach the floor with their toes.

Soon Lib showed that his interest in growing things was more than the ordinary pastime of a country boy. In a neighbor's home, he discovered a book on natural history, and he borrowed it to show his teacher, Mrs. Julia Field.

Could they study natural history? he asked her. Mrs. Field turned to the rest of the class to see if anyone else was interested. No one responded.

But Mrs. Field was a good teacher. No matter that she knew very little about the world of nature herself, she did not discourage his special interest. Every day she assigned him to read a page or two of the book he had borrowed, then to tell her what he had learned. And she challenged him even more.

"What did you see today, Liberty?" she would ask.

He mentioned birds or animals or trees.

"What kind of trees do you pass on your way to school? How tall are they? How are they growing?"

The horticulturist Liberty Hyde Bailey.
Brown Brothers.

At first, Lib didn't know the answers to her questions. But soon he taught himself to observe trees carefully, noticing their leaves and bark and the differences between various kinds of trees. He not only remembered what he saw, he always remembered the teacher who had trained him to observe nature systematically. Many years later, he dedicated one of the books he wrote to Mrs. Field.

Lib's love of learning became so obvious that even his father began encourag-

ing it. Whenever he went on a trip, he brought a book home as a present for his son. One of the first books Lib read from cover to cover had a complicated title—*Explorations of the Nile Tributaries of Abyssinia*—but it also had wonderful pictures of lions, elephants, and other wild animals.

Growing into his teens, Lib continued assisting his father on their farm but he always kept looking for new reading material. On a visit to a neighbor, he discovered a book by Harvard University's highly regarded Professor Asa Gray entitled *Field, Forest and Garden Botany*. Lib happily pored over its pages describing and classifying thousands of American plants.

By the age of fifteen, Lib had learned so much while working in the family's apple orchard about the procedure called grafting that his skill was known throughout their area. Grafting involved cutting buds from desirable trees and fastening them onto other trees, so that the grafted trees would produce fruit just like the fruit grown by the trees from which the buds had been taken.

Despite Lib's youth, he was asked to deliver a talk on the topic of grafting to the farmers of South Haven. But he still felt mystified as well as attracted by the whole subject of scientific botany. A new neighbor, Mrs. Lucy Millington, was a botanist, and she helped him by lending him additional books.

Approaching his nineteenth birthday, Lib was six feet tall, strong and wiry from all of his outdoor work. As a result of his reading, as well as his farm experience, he had already begun to think that the science of botany could help farmers grow better crops. But how could those who tilled the soil receive the latest information? Back then, agricultural colleges were just beginning to operate and they were not yet geared to transmit their recommendations to farmers.

So Lib came to a major decision. One day, working outdoors with his father, he stopped hoeing weeds to say, "Father, I am going to college."

"Bless you, my boy," Mr. Bailey said. "What will you do for money?"

Lib replied that he had saved a few dollars and he could borrow the rest of what he needed from a bank if his father would sign a note. Mr. Bailey agreed to do this.

And so in September of 1877, the nineteen-year-old Lib caught a train for Lansing to enroll in the Michigan Agricultural College. As the years passed, it would grow into Michigan State University, but then it had a total of only 150 students. Before he could start attending classes, he had to pass an entrance examination.

The examiner sat up front in one of the college classrooms. All of the candidates for admission were men, apart from one attractive young woman with dark hair and large dark-brown eyes, who was wearing a gold chain around her neck.

Bailey pulled his watch out of a pocket, glanced at it, and looked toward the woman. She reached for her gold chain, glanced at the watch attached to it, and then over at him. With this friendly flirting on his first day at agricultural college, Bailey made the acquaintance of Annette Smith, the daughter of a Lansing cattle grower— and his future wife.

Bailey plunged into college life with great relish, attending classes every morning, doing field work in the afternoon, studying in the evening. The students were paid eight cents an hour for the farm work they did. As small as this sum may sound, it at least helped to pay the students' expenses at a time when room rent for an entire semester was $1.25 and hearty meals three times a day for a whole week cost just $2.40.

During his senior year, Lib Bailey emerged as a campus leader. He organized and edited a student newspaper. His classmates elected him president of the college's natural history society and of the student government. He received his bachelor's degree in 1882, at the age of twenty-four.

A methodical man, Bailey by this time had made up his mind about how he would spend his life. He had already used almost twenty-five years for education. Now he would devote twenty-five years to earning a living, and then his last twenty-five years to doing whatever he wanted.

Although Bailey had made a brilliant record at Michigan, the small college had no place for him as a teacher. With his writing experience, however, he got a job as a reporter for the Springfield *Morning Monitor* in Illinois. He had a flair for journalism, scenting good stories wherever he went and writing swiftly under deadline pressure.

Bailey impressed his editors so much that they soon offered him a job as city editor at what was then a fabulous salary—twenty dollars a week. It was enough so that he and Annette could get married.

But on arriving home for a visit, he found a letter that changed his life. It came from one of his Michigan professors, who wrote that he had recommended Bailey for the post of assistant to Professor Asa Gray at Harvard. The famous botanist was looking for a young man to help him sort and classify a large collection of new specimens he had just received from England. Did Bailey want the job?

Of course he did. But there was a major problem—the pay was much less than he could earn at the newspaper. Even so, Bailey jumped at the opportunity. He moved to Massachusetts in 1883, when he was twenty-five. That same year he and Annette decided to get married anyway. Lib hoped that by doing some writing in the evenings he could earn extra money to supplement his small salary as Dr. Gray's assistant.

Bailey worked with Gray for two years, certain that a job in his field would surely turn up when he completed his task of cataloging the English plants. It came in a letter from his alma mater, the Michigan Agricultural College. Would he accept an appointment as professor of horticulture and landscape gardening, the first such post in the nation?

Bailey took the job without hesitating. Gray was surprised. "But, Mr. Bailey, I thought you were fitting yourself to be a botanist," he said.

"Yes, Dr. Gray, but a horticulturist ought to be a botanist," he replied.

Gray, an eminent botanist, disagreed. He believed that botany, the scientific study of plants in the laboratory and classroom, was a higher calling. To him, horticulture—the practical study of plants in the field—was something for farmers and gardeners, not scientists.

But Bailey believed that he could be both a horticulturist and a botanist, devoting himself to scientific research as well as to actual crops grown in fields and orchards. He set out to prove his point when he began teaching at Michigan in 1885. Right from the outset, his courses were very popular with students.

"He could make any subject come alive," one of them said. Promptly on the hour, Bailey would stride into his classroom, talking as he entered and only rarely referring to the books and notes he carried. A gifted teacher, he often used the works of poets like Edgar Allan Poe to enliven his lectures.

But he never forgot his farm roots. He brought samples of fruits and vegetables into the classroom for the students to examine. Look at this, he would say, holding up a large pumpkin attached to a small vine. How could so big a fruit be nourished by such a tiny vine, he would ask, trying to make the students think.

At examination time, he trusted his students and left the room while they answered the questions he had prepared. His tests were unusual. For example, he would say: "Tell us about strawberries," letting students write about any aspect of the fruit that especially interested them.

Still, classroom teaching was only part of his job. Bailey relished his op-portunities to work with students in the field. With them he improved the college's old apple orchard, pruned the raspberry patches, and conducted experiments involving many different crops.

When the apple trees began to produce a lot of fruit, Bailey issued this warning in the college newspaper: "Now boys, don't go over into that orchard. If you have occasion to go, however, don't steal any apples. But if you do steal apples, do not under any circumstances steal green ones."

An energetic man, Bailey also laid out experimental gardens for small fruits and vegetables, wrote numerous scientific papers, lectured to farmers in the neighborhood and horticultural societies across the nation, entertained visiting dignitaries, wrote books, and still found time to play with his infant daughter, the first of his two children.

Once a critic complained that the college grounds were not kept up as well as in the past. The president of the college replied: "That may be so, but Bailey's genius lies in other fields. You don't hitch a race horse to the plow."

One of Bailey's first lectures to an outside horticultural group bore the title, "The Garden Fence." He defined that fence as the wall of prejudice separating botanists from horticulturalists, the barrier between theory and practice. The time had come to tear it down, he said.

Bailey saw his job as educating not only students but also the general public and working farmers, too. In 1885, he addressed the first of his many books, *Talks Afield: About Plants and the Science of Plants,* to nonspecialists. A year later, he aimed his second book, *Field Notes on Apple Culture,* directly at apple growers.

His name became well known at other institutions, which called upon him to lecture and offered him jobs. The offer that interested him the most came from Cornell University in upstate New York, then starting an expansion program in practical agriculture. Would he become its first professor of horticulture, with sufficient funds to build facilities for all the agricultural experiments he could dream up?

Bailey arrived in Ithaca in 1888. He found that he and Isaac P. Roberts, an older professor, were the complete faculty in the field of applied agriculture, with a handful of students and only a few classrooms. Together, during the next several years, they built Cornell's ag school into one of the world's leading colleges.

Most of the work fell to Bailey, just thirty years old and filled with boundless energy. When he first turned up in Ithaca, the ground was frozen. Not willing to wait until it thawed, he began to build a house anyway, digging out icy dirt so he could start laying the foundation.

And he bounced into classes asking his students, "What do you know today that you did not know the last time we met?"

A skilled writer, Bailey published a steady stream of books, scientific studies, agricultural manuals, and encyclopedias about plants for both farmers and the general public. During his first year at Cornell, he wrote *The Horticulturalist's Rule Book,* containing much useful information for growers of both fruits and vegetables. Scores of other books and pamphlets followed.

Teacher, experimenter, speaker, home gardener, writer, and family man—how did Bailey manage to do it all? He often worked until midnight and rose the next morning at six o'clock to start another busy day. He wrote rapidly, his pen skimming over page after page, and what he wrote required little revising. He told anybody who asked how he accomplished so much that there were just two essential steps in any task, "to begin, and to get done."

Perhaps his greatest triumph, however, came in the political arena. When Bailey first arrived at Cornell, agricultural subjects were taught by a department that depended on the university for buildings and funds. But the ag department was growing and needed more than the university could provide.

Bailey believed that New York's legislature should create an independent college of agriculture. So he became a lobbyist, traveling often to Albany, the state capital, to plead his cause with legislators. He also encouraged farm groups to pressure their representatives to vote for an independent ag college.

Finally, in 1903, the governor of New York signed a bill establishing a State College of Agriculture at Cornell, which would receive direct funding from the state's treasury. Cornell students celebrated with a parade led by a big black bull from the college farm, fireworks, a bonfire, and a banquet.

Bailey became the new college's first dean. When he took charge, its faculty consisted of 9 teachers, offering 25 courses to a student body of 252. Ten years later, the faculty numbered 104, with 224 courses being given to 1,400 students.

Not all of this increase could be attributed to Bailey, of course. It was a period of tremendous growth in farming all over the United States, and also of educational programs for farmers. But Bailey was certainly the driving force behind Cornell's emergence as one of the world's outstanding centers for agricultural studies—noted, in addition, for its outreach to farms through its agricultural extension service and its promotion of nature study by school children.

Indeed, Bailey's contributions extended far beyond Ithaca. He became the first president of the American Nature Study Society, president of the Society for Horticultural Science, and chairman of President Theodore Roosevelt's Commission to Study Improvements in Rural Life.

Yet Bailey regretted that he had to give up classroom teaching when he became an administrator and a national figure. Still, he kept his office open so any student with a problem could stop in to consult him. Restless at a desk, he often jumped up to stride across the campus and survey the college's experimental gardens.

One student provided a picture of him during this period: "He was kind of lanky, with long arms, a hawk-like face, and long black hair. He [wore] a plain suit and a black felt hat, western style. His height not his clothes made him conspicuous."

As a relief from the tensions of his work, Bailey turned to poetry. Not only did he invite students to his home on Sunday evenings for conversation and poetry reading, but he also tried his hand at writing verse such as:

An illustration of apricots from Liberty Hyde Bailey's *Standard Cyclopedia of Horticulture*, Volume 1, 1914/15 edition.

From morning till night and
   everywhere
My days are full of their effort
   and care . . .
The peace of the wind is my
   undertone
I move with the crowd, but
   I live alone.

Nevertheless, he fully enjoyed some of the by-products of his position. When Theodore Roosevelt came to visit the college, Bailey acted as his host. Speaking to the students, Roosevelt praised Cornell's ag school as the foremost institution of its kind throughout the world. Then turning to his host, the retired president said, "Dean Bailey, it is none of my affair, but I should regard it as a calamity, not only to the state, but to the nation, if you do not continue to do your work as head of this college."

Even so, Bailey felt it was time for him to step down. In accordance with the plan he had made many years earlier, he aimed to spend the last third of his life doing what he really wanted— research. In 1913, at the age of fifty-five, Bailey resigned as dean of the College of Agriculture and began an important new phase of his career.

First, he revised his six-volume *Standard Cyclopedia of Horticulture*, a basic reference guide for plant growers. He also traveled extensively as a working botanist, collecting thousands of specimens that he dried and preserved.

On a trip to New Zealand, Bailey wrote a book he called *The Holy Earth*, which he hoped would live long after his technical botanical books had been forgotten. Half a century before there was any environmental movement, he expressed his philosophy that the use of the earth's resources must be founded on religious and ethical principles.

Five years before his death, Liberty Hyde Bailey sits amid some of his favorite botanical specimens. *George Silk*, Life *magazine/©1949 Time Warner Inc.*

During another trip, to the island of Jamaica in the Caribbean, Bailey's wife asked him the name of a palm tree she saw. When he said he didn't know, she teased him about his ignorance. Thus challenged, he applied himself to studying a form of plant life he had never paid much attention to—and became the world's leading expert on palm trees.

Honors poured in on him. In 1926, Bailey was elected president of both the Botanical Society of America and the American Association for the Advancement of Science. He also received medals from horticultural groups in England and France.

By 1935, when his personal collection of dried plants contained more than 125,000 specimens, Bailey had begun worrying about what would happen to them in case of his death. So he presented them all to Cornell—a collection now known as the Liberty Hyde Bailey Hortorium. Bailey himself coined the word "hortorium" to mean a collection of plants in both their natural and cultivated states.

Advancing age did not stop Bailey from taking new research trips. When he was eighty, he set out for Cuba, Mexico, and South America in quest of palm specimens. At ninety-one, he bought tickets to go to inspect the palm trees of Africa, the one continent he had not yet visited. But he fell and broke a leg, so he had to cancel this journey.

Bailey spent the remaining years of his life in Ithaca, the home of Cornell University. He died there on December 25, 1954, at the age of ninety-six.

Today he is remembered not only on the Cornell campus, where a building has been named for him, but at Michigan State, which considers him its most distinguished alumnus, and also in South Haven. There, the Liberty Hyde Bailey Museum welcomes visitors to the birthplace of a farm boy who rose to become one of America's foremost plant experts.

John Bartram 1699–1777
William Bartram 1739–1823

Pioneer American botanists

Around the middle of the 1700s, people as far away as Sweden developed a great curiosity about John Bartram. How had a Pennsylvania farmer, who had left school at the age of twelve, become the leading botanist in the American colonies? Bartram himself once told a visitor that he owed his special interest in plants to a clump of ordinary daisies.

While plowing a field, he recalled, he had stopped to pluck one of these white flowers for a closer look at its sunny yellow center. Then, marveling at the complexity he observed, he had made up his mind to seek more knowledge regarding all sorts of plants. But his son William remembered hearing something else.

According to William, his father had wished in his boyhood that he could study medicine. Obliged instead to work on the family farm, he had still made a habit of searching out medicinal plants—in those days, the only medicines available for treating many diseases were concoctions using various leaves or twigs or roots.

No matter what had originally motivated John Bartram, though, as an adult he managed to teach himself enough about plants to play a major role for several decades in acquainting Europe with the trees and flowers of North America. He also inspired similar efforts by the son he fondly called Billy. Together, they formed one of the most notable teams in the history of natural science.

The Bartrams' forebears were sober Quakers from Derbyshire in England, where their religious convictions had brought them increasing harrassment. When the English Quaker William Penn received a tract of land in the New World as payment for a debt, he encouraged fellow believers to move there. John Bartram's grandparents joined a group of eight families that settled just west of Philadelphia in 1683, founding a town they named Darby to remind them of their old home.

The future naturalist was born in this orderly farming community on March 23, 1699. But tragedy shadowed his early years. When he was three years old, his mother, Elizabeth Hunt Bartram, died after giving birth to another son, so John and his brother were raised mainly by grandparents.

Much later in his adventurous life, John Bartram described himself as having been a very timid child. During his boyhood, he wrote, he'd had "a slavish fear" of lightning in particular, causing him to hide indoors during thunderstorms and pray for protection.

Yet he tried hard to conquer his fears, telling himself firmly that few people were killed by lightning or the other hazards he dreaded. His success in changing his outlook was especially remarkable because of the horrible death of his father, the William Bartram after whom he would name his own son. John's father, venturing into Indian ter-

ritory with a plan for establishing a new Quaker outpost in North Carolina, was murdered there by Indians infuriated over white encroachments on their land.

Despite this awful event in 1711, when John was twelve, his Grandmother Bartram deeply impressed him with her Quaker philosophy opposing every type of violence, even violent thoughts. As a result, he never harbored hatred for all Indians because of his father's death at the hands of one band of them. When John Bartram's later travels repeatedly took him to remote areas where only Indians lived, he was able to meet them with a brotherly attitude untinged by any spirit of revenge.

Apart from the trauma of losing both his parents, John's youth passed peacefully. He attended the Quaker school only a short walk from the farm where he lived with his grandparents—a strict school that was in session every month of the year, with eight hours of lessons five days a week and four hours on Saturdays. Although he stopped going to classes around the time of his father's death, when his widowed Grandmother Bartram needed his help, John had probably already absorbed as much basic instruction as some high schools today offer their students.

And he must have been an outstand-

An oil portrait of John Bartram, painted about 1758 and attributed to John Wollaston. *National Portrait Gallery, Smithsonian Institution.*

ing pupil, judging by the ease with which he picked up information after he began putting concentrated effort into studying on his own. But this program of self-education did not get seriously underway for another several years.

In his own words, he was "a tall thin spare" young man just past his twenty-fourth birthday when he married Mary Maris, the daughter of a neighboring family, on April 25, 1723. Shortly afterward, his ailing grandmother died, leaving him her two-hundred-acre farm complete with cattle, a fine orchard, and tidy buildings. Because John Bartram liked being a farmer, he contentedly set about improving his property.

In 1724, the young couple had a son they named Richard. Bartram, who proved to be a most devoted parent, must have grieved deeply when this baby died before reaching his first birthday. Two years later, Mary Bartram gave birth to a healthy boy—but she herself died of an infection.

John Bartram never recorded his feelings when he was left alone to care for the infant Isaac. Fortunately, in less than two years he became engaged to the woman with whom he would happily spend the rest of his life. On October 10, 1729, he married Ann Mendenhall in a solemn Quaker ceremony.

No doubt he had been looking toward a fresh start in new surroundings when he had bought a farm right on the outskirts of Philadelphia the preceding year. Also, perhaps, he already had plans for creating a special kind of garden there. In any case, to welcome his new bride he built a handsome stone house on this land overlooking the Schuylkill River. With his own hands, he engraved both their names onto an outer wall of the structure that still stands more than two and a half centuries later.

Upon moving there, Bartram finally began to emerge as a most extraordinary farmer. Besides undertaking various fertilizing and irrigating projects that made his land produce twice as much as his neighbors harvested, he also started setting out specimens of every unusual plant he could discover. In a few years, he had created a botanic garden of sufficient interest to draw many visitors from Philadelphia.

Benjamin Franklin, already one of the city's leading citizens, found Bartram's garden—and Bartram himself—so fascinating that he came to see them often. Other notable Philadelphians were attracted by Bartram, too, but none had more influence on Bartram's future than a merchant with a novel hobby.

It involved the smearing of ink onto

the leaves of plants, then pressing the leaves onto paper, thereby making very accurate reproductions. This merchant sent some of his leaf prints done from specimens in Bartram's garden to an English business connection—a London wool dealer named Peter Collinson, who much enjoyed setting out plants from every part of the world at his own country estate.

The result was that a unique relationship started in 1733 between Bartram and Collinson, who never actually met each other because neither of them ever sailed across the Atlantic. Even so, by mail they became intimate friends as well as botanic colleagues. Bartram called the Englishman Mr. Collinson in the first letters he wrote to him, and the letters he received were headed: Friend John Bartram. Soon, though, they were Peter and John to each other as they pursued their remarkable partnership. In addition to their main interest of botany, they also collaborated on collecting many other types of natural phenomena, such as rocks, fossils, and birds' eggs.

To start with, Collinson asked Bartram to supply him with some native American plants. In return, he promised to ship back English varieties that might grow well near Philadelphia. It quickly became clear, however, that their exchange would work better if

Bartram knew the proper botanic names of everything they discussed.

Then Bartram confessed that he had always wished he could learn more about plant science—and asked Collinson what books he ought to read. But even though Philadelphia was one of the largest towns on the American continent, in the 1730s it did not yet have any public library; prodded by Bartram, Benjamin Franklin began taking steps to remedy this lack. Meanwhile, Collinson sent Bartram several of the important volumes on plants that European scholars had recently produced.

Because scientists of the era did much of their writing in Latin, Bartram hired a schoolmaster to tutor him in that language. Within just a few months, he could read Latin well enough to study his botany books—and yet living plants still appealed to him more than any books about them. So Collinson urged his American friend to range beyond the Philadelphia area in quest of notable wildflowers or trees or bushes.

In the autumn of 1736, Bartram saddled his horse and started out alone to follow the Schuylkill River to its source far from any colonial settlement. Although this journey into Pennsylvania's rugged mountains lasted only a few weeks and covered only a few hundred miles, it proved a good preparation for the many longer and more difficult

John Bartram's house near Philadelphia. *North Wind Picture Archives.*

expeditions he would undertake during the next thirty years.

Undaunted by rough trails or solitude, Bartram filled his saddlebags with clusters of seeds he gathered from interesting plants along his route—and he even dug up small plants, wrapping them with a little soil around their roots into ox bladders he tied tightly with string (a procedure quite like the use of plastic bags for such purposes today). On returning home, he packed what he had collected into wooden boxes for shipment to Collinson.

Because Collinson realized that Bartram was not a rich man who could afford taking time away from his farming, which supported his ever-expanding family, the Englishman decided around this period to pay Bartram a yearly fee himself. Collinson also arranged for several other English plant enthusiasts to pay similar fees, and Bartram gladly undertook to supply them, too.

In this way, the plain Quaker John Bartram came to have an important impact on the English landscape. He provided bushels of acorns that grew into stately oaks on many great estates, along with seeds of American cedars and sugar maples and numerous other native American species. His clients eventually included famous dukes and even the Prince of Wales, for the holder of that title in those days took a personal interest in turning Kew Gardens near London into one of the world's most noted horticultural centers.

As Bartram ranged ever further from Philadelphia on his expeditions, the size of his family also kept increasing. In addition to the son his first wife had given him, his second wife had eight children who survived to adulthood. When the eldest of all these sons and daughters began having children of their own, he wrote them a series of letters in which he summarized his opinions about how he believed babies should be raised. The letters amply prove that he must have been an unusually good father himself.

Besides objecting to the common practice then of keeping infants "swathed up not quite as tight as an Egyptian mummy," Bartram also disapproved of frightening children by telling them a big bear would catch them if they didn't do as they were bid. He suggested that parents should not "let a good Deed pass without praise nor a bad one without Rebuke"—a system he called "much better than all ye whip-ping, thumping, boxing, scolding & I know not what that is commonly used by parents."

Yet Bartram's guidance on the bringing up of children said nothing about how to avoid giving one child more love than any other. Perhaps because one of his sons clearly needed extra attention, this otherwise model father could not help favoring him. The boy who received special treatment was William, born with his twin sister Elizabeth on February 9, 1739.

From infancy Billy seemed not as sturdy as the rest of his family, although he had no particular health problem. Indeed, it was his restless nature that most set him apart. Bright as he appeared to be, he would flit from one occupation to another during his early years, doing well at whatever he tried but never sticking long with any chore. Because he was also small for his age, and very shy, his father often worried about his future.

Bartram's wish to keep Billy under his own watchful eye might have been the main reason why he decided—in the autumn of 1753, when Billy was fourteen—to take the boy with him on a plant-collecting journey into New York's Catskill Mountains. In addition, though, Bartram had a sociable disposition and he had often wished he could find somebody to accompany him when he rode off practically every spring and fall. Much to his satisfaction, the experiment of bringing Billy along worked out wonderfully.

Not only did Billy show by his behavior on the trip that he had inherited his father's strong feelings for nature, but he also demonstrated a real talent for making drawings of whatever they encountered. Bartram looked forward eagerly to sending his English friend Peter Collinson some of these sketches depicting features of the American wilderness much more clearly than any words could.

Even the hardships of the expedition failed to faze Billy. Because parts of the Catskills were so rugged, Bartram hired a local guide to escort them safely up and down some rocky slopes. As the three of them were proceeding on foot along a high ledge, with Billy in the lead, the boy noticed what seemed to be a large mushroom on their path, and he was about to kick it—when he suddenly saw that the object was actually a coiled rattlesnake.

Billy stopped and in a calm voice warned his father and the guide to watch their steps. Bartram's Quaker convictions against using any violence made him averse to killing the snake as it started slithering away from them, but the guide had no such scruples. He shot it, saying he never let a snake

escape him. Being unarmed, Billy still thought that he could have protected them all, if necessary, by using a tree branch to smash the rattler.

Owing to the success of this Catskill plant-collecting trip, Bartram took Billy with him again to the Catskills the following year. And they made several less extensive journeys together, but the time for establishing the young man in some career of his own was fast approaching. In this period he was attending the Philadelphia academy that a few years later would become the University of Pennsylvania—none of the other Bartram children had been given any such opportunity. Yet his exposure to higher education soon convinced Billy that he was not cut out to be a doctor, as his father had hoped. How, then, would he support himself?

Ben Franklin offered to take Billy under his own wing and train him as a printer. But Bartram objected that, apart from Franklin himself, printers were not very prosperous. In the spring of 1755, the perplexed father sought the advice of his English friend Peter Collinson.

His son Billy had just turned sixteen, he wrote, and "I want to put him to some business by which he may, with care and industry, get a reasonable living. I am afraid that botany and drawing will not afford him one, and hard labor don't agree with him . . . Pray, dear friend Peter, let me have thy opinion about it."

Like many others who ask advice, however, Bartram did not heed it. Although Collinson recommended encouraging Billy's artistic efforts, the young man's father apprenticed him to a Philadelphia storekeeper. But that did not solve the problem. During the next five years Billy drifted from one unsatisfying job to another, until his father agreed to let him try his luck working as an independent trader in North Carolina, where a relative had settled.

Even though that venture failed, too, it provided both father and son with opportunities to explore new areas rich in plant life. John Bartram found the Carolina mountains the most rewarding place for the collecting of new specimens that he had yet visited because the prevailing mists there gave off constant moisture, supporting an amazing growth of beautiful wildflowers and bushes.

This experience made him wish he could undertake still more ambitious expeditions along the continent's great rivers as well as into the territory of Florida, recently ceded by Spain to England. "Oh!" he wrote to Collinson, "if I could but spend 6 months on the Ohio, Mississippi & in Florida, I believe I could find more curiosities than

the English, French & Spanish have done in 6 score years."

Instead of bemoaning his inability to afford such extensive travel, though, Bartram boldly set about seeking assistance from no less a personage than King George III. First, to show that he deserved royal help, he shipped a box filled with choice specimens of American plants, addressed to the king himself. Then he began pulling whatever strings he could.

By the early 1760s, when Bartram embarked on this campaign, relations between England's American colonies and the mother country were beginning to become strained. So Benjamin Franklin, in London representing colonial interests, was able to do some unofficial prodding on Bartram's behalf. Meanwhile, Collinson enlisted the aid of many influential gardening enthusiasts. At last, in the spring of 1765, Collinson triumphantly informed Bartram of his appointment to the post of "King's Botanist" at a salary of fifty pounds a year.

Although the pay was less than Bartram had hoped for, he immediately asked Billy to accompany him to Florida. Their historic trip, marking the first real investigation of this region's exotic plant life, began in September of 1765, when the father and son sailed from Savannah, Georgia, bound for the

William Bartram's painting "Franklinia." *Courtesy of the Natural History Museum, London.*

old Spanish city of St. Augustine. Thanks to the prestige bestowed by John Bartram's new title and also to the renown his previous travels had brought him, the pair received a warm welcome from military officers at the fort there.

The next several months were the high point of John Bartram's life. Despite his having reached the age of sixty-six, he cheerfully endured the rigors involved in daily canoe travel through narrow inlets; he explored swamps and tramped the shores of uninhabited islands, always jotting down notes about the vegetation he found. Journeying hundreds of miles up and down the St. John's River, where only an occasional trading post or intrepid settler's plantation gave any sign of civilization, he never ceased marveling at nature's variety.

His son William Bartram was twenty-six when he joined his father on this expedition, and he still had not arrived at a fixed plan for his future. Happier away from the pressures of ordinary existence, he displayed a boyish streak of bravado early in the trip.

One afternoon when he was out walking with his father near the St. Augustine fort, he spied an enormous rattlesnake, grabbed a tree sapling, then clubbed the snake to death. What's more, he attached a rope to the creature and dragged it back to show it off at the fort. The commanding officer, who relished eating rattlesnake, ordered it served for dinner. Neither Billy nor his father could bear to taste a bite of it, yet the praise Billy got for his daring may have had something to do with a decision he soon announced.

He wanted to settle in Florida, Billy said, and he proposed buying a few slaves as well as a small plantation. Although his father foresaw another failure, his partiality toward this son made it impossible for him to object too strongly. He even gave Billy some money to make the required purchases. But the scheme ended in disaster.

Back in Philadelphia, John Bartram feared the worst when he heard nothing from his son for almost a year. At last, a Georgia friend relayed word that Billy had survived a serious bout of fever. However, his slaves had run away, his crops had been ruined, and he had lost every penny invested in this venture.

In the next several years, John Bartram himself received numerous honors. Ever since his first shipments of plants and his first letters to Europe had caused Peter Collinson to conclude that this American farmer had a superior mind, many of the leading scientists of the era had been coming to the same conclusion, because Collinson had encouraged Bartram to write directly to the most eminent men in the field of botany. Collinson had also delivered speeches incorporating Bartram's reports about some of his discoveries—speeches that were printed in the journals of some of Europe's outstanding scientific groups.

So it happened that the Swedish Carl Linnaeus, the towering figure in eighteenth century science, praised John Bartram as the greatest "natural botanist" the world had yet seen. A gold medal and a silver goblet were some of the prizes sent to Bartram from England. In 1769, he received word from Sweden of his election to membership in the Royal Academy of Science of Stockholm.

Bartram's pleasure at this news was sadly diminished because Peter Collinson had died the preceding year, ending a tie that had lasted thirty-five years. Also, the worsening tension between England and its American colonies much distressed him, for it threatened to cut off further shipments of American plants to English collectors. But Benjamin Franklin advised Bartram that in any case he should stop his "lengthy and dangerous travels" at his age, devoting himself instead to "a work that is much wanted and which no one besides is so capable of performing . . . the writing of a Natural History of our Country."

Bartram did not take Franklin's ad-vice, at least partly owing to his unwillingness to set himself up as an expert. Moreover, his mind was distracted by his worries about his son Billy, who still was just drifting aimlessly. Finally, in the summer of 1772, the thirty-three-year-old Billy sent his father a troubling letter from North Carolina.

Billy said he had spent most of the previous year reviewing his past and planning his future, as a result of which he had concluded that any sort of business career involved him too much with people and trivialities, leaving no quiet hours for his real interests—drawing and studying nature. So he was now determined "to retreat within myself to the only business I was born for, and which I am good for." In short, he would be departing soon on a solitary journey exploring more of Florida.

Although John Bartram despaired of ever seeing his son again, that decision put William Bartram on the road to fame. From 1772 through 1777, he traveled thousands of miles in Florida and neighboring territories, mostly alone and always carrying pencil and paper. A band of Seminole Indians he encountered gave him the name of Puc-Puggy, signifying Flower Hunter. But instead of collecting actual plants as his father had, he made drawings of them and described them vividly in the journal he kept.

When his drawings eventually

William Bartram four years before his death. *Independence National Historical Park Collection.*

reached London, they were praised as "exquisite." And when the journal was published, it attracted thousands of readers on both sides of the Atlantic—even inspiring poems by two of England's greatest poets, William Wordsworth and Samuel Taylor Coleridge. William Bartram's *Travels* still is considered a literary classic, owing to the richly emotional tone of passages like this description of a remote mountain scene: "How harmonious and sweetly murmur the purling rills and fleeting brooks, roving along the shadowy vales, passing through dark, subterranean caves, or dashing over steep rocky precipices . . ."

Unfortunately, John Bartram did not live to see the success of this son who had caused him so much concern. He died in his sleep at the age of seventy-eight, on September 22, 1777, about four months before William finally returned to Philadelphia.

Because William's health, never robust, had been weakened by his long southern wanderings, he never took another major trip. After being appointed professor of botany at the University of Pennsylvania, he turned down the post on the grounds of poor health. But

he and his brother John, who had managed their father's nursery business during the latter's last years, jointly preserved the famous Bartram Garden until John's death in 1812.

William, who never married, continued to live on the family's property with one of John's daughters and her husband. A few visitors still came to see the garden, and the nursery business kept operating on a small scale. In addition, William spent many happy hours drawing illustrations for books on botany and other natural sciences. It was just after he had finished writing the precise description of a plant for one of these volumes that William died suddenly on July 22, 1823, at the advanced age of eighty-four.

A generation later the Bartram Garden began falling into neglect. Weeds choked its once-neat rows as more and more factories were built in the area. Then around 1900 the city of Philadelphia, together with a group calling itself the John Bartram Association, started to restore the historic garden. Now, it looks much as it used to—and thousands of plant lovers visit it every year.

Hugh Hammond Bennett

1881–1960   American soil scientist known as the father of the soil
conservation movement

The wind blew fiercely in the West, piling up drifts of soil that covered some roads ten feet deep. Airplanes climbed to 20,000 feet to get above the clouds of dust in Texas, Wyoming, Nebraska, and North Dakota. In Kansas, visibility dropped to less than three hundred yards at midday. All over the Dust Bowl of the 1930s, the bones of starved cattle lay whitening under the occasional sunlight.

Far away in the nation's capital, during the spring of 1935 a small group of senators sat around a table. They were considering one of the many bills introduced in those early days of President Franklin D. Roosevelt's New Deal. Facing them sat an obscure civil servant, who seemed to know what he was talking about.

The witness, Hugh Hammond Bennett, spoke with a southern accent. He was a large and rumpled-looking man—his hair was ruffled, his tie twisted, and his vest half-buttoned. Despite his appearance, he held the senators' attention as he described the Dust Bowl crisis.

"On the 11th of May last year, we had for the first time since the white man came to America, one of those dust storms which came over Washington, almost blotted out the sun, reached a height of more than 8,000 feet and settled on the decks of ships three hundred miles out from the Atlantic coast," he said.

Bennett explained the reasons for the Dust Bowl. Drought had dried up the soil under the grasses of the Great

61

Plains, leaving it in a powdery condition. Then windstorms had swept up the loose soil, sending it swirling eastward, and continued to do so.

State by state, Bennett called out the roll of disaster in the Great Plains. He reported abandoned farms, soil clogging streams, and wind erosion that had already taken four million acres out of food production, besides damaging sixty million additional acres.

Although the senators seemed weary, Bennett did not hurry his testimony for a very special reason. He knew what was coming later that day. According to weather reports, another giant dust storm was on its way from the West—and, more than any words, that would surely have a dramatic impact on the lawmakers.

In midafternoon, as Bennett continued testifying, one of the senators interrupted him.

"It is getting dark," the senator said. "Perhaps a rainstorm is brewing."

"Maybe it's dust," another senator said.

Bennett nodded. "I think you are correct," he said. "Senator, it does look like dust."

Bennett had perfectly timed the storm's arrival as the climax of his testimony. The senators gathered at a window, watching as the dust blotted out the sun. Heavy with grit from the West, the air of Washington turned the color of copper, making it impossible to see the green grass around the capital.

A page boy entered with a telegram from Oklahoma City for one of the senators. It read: WORST OF ALL DUST STORMS NOW RAGING IN THIS CITY. STREET LIGHTS ARE ON. YOU CAN'T SEE THE LENGTH OF A BLOCK.

The senators needed no more convincing. They passed the first soil conservation act in the history of the United States—or of any other country—creating a Soil Conservation Service, with Bennett as its first director.

It was one of those rare times when the right man appeared at the right time to solve a major problem facing the nation. For years, Bennett had been a voice in the wilderness crying out that attention must be paid to the conservation of one of America's greatest natural resources, its soil. Now the opportunity had come to practice what he had preached.

Who was the man the Congress turned to in this time of national peril?

Hugh Hammond Bennett was a soil scientist, just one of tens of thousands of government employees quietly doing their jobs in Washington. In several foreign lands—in Mexico, in Cuba, and in Brazil—he had already received honors for his contributions to agriculture. But he and his profession were still largely unknown in the United States.

Called upon to cope with one of nature's greatest calamities, Bennett was ready. At the age of fifty-four, he organized the nation to protect its foundation, the land itself.

His fellow workers at the Department of Agriculture called him "Big Hugh" because of his size and his appetite. He was six feet one inch tall, but somehow seemed larger because of his rumpled appearance. One friend described him as a walking filing cabinet, his pockets filled with notes, clippings, and memos.

Bennett paid no attention to how he looked. On one occasion, when he was getting ready for a formal party in a foreign country, he found himself without the customary black tie. He knotted two black socks together as a substitute. "It looked fine, too," he said later with a laugh.

His colleagues knew him as a man who loved to eat. Once, one of them arranged a lunch for him by sending over a menu and asking Bennett to check his choice. Bennett checked everything and then ate it all.

He lived in Washington with his second wife, Betty Virginia Brown, and their son, Hugh Hammond Bennett, Jr. His wife tried her best to improve his appearance when he went to testify before Congress, but Bennett somehow always achieved an untidy look in minutes.

No matter where he lived, he maintained a personal connection with the soil by planting a garden. One year, his son recalled, he planted twenty-four different varieties of black-eyed peas to see how they grew and tasted.

Although Bennett worked at a desk in Washington, he did not like it. He preferred to go out to farm country, into the fields, talking to active farmers. When he traveled, he usually refused to stay in hotels. Instead, he camped out in the open, even cooking his own meals.

"The best way is to put everything in one pot but the coffee," he said. "Some people might call it a chowder or a stew but it isn't. It is a sort of slum gullion. And there's nothing quite so good if you are really hungry and tired and camping out."

Bennett's love of the outdoors grew naturally from his farm upbringing. He was born on April 15, 1881, just outside Wadesboro, North Carolina, not far from the South Carolina border. One of nine children, he lived on a plantation owned and operated by his father, William Osborne Bennett. His mother, the former Rosa May Hammond, came from a family of cotton exporters.

Once the soil of the area had been fertile, producing large quantities of cotton, a major crop of the South. But when Bennett was a boy, the land clearly showed the ravages of a system

Hugh Hammond Bennett. From *Big Hugh: The Father of Soil Conservation*, by Wellington Brink. New York: The Macmillan Co., 1951.

that kept cutting down trees to make more fields for more cotton. Whenever it rained, water rushed down the cultivated slopes, creating gullies almost everywhere.

Farmers tried to prevent erosion by building level terraces on sloping ground, but that didn't always work. On the Bennett farm, Hugh and the other boys helped their father lay out the terraces. One day when he was about ten years old, Hugh stopped to ask why they were doing all this work.

"To keep the land from washing away," his father replied. Hugh never forgot those words.

Hugh rode a mule to school in Wadesboro, about three miles from his home. When the mules were needed for farm work, Hugh and his brothers walked. Although the Bennetts were not a poor family, the boys had to work to pay for a college education.

In the summer of 1896, when Hugh was fifteen, he cut and split wood to earn enough to enroll that autumn at the University of North Carolina in Chapel Hill. A pile of two hundred cords of wood sat on the plantation, ready for sale. But before it could be sold, a hunter set fire to nearby brush to scare out some game. Wind carried the flames to the woodpile, sending Hugh's hopes of going to college that year up in smoke.

He did go to Chapel Hill the follow-ing year, studying geology and chemistry. A job as a lab assistant helped Hugh to pay his expenses, but after two years his funds were exhausted. He dropped out to earn more money by working awhile for a Wadesboro druggist, finally graduating from college in 1903 when he was twenty-two.

By chance, he recalled later, he saw an advertisement announcing a civil service examination for the post of chemist in the Bureau of Soils of the United States Department of Agriculture. Bennett passed the test with the highest grade of any applicant and went to work surveying soils in Davidson County, Tennessee, at a salary of one thousand dollars a year.

On foot or riding a horse, Bennett and his fellow workers covered miles of fields and hills. Using an augur three to five feet long, they drilled into the soil to observe and classify it. In those days before soil maps were common, they made their own. They measured distances by adjusting their steps to three feet on the average or by record-ing the revolutions of a buggy wheel. Then they noted the varying soil types on their maps.

From Tennessee, Bennett went on to do similar mapping in Virginia, Alabama, and upstate New York. Next, he was sent back to Virginia with instruc-tions to find out why Louisa County in the middle portion of the state had a reputation for having unusually poor soil.

In 1905, the twenty-four-year-old Bennett and a fellow mapper made a simple observation. They looked at two pieces of adjoining land, one soft and loamy and the other clay that was as hard as a rock. The good soil bordered on wooded land, covered with forest litter. The other piece was a field that had been farmed for a long time.

Bennett later recalled: "We figured that both areas had been the same originally and that the clay of the cultivated area could have reached the surface only through the process of rainwash— that is, the gradual removal, with heavy rainfall, of a thin sheet of topsoil." The technical term for what they observed was sheet erosion, or the slow washing away of thin layers of soil by the action of rain.

Erosion was not a new discovery, of course. From the earliest colonial days, progressive farmers had noted that heavy rains carried topsoil away. They saw gullies created by rushing water on some farm fields, making the land useless for crops. On other fields, after crops were harvested, sometimes the wind blew topsoil away, too, making the land less fertile.

Year after year, in some areas farmland became worn out and produced smaller crops. The normal solution for many early farmers was to move west, where land was abundant and available for the taking. But some farsighted farmers worried about the land and tried to find ways of saving it. They experimented with new kinds of plowing, filling in gullies, rotating crops, and making terraced fields on hillsides.

Still, those early conservationists were too few in number to make a major impact. They had no soil scientists to advise them, no program of research, no help from the government. Their individual conservation efforts worked on their own farms, but few listened to them.

As late as the early 1900s, officials in the Bureau of Soils in Washington believed that the soil was indestructible, that it was "the one resource that cannot be exhausted." And so, when Bennett reported his findings that rainfall caused gradual soil erosion, they fell on deaf ears.

Two years later, in a soil survey of Fairfield County in South Carolina, Bennett reported that 136,000 acres of formerly good cropland had been ruined for farming by gullies or swamps caused by erosion. Although his report—the first large-scale survey of the devastation caused by soil erosion—was printed, it was ignored by farm officials and farmers alike.

No matter that his reports attracted

little notice, Bennett was not discouraged. He continued to work in various parts of the country and even received promotions. At the age of twenty-six, in 1907, he married Sara McCue. But she died shortly after giving birth to a daughter.

In 1909, Bennett went to the Panama Canal Zone as part of a commission to study its agricultural possibilities. Later, he acted as chairman of an expedition to survey the soils of Alaska in preparation for building a railroad. When the United States entered World War I in 1917, he served as a lieutenant in the army's corps of engineers. Then after the war, he traveled frequently to countries in Central and South America to help with soil and farm problems.

During all those years, though, Bennett's main occupation remained trying to convince the American public and Congress of the dangers of soil erosion. He spoke at farm meetings and to any scientific group that would hear him, in addition to writing many papers and reports.

One of his reports, *Soil Erosion, a National Menace*, published in 1928, finally made an impression. Bennett and his coauthor, W. R. Chapline, estimated that five hundred million tons of soil—an incredible amount—flowed into the sea each year as the result of erosion.

Called to testify before a committee of the House of Representatives, Bennett persuaded it and the Senate to appropriate $100,000 to gather data on soil erosion across the nation. It marked the beginning of the scientific study of soil erosion—twenty-four years after Bennett's first report about the problem back in Louisa County, Virginia.

He set up ten research stations around the country to measure soil and water losses after rainfall. Slowly, his ideas of soil conservation began to win converts. But they also drew attention from some other government workers who saw his new network as a means of obtaining appropriations and power in the new administration of President Franklin Roosevelt.

Bennett heard about one of the new proposals—to spend $5 million on a new program of terracing land. He stormed into the office of the assistant secretary of agriculture, Rexford Guy Tugwell.

Tugwell welcomed him warmly. "It's good to meet at last the man whom I have always looked on as the father of soil conservation," he said. "What can I do for you?"

Bennett told him that more harm than good had been done by putting terraces in the wrong places. Then he proceeded to outline his ideas about a whole range of soil conservation practices.

"That sounds reasonable to me," Tugwell said. "I'll see what I can do."

For once the government bureaucracy acted swiftly. Within just a few months a new agency was set up, called the Soil Erosion Service. It was the first erosion control agency in any major country of the world.

For Bennett—and the nation—September 19, 1933, became an important date. At last his dream was realized. He became director of the new Soil Erosion Service in the Department of the Interior, with enough funds available to carry out his mission of saving the nation's soil.

Bennett went to work quickly. From his years in the field, he knew the right people to hire. He gathered teams of engineers, crop experts, biologists, foresters, and soil surveyors. In a few months, he had forty erosion control projects under way covering four million acres in thirty-one states.

To do all this work, Bennett used the labor of thousands of men in the CCC—the Civilian Conservation Corps, recruited from the unemployed in the nation's cities as part of the New Deal program for coping with the Great Depression of the 1930s. He also hired hundreds of recent graduates of agricultural and engineering colleges to train in soil erosion control.

Their work aroused such enthusiasm

that, within a year, Bennett received more than double the amount of money his agency had originally been granted. In addition, President Roosevelt called him to the White House to congratulate him personally on "the good job" he was doing.

"You want to know how I found out about it?" Roosevelt asked.

"Yes, sir," Bennett said.

"They're after you, Bennett," the President replied, referring to jealous colleagues. "And when they're after somebody, he's usually doing a good job."

Then, right after Bennett's dramatic testimony the day the dust storm from the West hit Washington, Congress changed the name of the Soil Erosion Service to the Soil Conservation Service, making it a permanent part of the United States Department of Agriculture because its work was so closely connected with farmers.

States throughout the nation set up conservation districts in which farmers themselves organized to save their soil, with the help of Bennett's technicians. In 1937, the Brown Creek Soil Conservation District, which included the Bennett family farm in North Carolina, became the first official conservation district in the country.

Bennett saw farmer cooperation as the keystone to the success of the con-

Young men march in step for the C.C.C. (Civilian Conservation Corps). *Brown Brothers.*

servation districts. Aided by Soil Conservation Service experts, farmers built drainage ditches, ponds, and terraces. They installed underground tile drains, planted windbreaks, grew cover crops to hold the soil in place, and rotated crops like corn and alfalfa. Some farmers found that, by conserving their soil, they doubled their production—and increased their income.

By that time, Bennett had learned that doing good work in the field was only half of his job. The other half was convincing Congress to keep support-

ing his agency—and Bennett became a master at it.

He delighted in using simple illustrations when he appeared before congressional committees. Once he brought in a plow to demonstrate how it turned over the soil. Another time, he showed a 100-year-old fence post made of locust that had grown in a gully.

His favorite trick, though, was to spread a thick bath towel out on the table in front of him, then pour a pitcher of water on it. The towel absorbed most of the water. Next, he lifted the towel

Two government posters of the 1930s promoting conservation: PLAINS FARMS NEED TREES by Joseph Dusek, Chicago, Illinois, and SPARE OUR TREES by Stanley T. Clough, Cleveland, Ohio. *The Library of Congress.*

and poured water on the smooth table-top and watched it run over onto the rug.

"I didn't say anything right away—just stood there looking at the mess on the floor," he noted.

Then he explained to the committee that the smooth tabletop resembled bare eroded land, while the towel represented well-managed land that could absorb rainfall. The simple demonstration convinced Congress to vote

him the money that he requested.

Bennett became increasingly known as the man with the answers to the problems of soil erosion. He received many medals and honorary degrees, besides being nominated for a Nobel Prize. But the honor that pleased him most was North Carolina's proclamation of Hugh Hammond Bennett Conservation Day, when thousands of people came to Wadesboro for a parade, speeches, and a barbecue feast.

Bennett retired from government service in 1952, when he was seventy-one years old. He continued to serve as a consultant on soil problems to many foreign governments until his death on July 7, 1960, at the age of seventy-nine. He was buried with full military honors in Arlington National Cemetery.

The *Milwaukee Journal* commented: "Great men are memorialized in stone and metal, but the earth itself is being carved into a memorial to Hugh Bennett."

Luther Burbank

1849–1926 American horticulturist whose experiments led to the development of new varieties of cultivated plants

What Luther Burbank remembered best about his boyhood was a fabulous discovery that he made one winter afternoon. Walking through a patch of woods near his family's farm in Massachusetts, he was feeling so fed up with cold weather that he kept kicking at the snow on the ground and calling it names. Then suddenly he saw a green place ahead of him.

"I could not believe my eyes," he wrote many years later. But when he ran down into the magic little hollow, he found that green grass and vines really were growing there. He even spied a few clumps of yellow buttercups.

Carefully inspecting this amazing oasis, Lute soon figured out the reason for its existence. Thanks to a warm spring of water bubbling up from far below the earth's surface, enough heat

was being provided to "fool" these plants. The thought that nature itself could play such tricks excited his lively mind tremendously. Long afterward, when Luther Burbank's own experiments with plants had brought him great fame, he would say that coming upon the winter buttercups had inspired his whole career.

And it was a remarkable career. Burbank's work as a plant breeder who introduced dozens of new varieties of fruits and flowers attracted an immense amount of publicity during his lifetime. The seeming magic he achieved made many people put him into the top rank of American heroes—despite grumblings among scientists that his accomplishments were being much exaggerated.

Then after his death, the opinion of

those experts who had condemned him as a "nature-faker" gradually prevailed, and he was almost forgotten. In recent years, however, the verdict has changed again. Now, even though plant science has advanced enormously since his era, it seems that Burbank actually deserved a lot of the praise he received in his own day.

The subject of all this attention was born on March 7, 1849, into a family that had never stood out in any particular way. His father, Samuel Walton Burbank, combined farming with running a small brickyard, while his mother, Olive Ross Burbank, was the daughter of a cabinetmaker. On both sides, his ancestry could be traced back to plain farm people from England or Scotland who had crossed the ocean seeking better lives.

In the New England of Luther Burbank's youth, large families were much more common than they are today. Sadly, the death of babies was common, too, and many women died as the result of infections associated with childbirth. Still, in the Burbank farmhouse outside the town of Lancaster, about thirty miles west of Boston, an unusual number of these tragedies occurred.

Long before Luther's birth, his father had married for the first time, and this first wife had eight children. But only three of them were still alive when their mother died. Then Samuel Burbank's

second wife and her two children had died. Samuel's third wife—Luther's mother—had already gone through the misery of losing her first two sons by the time Luther arrived.

Thus, even though Luther was listed in the family Bible as his father's thirteenth child, he only knew two older brothers and one sister. During the next few years after his birth came another boy, Alfred, and a girl, Emma, who both grew into sturdy youngsters. Lute himself was always small for his age, however, and his parents worried about his health.

So he was never pressed to do chores that might tax his limited strength. Lute often helped his mother in her flower garden, instead of assisting his father with heavier work around the farm. A shy boy, he spent many hours playing alone. But he laughed easily, and he seemed to have a gift for making people like him.

At the age of five, Lute started attending a little school not far from his home, where his much-older brother Herbert was the teacher. On snowy days, Herbert pulled him to school aboard a sled. Besides doing well with his lessons, Lute kept thinking up diverting pastimes. Many years later, he listed what he had enjoyed best:

Every child should have mud pies, grasshoppers, water bugs, tadpoles, frogs, mud-turtles, elderberries, wild strawberries, acorns, chestnuts, trees to climb, brooks to wade in, water-lilies, woodchucks, bats, bees, butterflies, various animals to pet, hayfields, pine cones, rocks to roll, sand, snakes, huckleberries and hornets; and any child who has been deprived of these has been deprived of the best part of his education.

Yet probably the most important part of Lute's education came during the many walks he took with a grown cousin, a man who was more successful in the eyes of the world than any other of his relatives. Levi Sumner Burbank, the eldest son of one of Lute's uncles, had risen to become the president of Paducah College in Kentucky. Then the outbreak of the Civil War had brought him home again.

Lute was twelve years old when Cousin Levi, noted as an expert in the science of geology, came back to live in Lancaster. Soon this boy with such a fondness for nature was accompanying this eminent collector of rocks on frequent outings around the countryside. In effect, Lute received private lessons in every aspect of nature study from a professor who knew just how to explain even the most complicated topics so that they seemed "alive and exciting and never dull and tedious."

Cousin Levi "had read more books and understood them better than any one else I knew," Luther Burbank would write many years later. Looking back, Burbank thought that the experience of walking and talking with him had shaped his own future course in many ways. Nevertheless, this course by no means appeared clear during his early years.

Because his father's health was failing, as Lute entered his teens he had to work for months at a time driving a wagon that delivered bricks. Then, when he was fifteen, he enrolled at the Lancaster Academy, where he spent the next four winters as a student. Summers, he stayed with relatives in the city of Worcester and worked at a plow factory.

He did so well there, figuring out ways to improve the machinery, that he was offered a permanent job when he was nineteen. But Lute was positive that he did not want to spend his life in a factory—even if he could not yet see how else he might be able to earn money more happily. Prodded by his ailing father, he began assisting in the office of a local doctor; in those days, it was possible to qualify as a physician without any special schooling.

At the public library, though, Lute kept borrowing books that interested him much more than medical studies did. Charles Darwin, Henry David Thoreau, and Alexander von Humboldt—all outstanding naturalists— were his favorite authors. In the year he turned twenty, the death of his father upset him so deeply that he quit the work he could not find rewarding and embarked on a bold adventure.

Aboard a fishing boat off the coast of Canada, Luther Burbank finally decided that he had to trust his own feelings about his future. Soon after returning from the voyage, he used his small inheritance to buy seventeen acres of unusually fine soil a few miles beyond Lancaster. Here he began growing vegetables to sell in nearby cities.

Yet Burbank was well aware that he could not prosper by offering just ordinary vegetables. Recalling the winter buttercups of his boyhood, he aimed to bring his peas and corn to market at least a few weeks earlier than other growers could—or even to develop better-tasting varieties. A book he had recently gotten from the library had set his mind to exploring all sorts of thrilling possibilities along these lines.

The book was Charles Darwin's *Variations of Animals and Plants Under Domestication*. In it, the famous British naturalist described how plants could be changed by brushing the pollen from one type of flower onto the little spikes within the blossom of a related flower. Then the seeds produced by any plant that had been treated this way might yield some surprises. The resulting new plants could even be superior, from one standpoint or another, to either of their parents.

Down through the ages, many plant improvements of the sort Darwin discussed had come about accidentally, when birds or insects "crossed" one variety with another. Also, observant gardeners all over the world had sometimes practiced an elementary kind of plant breeding. What struck Burbank as such an enormous challenge, though, was purposely to undertake the breeding of new plants on a more ambitious scale than had ever before been attempted.

As it happened, however, Burbank's first great triumph resulted from a happy accident.

Soon after buying his farm, he started concentrating on potatoes because insect pests and plant diseases were keeping farmers from growing the type of good-sized white potato people wanted. But potato plants, unlike most others, practically never produced seeds—new crops were sown by setting out rows of old potatoes, whose sprouts grew into plants beneath which clusters of tubers just like the parent potato soon formed. So how could a better potato conceivably be developed?

One day when Burbank was out walking through his field of potatoes, he was astounded to find his answer. Atop one plant of the Early Rose variety— the best then available—he spied a seedpod! While the odds against making such a discovery were probably a million to one, he knew exactly what to do.

As soon as the seedpod ripened, Burbank carefully cut it open. Inside were twenty-three seeds. The next spring, he planted them and all of them came up. But with the touch of genius he himself could never explain, he selected one plant as the best of the lot. From this plant came such outstanding potatoes that they are still this country's most popular baking variety.

In the autumn of 1875, Burbank sold a large sack of his superior potatoes to a Massachusetts seed company for one hundred fifty dollars, saving only ten potatoes as a sort of insurance. He also sold his farm. Bent on experimenting with plants, rather than becoming a businessman, he had decided to move to a more favorable climate where he could work outdoors every month of the year. That October, at the age of twenty-six, he boarded a train for California.

Actually, Burbank had a few other reasons for taking this great step. Around the time of his birth, the discovery of gold in California had spurred

his oldest brother George to join the rush of westbound fortune seekers. While George had never gotten rich, his glowing letters about the endless sunshine he had found had already lured Luther's younger brother Alfred to try his luck there. In addition, Luther's own hopes for winning the heart of a girl named Mary had just been dashed.

Yet Luther Burbank's arrival in California, for whatever reasons, could not have been better timed. Owing to the recent completion of railroad tracks linking the West Coast with the rest of the country, suddenly it was possible to ship California crops all over the United States. So a great agricultural expansion had started—and anybody who could help growers produce better varieties, especially of fruit, was almost bound to succeed.

Still, Burbank did not immediately thrive. Settling in the small city of Santa Rosa, about two hours north of San Francisco, he lived at first in a small shed his brother Alfred built for them. While Alfred earned money as a carpenter, Luther worked at a nearby plant nursery. Perhaps from the steamy atmosphere of the greenhouse there, he fell ill with a high fever.

Then his mother and sister Emma came hurrying from Massachusetts to take care of him. Mrs. Burbank bought a house in Santa Rosa with four acres of adjoining land. Here, after another few years of making only a small income growing and selling his own variety of potatoes, Luther Burbank finally began his rise to fame.

Early in the spring of 1881, a local banker came to him with an amazing request. Warren Dutton wanted to raise prunes on a big scale, and he wanted to get started as soon as possible. Could Burbank supply him with 20,000 little plum trees no later than December first?

An order for so many plum trees was remarkable enough—the idea of growing this kind of fruit, which could easily be sun-dried and then shipped east without any danger of spoilage, had only lately struck some canny Californians. But to ask for so many trees so quickly was to expect something like a miracle. Normally, it would take several years to produce plum trees ready to be set out in an orchard.

Yet as Burbank was about to tell Dutton that nobody could possibly fill his order, he stopped and thought a few seconds. Almond trees were not hard to start by simply planting almond seeds. And almond trees were notably fast-growing. Why not try turning 20,000 almond seedlings into plum trees within a single growing season?

The practice of grafting buds from one kind of fruit tree onto the twigs of another had been common for centuries. Nevertheless, nobody had ever accomplished such a large-scale transformation so dramatically. When Burbank delivered 20,000 healthy little plum trees by the promised date, word of his achievement spread rapidly.

Soon Burbank was operating a nursery business that brought him a comfortable income. In 1884, he purchased additional land—and indicated his underlying goal by calling this plot his Experimental Gardens. The first project he undertook at the new site resulted from his having come across a book in which an American sailor who had visited Japan described an incredibly delicious red plum that he had eaten there.

Burbank managed to find the name of an English merchant living in Japan and sent him an order for a large batch of seeds and cuttings from fruit trees. Within three years, Burbank was satisfied that he had duplicated the marvelous Satsuma plum with blood-red flesh the sailor had written about—besides developing several other outstanding varieties. So his 1887 catalog offered growers a dozen kinds of trees that would produce these novelties.

As a result, Burbank's nursery trade increased to such an extent that, once again, he demonstrated his lack of interest in merely becoming prosperous. He sold off his business, then took a trip back to Massachusetts where he much enjoyed letting old friends gather how well he had done. When one of them asked him what he would raise if he still had a farm in New England, his answer was: "I think I would try to raise enough money to get to California."

Aboard the train taking him westward once more, Burbank met a young widow from Denver who seemed very agreeable. On September 23, 1890, at the age of forty-one, he married Helen Coleman. But right from the outset she complained about her husband's absorption in his work, and she called his mother "an old vicious cat." After much unhappiness, in 1896 Burbank and his wife were divorced.

By then he was no longer just locally celebrated as a man capable of working magic with plants. Thanks to the Satsuma plum, Burbank had become famous all over the country. In leading newspapers and magazines, he was called the greatest "plant wizard" who had ever lived.

The writers who kept coming to interview him made much of Burbank's modest personality. Describing him as a man of medium size, with lively blue eyes and a boyish manner, the stories about him said he would much rather avoid being photographed or otherwise interrupted.

Yet Burbank himself could not seem to help making grandiose claims about his work. On the covers of his catalogs—for he still kept selling plant novelties in order to finance his experimenting—he printed highly flattering tributes from his customers. "What Shakespeare was to poetry and the drama Luther Burbank is to the vegetable world," one of these proclaimed.

Among agricultural scientists, this sort of puffery stirred increasing antagonism. To start with, some of the major figures at research centers generously praised Burbank. Liberty Hyde Bailey, the dean of Cornell's College of Agriculture, whose books on botany had won him international renown, visited Santa Rosa in 1901, and he was very favorably impressed. Bailey wrote:

Luther Burbank is not a wizard. He is an honest, straightforward, careful, inquisitive, persistent man. His new plants are the results of downright, earnest, long-continued effort. He earns them. He has no other magic than that of patient inquiry, abiding enthusiasm, an unprejudiced mind, and a remarkably acute judgment of the merits and capabilities of plants.

Bailey even excused Burbank's failure to keep any scientific records of his experiments. But another professor assigned by a foundation to study Burbank's methods became more and more distressed by Burbank's reliance on his

Luther Burbank offers flowers to the tennis champion Helen Hull Jacobs. *The Bettmann Archive*.

Luther Burbank with his famous Shasta daisies, named after a mountain in California's Cascade Range. (In the lower right-hand corner, an oval inset of Mount Shasta's snowcapped peaks.) *Stark Brothers Nurseries.*

own memory rather than any written account of the crosses he made. In 1905, this foundation created by the millionaire industrialist Andrew Carnegie had awarded Burbank what was supposed to be the first of a ten-year series of $10,000-a-year grants. Four years later, however, the grants were discontinued.

Yet the general public marveled over a new flower Burbank had recently introduced—the Shasta daisy, a much prettier and more hardy version of a wild white daisy he had found growing near California's Mount Shasta. Also, new fruits and berries that he offered in his annual catalogs were proving very popular. Reaching for an even greater triumph, Burbank promised that the western deserts would be soon transformed into valuable pasture land nourishing huge herds of cattle because he now aimed to produce *spineless* giant cactus.

The flood of publicity about this cactus project hurt Burbank seriously in the scientific community. For many reasons, both botanic and agricultural, there was no possibility of creating a truly spineless cactus on which animals could feed. At meetings of plant experts, speakers ridiculed "the sage of Santa Rosa," reciting verses like:

O, Mr. Burbank, won't you try and
   do some things for me?
A wizard clever as you are can do
   them easily.
A man who turns a cactus plant into
   a feather bed
Should have no trouble putting
   brains into a cabbage head.

In this same period, Burbank's reputation suffered further when a set of expensive books he had let promoters publish about his work turned out to contain many unjustified claims. In addition, some business difficulties cast him in an unfavorable light. Nevertheless, to the majority of Americans he remained a hero.

In 1915, the famous automobile manufacturer Henry Ford paid Burbank a visit, along with the inventor Thomas Alva Edison. Pictures of these three chatting together appeared in newspapers all over the country, with captions exalting the trio as the nation's greatest men.

The following year, Burbank again made headlines. At the age of sixty-seven, on December 21, 1916, he married his secretary, Elizabeth Jane Waters, who was in her twenties. Till then his adoring sister Emma had kept house for him.

A year later, California's state board of education published a booklet about nature study featuring Luther Burbank's work—and this was used by schools everywhere, spreading Burbank's fame among the coming generation. Although Burbank himself became increasingly frail, he still spent a few hours every day in his Experimental Gardens, and he still kept hoping to give the world a spineless cactus.

Early in the spring of 1926, Burbank suffered a heart attack. Although he seemed to be getting better, shortly after his seventy-seventh birthday, on April 11, 1926, Luther Burbank died.

During the next several decades, as plant science vastly expanded its horizons, Burbank's reputation kept diminishing. Even so, at least three of his discoveries—the Burbank potato, the Satsuma plum, and the Shasta daisy—

have turned out to rank among the most successful varieties any plant breeder has ever introduced.

In addition, all the publicity that Burbank received now seems to have served the very worthwhile purpose of stimulating research at state agricultural colleges. Among many other benefits, this research has helped to make Burbank himself a more respected figure—because at least some of his ideas that struck scientists of his day as quirky or just plain wrong have come to be regarded as possibly valid.

Also, Burbank's ability to select the most promising plant from among hundreds or even thousands of apparently identical seedlings continues to arouse the awe of experts. Citing this talent, along with his mass-production methods, the writer of a recent book about him summed up his career by calling Luther Burbank "the Henry Ford of the art of plant-breeding."

John Burroughs

1837–1921   American observer of nature; author of nature essays

As a boy, he was a prize berry picker. On his family's hilly farm in a remote and beautiful area of New York's Catskill Mountains, he worked hard, too, at hoeing long rows of corn every summer and at digging potatoes every autumn. Always, though, he kept storing up intensely vivid impressions of birds and trees and everything else comprising the marvelous world of nature.

John Burroughs used these boyhood memories throughout his remarkable successful career as a writer about nature. Over a period of sixty years, his many books and magazine articles made him one of the best-loved figures of his era among ordinary readers. In addition, his work led to warm friendships with some of the nation's outstanding personages—including President Theodore Roosevelt, Henry Ford, and the great inventor Thomas Alva Edison.

Burroughs himself never ceased being awed by the fame his writings brought him. Although in his later life he traveled widely, he still felt most at ease in a familiar, simple rural setting. So he spent at least part of every year back in the Catskills, renewing the ties he had formed there during his youth.

The seventh child in a large family—altogether, he had six brothers and three sisters—John Burroughs had been born in a plain farmhouse on April 3, 1837. His parents were Chauncey A. Burroughs and Amy Kelly Burroughs, both descended from early settlers who had left England or Ireland before the United States gained its independence. One of John's grandfathers had served as a soldier under the command of General George Washington during the American Revolution, but, otherwise, none of his ancestors had stood out in any way.

While John never thought of his family as having been poor, money was certainly scarce in the agricultural community where he grew up. It was not easy to prosper there, given the rocky soil and the short growing season of this mountain region. Even so, the Burroughs farm offered a rich variety of scenic vistas from its high meadows above the small village of Roxbury—and these surroundings provided a wonderful training ground for a future naturalist.

Yet only limited schooling was available in the area. Most farm boys and girls attended classes just a few months every winter, when they could be spared from field or kitchen chores. Then, around the age of twelve, they became full-time farmers or mothers' helpers. So nobody could have expected any local child to do much reading, let alone learn enough to turn into a famous writer. As an adult, Burroughs would always remember that, despite the deep affection linking every member of his family, neither his parents nor any of his brothers and sisters did more than merely glance at his own

first book when he proudly brought it home to show it to them.

Somehow, though, John alone felt a constant thirst for learning during his childhood. He avidly read any books he could borrow at the one-room school he went to from the age of five onward, and he developed a special fondness for high-sounding words. Once at a lecture in the village, the speaker said something about the *Encyclopaedia Britannica*. John had not the slightest notion of what the man meant, but the mere words delighted him to the extent that he went around for weeks saying them to himself. "What a fine mouthful it was!" he remembered long afterward.

Because John seemed so bent on studying, his father let him go to school winter after winter until he had learned as much as the local teacher could teach him. By then John was sixteen—a tall, skinny young fellow determined to acquire some higher education. When his father told him that no money could be spared for any such purpose, John made up his mind to earn enough himself.

In the spring of 1854, shortly before his seventeenth birthday, carrying a black oilcloth traveling bag and with just a few dollars from his mother in his pocket, John set out on foot to try his luck beyond the mountains. Leaving home this way was the bravest step he

John Burroughs in his Catskills cabin, 1910. *The Bettmann Archive.*

ever took, for he felt extremely strong ties to his native landscape as well as to his relatives. Also, because he was very shy, he feared he would have a difficult time living among strangers.

Still, the young Burroughs had already begun to dream of becoming a writer. Spurred by this ambition, he sought work using his head rather than his hands. Despite the gaps in his knowledge, he managed to get hired

as the teacher at a rural school like the one he had just left, down near the Hudson River outside the town of Kingston. His pay was eleven dollars a month, plus food and lodging supplied by families of his pupils. He found "boarding 'round," which meant moving into a new household every month, even more of a test than standing up in front of a roomful of students.

After five months Burroughs had

saved fifty dollars, enough to pay for a semester at a new academy grandly named the Ashland Collegiate Institute. At this glorified high school in a mountain village only about thirty miles from his home, he learned some basic algebra and chemistry, besides discovering to his satisfaction that the compositions he wrote were highly regarded by the faculty. But his money ran out before he could advance any further, and he had to go back to teaching.

After he had accumulated some savings again, Burroughs enrolled for another term of schooling himself—this time at the Cooperstown Seminary in Cooperstown, New York. During the three months he spent there he read some of the essays of Ralph Waldo Emerson, and this eminent author deeply influenced Burroughs's own thinking. "I got him in my blood," Burroughs said later, "and he colored my whole intellectual outlook."

If Burroughs could have continued his studies uninterruptedly, perhaps he would have had quite a different sort of career focused on complex questions about Emerson's philosophy. As it was, however, he had to resume working after just one semester at Cooperstown, which turned out to be his last taste of higher education. From then on, he kept reading widely on his own but he never could spare the time to be a stu-

dent again. For a young woman with dark curly hair and definite ideas regarding his every action had already begun playing a large part in his life.

Ursula North, the daughter of a farm family from the neighborhood of his first teaching job, had originally attracted Burroughs because her positive manner awed him. How wonderful always to be so sure of yourself, he thought. Opposite as John's and Ursula's temperaments were, they fell in love with each other. On September 12, 1857, when he was only twenty and she a year older, they were married at her parents' home.

But the young couple immediately displayed differing outlooks that were not a good omen for a happy future together. Although John preferred continuing to teach until he could make his mark as a writer, Ursula wanted him to become a salesman as a step toward operating his own business—so they could afford a fine house in some thriving town. For the first year and a half of their marriage they debated this issue mostly by mail, while Burroughs taught off and on at various country schools and his wife remained at home with her parents.

The debate by no means ceased after the couple finally set up housekeeping in February of 1859. Despite the fact that Burroughs did try repeatedly to enter the world of business, none of these efforts brought the sort of opportunity his wife kept prodding him to find. Possibly he might have done better at this quest if he had not been striving so eagerly, in this same period, to prove that he really could win attention as a writer.

Even before marrying, Burroughs had begun sending short pieces on various topics to country newspapers. His contributions usually were printed anonymously, and he received little or no money for them, but they encouraged him to aim higher. In 1860, at the age of twenty-three, he put several months into composing a serious essay very much in the style of his literary idol, Ralph Waldo Emerson. He sent it to the nation's leading magazine, the *Atlantic Monthly*.

On receiving this essay titled "Expressions" from an unknown writer whose complicated sentences sounded so Emersonian, the editor suspiciously asked an underling to go through Emerson's works to make sure that no early opus by the master had simply been copied. When the search yielded no evidence of any borrowing, the *Atlantic* printed "Expressions" without giving the name of the author, as was its custom then. Many readers thought, therefore, that Emerson actually was the author.

But Burroughs himself was elated by this triumph. Fortunately, though, he had already made a few literary friends who advised him against continuing to model himself so closely on another writer. Find your own voice, they urged him. The notion of practicing his chosen craft by tapping his boyhood memories of nature's wonders struck him, and he started a series with the general title of "From the Back Country."

When a weekly of those days, the *New York Leader,* published the series, Burroughs and his wife reacted very differently. While she kept muttering bitter words about his "eternal scribbling," he grew increasingly certain that he was on the right track. It gave him a great sense of inner peace to put all that he had seen and heard and felt during various outdoors experiences— for instance, walking through a snowy woods or watching hordes of passenger pigeons fly southward—into clear and interesting prose.

Even if Burroughs could not be aware of it yet, he was creating a new type of informal writing about nature that would eventually win him fame. But another few years of private difficulties followed his first efforts in this direction. At last, Burroughs gave up trying to change himself for his wife's sake.

In 1863, when he was twenty-six, he went alone to the nation's capital. Burroughs sent several long letters to his wife soon after his arrival in Washington setting forth the conditions he thought they should agree to before she joined him there. Summing these up, he wrote:

I grant you the utmost freedom to choose and act for yourself; have and see what friends you please, go and come when you please. . . . I shall love you the better for being thus free. I only ask the same for myself: To dress as I please, wear my hair and hat as I please, read and study and think and walk . . . when I please. . . . In this way we can live in peace and love. . . . Am I not right?

Apart from his domestic difficulties, Burroughs had two specific reasons for going to Washington. With his retiring temperament, he could not bring himself to volunteer as a soldier in the great Civil War tearing the country apart. But he thought he could help the Union cause at least indirectly by working in some government office. Also, he yearned to become personally acquainted with a man he hugely admired—the controversial poet Walt Whitman, who was then devoting himself to caring for wounded soldiers in Washington hospitals.

Burroughs succeeded on both counts. He found a post at the Treasury Department and, with his gift for win-

ning friends, forged a close relationship with Whitman. A few evenings a week, over oyster suppers, an association of major importance to the careers of two seemingly very diverse literary figures was firmly established.

Because Whitman's recent book *Leaves of Grass* had ignored many of the conventional rules concerning the writing of poetry, it had upset or even infuriated numerous readers. But Burroughs, sensing genius where others saw only a disregard for valued traditions, took on the mission of explaining his new friend's greatness to less perceptive people. His own first book *Notes on Walt Whitman as Poet and Person*, which was published in 1867, provided the first solid defense of Whitman's work. It also gave Burroughs himself a new stature among influential figures like the editor of the *Atlantic Monthly*.

Burroughs even helped Whitman more specifically. After the assassination of President Lincoln, when Whitman was writing his moving poem about the tragedy called "When Lilacs Last in the Dooryard Bloom'd," he consulted his nature-loving friend because he needed to refer to a bird that would enhance the poem's mood of mourning. Burroughs suggested one of his boyhood favorites—the hermit thrush, whose song seemed to him to express the deepest solemnity imaginable. "That's my bird!" Whitman exclaimed.

In the ten years that Burroughs spent at the Treasury, where he sat facing a vault filled with money and served as hardly more than a guard, he had plenty of time for his writing. During this period, the nature essays he sent to many magazines showed a growing mastery of his craft. One of these essays, "In the Hemlocks," celebrated the same bird he had recommended to Whitman, in a passage typical of the personal style Burroughs was developing:

Ever since I entered the woods, even while listening to the lesser songsters . . . a strain has reached my ears from out of the depths of the forest that to me is the finest sound in nature—the song of the hermit thrush. I often hear him thus a long way off . . . and through the general chorus of wrens and warblers I detect this sound rising pure and serene . . .

In 1871, when Burroughs collected several essays including "In the Hemlocks" to make his first book about nature, the reaction of literary critics was very favorable. "It is a sort of summer vacation to turn its pages," the noted novelist William Dean Howells wrote. Many others compared Burroughs with Henry David Thoreau, although Burroughs himself modestly disagreed. He said that his own goal was only to picture nature artistically while Thoreau had aimed to teach moral lessons based on nature's example.

But Burroughs could not deny that his long-dreamed-of career had finally been launched. Although his wife had joined him in Washington and they were living fairly amicably in a small brick house that she kept spotless, he still felt dissatisfied because he craved more rural surroundings. Even if his kind of writing would probably never earn enough money to live on, he impulsively resigned his job soon after his nature book came out.

Thanks to his Treasury connections, Burroughs was able to arrange for part-time employment as a bank examiner traveling up and down the Hudson Valley. So, in 1873, when he was thirty-six, he bought about ten acres of neglected land overlooking the river a few miles below Kingston. There, within easy reach of the Catskills, he built the home that would soon become a sort of shrine to nature lovers all over the country.

Since the house had to suit his wife's more elaborate tastes, Riverby, as they called it, was bigger and gloomier than he had hoped, filled with stiff-looking furniture. Yet Burroughs plunged energetically into planting fruit trees as well as various vegetable crops, creating an actual working farm to supplement his bank-examining and literary income.

Next, he built himself a woodsy studio—a separate building solely for his writing. So many visitors found their way there, though, that eventually he constructed a still more isolated hideaway a few miles off, a rustic structure made from slabs of trees he cut himself. This he called Slabsides. As his fame grew, Burroughs was often called the Sage of Slabsides.

By 1885, he found it possible to give up his periodic travels to banks in the area because his farming and his writing brought in sufficient money to satisfy his simple needs. Before then, though, an event of huge significance to him had made him increasingly unwilling to leave home. On April 15, 1878, when he was forty-one and had long since despaired of having any children, his wife had given birth to a son they named Julian—and Burroughs doted on the boy.

But even after he no longer had to take trips for bank business, much of his time was occupied by obligations resulting from the popularity of his writing. Groups of students at Vassar College, just across the Hudson River, often came to see him, and many other groups came, too. The parade of visitors became nearly unceasing in the 1880s when school systems all over the coun-

try started introducing nature study into their programs, using works by John Burroughs as their textbooks.

Simply dressed in country clothes, with a flowing beard that was beginning to turn white, Burroughs gave the impression of being almost a Biblical figure. In an era known as the Gilded Age, when many Americans seemed obsessed by a frenzy for making and spending a lot of money, the Sage of Slabsides struck those who worried about the current emphasis on wealth as a most refreshing symbol of old-fashioned values.

Even readers who could not pay personal visits showered Burroughs with approving letters—probably more fan mail than any previous American author had ever received. In addition, colleges awarded him honorary degrees, and officials of all sorts of organizations wrote asking him to deliver lectures.

Shy as Burroughs still considered himself, he could not help enjoying most of this acclaim. He had always liked getting to know people who shared his enthusiasms, sometimes taking the initiative himself and addressing letters of praise to other writers whose work he admired. Now he discovered, much to his own surprise, that he was really quite good at standing up in front of an audience to talk about his beloved outdoors.

And Burroughs vastly expanded his acquaintance with nature during the latter part of his life. Besides two trips to England, he ventured far and wide elsewhere when invitations he could not resist were extended by some of the country's most prominent individuals. In 1899, when he was sixty-two, he joined a summer cruise to Alaska organized by Edward H. Harriman, the millionaire railroad builder. Four years later, he accompanied President Theodore Roosevelt on a camping tour of Yellowstone National Park. With John Muir, the noted geologist and all-around expert on the West, he explored Arizona and California in 1909. At the age of seventy-two, he even sailed off with Muir to see the gorgeous flowers of Hawaii.

Yet all of this roaming, along with winter journeys to the warmth of Florida or the Caribbean as his advancing age made him dread cold weather, failed to shake his lifelong devotion to the Catskill area of his youth. He never felt quite at ease in any other landscape. Although each of his expeditions stirred him with a new excitement over nature's astounding variety, Burroughs heaved a sigh of relief upon returning to Riverby and, especially, to his own Slabsides.

Nevertheless, so many visitors dropped in on him there that the problem of finding time for his writing bothered him increasingly. Throughout all the years since he had left his family home as a youth, he had continued to spend a few weeks every summer back in Roxbury helping out with farm chores and renewing ties with his relatives. Even after the death of his parents, he remained close to his brothers and sisters.

In 1910, when John Burroughs was seventy-three, the notion of creating a new retreat where he could write uninterruptedly struck him. Why not fix up the unoccupied old Roxbury farmhouse facing his favorite vista in the entire world? Before starting on this project, though, he prudently looked into legal questions regarding the land's ownership and found that acquiring a clear title would cost more money than he had. But a rich friend quickly offered to take care of the matter.

Henry Ford had begun the friendship by, out of the blue, sending Burroughs a fan letter and then a brand-new Ford automobile—in gratitude, he wrote, for the pleasure many Burroughs essays had given him. When Burroughs kept bumping the car into trees or fence posts because he never could keep his eyes on the road when there were hawks or wild orchids to be noticed, his son Julian took over the driving. Julian, running the Riverby farm now,

Magnifying glass in hand, John Burroughs observes a small specimen. *Courtesy Department Library Services, American Museum of Natural History.*

had also provided his father with three adored grandchildren.

Ever since Ford's gift of the auto had led to a personal visit, he and Burroughs had become fast friends. With other eminent nature lovers, including Edi-

son and the tire manufacturer Harvey Firestone, Burroughs and Ford had taken several camping trips in the Adirondack Mountains. So Burroughs let Ford help him again with the money needed to gain unquestioned ownership of the farm where he had been born.

From then on, Burroughs spent much of every summer writing contentedly in the remodeled farmhouse he named Woodchuck Lodge because of the prevalence of these creatures in the vicinity. Of course, human visitors soon found their way here, too, and Burroughs could not help welcoming them. Still, he managed to continue turning out at least a few new magazine pieces every summer—his output, during his long career, would fill a total of twenty-seven books.

While his nature essays remained his most popular works, Burroughs also published thoughtful articles about such topics as Charles Darwin's writings on evolution, which he defended as a huge contribution to the world's store of knowledge. Some critics said that Burroughs himself had a much keener mind than he was usually given credit for, but he brushed aside such compliments. Roaming the outdoors and then describing what he had experienced in a way that gave pleasure to those who read his words was the summit of his ambition, he insisted.

Burroughs kept on doing this in his old age despite his increasing frailty. Although his wife's temper had somewhat mellowed after he won fame, she became more trying than ever for several years before her death in 1917. He was eighty years old then, and he went right on working—until he fell ill during the winter of 1920, while he was in California. En route home, as his train was rolling through Ohio, Burroughs died on March 29, 1921.

Five days later, on what would have been his eighty-fourth birthday, his body was buried beside a huge boulder in a high meadow of the Catskills farm of his boyhood. Over the years since then, changes in literary tastes have dimmed his fame but Burroughs has by no means been forgotten. Both his burial place and the nearby Woodchuck Lodge, along with Slabsides as well as Riverby about an hour's drive to the southeast, have all been preserved as national landmarks—and hundreds of people still visit them every summer.

Rachel Carson

1907–1964   American marine biologist whose book *Silent Spring* aroused worldwide concern over environmental pollution

Not very long ago, hardly anybody worried about protecting our environment. Only a handful of experts even suspected that air pollution and water pollution, caused by man's own activities, had begun to reach dangerous levels— levels high enough to harm many forms of life. Then, in a book called *Silent Spring*, an unassuming woman sounded an alarm heard all over the world.

In 1962, when this powerful book appeared, Rachel Carson already was a well-known writer. Several of her earlier works about the sea and its creatures had given her the reputation of being a scientist with a poet's gift for describing the wonders of nature. But her previous modest reputation was far surpassed by the outpouring of praise, and also abuse, that *Silent Spring* brought her.

Because her book condemned some of the most widely sold chemical sprays used to kill insects and control weeds, major corporations manufacturing these products mounted a large-scale attack against it. Their main tactic was to ridicule the book's author, implying that a woman's words about chemistry or similar weighty subjects could not be trusted. Even so, millions of readers were aroused by her warning—and Rachel Carson has come to be considered as, in effect, the founder of today's broad-ranging environmental protection movement.

But she herself took little part in any organizing efforts. Beyond her reluctance to make speeches or other public appearances, Carson had a serious illness by the time *Silent Spring* was published. Nevertheless, she kept defending her book as best she could until her death only two years later.

Rachel Louise Carson's whole career was filled with unpredictable drama. Born in the western part of Pennsylvania on May 27, 1907, she had no reason to be enchanted by oceans. The town of Springdale, where she lived, was several hundred miles inland from the Atlantic Coast, and her family could not afford any seaside vacations. Even so, years later she would write: "As a very small child I was fascinated by the ocean, although I had never seen it. I dreamed of it and longed to see it, and I read all the sea literature I could find."

This outwardly shy girl, who found great excitement in the pages of books, was the youngest of her parents' three children. Her father, Robert Warden Carson, besides being a part-time farmer, sold insurance without much success. Her mother, Maria McLean Carson, was the daughter of a Presbyterian minister and had taught in a local school before getting married.

Thanks to her mother's warm encouragement, Rachel started writing stories and poems at an early age. When she was ten, she entered a contest sponsored by the children's magazine *St. Nicholas* and won its Silver Badge prize. The following year, she sent the magazine an essay about St. Nick himself, which she had written for her English class in school. The magazine paid her

three dollars for it, so she could jokingly say after she became famous that she had been a professional writer ever since the age of eleven.

During this period, Rachel's other deep interest was exploring the outdoors. "I was rather a solitary child," she later recalled, "and spent a great deal of time in woods and beside streams, learning the birds and the insects and flowers." Contented as she seemed, though, she must have often felt lonely.

For her girlhood lacked a lot of the fun and friendships that most other girls valued above reading and writing and nature study. No matter that she never told any interviewers years afterward about having felt cut off from her classmates, the way her classmates felt about her can easily be guessed. Here is the verse that was printed beside her picture in her high school yearbook:

> Rachel's like the mid-day sun
> Always very bright
> Never stops her studying
> Until she gets it right.

Yet, owing to her good marks in high school, Rachel earned a scholarship offered by the Pennsylvania College for Women in Pittsburgh. There an outstanding teacher recognized her literary talent and urged her to pursue her ambition of becoming a writer. But during her sophomore year a required course

Rachel Carson, at fifteen, sits with a favorite teacher, Marguerite Howe, of the Springdale High School, Pennsylvania. From *Sea and Earth: The Life of Rachel Carson*, by Philip Sterling. New York: Thomas Y. Crowell, 1970.

in biology opened her mind to so many new possibilities that she could not decide whether to concentrate on science instead.

"I thought I had to be one or the other," Carson explained long afterward. "It never occurred to me, or apparently to anyone else, that I could combine the two careers." Finally, in the middle of her junior year, she opted to major in zoology—the branch of biology devoted to animal life.

Plunging into catching up on laboratory courses she had missed, Rachel suddenly found it easy to make friends among students having similar goals. During her senior year, she was elected president of the college's science club. What's more, she did so well on her exams that she graduated, in the spring of 1928, with high honors.

At the age of twenty-one Rachel Carson was a studious young woman with a quiet sense of humor who looked forward to qualifying as a college science teacher. Toward that end she enrolled at Johns Hopkins University in Baltimore, and for the next two years she took advanced courses leading to a master's degree. Most importantly, however, she spent those two summers working on research projects at the Woods Hole Marine Biological Laboratory in Massachusetts—at last, getting a firsthand acquaintance with the sea.

Carson found this experience just as thrilling as she had anticipated. In almost a mystical way, she felt that her own destiny was somehow linked with the sea and its tides, its shores, its amazing variety of water-supported life. But she had no idea yet of how she might go about fulfilling that destiny.

While puzzling over her future, Carson worked as a lab assistant and taught on a part-time basis at Johns Hopkins or at the University of Maryland. Also, she kept trying—unsuccessfully—to interest all sorts of magazines in printing poems she wrote. Around the middle of the 1930s, she thought of a new possibility and began writing short pieces about some of her shorefront wanderings, several of which the *Baltimore Sun* accepted.

But a combination of personal and national crises forced her to search for a more dependable income. In 1935, during the depth of the Great Depression, when millions of Americans were out of work, her father died. At the age of twenty-eight, she found herself obliged to support her mother as well as herself.

Fortunately, Carson heard from scientist friends about a promising opportunity. At the Bureau of Fisheries in Washington, a series of radio broadcasts, "Romance Under the Waters," was being planned—and the government agency needed a writer trained in marine biology. Although the job would be only temporary, she was overjoyed to get it.

Carson's pay for writing what she and her new co-workers laughingly called "Seven-Minute Fish Tales" was just $19.25 a week. If the job lasted a whole year, her annual income would amount to merely $1,001. Even though in those days a good lunch in a government cafeteria could be bought for a quarter, and prices for everything else were also much lower than they would be today, it still wasn't easy for Rachel and her mother to manage on such a small income.

Furthermore, within the year the Carsons were confronted by another family tragedy. Rachel's married sister Marian died at the age of forty, leaving two little girls who now needed a home. Rachel and her mother unhesitatingly took Marjorie and Virginia to live with them. But that meant Rachel urgently needed a steady and larger salary.

Had she been a man, it would have caused no surprise when she signed up to take an exam being given by the government agency where she was working on a temporary basis. The test was part of the civil service procedure for filling any vacant post permanently. In effect, she wanted to continue on the job she was already doing—but as a regular staff member who would also receive more money.

Although women only rarely competed for scientific positions then, Rachel Carson got the highest score. In August of 1936, she became a full-time employee of the Bureau of Fisheries with a salary of $2,000 a year.

Relieved of severe money worries, Carson now could enjoy more of the comradeship of working among people with similar outlooks. Besides weekend bird walks in rural areas around Washington, she and her associates frequently got together in the evening to celebrate birthdays or other occasions. These office friendships were especially important to her because of all the responsibilities she had at home. With her mother and her young nieces, she was now settled in a rented house just outside Washington, in Silver Spring, Maryland.

Yet the professional advantages of her post overshadowed any other benefits. Given Rachel Carson's unusual gifts both as a writer and as a specialist in the science of the sea, it would be hard to think of a better place for her than the one she occupied. And her exceptional talents were recognized there very soon.

Right after she completed the series of radio scripts to which she had originally been assigned, Carson was asked to prepare "something of a general sort about the sea" for a new broadcast. This request inspired her to work late many nights, struggling to find just the right words to express complicated ideas in a simple way. Still, she felt very uncertain about whether she had succeeded when she showed the resulting manuscript to Elmer Higgins, the chief of the agency's biology division.

After reading it, he handed it back to her and said, "I don't think it will do." His eyes were twinkling, though, as he asked her to try again on the assigned task.

Then Higgins, with an outright smile, added that she really should send what she had already written to one of the nation's leading magazines, the *Atlantic Monthly*—because her script was much too good for the sort of broadcast he had in mind.

So it happened that, in September of 1937, the *Atlantic* published an article called "Undersea." Even its first few sentences gave evidence of a remarkably vivid kind of writing, along with a sure grasp of scientific fact:

Who has known the ocean? Neither you nor I, with our earth-bound senses, know the foam and surge of the tide that beats over the crab hiding under the seaweed of his tide-pool home; or the lilt of the long, slow swells of midocean, where shoals of wandering fish prey and are preyed upon, and the dolphin breaks the waves to breathe the upper atmosphere. Nor can we know the vicissitudes of life on the ocean floor, where the sunlight, filtering through a hundred feet of water, makes but a fleeting, bluish twilight, in which dwell sponge and mollusk and starfish and coral . . .

Rachel Carson's wonderfully interesting way of writing about the sea stirred many ordinary readers. In addition, though, it also captured the attention of two major literary figures who immediately got in touch with this as-yet unknown author. From that *Atlantic* essay, Carson herself said twenty-five years later, "everything else followed."

Only a few days after "Undersea" appeared in print, she received a glowing fan letter from an editor at one of the country's leading book publishing companies. Did she have any ideas for expanding her magazine piece into a book? If so, the firm of Simon and

Schuster would like to talk over this project with her.

Then a couple of days afterward came an immensely enthusiastic note dashed off by one of the most eminent authors of the era, Hendrik Willem van Loon, whose *The Story of Mankind* had recently been a record-breaking bestseller. He urged Miss Carson to visit him so he could explain more fully why he hoped she'd undertake a whole book on the previously neglected subject.

As a result, early in 1938 Carson signed a contract committing her to hand in the manuscript for a book on December 31, 1940. Because she still felt uncertain about such an ambitious undertaking, she hardly mentioned it to anybody outside of her family. Also, because she could not possibly give up her regular salary she continued working as usual at the Bureau of Fisheries, doing extra research on her own time.

At the Woods Hole laboratory in Massachusetts, where she spent several summer weeks, staff members became very curious because "Ray," as her friends called her, kept delving into matters obviously not connected with the government booklets she was assigned to by her Washington office. Only "Buzzie" and "Kito" could have known what she was up to.

These were Carson's two cherished Persian cats, who after she returned home played every evening on the writing table in her bedroom amid piles of notes and pages of preliminary typing. Although she enormously enjoyed doing research, she found the writing part of her project a terrible strain owing to her need to keep seeking precisely the right way of expressing her every thought. So she felt a great sense of relief when she finally delivered the manuscript—on the exact date it was due.

Carson's first book *Under the Sea-Wind* came out, most unluckily, only a few weeks before the Japanese attacked Pearl Harbor on December 7, 1941. Then the nation's involvement in World War II overshadowed everything else. Although some very favorable reviews had already appeared, the book attracted hardly any readers.

Throughout the war, Carson was so busy with her government work that she had little time to grieve about her book's sad fate. When her agency merged with another one—forming a branch of the Department of the Interior known as the Fish and Wildlife Service—she became the editor-in-chief of a variety of official publications, besides continuing to write many bulletins herself. The field trips she had to take to such nature preserves as the Everglades in Florida were the part of her job she liked best.

Although Carson told her friends that

she would never again put long hours into outside work that brought little reward, when the war was over she started looking for some stimulating new occupation. Unable to find any better-paying job she decided, after all, to try writing another book about the sea. This time she would cover many aspects she had had no room for in her first book, besides describing the great advances the war itself had brought in the science of oceanography.

And, this time, Carson's effort was not wasted. In 1951, her second book, *The Sea Around Us,* became the nation's number one best-seller. Suddenly, at the age of forty-four, this self-effacing woman found herself a literary celebrity. Then the following year, when her first book was reissued, it, too, made the best-seller list.

Medals and other awards rained down on her. Carson, at first taking just a leave of absence from her government post, did her best to preserve her personal privacy. Now that she could finally afford to live more comfortably, she built a new house on a few secluded acres in Silver Spring, and a summer cottage perched on rocks overlooking Sheepscot Bay near West Southport in Maine. At last, she had a place where she could satisfy her lifelong yearning to awaken and go to sleep within sight of the sea.

Working on a further expansion of

Rachel Carson examines seashore vegetation. *Erich Hartmann/Magnum Photos.*

her oceanographic writing—the book that became *The Edge of the Sea*—Carson soon realized that she could safely retire from her government job. Then she had time to teach herself such special skills as photographing the beautiful details of tiny natural phenomena visible only when magnified by microscopes. It appeared that she might be able, while looking after just her aged mother now that her nieces were grown up, to spend many happy years doing what she most enjoyed.

But, in 1957, her niece Marjorie died

and, in a sad repetition of this family's troubled past, left a five-year-old boy who needed a home. Around her own fiftieth birthday, Carson adopted her great-nephew Roger, aiming to bring him up as her son. The following year her mother, nearing the age of ninety and still a source of warm encouragement, fell ill and died.

By this time, though, despite her personal problems and her desire to stay out of the spotlight, Carson had already started working extremely hard on a new project. This book would be very different from her others. And she knew that it was bound to involve her in bitter controversy.

What led Rachel Carson to write *Silent Spring?*

Ever since around 1945, a variety of evidence had been making her more and more certain that the increasing use of deadly poison sprays to kill insects threatened to upset the whole balance of nature. In her own words:

For the first time in the history of the world, every human being is now subjected to contact with dangerous chemicals. . . . They occur virtually everywhere. They have been recovered from most of the major river systems and even from streams of groundwater flowing unseen through the earth. . . . They have been found in fish in remote mountain lakes, in earthworms burrowing in soil, in the eggs of birds—and in man himself.

Carson focused much of her research on the effects of the substance known as DDT (its full name is dichloro-diphenyltrichloroethane). During the war, this seemingly miraculous white powder had been widely used to kill the mosquitoes that spread malaria and the lice that caused typhus. So, with the coming of peace, airplane spraying of DDT had been welcomed in many areas where various insects were damaging trees or crops.

Because some pests had developed an immunity to DDT, a growing number of other new chemical substances were also being sprayed over thousands of acres of farms, forests, and even suburbs. Quietly, several scientists had noted some very disturbing facts casting serious doubts on the safety of all this spraying. Yet most people had no idea of the dangers involved—until Rachel Carson dramatized the issue in her first chapter of *Silent Spring.*

"There was once a town in the heart of America where all life seemed to live in harmony with its surroundings," she started out. Then she went on to describe the strange blight that crept over the area, as if an evil spell had afflicted the community. Farm animals, household pets, even people fell ill mysteriously, and when spring came there was a strange stillness because no birds were singing cheerily in the trees and meadows.

"No witchcraft, no enemy action had silenced the rebirth of new life in this stricken world," Carson wrote. "The people had done it themselves."

Carson proceeded to explain that, although no particular community had yet experienced all of the misfortunes she had listed, everything she described had actually happened already in one place or another. Detailed information regarding these events, along with a clear account of exactly how DDT and other poisons are absorbed by the cells of all living creatures, occupied the remaining three hundred pages of her book.

It took Carson almost five years of intense effort to write *Silent Spring*. During these difficult years, she often doubted whether it would accomplish anything more than merely angering the manufacturers earning millions of dollars from the sale of pesticides. She was right about the furious reaction from this highly profitable industry. In addition, influential farm groups insisted that the sprays were necessary to produce enough food for the world's expanding population.

Nevertheless, the book had a huge impact on the general public. Even before it was actually published, excerpts from it in the prestigious *New Yorker* magazine made opinion leaders hail Carson as a great crusader whose work would have lasting significance. Comparing her with Harriet Beecher Stowe, whose *Uncle Tom's Cabin* had exposed the evils of slavery a century earlier, they predicted that Rachel Carson's *Silent Spring* would awaken people everywhere to the perils of tampering with our natural environment.

Tragically, though, by 1962 when the furor over *Silent Spring* turned Rachel Carson into an internationally famous figure, she was already suffering from bone cancer. So she could take little part in the many ceremonies honoring her, or in the many debates where her point of view was angrily challenged. On April 14, 1964, nearing her fifty-seventh birthday, this shy woman who inspired a whole new era of environmental concern died at her home in Silver Spring.

Since then, the crusade that she started has continued to arouse controversy—accomplishing some of its goals, but still failing to achieve others. Most notably, it has brought about the establishment of many governmental agencies charged with guarding against the pollution of our air, water, and soil. In the United States and a number of other countries, these units have outlawed DDT as well as several other similarly long-lasting substances. Also, rules regulating the use of less dangerous poisons have been widely adopted.

Although pollution of various kinds continues to be a major problem, Rachel Carson has by no means been forgotten. Several nature preserves have been named after her, among them a portion of the Maine coast now known as the Rachel Carson National Wildlife Refuge. In addition, many environmental education programs have been established in her memory, and her picture has appeared on a United States postage stamp.

Perhaps she herself would have been most impressed by the tribute paid to her in 1980, sixteen years after her death. Then-president Jimmy Carter awarded her the highest honor any American not in the armed forces can receive—the Presidential Medal of Freedom, which her adopted son accepted on her behalf. As he handed Roger the medal, President Carter said:

Never silent herself in the face of destructive trends, Rachel Carson fed a spring of awareness across America and beyond. A biologist with a gentle, clear voice, she welcomed her audiences to her love of the sea, while with an equally clear determined voice she warned Americans of the dangers human beings themselves pose for their own environment. Always concerned, always eloquent, she created a tide of environmental consciousness that has not ebbed.

George Washington Carver

1864–1943   American botanist and agricultural researcher

A band of armed men galloped up the road leading to the Carver farm in southwestern Missouri. For Moses Carver the sound of the thundering hoofbeats was a signal to hide. Twice before, the farm near the village of Diamond Grove had been raided by masked men seeking money and loot.

Moses and his wife, Susan, were hard-working farmers in a corner of Missouri that was a battleground between rival gangs, called bushwackers, in the waning days of the Civil War. Some of those gangs supported the Union and others the slave-holding Confederate states, but all were interested in robbery and money. Although the Carvers owned a few slaves to help them on the farm, they were staunch Union supporters. That made them a target for the anti-Union groups.

Carver and his wife fled to a nearby wooded area with Jim, one of their slaves. Jim called to Mary, his mother, to follow them. But she was confused and looked for a blanket to cover her baby, George. Before she could leave, the masked men broke into the farmhouse. Finding no money, they seized Mary and her baby and carried them off.

Moses Carver hired a neighbor to track down and rescue Mary and the child. In six days, the neighbor returned—with a bundle wrapped in his coat and strapped to the back of his horse.

It was the baby George, just barely

alive. He had been abandoned by the kidnappers, but no trace of his mother was ever found. Moses Carver rewarded his neighbor with a racehorse worth $300 for bringing back the infant.

George's future seemed very dim. Not only was he sickly, but he was an orphan and black. He never knew his father, who had died before his birth, and his mother had disappeared. He never even knew exactly when he was born, but it must have been during the early days of 1864.

The Carvers were a kindly couple, though, and they raised George along with his older brother as members of their family. A frail child, George did not work in the fields the way Jim did but helped Mrs. Carver in the house, learning how to cook, mend, and even embroider.

George struggled for an education. It wasn't easy for a black, no matter how gifted, to get ahead in the United States after the Civil War, despite the ending of slavery. Black people were still segregated because of their color, and they were also restricted in many other ways. Sometimes their very lives were threatened by outbreaks of mob violence.

During his formative years, George faced all of these problems and yet he grew up without bitterness in the pleasant all-white surroundings of the Carver farm. He and his brother even went to the same church the Carvers attended. Nevertheless, George was not permitted to enter the weekday school for local children because he was black.

That first experience of racial prejudice came as George was hungering for more education than the Carvers could give him at home. He had quickly mastered the alphabet and longed to learn more. Somehow, the sickly orphan boy had developed an intense curiosity about everything around him.

He was especially interested in plants. Even as a young child, he became known in the neighborhood for his ability to care for them. He observed where they grew best and learned to treat ailing plants so well that he was called "the plant doctor."

Years later, he recalled that as a boy he had thirsted for more knowledge: "I wanted to know every strange stone, flower, insect, bird, or beast. No one could tell me. My only book was an old Webster's Elementary Spelling Book, and I would seek the answer here without satisfaction. I almost knew the book by heart."

The Carvers sympathized with George's quest. When he was twelve, they let him to go off to Neosho, about eight miles away, where there was a school for black children. He made his way to Neosho alone, with all his possessions tied in a big handkerchief. When he arrived, he entered an all-black atmosphere for the first time.

George lived with a childless black couple, Mariah and Andrew Watkins, who took him in and treated him like a son. At their home, he learned how to wash clothes and iron them smoothly without a wrinkle, a skill that proved helpful later on. Daily, he went to the crude tumbledown cabin that was the black school attended by about seventy-five other children.

After a few months, George's brother Jim came to Neosho, too. He accompanied George to classes for a while, but learning just reading and writing was enough for him. He left school to work on building houses. George, however, soaked up everything the young schoolteacher could offer and still wanted to know more.

When George heard that a black family was moving west to Fort Scott, Kansas, he asked to go along. At the age of thirteen, he set out with them—but he was really on his own now. On arriving in Fort Scott, he arranged to stay at the home of a blacksmith in return for cooking meals and doing other household chores. "I found employment just as a girl," he said later.

Although George went to school in Fort Scott, the big lesson he learned there had nothing to do with books.

While he had met prejudice before, no previous experience had prepared him for the horror of what happened one afternoon in 1879. Thirty masked men broke into the town jail and took out a black man accused of attacking a white girl. They tied a rope around his neck, dragged him five blocks, hanged him from a lamppost, and then burned the body.

That decided Carver. Fort Scott was no place for him, and he moved on to a Kansas town called Olathe. There, he went to school again while living with a black couple, Lucy and Ben Seymour. He helped Mrs. Seymour in her laundry business, shined shoes, did odd jobs, and also cooked for the family of a barber.

When George was sixteen, the Seymours decided to settle in the nearby town of Minneapolis, Kansas, and he accompanied them. He opened his own small laundry business in a ravine called Poverty Gulch, but he also went to the local school with mostly white students. In addition to attending classes, he gardened, painted a little, learned to play the accordion, and attended church faithfully.

Still, he faced a problem. There was another George Carver in Minneapolis, and sometimes their mail got mixed up. So he picked a middle initial at random, identifying himself as George W. Carver. When someone asked him if that stood for Washington, he replied, "Why not?" and became known as George Washington Carver.

Four happy years did not quench his thirst for more education. At the age of twenty-one, Carver applied for admission to Highland College, a small religious school in the northeast corner of Kansas. An official of the college wrote back that his grades were satisfactory and he would be admitted with the class starting in September 1885.

When George arrived there, he eagerly went to the office of the principal.

"I am George W. Carver, sir," he said.

"Yes?"

"I have come to enroll at Highland. Your letter said—"

"There has been some mistake," the principal interrupted him. "You didn't tell me you were a Negro. Highland College does not take Negroes."

It was a crushing blow. For the next several years, Carver wandered through the farming areas of Kansas, working at odd jobs. Everywhere he went he set up a small laundry business, spending fifteen cents for a washboard and twenty-five cents for a tin tub. In the mostly all-white communities of the frontier, he was welcomed for his working skills and friendly manner, and the hurt of the rejection from college faded.

One of the towns he stopped in was Winterset, Iowa. At church one Sunday morning he obviously attracted attention, not only because of his color but because of his clear tenor voice. A white couple, Dr. and Mrs. John Mulholland, invited him to their home.

The Mulhollands became friends and mentors. Impressed by Carver's artistic abilities, they persuaded him to apply for admission at Simpson College in Indianola, despite his rebuff at Highland five years before.

And so in September 1890, Carver once more presented himself in the office of a college president.

"My name is George Carver, sir," he said.

There was no hesitation this time.

"Welcome to Simpson," the president said, reaching out to shake Carver's hand.

At the age of twenty-six, Carver thus became a college student, the only black on the campus. He was six feet tall, thin, with a high-pitched voice, a black moustache, and a shy manner. Quiet and respectful, he got along in white communities by keeping his feelings to himself. Everywhere he went he made friends, most of them white, who were attracted to him by his friendliness, hard work, and many talents.

At Simpson, Carver set up a laundry in a shack not far from the campus to earn money for his fees and upkeep. He registered for classes in grammar, arithmetic, essay writing, piano, and singing, but was rejected at first for art, which he wanted to study above all else. He persisted, finally winning permission to enter the painting class.

His work impressed the young teacher, Etta Budd. She convinced him, though, that he would not be able to make a living as an artist. Knowing of his love of plants, she suggested that he study agriculture at Iowa State College in Ames, where her father was a professor.

Carver followed her advice. The following year, in 1891 when he was twenty-seven, he entered Iowa State, one of the nation's leading centers of agricultural research and education. Once again the only black on the campus, Carver overcame some initial distrust and became one of the most popular students.

He was active in prayer meetings, wrote the class poem, attended meetings of the debating, German, and art clubs, rose to the rank of captain in the Reserve Officers Training Corps, played the guitar, and even became a masseur, rubbing the aching joints of members of the football team.

Lacking money, Carver did menial jobs to earn enough to pay for his fees and food. Still, he found time for his favorite occupation of painting, as well as his classwork. His paintings of flowers were so good that some of his fellow students bought him a new suit and a railroad ticket so that he could exhibit them at a state show in Cedar Rapids. His "Yucca and Cactus," selected as part of Iowa's display at the World Columbian Exhibit in Chicago in 1893, won an honorable mention in competition with the world's best artists.

More than anything else, though, Carver's work with plants won him the respect of the Iowa State faculty. His ability to raise, crossbreed, and graft plants was considered extraordinary, even in that center of agricultural research. He became known as "the green thumb boy," a man with a natural instinct for making plants thrive.

After he received his bachelor's degree in 1894, Carver began to work as assistant botanist in the college's experiment station while studying for a master's degree. He specialized in mycology, the study of mushrooms and related types of fungus. The collection of fungi he started grew to contain 20,000 specimens, and his professor called him "the best collector I have ever known."

In 1896, Carver received a master's degree, becoming the only black man in America with a graduate degree in agriculture. At the age of thirty-two, he faced his future. He could stay at Iowa and continue his work there, but he had another option. Booker T. Washington, well known for his leadership of the Tuskegee Institute in Alabama, invited him to help educate blacks in the South.

"I cannot offer you money, position, or fame," Washington wrote. "The first two you have. The last, from the place you now occupy, you will no doubt achieve. These things I now ask you to give up. I offer you in their place work—hard, hard work—the task of bringing a people from degradation, poverty and waste to full manhood."

Arriving in Tuskegee in October of 1896, Carver found quite a contrast to the beautiful campus he had known in Iowa. Founded only fifteen years earlier, the institute occupied an abandoned plantation and some frame buildings put up by students. As head of the new agricultural department Carver had one ax, a hoe, a blind horse, and twenty acres of tired-looking soil. There were thirteen students to work with him, but no building or equipment for them to use.

Carver set about making plans. First, he told his students that they would have to build a laboratory. Under his direction, they searched the junk piles on the campus, picking up discarded bottles, rusty pans, flatirons, old wire.

They converted the bottles into lamps, made a Bunsen burner by putting a wick into an ink bottle, used a heavy battered cup as a mortar, and pounded holes into pans to make strainers to sift soil samples.

Dividing the twenty acres at his disposal into different plots, Carver supervised the students in preparing for planting. He himself drove a plow to till the soil. In his high-pitched voice he shouted, "Plow deep. Help those roots get down where the good is."

Since they could not afford to buy fertilizer, Carver made his own. His students gathered leaves from the woods, collected potato peelings from the dining hall's kitchen, and cut weeds, piling all this together to decay into rich black compost. Many years before there was any organic gardening movement, Carver applied its basic principles for soil enrichment.

By the end of his second year at Tuskegee, production on its agricultural land rose to 265 bushels of sweet potatoes an acre—more than six times the usual harvest. When he finally planted cotton, the region's main crop, his yield was far more than that of any other farm in the area. These results illustrated the lesson that Carver taught his students: "There is no richer plant food than the things we ignore or throw away every day."

George Washington Carver holds a prize sweet potato. *The Bettmann Archive*.

Just a year after his arrival, Carver's agricultural department had become the busiest place on the campus. His original thirteen students had grown to seventy-six. In addition to teaching, Carver collected fungi and grasses of Alabama. That summer, he went off to Washington for a conference called by the United States Department of Agriculture.

There, Carver met one of his professors from Iowa who had become the new secretary of agriculture. James C. Wilson asked if there was anything he could do for Carver. Yes, Carver said, inviting Wilson to the dedication of a new agricultural building in Tuskegee. Wilson came, and his presence marked the first official recognition of the Tuskegee Institute by the United States government. Carver's reputation as a man who got things done soared.

Carver saw his mission as much broader than only teaching the students who came to Tuskegee. He carried the message of balanced farming to the poor black farmers of Alabama and the rest of the South. He persuaded them to grow healthful vegetables to feed their families, along with their basic money crop of cotton.

On Friday evenings, he drove a wagon pulled by a mule into the nearby countryside to show new methods of farming to the black farmers who could

not come to Tuskegee. He urged them to plant sweet potatoes and peanuts as well as cotton, and showed farm wives how to pickle and can foods.

Despite all of these activities, Carver still saved time for the things he enjoyed. He played the piano at church on Sunday evenings, taught a Bible school, and continued painting pictures. Although he would always stop whatever he was doing to advise students or farmers, he refused to take part in any purely social activities on the campus. He lived simply, dressing in shabby old clothes and letting his pay checks mount up uncashed on his desk. Asked once why he did not get married, he replied that he did not have time.

As his work expanded, Carver became the target of criticism on the campus. Some faculty members considered him an outsider because he had not grown up in the South. Others were jealous of his achievements, his connections with government officials, and his friendships with whites.

But everyone agreed that he was a poor administrator of the many programs that came under his direction. That problem was solved in 1910, when he was relieved of his teaching duties and given what had been his dream from the start—a first-class laboratory for agricultural experiments.

That lab made Carver world famous. Out of it flowed a series of products that transformed the farm economy of the South, then dependent on cotton as the major crop. Although his work resulted in many useful innovations involving farming practices, even more importantly he "invented" dozens of everyday products created from sweet potatoes and peanuts.

One of the many bulletins issued by his laboratory described how to use sweet potatoes to make flour, sugar, bread, or even "mock coconut." Carver wrote so much about new uses for the sweet potato that he became known as the Sweet Potato Man. Altogether, he developed more than a hundred products from sweet potatoes.

Then, in September of 1919, Carver unassumingly opened the most celebrated phase of his career. Robert Russa Moton had succeeded Booker T. Washington as head of Tuskegee, and Carver told him: "I am sure you will be pleased to know that I have today made a delicious and wholesome milk from peanuts."

To dramatize Carver's work on finding new uses for the peanut, the institute invited nine local business people to lunch. The menu included soup, chicken patties, creamed vegetables, bread, ice cream, cookies, and coffee. At the end, when Carter announced that everything served at that meal had been made from peanuts, the audience burst into loud applause.

Then Southern farmers began to convert some of their cotton fields into peanut patches. Soon their barns bulged with sacks of the nuts—so many that they caused a major problem. One farmer came to Carver and demanded to know who would buy all those sacks.

Carver went back into his laboratory, seeking a solution. First, he ground peanuts into a fine powder. Then he heated the powder, squeezed it, and extracted the peanut oil. He used the oil and the peanut meal and, like a magician, he made peanut butter.

Also, he made peanut flour, milk, ink, dyes, shoe polish, shaving cream, margarine—and, much more important, peanut cooking oil. Carver even found ways to use mounds of seemingly useless peanut shells for making insulating boards, fuel briquettes, and synthetic marble.

Following his guidance, the peanut industry grew rapidly. The growers organized a United Peanut Association of America and invited Carter to speak at a meeting in Montgomery in 1920. He arrived carrying two heavy cases of his samples but was refused admission because he was black.

At that time, segregation by race was the custom in the South. Carver was

George Washington Carver in later years, at work in his laboratory. *The Bettmann Archive.*

not surprised or angry. It had happened to him before. Recalling this episode later, he said it would have been easy to walk away in anger. But, he said, "God reminded me that I had not come to Montgomery to indulge my personal feelings . . . I had come to help thousands of farmers I had persuaded to get into peanuts in the first place."

So he sent word to the meeting's sponsors that he had arrived. Taken around to the rear, he was brought upstairs in a freight elevator. Standing before the audience, Carver did not mention his problems in reaching the auditorium. He talked about peanuts.

Opening his cases, he took out bottle after bottle and mentioned their contents: leather stain, Worcestershire sauce, milk, coffee, soap, shaving lotion, face powder, cheese, instant coffee, instant coffee with cream, buttermilk, evaporated milk, fruit punch. All, of course, had been made with peanuts. The audience cheered.

Carver became lastingly identified as the Peanut Man after he testified before a committee of Congress in 1921. The committee, considering a tariff on imported peanuts, heard many witnesses before it was Carver's turn late in the afternoon. He was given ten minutes to speak.

With his familiar package of peanut products in front of him, Carver began to explain them as he pulled them out one by one. He showed some chocolate-covered peanuts and a breakfast food. "I am very sorry you cannot taste it, so I will taste it for you," he said.

Everybody laughed. One after another, Carver displayed salted peanuts, peanut flour, peanut skins used for dyes, and peanut mash used for feeding cattle.

The committee chairman, impressed by Carver's presentation, said: "We will give you more time."

So Carver continued to pull things out of his case—samples of the more than 300 products he had made from peanuts. "You have seen just about half of them," Carver said almost two hours after he had started.

"Well, come again and bring the rest," the chairman said.

Carver's showmanship and quiet humor charmed the congressmen so much that they applauded as he left the witness stand. More important, Congress voted a tax on imported peanuts to support the domestic peanut industry.

He returned to Tuskegee a hero. Honors poured in on him, including medals from the white United Daughters of the Confederacy and the National Association for the Advancement of Colored People. Despite all his awards, though, Carver still shared the humiliations of segregation along with his less-famous brothers and sisters.

During his forty-seven years at Tuskegee, race relations in the United States were probably at their worst. Carver himself was never physically threatened as many other blacks were, but he suffered many insults. He was never able to eat at the scientific meetings he addressed. He could not attend a Montgomery concert by the famed pianist Paderewski because blacks were not permitted in the theater. When a pipe organ in his own town of Tuskegee was dedicated to him, he stayed home from the ceremony because it was held at a white church.

Carver found inner strength in his belief that God had put him on earth to calm troubled waters by work useful to all. Throughout his life he had white friends, but he always felt called upon to do all he could to bridge the gap between the races.

Carver died on January 5, 1943, at the age of seventy-nine. But his name lives on in the annals of agricultural research and at the many schools named for him. Also, now there is an official historical marker at the Missouri birthplace of the slave boy who rose to become a world-renowned plant scientist.

Jacques-Yves Cousteau

1910–   French underwater explorer

"When I was four or five years old, I loved touching water," Jacques Cousteau once said. "Water fascinated me—first floating ships, then me floating and stones not floating. The touch of water fascinated me all the time."

At summer camp in Lake Harvey, Vermont, when he was ten years old, he made his first dive underwater. It came at the direction of an instructor named Mr. Boetz, whom Jacques disliked intensely.

"He forced me to ride horses and I fell a lot," Cousteau said years later. "I still hate horses." But Mr. Boetz also made him clear the bottom of the lake of dead branches so that the other campers could dive into the water without danger. Jacques liked that.

Under the diving board, the lake was full of dead twigs and branches. "I worked very hard, diving in that murk without goggles, without a mask, and that's where I learned to dive," he said. "I became a good swimmer."

From that love of the water came a career that made Cousteau internationally famous. A restless man with an unquenchable sense of adventure, he combined three loves—for gadgets, for filmmaking, and for the sea—in his work. He invented the Aqua-Lung, making lengthy dives possible; then he spent the rest of his life exploring and photographing beneath the sea.

Through his films and television shows, Cousteau brought the wonders of the teeming underwater world to hundreds of millions of people. In addition to awesome fish, coral, and sunken

117

vessels, viewers saw a thin, tall man who looked somewhat like a wading bird, with pale blue eyes, a long hooked nose, and a smile always ready to burst forth as he talked about the marvels he discovered.

Cousteau was born not far from the Atlantic Ocean in the small village of Saint-André-du-Cubzac, near the city of Bordeaux in France, on June 11, 1910. His father, Daniel Cousteau, served as the business manager for some rich Americans. That required him to travel a lot, taking his family with him.

They landed in New York in 1920. With his older brother, Pierre, the ten-year-old Jacques attended an American school where he quickly learned to speak English. Playing stickball on the streets of New York, he got used to being called Jack. After his summer at camp in Vermont, the Cousteaus returned to France.

At school in Paris, Jacques often got low marks because he kept so busy with other interests. Machines fascinated him. When he was only eleven years old, he built a model of a machine for loading cargo onto ships that was almost as tall as he was. An engineer friend of his father's said the boy's crane moved in such a unique way that it could be patented.

Two years later, Jacques took up writ-

ing. He wrote a book he called *An Adventure in Mexico*, lettering and illustrating it by hand. Then he made copies of his manuscript by running it through a mimeograph machine.

Next, he bought a secondhand movie camera and started to take pictures, almost completely neglecting his schoolwork. One day his father found a stack of home-printed stationery in his son's room headed: FILMS ZIX—Jack Cousteau producer, director, and chief cameraman.

When Jacques came home, his father asked him how he had gotten the movie camera.

"I saved for it," Jacques told him.

"Well, you had better let me keep it until you catch up in school," his father said.

Jacques's schoolwork improved rapidly. A month later, he got his camera back. Years later, he said: "My films weren't much good. What I liked was taking the camera apart and developing my own film."

His scientific bent was illustrated by a rash schoolboy prank. Would a strongly thrown stone make a small hole in glass or break a window? He experimented on seventeen windows at school—and they all broke. He was expelled in disgrace.

Shipped to a strict boarding school in the Alsace region of France, Jacques changed. Under the influence of discipline and challenge, he began to study, often keeping at his books until late at night. At the age of nineteen, he easily passed the entrance examinations for the French naval academy in the city of Brest.

"There was no naval tradition in my family," he later explained. "I thought it was a good way to go places."

Taking along his camera, Cousteau went with a group of cadets on a one-year cruise around the world aboard a training ship. But the life of a naval cadet was not all play and sightseeing. He studied hard, even using a flashlight under blankets at night to read. He finished second in his class in 1933 and, at the age of twenty-three, became a naval officer.

After serving briefly aboard a warship, Cousteau entered the French naval flying school, preparing to be a fighter pilot. Just before graduation, however, he had an accident that changed his life.

Borrowing his father's sports car one night, he went speeding along a deserted mountain road on his way to attend a friend's wedding. As he rounded a sharp curve, the car lights suddenly went out. Cousteau slammed on the brakes. The car flew off the road into the blackness and rolled over several times.

Cousteau awoke bleeding, with several ribs broken, one arm broken in five places and the other paralyzed. Despite great pain, he crawled to a nearby darkened farmhouse at two o'clock in the morning.

"Go away," an angry woman cried out in French.

"Madame, if you saw me you would not say that," Cousteau answered.

She opened her door, then sent for a doctor, and Cousteau was taken to a hospital. The doctors there wanted to amputate his right arm. "I forbid you to cut it off," Cousteau said. They told him, though, that he would never recover the use of either arm.

Yet Cousteau refused to accept the doctors' discouraging verdict. Day after day, week after week, he persisted in a dogged program of whirlpool baths and other treatments. By sheer willpower he kept trying to move his fingers. After eight months of effort, he finally moved one finger.

Two months later, he could bend two fingers and one of his wrists. Still, he would not give up hope of further improvement. This was a terrible time, he recalled long afterward, but it never affected his optimism. "It was a test for me," he said.

Cousteau passed that test. Although his right arm remained slightly twisted for the rest of his life, otherwise he recovered almost completely. His aim of becoming a pilot had to be abandoned, but he stayed in the navy.

While still recuperating, Cousteau was assigned to shore duty at Toulon, a port on the Mediterranean. There, he spent hours working to regain strength in his arms by swimming in the sea. One day in 1936, a fellow officer, Philippe Tailliez, gave him a pair of small goggles obtained from a Japanese pearl diver. Cousteau put them on, then plunged below the water's surface —and that first underwater dive with goggles gave his life a new direction.

As he later recalled: "I saw fish. Standing up to breathe, I saw a trolley car, people, electric light poles. I put my eyes under again and civilization vanished. I was in a jungle never before seen by those who floated on the opaque sea."

Sometimes, Cousteau mused many years afterward, we are lucky enough to know instantly that we have reached a great turning point. "It happened to me that summer's day when my eyes were opened to the world beneath the surface of the sea." He was twenty-six years old then, a young naval officer and a bachelor.

On the beach, Cousteau met Frederic Dumas, a civilian who speared fish underwater with a curtain rod. Soon Cousteau, Tailliez, and Dumas began working together to dive deeper, to see more, to stay underwater longer. They fashioned masks from inner tubes to help them see and air tubes from garden hoses to help them breathe.

Only one interest distracted Cousteau from his underwater experiments. In Paris, he had met a young woman named Simone Melchior, whose father was a former naval officer and who came from a long line of admirals in the French navy. Once she said she regretted not having been born a boy so that she could go to sea herself.

After marrying Cousteau in 1937, she did go to sea. The couple had two sons, Philippe and Jean-Michel, but Simone Cousteau shared all of her husband's adventures.

At the outset, Cousteau and his friends Tailliez and Dumas tried to work around the restrictions that faced underwater divers. Without an outside source of air, divers could go below only for brief periods, holding their breaths. They knew that over the centuries men—and some women, too—had dived for sponges, coral, and pearls but were limited in their time underwater. Waterproof suits had been developed, with air pumped down into helmets from the surface, but they were heavy and clumsy, and even dangerous if the diver fell.

The outbreak of World War II in 1939

Jacques-Yves Cousteau (right) and an unidentified companion adjust underwater equipment. *Robert Capa/Magnum Photos.*

interrupted their research. Cousteau, as an active naval officer, became a gunnery specialist. However, the war was over for France before he saw much action. When the Germans captured Paris and the French surrendered in 1940, he remained at Toulon. With the French fleet disarmed, he served as an artillery officer on the hills around the Toulon naval base.

That left a lot of time for what really absorbed him—his experiments under the sea. Cousteau found that breathing pure oxygen was dangerous, that coating oneself with heavy grease as protection from cold water was useless, and that hot drinks and alcohol do not restore body temperature after dives in cold water.

Gradually, Cousteau became convinced that a self-contained compressed air lung was the only practical way to supply enough air for underwater swimming. It had to be automatic, too, with a valve that let in air for divers to breathe and then shut when they exhaled—requiring no action on their part, thus freeing them to concentrate on their exploring.

In Paris, Cousteau visited the offices of Air Liquide, a company where his wife's father worked. He was introduced to an engineer there named Émile Gagnan. As Cousteau began explaining what he had in mind, Gagnan reached onto a shelf behind him and brought down a small gadget.

"Something like this?" he asked.

By coincidence, Gagnan had been working on a valve to feed cooking gas automatically to automobile engines. At that time of great hardship in France, with German troops occupying the country, gasoline was not available. So ingenious engineers were trying to find ways of burning charcoal and natural gas to provide fuel for cars.

In a few weeks, Gagnan and Cousteau converted Gagnan's gadget into an automatic air regulator. Cousteau tested it on a dive in the Marne River outside Paris, and it worked perfectly when he swam horizontally underwater. But when he stood on his head, the air supply almost stopped. How could he dive if he couldn't breathe going down?

Riding back to Paris, Gagnan and Cousteau found the answer. The intake and exhaust valves were on different levels on the regulator. That changed the flow of air when he dived, but when

he swam horizontally the valves were on the same level and worked properly. It was a simple matter to place the two valves together.

One morning in June of 1943, Cousteau picked up the improved diving mechanism. He and Gagnan called it a Self-Contained Underwater Breathing Apparatus—scuba for short—but they patented it under the name of Aqua-Lung.

It consisted of three moderately sized cylinders of compressed air, linked to an air regulator the size of an alarm clock, to be strapped on the diver's back. From the regulator, two tubes carried air for breathing to a mouthpiece.

Cousteau began the first real test of the new Aqua-Lung in a secluded cove near Toulon. He wore a watertight mask over his eyes and nose, and rubber flippers on his feet. Under the fifty-pound weight of the apparatus, he waddled into the water and swam down to a depth of thirty feet. He experimented by doing somersaults, loops, and barrel rolls, then even stood upside down, balancing himself on one finger.

Swimming toward a cave, Cousteau found it full of lobsters. He picked a pair and rose to the surface, then handed them to his wife who was swimming there to monitor his movements. Not only did the Aqua-Lung pass its first test successfully—but also, at a period in war-ravaged France when food supplies were scarce, it provided some wonderful meals for its inventor's family.

Delighted as he was by the new Aqua-Lung, Cousteau knew that the only way other people could see the wonders of the deep was through photography. It was very difficult to buy movie film then, though, and even to ask for any was to risk being investigated by the German secret police.

So Cousteau and his wife visited photography shops all over Toulon and the nearby city of Marseilles, purchasing thirty-five-millimeter film for still cameras. Under blankets because they had no darkroom, they spliced the rolls together to fit an old movie camera they had bought for twenty-five dollars. They made a watertight case for the camera and began to take the world's first underwater pictures.

They filmed Dumas feeding fish. Then they visited a sunken steamer, something that people had never seen before. Cousteau took pictures of his friends swimming among fish near the submerged vessel and showed them as they swam over barnacled railings to explore its decks. Two of their short motion pictures won prizes at the new Cannes Film Festival.

It was great fun for them. But for Cousteau, still on active naval duty, the war and the enemy were ever-present dangers. He worked with the French resistance movement to thwart the occupying German troops while his diving experiments cloaked his undercover activities.

When the war ended, Cousteau convinced his superiors to assign him full time to underwater research. He quickly recruited a staff that performed dangerous work, locating and dismantling underwater mines, finding shipwrecks, and filming torpedoes launched from submarines.

That was only the beginning of Cousteau's fame. Magazine editors, television producers, and moviemakers sought him out for more films and pictures. He learned to be a celebrity, talking readily to reporters with the aim of raising money for his experiments. He sparkled with ideas for ship design, salvage, underwater pipelines, offshore drilling, and even mining the sea floor.

One thing Cousteau did not foresee: that his Aqua-Lung would spawn the whole new sport of scuba diving. By the end of the 1950s, millions of people were using the Aqua-Lung to discover for themselves the thrill of swimming underwater and the beauties of the world below the water's surface.

But Cousteau himself was more interested in scientific research. What he really needed was a ship especially designed for his kind of ocean study. In 1950, he found her in a surplus minesweeper built in the United States for the British navy. He named his vessel *Calypso* after a water nymph in Greek mythology.

Aboard the *Calypso*, Cousteau at the age of forty began a new chapter in scientific ocean research that the public shared through his books and movies. The *Calypso* was a wooden ship, 139 feet long and 25 feet broad, with much special oceanography equipment. Its most unusual feature was an underwater chamber known as "a false nose," in which an observer could lie flat to look out as the ship cut through ocean waters.

Cousteau's motto became: "We must go and see for ourselves." From 1951 on, he and his *Calypso* went everywhere—to the Red Sea, the deep trenches of the Atlantic Ocean, the Indian Ocean, the Pacific off Alaska, Antarctica, the Mediterranean, and even up great rivers like the Amazon and the St. Lawrence.

Cousteau operated a friendly ship, with everybody treated equally. Officers and men ate together; nobody wore a uniform. Surprisingly, for a naval officer, Cousteau was very relaxed about clothing and dress codes, although he insisted on strict safety rules.

Off-duty life on the *Calypso* centered on the mess hall, where wine came with meals in the French fashion. Cousteau joined in the plotting of practical jokes and played games like Scrabble with the crew.

But he was very serious about his work. Everywhere he went, he and seamen conducted research along with the scientists and divers who sailed with them. They took thousands of pictures of fish, sunken ships, caves, and coral formations. In 1953 Cousteau's book *The Silent World*, written with Frederic Dumas, became a best-seller. Four years later, his film with the same title won an Academy Award as the best documentary of the year.

In 1957, after Cousteau retired from the French navy with the rank of captain, he became director of the Oceanographic Institute in Monaco on the Mediterranean. Besides supervising an aquarium, museum, and library there, he also spent part of every year in Paris. Still eager to explore more of the underwater world he had discovered, he often went to sea again.

To go deeper into the water and stay there longer, Cousteau invented various new contrivances including a two-man diving saucer, a one-man mini submarine that traveled on the sea bottom, and "a house under the sea" in which men lived under the water for weeks at a time. He also developed a series of cameras capable of taking better pictures underwater.

These ventures were very expensive. How did Cousteau get the money for them? The French government, along with his family and friends, financed his early expeditions. His wife even sold her jewelry to help pay the bills. Later on, in addition to his earnings from his writing and his films, the growth of television provided substantial sums— American networks paid for many of his trips, in return for the right to show his films.

For Cousteau, underwater diving was a family affair. His wife Simone, who accompanied him everywhere, was probably the world's first woman scuba diver. When one of his sons was only five and the other seven, their father had outfitted them with miniature Aqua-Lungs, and they, too, had learned to swim underwater, although with some difficulty.

The problem was that they could not stop talking despite the masks around their noses and their mouthpieces. In a short time, the masks started to fill with water and they were in danger of drowning. As Cousteau later recalled, "I seized the waterlogged infants and hauled them out of the water." Then he gave them a lecture on the theme that the sea was a silent world

so little boys must "shut up when visiting it."

When the boys grew up, Jean-Michel became an architect. Philippe, after a brief period as an independent filmmaker, devoted himself to assisting his father. After Philippe tragically died in an airplane accident in 1979, his brother took over as vice president of the Cousteau enterprises.

Throughout Cousteau's career, he was constantly asked one question: Is underwater diving safe?

Yes, he would always answer, if proper precautions were taken. He insisted on safety first and constant training. The basic rule on the *Calypso* was: Never take any unnecessary risks.

What about sharks?

As protection, Cousteau and his fellow divers always carried a "shark billy"—a stout wooden stick about four feet long, studded with nails at the end—whenever they were in waters where sharks were common.

"It is employed, somewhat in the manner of the lion tamer's chair, by thrusting the studs into the hide of an approaching shark," he explained. "The nails keep the billy from sliding off the slippery leather, but do not penetrate far enough to irritate the animal. The diver may thus hold a shark off at his proper distance."

To Cousteau, the greatest danger in

Jacques-Yves Cousteau, aboard ship, looks out to sea. *The Bettman Archive.*

the sea—and all around us—is pollution. He once told a congressional hearing in Washington that he was appalled at the amount of trash that the *Calypso* had encountered at sea.

"People do not realize that all pollution ends up in the sea," he said. "The earth is less polluted. It is washed by rain which carries everything into the oceans, where life has diminished by 40 percent in twenty years."

Cousteau believed that the damage to marine life could be stopped through education and favored using television as a means of reaching the public. But that was not enough. In 1973, he organized the Cousteau Society as a nonprofit agency dedicated to "the protection and improvement of life" on the planet Earth. The society, based in Norfolk, Virginia, has attracted more than 300,000 members.

Over the years, Cousteau collected dozens of medals and awards from governments and private groups, as well as honorary degrees from many universities. He wrote more than fifty books and made more than sixty television documentaries about his life under the sea.

Once when he was called the first "man-fish" to explore a whole new underwater world, Cousteau said: "Diving is the most fabulous satisfaction you can experience. I am miserable out of water. It is as though you have been introduced to heaven and then find yourself back on earth. The spirituality of man cannot be completely separated from the physical. But you have made a big step toward escape simply by lowering yourself in water."

Charles Darwin

1809–1882   English naturalist; developer of the controversial theory of evolution

In his old age, Charles Darwin cheerfully admitted that he had been a very ordinary boy—a boy who even seemed rather dim-witted. One day his father had lost his temper and told him: "You care for nothing but shooting, dogs, and rat-catching, and you will be a disgrace to yourself and all your family."

What's more, the head of the boarding school the young Darwin attended, upon being asked what profession this pupil should aim for, answered: "It doesn't matter. He'll never make a success of anything."

Yet the shy, likable subject of these negative comments went far beyond merely becoming the most outstanding naturalist of his own era. He also became one of that small handful of individuals throughout recorded history whose ideas have continued to influence every thinking person everywhere.

Darwin's theory of evolution—holding that all forms of life have gradually changed, developing new traits as the result of a process he called natural selection—still arouses great controversy among deeply religious people. They accept the Bible's version of God's creation of every living creature as the literal truth. Despite continuing dispute, however, a century after Darwin's death there can be no doubt about the lasting impact of his basic conclusions.

The man around whom so much argument has swirled could hardly have had a more peaceful early life. Born on February 12, 1809, Charles Robert Darwin belonged by birth to England's comfortable upper class. His father, Dr. Robert Waring Darwin, was a highly regarded physician in the town of Shrewsbury. His mother was Susannah Wedgwood, whose family owned the famous Wedgwood pottery works where plates and bowls of elegant simplicity were produced for shipment all over the world.

Charles was the second son, and the fifth of six children, in the Darwins' fine house near Shrewsbury. Only the death of his mother, when he was eight years old, marred the happiness of his boyhood. Then his eldest sister, Caroline, took over responsibility for looking after him.

Caroline, giving lessons to Charles and their younger sister Catherine, found that the little girl learned much more quickly than their brother. So she tried hard to make Charles improve, but her efforts had just one effect. Every time Charles entered a room where Caroline was, he asked himself: "What will she blame me for now?" Because pleasing her seemed impossible, he acted as if he didn't care about anything that books contained.

Already, though, Charles had a passionate interest in nature's wonders. Whenever he spied a wildflower he had never before noticed, he made a point of finding out its name. Also, he appeared to be a born collector—he practically never returned from an outdoors ramble without some plant or rock or shell to add to one of his collections.

A year after his mother's death,

Charles spent a brief period attending a local day school. Then at the age of nine, he entered a noted boarding school. This experience was less painful than it might have been because the Shrewsbury School was located only a mile from his home, so he could still spend a lot of time wandering in familiar woods and fields with his favorite dogs.

Years afterward, when Darwin wrote the story of his life for his own children, he gave an example of the kind of trick older boys at this school often played on newcomers:

A boy of the name of Garnett took me into a cake-shop one day, and bought some cakes for which he did not pay, as the shopman trusted him. When we came out I asked him why he did not pay for them, and he instantly answered, "Why, do you not know that my uncle left a great sum of money to the Town on condition that every tradesman should give whatever was wanted without payment to anyone who wore his old hat and moved it in a particular manner?" and he then showed me how it was moved. . . . He said, "Now if you like to go by yourself into that cake-shop . . . I will lend you my hat, and you can get whatever you like if you move the hat on your head properly." I gladly accepted the generous offer, and went in and asked for some cakes, moved the old hat, and was walking out of the shop, when the shopman made a rush at me, so I dropped the cakes and ran for dear life, and was astonished by being greeted with shouts of laughter by my false friend Garnett.

For seven years, from 1818 to 1825, Charles remained at the Shrewsbury School, mostly enjoying himself and even learning a little Latin and Greek. But he put much more effort into learning on his own how to preserve the skins of the varied birds and small animals he shot. He also carefully saved all the insects he caught.

Despite the undistinguished record Charles made as a student, in the autumn of 1825, when he was only sixteen, his father sent him to the University of Edinburgh in Scotland. He went with his older brother Erasmus—Dr. Darwin wanted both of his sons to follow in his own footsteps by preparing there to practice medicine. But Charles found many of the lectures he was supposed to attend terribly dull.

Furthermore, he discovered that he could not bear watching his first surgery lesson. In those days, there were no anesthetics to put patients to sleep before a surgeon began his work. Charles felt such anguish himself at the sight of a patient about to be cut that he fainted, and after he revived he vowed he would never again enter the operating room.

Yet Charles did not waste the two years he spent in Edinburgh. Because he was so fascinated by rocks, he searched out lectures on geology. Likewise, he gained a good deal of knowledge about sea creatures—he even presented a few reports about his own shorefront findings at meetings of scientific groups. When he was eighteen, however, his father called a halt to such activities.

Among families like the Darwins, only a few professions were considered suitable. Since Charles clearly was unfit for a medical career, the strong-minded Dr. Darwin proposed making him a clergyman instead. This idea struck Charles as more appealing because he still felt no doubts about the teachings of the Church of England that he had absorbed during his early childhood. Also, he knew that, after being ordained, he would probably be assigned to a country parish where he would have plenty of leisure for continuing his nature studies on his own.

So, in the autumn of 1827, young Darwin willingly transferred to one of Britain's leading learning centers—the world-famed university at Cambridge. Enrolling here as a candidate for the ministry, he joined a group of not overly studious comrades who cared more about extracurricular events like shooting parties than about winning top honors on the exams they took. A tall, broad-shouldered fellow with an agreeably animated manner whenever he spoke of something that interested him, he became quite popular despite his shyness.

Again, though, Darwin's bent for observing nature took precedence over all else. His main goal during his Cambridge years was to add to his collection of unusual beetles. One day, when he was out walking amid some old trees, he tore away a scrap of bark and saw two rare beetles. He seized one in each hand. But then he saw a third and new kind, so he popped the one that he held in his right hand into his mouth. "Alas," he wrote long afterward, "it ejected some intensely acrid fluid, which burnt my tongue so that I was forced to spit the beetle out." Many years later, he still regretted losing this beetle as well as the third one.

Much more significantly, at Cambridge Darwin attracted the attention of several leading professors in various fields of natural science, for he kept displaying signs that he might have an exceptional mind. During informal Friday evening gatherings held by an eminent teacher of botany, Darwin showed a surprising grasp of a subject he had mostly taught himself. On summer rock-hunting expeditions, he similarly impressed a noted geologist. In addition, he seemed to possess a special gift for finding new ways to explain facts he observed.

Yet Darwin was still supposed to be studying for the ministry. After he earned his Cambridge degree in the spring of 1831, he went on another geological tour through the mountains of Wales, not far west of Shrewsbury—planning to take steps toward being ordained when he returned.

But a happy chance changed Charles Darwin's plans. When he got home, he found a letter from the Cambridge botanist whose Friday evening gatherings he had so much enjoyed. Professor John Stevens Henslow had been asked to recommend a candidate for a great adventure.

H.M.S. *Beagle*, a British Navy warship especially equipped for surveying coastal waters, was about to undertake mapping the entire coast of South America as well as some groups of islands. The voyage would last at least two years, probably longer—and because so little was known about the plants, animals, and rocks of the areas to be investigated, it seemed advisable to have a naturalist join the ship's company.

Would Darwin accept this post, Henslow asked.

Darwin was tremendously excited by the letter. But since no pay went with the post and he would have to depend on his father to advance money for his expenses, his first step was to consult

Charles Darwin's ship, H.M.S. *Beagle*, 1872. *Culver Pictures.*

his father. Dr. Darwin shook his head firmly.

Such a trip was bound to be dangerous, he said. At the very least, it might cause lasting health problems. And it would put off his son's entry into the ministry unnecessarily. Nevertheless, the doctor added, if Charles could find one sensible man who disagreed with his own outlook, let this gentleman try to convince him.

Charles, having reached the age of twenty-two without ever having defied his father, wrote to Professor Henslow saying he could not go on the voyage. Then, with the aim of raising his low spirits, he rode over to visit his Wedgwood relatives—he was particularly fond of his cousin Emma.

As soon as her father heard why Charles was feeling disappointed, Uncle Josiah called for his horse. An hour or so later, he and Charles were back at Shrewsbury, Charles listening with rising hope while Uncle Jos patiently refuted every one of Dr. Darwin's arguments against the voyage. That same afternoon another letter went off to Professor Henslow, canceling the one mailed that morning.

On December 27, 1831, H.M.S. *Beagle* set out from the English harbor of Plymouth. Nearly five years elapsed before it returned safely. Because the young naturalist aboard proved to be a genius, this cruise would become one of the most famous seafaring ventures in all history.

The *Beagle,* very small by modern standards, measured only ninety feet from stem to stern. Seventy-four people somehow worked and slept in the limited space available. Darwin shared a cabin less than fifteen feet square with Captain Robert FitzRoy and one other officer. When the exceptionally tall Darwin wanted to stretch out on his hammock, he had to remove the top drawer of his chest and put it on the floor so he would have room for his feet.

During the first weeks of the voyage, Darwin spent most of his time thus stretched out while the ship pitched and rolled. Seasickness afflicted him to the extent that he could eat nothing except raisins. Still, he managed to remain enthusiastic as he made plans for exploring ashore once they reached South America.

Stowed in his locker were a supply of notebooks in which Darwin would keep detailed accounts of the natural phenomena he found. In addition, he had brought along a small microscope, binoculars, a geological magnifying glass, and a jar of alcohol for preserving notable specimens. This simple equipment, plus a few books by leading naturalists, would be all he could rely on to help him—but his greatest asset was his own inquiring mind.

Sixty-three days out of England, the *Beagle* reached the coast of Brazil. Darwin went ashore then, as he would do repeatedly, sometimes for several weeks at a time while the vessel went about its mapping task. The lush tropical scene of coconut palms and bananas growing in great bunches around the town of Bahia thrilled him. That evening, he wrote in his diary: "Delight is a weak term to express the feelings of a naturalist who for the first time has wandered by himself in a Brazilian forest."

At Bahia, Darwin set the pattern he would follow throughout the expedition. Exploring on foot or by horseback, alone or with native guides during longer outings, he collected all sorts of specimens—insects and birds, even small animals, as well as rocks and parts of plants. Each night he worked at carefully preserving and labeling everything he had gathered. "I shall have a large box to send very soon to Cambridge," he wrote to Professor Henslow.

Also, Darwin put down complete descriptions of his findings in his notebooks so that he would be able to provide European specialists with a great deal of new information about South American plant and animal life. But valuable as his data proved to be,

if he had done no more than this technical job probably his name would hardly be remembered.

In addition, though, Darwin's letters home, and the diary he kept so diligently, gave such vivid pictures of his travel experiences that even nonscientific readers found them fascinating. So his high-spirited accounts of sitting around campfires with South American cowboys, eating delicious ostrich dumplings or roast armadillos, could have earned him at least limited fame as a writer of true adventure stories.

Yet the real reason Darwin's name continues to be known everywhere more than a hundred years after his death is that, throughout his travels, he kept noticing surprising mysteries and trying to explain them.

Why did fossil remains he had found of ancient creatures that had long since disappeared from the earth have so many features resembling those of existing creatures?

And how could the vast changes in the earth's surface clearly indicated by the different layers of rock in the Andes Mountains have occurred during a comparatively short period? For, according to the Bible, God had created the earth as well as all forms of life only about 4,000 years earlier.

But the most compelling question struck him toward the end of the cruise, when the *Beagle* had just departed from the Galápagos Islands. About 500 miles off the coast of Ecuador, the Galápagos were eerie specks of land—mostly black sand and boulders, with hardly a trace of green. Still, an amazing variety of animal life inhabited these seemingly inhospitable islands. Although the giant turtles were the species previous explorers had especially marveled at, to Darwin the birds provided even more of a puzzle.

Wasn't it beyond belief that any higher power would have bothered to create unique types of finches on each of these strange little islands in the Pacific Ocean? How otherwise, then, could his own findings be explained? For, as soon as Darwin began to study his Galápagos specimens carefully, he saw clear differences in the beaks of finches he had collected on islands only fifty or sixty miles apart.

It was from these Galápagos finches that Charles Darwin conceived his world-shaking theory of evolution, some writers would later say. Even if they were putting a complicated and painstaking process very simply, in a way they were right. Still, more than twenty years would elapse before the finches—plus a whole lot else—led Darwin to publish his historic book *The Origin of Species*.

Even during the final months of the long voyage, he realized that his own former faith in the Bible as the basic authority on natural history had gradually disappeared. From the weight of the evidence he himself had collected, he had become convinced that the earth must be millions of years old. Furthermore, he felt certain that all the different forms of life could not have been created with an unchangeable identity but, instead, had been evolving over the centuries in some way nobody yet understood.

Testing these ideas as the *Beagle* sailed homeward, Darwin got a taste of what lay ahead of him. Captain FitzRoy, a hot-tempered man only about thirty years old, took his religious beliefs so seriously that he almost exploded when he heard what his cabin mate had on his mind. Always anxious to avoid dispute, Darwin quickly changed the subject.

Indeed, after landing back in England on October 2, 1836, Darwin gave no immediate signs that he was mulling over any revolutionary theory. He seemed to enjoy the modest fame his adventure brought him—the boxes he had sent to Cambridge had insured his warm welcome at scientific meetings, then his account of his travels published a few years after his return won him a wider reputation as a promising young naturalist.

As a result, Darwin felt sufficient self-confidence to take a major personal step. On January 29, 1839, shortly before his thirtieth birthday, he married his cousin Emma Wedgwood. Following a brief period in London, which he and his country-bred wife both found impossibly noisy and dusty, they moved to a rambling stone house on eighteen acres of rural land outside the village of Downe, only about twenty miles south of the bustling capital city.

Over the next forty years, Darwin hardly ever left his own secluded property. Surrounded by his large family—he and his wife had seven cherished children, besides three others who died early—he constantly kept diverting himself with projects for adding rooms or improving his grounds. The reason he rarely traveled even as far as London was a baffling illness that made him almost an invalid.

A century after Darwin's death, experts of all sorts still cannot agree about what ailed him. While he undoubtedly suffered repeated bouts of acute stomach upsets and general weakness, no doctor then or now has been able to diagnose the cause. Although some insist that he must have been infected by a rare tropical bug during his South American journey, others say his trouble was really psychological—that his symptoms were an inner protest against the way his overbearing father had treated him, or even against the threat to established patterns of thought posed by his own ideas.

In any case, from being an adventurous young man who could not see a mountain without wanting to climb it, Darwin turned remarkably rapidly into a stoop-shouldered and white-bearded stay-at-home. Yet despite the fact that walking more than half a mile exhausted him, he still managed to accomplish an incredible amount of scientific work.

Thanks to the money left to him and his wife by well-off relatives, Darwin had no need to earn enough to support his family. So he could concentrate on expanding his grasp of natural science in order to provide a more solid foundation for his surmises about evolution. Toward that end, he spent hour after hour probing the structures of many kinds of tiny creatures at a table in his study. In addition, several leading figures from England's scientific community, who had become close friends of his, regularly visited him and kept him informed of all sorts of new research being carried out elsewhere during this very active period in the advancement of science.

Thus, isolated as he was but constantly reading and writing and thinking, Darwin kept finding more and more support for his revolutionary con-

Charles Darwin at the age of thirty-one. *Royal College of Surgeons of England.*

clusions. As early as 1837, he had opened his first notebook on the subject of evolution. In this and its successors he collected a huge amount of evidence backing up his theory, but he also had to answer a crucial question.

By what means had evolutionary changes occurred?

Despite the progress science was making in the middle of the 1800s, great gaps remained. Because the whole subject of heredity had yet to yield any of its secrets, Darwin could not possibly show the mechanism whereby individual members of a species inherited any given trait. Nor could he discuss what are now known as mutations—sudden changes in genes, causing notable differences between offspring and their parents.

Instead, Darwin had to rely on intuition and answer the basic question with two phrases that have since entered the language—"natural selection" and "the survival of the fittest."

Suppose, he said, that individual finches or elephants were born varying in some way from others of the same species. Then if their variation helped them adapt better to the climate of their area or gave them a special advantage when competing for the available food, nature itself would, in effect, select them to thrive and reproduce themselves while less-adaptable relatives died out.

It was this concept of natural selection that probably accounts for Darwin's own survival among the ranks of great thinkers. For, during the decades when he continued to delay publishing any major work, evolution itself was "in the air," as many writers would later put it. As far back as the 1700s, the general idea had been proposed a few times— Darwin's physician-grandfather Dr. Erasmus Darwin was among those who had written fancifully on the subject. More recently, though, other minds had begun considering the topic more deeply.

Indeed, when Darwin finally, in 1859, published his great book about evolution, a plant collector named Alfred Russel Wallace had already arrived independently at even the crucial mechanism of natural selection. The remarkable story of how this now nearly forgotten man might have received the credit—and blame—that Darwin received instead will be told in the separate chapter about Wallace's life.

Apart from the difference it would have made in Darwin's own reputation if someone else had introduced the concept of evolution, possibly the world's reaction might have been different, too. Because Charles Darwin was such a kindly and unargumentative English gentleman, the controversy his *The Origin of Species* provoked perhaps was less bitter than it would have been had someone more assertive attempted to force people to accept his views.

As it was, one of Darwin's warmest friends—the noted zoologist Thomas Henry Huxley—assumed the role of "Darwin's bulldog" when critics began ridiculing the whole idea of evolution. Beyond the intense religious objection to any theory denying the Bible's complete truthfulness, the opposition focused on a single point.

Since Darwin had anticipated how much heat would be generated if he applied his theory to human beings, he had concentrated in his book on other forms of life. But that did not stop critics from immediately hooting that anybody who believed Darwin must believe also that men had descended from apes. A leader of the Church of England, hoping to demolish Darwinism once and for all, seized on this issue during a tense debate about evolution at Oxford University.

Bishop Samuel Wilberforce, reaching the climax of his argument, turned toward Thomas Huxley and demanded to know: On which side of his family would he be willing to admit he had monkeys as ancestors?

Huxley did not hesitate. In a voice dripping with scorn, he said that he would far rather have sensible simian creatures as his forebears than the kind of men afraid to face the truth.

His words caused such an uproar that one lady in the audience fainted away. Yet even if Huxley failed to end all opposition to Darwin's theory, within just a few decades practically every reputable scientist—and a large number of ordinary people—had accepted evolution as beyond doubt. Many churchmen along with their flocks found it possible to modify their belief in the exact factual accuracy of the Bible while still retaining their religious faith. However, many others—especially the members of some fundamentalist groups in the United States—more than a century later continue to regard Darwinism as dangerous nonsense.

But even though, over the years, vast advances in many branches of science have undermined some of Darwin's surmises, among the science minded he remains a towering figure whose theory of evolution ranks him with geniuses like Galileo, who proved that the earth revolves around the sun, and Newton, who discovered the laws of gravity.

Yet the unassuming Darwin himself, during the two decades following the publication of his *Origin*, continued to live quietly at Downe. He wrote one other major work, *The Descent of Man*, devoted to specific evidence about the evolution of human beings, and he also kept assembling data for several less controversial books on such topics as honey bees and wild orchids.

At the age of seventy-three, Darwin

suffered a heart attack. On April 20, 1882, after telling his wife that he wished to be buried on the grounds of his beloved home, he died peacefully. But Mrs. Darwin found it impossible to obey his last request.

A committee led by members of the British Parliament insisted that Charles Darwin had earned the honor of being laid to rest among the nation's heroes— in the great London cathedral of Westminster Abbey. Accordingly, his body was taken there to be buried with much ceremony right beside the grave of Sir Isaac Newton.

In many other countries, too, Darwin's death inspired long and thoughtful articles about how much he had influenced human thought. The editor of a leading German daily held that no other figure of the era would prove to be as important. "Our century," he wrote, "is Darwin's century."

Jean Henri Fabre

1823–1915   Expert observer of insects

Seated on a stone at the bottom of a ravine, a man wearing a wide-brimmed black hat stared down at the sandy soil around his feet. Three women walked along the path in front of him on their way to pick grapes at a nearby vineyard, but he didn't look up.

Hours later, the three women passed once more, carrying baskets filled with grapes on their heads. The man was still sitting in the same place, motionless, and his eyes were still peering downward. As the women went by, one of them tapped her forehead and the other murmured, "A poor dumb one, alas."

They were mistaken. They had seen Jean Henri Fabre at work, studying wasps on the sunny slopes of the Rhone Valley in his native France. An amaz-ingly patient man, Fabre spent much of his life observing many types of insects—and then writing about every aspect of their behavior as no other scientist had ever done before.

Fabre was "an incomparable observer," according to the eminent naturalist Charles Darwin. Victor Hugo, the famous French novelist, called Fabre "the insects' Homer" because of the poetic way he described these creatures and their habits.

Despite science's great advances since Fabre wrote his books, today they are still regarded as some of the most accurate and readable accounts that we have of the lives of bees, wasps, ants, flies, and spiders.

For Fabre, the insect was not the lowest of creatures, to be stamped on as a pest or to be killed by chemical sprays. He saw the work of God in the intricate beauty of the spider's web, in the strange light given off by glow-worms, in the untiring work of various beetles, and even in the paralyzing attacks of hunting wasps.

All around him he saw the world of insects flourishing, as it continues to flourish today. Constituting nine-tenths of the earth's animal population, insects fly through the air, crawl on the ground, and burrow underground, besides gnawing into trees and other growing things.

For farmers, weevils and maggots are pests to be destroyed. For people in houses, bees, wasps, flies, and mosquitoes are annoyances to be avoided or killed if necessary. But somehow the insects survive and, some think, will outlast man himself on the planet Earth.

This wondrous world of insects fascinated Fabre from his earliest childhood. He was born on December 21, 1823, in the village of Saint-Léon in Provence, a region of southern France where the sun shines brightly and the wind blows fiercely from the Mediterranean Sea. His father was Antoine Fabre, a far from prosperous farmer, and his mother was the former Victoire Salgues, daughter of the local tax collector.

The Fabres were so poor that the infant Henri was sent to live with his grandparents. They had a farm outside the neighboring hamlet of Malaval. He spent his earliest years there, helping to tend cows by day and listening to the stories of his grandmother in the evenings.

Long afterward, he remembered his first scientific discovery. At nightfall, a sort of singing that seemed to be coming from a patch of woods near his grandparents' house attracted his attention. He went out, but the sound of his steps made the song stop. Stubbornly, he returned night after night.

"Whoosh!" he later wrote. "A grab of my hand and I hold the singer. It is not a bird, it is a kind of a grasshopper. I now know from personal observation that the grasshopper sings."

When Henri was seven years old, his parents brought him home to attend a local school. He learned to read and write and do simple arithmetic. Best of all, though, he liked his daily chore of driving ducks to the pond near his home.

At the pond, Henri picked up stones that shone like diamonds. He also found a beautiful blue beetle, which he put in an empty snail shell that he covered with a leaf. He filled his pockets with oddly shaped stones that looked like little rams' horns.

When Henri returned home one evening, his pockets bulged with his finds. "You rascal," his father shouted at him. "I send you to mind the ducks and you amuse yourself picking up stones. Make haste, throw them away."

Henri was ten years old when his father tired of the harsh life of a farmer. The family moved to the village of Rodez, where his father opened a café. The boy attended school there, paying his fees by serving at Sunday Mass in the local chapel.

In his Latin studies, Henri paid particular attention to the works of Virgil, the great Roman poet. He liked Virgil's verses about bees, crows, cicadas, turtledoves, and nanny goats because of his own acquaintance with all these creatures. While he was a good student, though, his father was a bad businessman.

After four unprofitable years in Rodez, the Fabres moved to the city of Toulouse and then to Montpellier. His father still could not earn a living for the family—so Henri, at the age of fifteen, went off on his own. He sold lemons at fairs, worked on the construction of a rail line, and at times even picked grapes growing near the road for food if he had nothing else to eat.

But somehow the love of learning had been instilled in him. Henri took the entrance examination that was given by a government-supported school for teachers in the town of Avignon and passed with the highest grades. After three years of study, he received a diploma as an elementary-school teacher in 1841, when he was eighteen.

Fabre's first assignment as a teacher took him to a village near Avignon, where the school was in a cellar. He had fifty unruly boys in his class, some of them as old as he was. Yet he managed to keep order among his students, teach them basic subjects—and even learn from them.

In May when the weather moderated, he took the boys outside to teach them geometry by laying out triangles and polygons on the ground. But he noticed something suspicious. Each time one of the boys bent down to put in a stake, he picked up a piece of straw and licked it. Fabre asked what they were doing. They told him they were sucking up honey from the nests of big black bees that made their hives of pebbles.

Even though Fabre could scarcely support himself on the meager wages of a teacher, he was so fascinated by the bees that he bought a book about insects. In it, he found the names of some men who had spent their lives studying the habits of the insects pictured on its pages.

As he read the book for the hundredth time, he remembered later, a voice within him seemed to whisper, "You also shall be of their company."

Fabre had found his life's work. No matter that he was a poor schoolteacher earning only enough for bread and a little red wine, he determined that he would learn more about the magnificent insects depicted in his book. He realized, however, that first he needed a better general education.

To start with, he taught himself algebra. While still teaching at the elementary school, he earned degrees in mathematics and physical sciences—also finding the time to court a local young woman named Marie Villard. They were married in 1844, when he was twenty-one.

But Fabre had to wait five years before he received an appointment as a teacher in a lycée, the French equivalent of our high schools. In 1849, he became a professor of physics and chemistry at the lycée in Ajaccio, the main city on the French island of Corsica. Despite his grand title, he was a high school teacher who received very little pay.

Still, around him stretched a wonderland of flowers, plants, and sea shells. He collected all the shells he could find until a visiting biologist gave him an important lesson.

"You interest yourself in shells," the biologist said. "That is good, but it is not enough. You must look into the animal itself."

Using a scissors and needle, the biologist showed him how to cut open a snail. Then he spread out the internal organs and explained their functions. Fabre never forgot the lesson.

After three years on Corsica, Fabre suffered an attack of malaria. When he recovered, he secured a post at the lycée back in Avignon. With his wife and two young children, he returned to the south of France in 1852.

A gifted teacher, Fabre instilled a love of nature in his students. On his own, he kept delving more deeply into the study of entomology, as the science devoted to the study of insects is called. One evening sitting before the fire at his home he read a paper by an insect expert named Léon Dufour, describing the peculiar habits of hunting wasps.

According to Dufour, these wasps captured small beetles and preserved them as food for their young. Dufour assumed that the beetles were dead, kept from rotting by a sort of embalming fluid injected by the wasps. The story fascinated Fabre, so he decided to investigate it himself.

In the fields near Avignon, he found some wasp nests with beetles inside. Examining them carefully, he made sure that the beetles were not dead. He was able to prove that the parent wasps had preserved them alive by an injection so they could feed their young on fresh food.

It was the first of Fabre's insect discoveries. He wrote a description of the fantastic process for the French scientific publication *Annals of the Natural Sciences*. His paper, published in 1855, started a long series of scientific articles that he contributed about many kinds of insects.

Fabre's debut as a writer marked the beginning of a very slow rise to fame. When his first paper appeared in print he was thirty-two years old, struggling to make ends meet. His salary at Avignon was even less than he had earned in Corsica although, by now, he had five children to support. So he spent evenings and days off either tutoring students or writing textbooks to earn extra money.

A shy man, Fabre refused to take part in the politics of the school and never sought advancement. During his years at Avignon, he never received a promotion or a raise in salary. His colleagues, jealous of his abilities, privately called him "the fly," referring to his love of insects.

Yet even though Fabre preferred to work quietly and alone in his corner of France, news of his discoveries gradually spread throughout the scientific world. In London, Darwin read Fabre's papers about the instincts of insects. In Paris, an important French official also was impressed by the writings of the obscure schoolteacher.

Victor Duruy was minister of public education under Napoleon III, then emperor of France. Duruy visited Avignon and, after observing Fabre at work, asked: "What do you want for your laboratory?"

Fabre, who sought favors from nobody, replied that he expected nothing.

"What, nothing!" Duruy exclaimed. "You are unique there. The others overwhelm me with requests, their laboratories are never well enough supplied. And you, poor as you are, refuse my offers!"

Six months later, Fabre received a letter summoning him to call upon the minister in Paris. He wrote back that he was busy and could not make the trip. A second letter arrived, signed by Duruy himself. It said: "Come at once, or I shall send my gendarmes to fetch you."

The next day, Fabre entered Duruy's office. The minister welcomed him and handed him a copy of the government's official newspaper.

"Read that," he said. "You refused my chemical apparatus, but you won't refuse this."

Fabre looked at the paper and was astonished to find his name among the new members of the Legion of Honor, a select company of France's most distinguished men. Duruy pinned the red ribbon of the legion on Fabre's lapel, kissed him on both cheeks in the French style, and made him telegraph the news to his family.

Duruy was not finished. He presented Fabre with a gift of scientific books and 1,200 francs for his expenses in coming to Paris. The following day he even took Fabre to visit the emperor. Fabre was not impressed.

"I had had enough of Paris," he wrote later. "Never had I felt such tortures of loneliness as in that immense whirlpool of humanity. To get away, to get away was my one idea."

Returning to Avignon, he put the ribbon of the Legion of Honor in a drawer. Although he considered it a tribute to his work, he never took it out and did not wear it on his lapel as almost all other winners of the award did.

About the same time, in 1865, Fabre had an unexpected caller. It was Louis Pasteur, already famous for his chemical discoveries. He had come south with the mission of rescuing the silkworm industry from a terrible plague that threatened to wipe it out.

Pasteur wanted to see some silkworm cocoons. Fabre fetched them.

Shaking one, Pasteur exclaimed: "It rattles! There must be something inside."

"Why, yes."

"But what?"

"The chrysalis."

"What's that?"

"I mean the sort of mummy into which the caterpillar turns before it becomes a moth," Fabre said.

"And in every cocoon there is one of those things?" Pasteur asked.

"Of course. It's to protect the chrysalis that the caterpillar spins."

"Ah," said Pasteur, now satisfied.

Fabre learned a lesson from that encounter. Although Pasteur obviously knew nothing about insects, he had quickly found out enough to conquer the silkworm disease. The lesson had an important influence on Fabre.

"I have made it a rule to adopt the method of ignorance," he wrote later. "I read very little. Instead of turning over the leaves of books, an expensive method which is not within my means, instead of consulting others, I set myself obstinately face to face with my subject until I contrive to make it speak."

Busy as he was as a teacher and a researcher, Fabre also found time to give a series of free lectures for girls— something most unusual in those days when few girls in France went to school. Here is how he described his lectures:

"I taught those young persons what air and water are; whence the lightning comes and the thunder; by what devices our thoughts are transmitted across the seas and continents by means of a metal wire; why fire burns and why we breathe; how a seed puts forth shoots and how a flower blossoms."

But Fabre's lectures offended church leaders. He was denounced from the pulpit as a dangerous man for daring to teach science to girls. Then his landladies, two old and religious women, informed him that he would have to move out of the home he rented from them.

Fabre dramatically told his wife: "It is all over, the downfall of my hopes is complete." Even his important friend in Paris could not help him. For Minister of Education Duruy, too, had lost his job as the result of pressure from church officials who opposed his reforms of the French school system and particularly his attempts to provide public education for girls.

At this crisis in his life, Fabre found help from a new friend—John Stuart Mill, the eminent English economist. They had met while Mill was vacationing in Avignon and had enjoyed many thoughtful discussions together. When Fabre appealed to Mill for money to help him move, Mill immediately offered whatever was needed.

In 1870, at the age of forty-seven, Fabre's life changed completely. Leaving Avignon, he settled in the tiny village of Orange with his wife and children. From then on he devoted all his time to observing and writing about his favorite insects, earning his living by writing textbooks.

Before the end of that decade, in 1879 Fabre achieved his dream of acquiring a piece of land he could call his own. He bought a tract of stony wilderness considered worthless for farming, just outside the village of Sérignan, where he spent the rest of his life.

"This is what I wished for," he wrote, "a bit of land, oh, not so very large, but fenced in to avoid the drawbacks of a public way; an abandoned, barren, sun-scorched piece of land, favored by thistles and by wasps and bees. Here, without distant expeditions that take up my time, without tiring rambles that strain my nerves, I could contrive my plan of attack, lay my ambushes and watch their effects at every hour of the day."

At Sérignan, Fabre began to put together all his observations in a grand series of books. He wrote them, one by one, over the years—*The Life of the Spider, The Life of the Fly, Hunting Wasps, The Sacred Beetle, The Life of the Grasshopper*, and many others. They established him as one of the outstanding scientific writers of all time.

Content at last on his own land, Fabre became known as the hermit of Sérignan. He hated to go away even for a few hours. But he was not alone. He made his children active collaborators

A drawing by E. J. Detmold. From *Fabre's Book of Insects*. New York: Dodd, Mead & Co., 1926.

in his work. Here is one of his stories about his seven-year-old son Paul:

My assiduous companion on my hunting expeditions, he knows better than anyone of his age the secrets of the cicada, the locust, the cricket, and especially the dung-beetle, his great delight. Twenty paces away, his sharp eyes will distinguish the real mound that marks a burrow from casual heaps of earth; his delicate ears catch the grasshopper's faint stridulation, which to me remains silent. He lends me his sight and his hearing; and I, in exchange, present him with ideas, which he receives attentively, raising wide blue questioning eyes to mine.

Fabre would rise at six in the morning and stay in his laboratory until noon, conducting experiments or recording what he had seen the day before. After lunch, he went into the fields observing, always observing the plant and insect life around him.

Wherever he went, Fabre smoked a pipe that kept going out as his attention strayed so he was constantly relighting it. But he was even better known for the wide-brimmed black felt hat he always wore. Almost every existing picture of Fabre shows him wearing this hat.

Jean Henri Fabre (seated) with his wife (second from left), his daughters on either side of her, his goddaughter, and his nephew. *Courtesy Department Library Services, American Museum of Natural History.*

Fabre did his writing at a small table in his laboratory. Dipping his pen into an inkwell, he wrote down his observations using clear language free of any scientific jargon. Less interested in making discoveries than in understanding the familiar, he often tried simple experiments to establish facts about common insects.

For instance, Fabre wanted to find out whether cicadas can hear their own chirping. So he borrowed two guns used in the village on feast days and fired them under a tree in which cicadas were merrily singing. The cicadas went right on with their song. He concluded, therefore, that these insects were unable to hear any sound—including the happy music they made themselves.

For thirty-six years Fabre lived in obscurity in Sérignan. His first wife died there, and he remarried. Most of his children left to follow their own careers, but some remained to care for him. All this time, his work never stopped.

In 1910, when he was eighty-seven years old, Fabre's friends decided that it was time to celebrate his life. Neither government officials nor scientists came to the party at which Fabre's neighbors honored him. Yet he was not completely forgotten by the outside world.

In Sweden, the Royal Academy of Stockholm awarded him its medal for outstanding scientific achievement. Besides receiving various French literary prizes, he was also nominated for a Nobel Prize. And the president of France made a special trip to Sérignan to visit Fabre on the occasion of his ninetieth birthday.

Ailing then, Fabre died on October 11, 1915, as he was approaching the age of ninety-two.

Shortly before his death, a young man told him that Sérignan was considering putting up a statue in his honor.

"Well, well," Fabre replied, "I shall see myself but shall I recognize myself? I've had so little time for looking at myself."

"What inscription would you prefer?" the young man asked.

"One word: laboremus," Fabre said, giving the Latin word meaning "Let us work."

Alexander von Humboldt

1769–1859   German natural scientist and explorer

Look at any collection of maps of the world and you will find:

The Humboldt Current off the coast of South America
The Humboldt Glacier in northern Greenland
The Humboldt Mountains in China
The Humboldt Peak in Colorado
The Humboldt Bay in New Guinea
The Humboldt State Redwood Park in California
The Humboldt River in Nevada

What's more, cities have been named after Humboldt in the Canadian province of Saskatchewan as well as in Illinois, Iowa, Kansas, Minnesota, Nebraska, South Dakota, and Tennessee. And three states have Humboldt counties—California, Iowa, and Nevada.

Who was Humboldt and what did he do to be honored in so many geographical areas all over the world?

His story starts more than two hundred years ago in a brick house in the center of the German city of Berlin. There on September 14, 1769, a boy was born to Major Alexander George von Humboldt and his wife, the former Maria Elisabeth von Hollwege. Like her husband, an aide to the duke of Brunswick, she came from the upper level of German society—the "von" in their family names indicated their elite status.

This aristocratic couple's second son was christened Friedrich Heinrich Alexander von Humboldt but called Alexander. With his brother Wilhelm, two years his senior, he grew up before

151

Berlin had become the capital of Germany. It was a small city in those days, with a population of about 150,000.

Only a short carriage ride away, the family had a country estate where the boys spent much of their youth. Their father loved nature, so he often took them on walks in the pinewoods at their country home. They went with him, too, when he inspected his fields of grape vines and mulberry bushes or visited a nearby lake bordered by tall reeds as well as sandy beaches. When Alexander was ten years old, however, his father died.

Unfortunately, his mother was a woman lacking in warmth or even affection for her sons. She left their care to servants and their education to tutors. Wilhelm, a bright and noisy boy, had an easy time becoming everybody's favorite. Alexander, with frequent headaches and bad moods, seemed slower to learn. But he was so talented at drawing and painting that his mother let him put his art works on the walls of her bedroom.

Raised almost as twins, the brothers took their lessons together. In addition to German, they studied French, Latin, Greek, and history. Because their tutors believed in the then-fashionable educational theories of Jean Jacques Rousseau—holding that children should be raised as close to nature as possible—the boys also were given many opportunities to learn about the natural world around them.

Alexander felt more comfortable outside than at home. He collected butterflies, insects, plants, and flowers in jars and boxes. After writing labels on each container, he put them on display in the room he shared with his brother. His exhibit resembled a shop kept by someone selling medicines, then called an apothecary, so Alexander became known in the family as "the little apothecary."

He also liked to sit in the woods, dreaming about faraway adventures after reading about the voyages of famous explorers. Later he recalled: "From my earliest youth, I had an intense desire to travel in those distant lands which have been but rarely visited by Europeans."

As Alexander grew into his teens, his interests expanded to include everything around him. He showed his dried plants and flowers to a botanist, who taught him the scientific way to classify them. He also learned how to put order into his rock collection. His drawings of flowers were so good that a well-known artist gave him lessons. In addition, he attended lectures on physics and philosophy.

At one of these lectures, Alexander heard about the American Benjamin

Alexander von Humboldt as a young man devoted to the study of botany. *Bibliothèque Nationale, Paris.*

Franklin and his new lightning rod. He begged his mother's permission to build one—and soon their home had one of the first lightning rods in Germany.

In 1789, twenty-year-old Alexander joined his brother at the university in the German city of Göttingen. It was Germany's foremost learning center, and he immediately felt at home in its exciting intellectual climate. He became a member of the Philosophical Society, read Greek and Latin works in the evenings, and began to write a study of the geology of the Rhine River Valley. He even asked for special permission to work in the library on Sundays.

One of his professors introduced him to a visiting celebrity. Georg Forster was an explorer and author who had accompanied Captain Cook on a voyage across the Pacific Ocean. Under Forster's influence, Humboldt decided upon a life in exploration and science—no matter that his mother had planned a career in finance and government service for him.

With Forster, he traveled to England taking notes on everything he saw—churches, museums, botanical gardens, and wool factories. They went on to Paris just a year after the French Revolution had turned France upside down. Humboldt sympathized with the aims of the revolution, but his concerns for

freedom took second place to his determination to be a scientist.

On his return to Germany, he obeyed his mother's wishes and enrolled in the Hamburg School of Commerce. But he had his own plan as well. He applied for admission to the Mining School at Freiburg, which offered the finest scientific training in Europe for anyone intending to become an explorer. Yet this ambition struck his family as very odd. His brother Wilhelm wrote that Alexander "maintains peculiar ideas for which I really don't care."

In Hamburg, Alexander attended classes faithfully. He also spent a great deal of time in the library, reading books about botany, geology, mathematics, and travel. Not hearing from Freiburg, he wrote directly to the government minister of industry and mines, who was much impressed by his paper on Rhine geology. As a result, Humboldt was admitted to the school.

From six o'clock in the morning until noon, he went underground in mines to study rocks, minerals, and mining methods. In the afternoon, he attended classes. In the evening, he either went on botany excursions or read books on geology, botany, and chemistry. "I have never been so busy in all my life," he wrote to a friend.

He spent so much time on his studies that he did not even attend the wedding of his brother Wilhelm. Alexander himself never married, although he always felt comfortable in the presence of women. His new sister-in-law once observed, "Alexander will never be inspired by anything that does not come through men." Indeed, he had numerous close friendships with other men at school and in his travels.

In 1792, at the age of twenty-three, Humboldt finished his studies and received an appointment as inspector of mines, a job he thoroughly enjoyed. A perceptive young man, he increased the output of the mines under his supervision by improving their working conditions. He also showed his concern for the welfare of the miners by setting up a school for miners and paying the salary of its teacher from his own pocket.

In the mines, Humboldt noticed mosses and lichen that grew on the walls. How could they grow without light? He tested them under varying conditions, then published his findings in a book he called *The Freiburg Flora*. It came out in 1793 and brought him a gold medal along with a promotion to a higher rank in government service. More important, it also brought him recognition from other scientists.

That did not satisfy Humboldt. A restless man, he wanted to travel and explore the world, not remain stuck in the mines of Germany. His opportunity did not come until 1797, when the death of his mother left him with sufficient money to devote himself to his scientific interests. That same year, he showed his versatility by publishing two volumes about his research into the effects of electric currents on human muscles.

While considering where to go on a new scientific expedition, he went to Paris to visit Wilhelm and his wife Caroline. Humboldt was twenty-nine years old then—of medium height, with unruly brown hair, bright blue eyes, a large mouth, and some scars on his forehead left by a mild attack of smallpox.

Caroline introduced him to the wide assortment of friends she regularly entertained. At her home German and French artists and scientists mixed easily, despite threats of war between their two countries. Humboldt met the aging explorer Louis de Bougainville, who urged him to come along on a trip around the world. He also talked with the famous zoologist Baron Georges Cuvier and other leading scientists.

In a French botanist named Aimé Bonpland, Humboldt found the traveling companion he thought would be most congenial. Together, they planned an expedition to Egypt but various problems arose. Instead they decided to explore the Spanish colonies of South

America, with Humboldt paying all the expenses.

They sailed from Spain on June 5, 1799, on the frigate *Pizarro*, following the route of Christopher Columbus to the New World. Landing in Venezuela in the middle of July, they began a five-year series of discoveries—and these would make Humboldt the second most famous man in Europe. Within just a few years, only France's Emperor Napoleon was more renowned.

Although it would take Humboldt a long time to publish all his findings, his letters home were read avidly by other scientists. "We run around here like mad," he wrote to his brother, explaining that he was overwhelmed by all the new kinds of flowers, plants, birds, animals, and rocks he kept encountering.

What made Humboldt different from many previous scientific explorers, however, was the breadth of his interests and knowledge. Not content merely to collect new specimens, facts, and data, he related them to one another.

As one biographer put it, Humboldt connected what he saw—for instance, he connected earthquakes with land forms, and rock formations with soil types, and climate conditions with human behavior.

In 1800, Humboldt and Bonpland went down the Orinoco River to the heart of the Amazon jungle, where they found wonderful sights as well as amazing animals like jaguars and alligators. It was so hot that they did most of their traveling during the night. By day, the mosquitoes were so thick that they found it almost impossible to move or take notes. But the Indians they met in the jungle were friendly.

They were fascinated by the Otomaco Indians, who ate soil in times of famine or flood. Humboldt reported: "This earth is a very fine sticky substance of yellow grayish color, which turns red in roasting." The Indians apparently thrived on their unusual diet.

By September, the two explorers had covered 6,443 miles of some of the least known and most dangerous areas in the Amazon jungle. They collected 12,000 plants—barely one-tenth of the new plants they saw. Humboldt had also established the connection of the water systems of the Orinoco and Amazon rivers and measured the height of the coastal mountain ranges. By sailing ship, they sent their collections and reports back to Europe where they created a sensation in scientific circles.

Their next stop was Cuba, where they visited sugar, indigo, cotton, and tobacco fields. What impressed Humboldt the most was the misery of the black slaves who worked in these fields.

From that time onward, he became an indignant opponent of slavery and the slave trade.

Early in 1801, Humboldt and Bonpland returned to South America, this time to Colombia. Day after day, in canoes paddled by Indians, they moved up various rivers through the jungles toward the town of Bogotá. It took almost three months to get there, but waiting for them was a well-known botanist, José Celestino Mutis, a pupil of the famous Linnaeus.

After comparing botanical notes with Mutis, Humboldt and Bonpland continued their jungle journey to Quito, arriving on January 6, 1802. Welcomed by the Spanish families settled there, Humboldt disappointed the ladies by vanishing at night to study the stars.

He was most fascinated, though, by the varied vegetation in the Andes Mountains. In the lowlands, palms and bananas grew. Further up, coffee and cotton flourished. Up a little higher, Indians cultivated grain and potatoes. Near the summits of the high peaks, llamas and sheep grazed on alpine herbs.

It became clear to Humboldt that the Andes could be compared to a stepladder, with distinct forms of life on each step. This was something never noted by scientists before—that the environment determined the diversity of animal and vegetable life. Moreover, each area displayed an orderly balance between soil and weather conditions and life itself.

Near Quito, the peak of Chimborazo, the highest in the Andes, challenged Humboldt. He and Bonpland climbed through the clouds, sometimes sick from nausea and giddiness caused by the altitude, but always noting where various kinds of vegetation grew. They finally reached the top, 20,577 feet above sea level, the highest that men had ever climbed up to that time.

After almost a year more in South America, the two explorers sailed north to Mexico, arriving early in 1803. For a mining expert like Humboldt, Mexico's fabulous silver mines made a rich field for research. Everywhere he went he made maps, studied the geology, inspected mines, delivered lectures, and collected data on the way people lived. He acted almost like a vacuum cleaner, sucking up all kinds of information.

At last, in 1804, it was time to leave Latin America. But Humboldt had one more mission in the New World. He had made up his mind to visit Thomas Jefferson, the president of the United States, to talk with him about the wonderful things he had found in South America and Mexico.

Humboldt's visit could not have been

timed better. He arrived with his maps of Mexico just after the United States had purchased the Louisiana Territory from France. Jefferson was very interested in Humboldt's maps and in all the facts he had collected about mines, roads, and commerce along the United States' new border with Mexico.

Talking to Jefferson, Humboldt also told him about the origin of the name America. "I believe [I] have earned a modest merit by [proving] that Amerigo Vespucci had no part in the naming of the new continent," he wrote later. Humboldt had explained to the president that the name America had first been used by a mapmaker illustrating Vespucci's travels years after his voyage to the New World.

On August 1, 1804, Humboldt returned to France to find himself famous at the age of thirty-four. He lectured to crowds of notables, arranged an exhibit of his plant specimens at the botanical garden in Paris, and planned to publish detailed accounts of his findings in several languages.

First, though, Humboldt traveled to Switzerland and Italy on a mission to measure the earth's magnetism with a new friend, Joseph-Louis Gay-Lussac, a French scientist. In Rome, he had a reunion with his brother Wilhelm, who was representing the German state of Prussia at the Vatican and had become a well-known patron of the arts.

Humboldt also returned to his birthplace to receive many honors. He was named a member of Berlin's Academy of Sciences and given various awards including a government pension. In addition, Prussia's king asked him to take part in Paris negotiations with the French emperor Napoleon, who had just defeated Prussia's army.

After Humboldt resumed living in Paris, he found himself with money problems for the first time in his life. He had spent lavishly on his South American travels and on establishing himself as a generous host in France's stylish capital city. But the recent wars in Europe had cut his income from his land holdings. To earn what he needed, he decided to write thirty volumes about his explorations and his findings.

So he settled into a diligent routine. After rising early, he went to one of the great libraries of Paris and worked until seven at night with only a brief interruption for lunch. After dinner with friends, he visited at the homes where artists and scientists gathered. But at midnight he returned to his studio to read or write again. Four hours of sleep a night was all he needed.

In those years, life in Paris was exciting politically. It was the era of the Napoleonic wars, with many French victories at first. Even after Napoleon declared war on Prussia once more in 1813, Humboldt remained in Paris, safe

Simia ursina.

An illustration of a monkey. From *The Collection of Observations of Zoology and Comparative Anatomy*, by Alexander von Humboldt. *Bibliothèque Nationale, Paris.*

in his scientific pursuits. When Napoleon was finally defeated, Humboldt acted as a guide to Paris for the Prussian king.

His books came out, one after another. Among them were a geographic history of Mexico, a personal narrative of his South American findings, a geological treatise on the rocks of the New World, and a survey of conditions in Cuba. Altogether, Humboldt wrote seventy books himself or in collaboration with others.

Although he loved the social and intellectual climate of Paris, after several decades there Humboldt obeyed a summons from the king of Prussia and moved back to Berlin. The famous German thinker Johann Wolfgang von Goethe wrote to a friend that Humboldt had dropped in: "What a man he is! I have known him for so long and yet he amazes me all over again. One can truly say that he has no equal in information and lively knowledge."

In Berlin, Humboldt organized a series of free scientific lectures open to the public, something unusual for that period. Royalty, society women, professors, and students crowded into a concert hall to hear him talk about his findings and his outlook.

During 1827 and 1828, he delivered sixty-three lectures in which he described an orderly universe that followed a cosmic design—with plants and animals on earth also existing in a pattern of unity. It was a theme Humboldt developed later in what he regarded as his major work, a book he called *Kosmos: A Sketch of the Physical Description of the Universe.*

Because of his influence, a meeting of German scientists convened in Berlin in 1828. About six hundred scientists attended and elected Humboldt as their president. That meeting is seen by historians as an important step in the recognition of science as a unifying force in a country that was divided by politics and religion.

Restless as usual, Humboldt accepted an invitation the following year to visit Russia. Despite his age—he was sixty by then—he inspected mines, collected rocks, discovered Russia's first diamond fields, made astronomical observations, and traveled all the way to the Chinese border. His reports on Russian Asia, in those days a mysterious and inaccessible area, led many people to call him another Marco Polo.

For the rest of his long life, Humboldt remained a great scientific hero as well as a respected aide to the king of Prussia. He often helped young scientists advance in their own careers, and he was regarded as the principal patron of the intellectual endeavors of his era.

Humboldt continued to speak out against slavery, both in the United States and in his own country. He wrote

A lithograph of Alexander von Humboldt in his study. *Collection of The Corcoran Gallery of Art.*

many letters condemning the slave system of the American South, but did more than that in Germany. There, in 1858, slavery was outlawed, largely because of Humboldt's humane views and his pressure on the German government.

In 1858, the American secretary of war, John B. Floyd, wrote to Humboldt, reporting that many places in the United States had been named for him:

Never can we forget the services you have rendered not only to us but to all the world. The name of Humboldt is not only a household word throughout our immense country, from the shores of the Atlantic to the waters of the Pacific, but we have honored ourselves by its use in many parts of our territory, so that posterity will find it everywhere linked with the names of Washington, Jefferson, and Franklin.

On May 6, 1859, a few days after finishing work on a book about geology, Humboldt died in Berlin at the advanced age of eighty-nine.

Aldo Leopold

1887–1948   American wildlife specialist and early environmentalist

At boarding school, the other boys called him "the naturalist." That was because he spent an hour or two almost every afternoon tramping through nearby woods, carrying a notebook and his grandmother's opera glasses. On returning, he often dashed off letters to his family filled with excited reports about his discoveries, such as:

Perfectly motionless, a bird with spread tail and greenish back perches on the trunk of a sapling. He turns! a flash of black and gold! and Ye Gods!—a Hooded Warbler!

From this kind of enthusiasm about the world of nature—along with a good scientific training and a gift for expressing complicated thoughts vividly—Aldo Leopold would forge an extraordinary career. Starting as a pioneer forester, he went on to become a wildlife specialist, then an influential college professor. In these varied roles, he did so much toward preserving vast areas of American wilderness during the first half of the 1900s that he won at least a modest fame among the conservation-minded.

But a small book Leopold wrote, which was not even published until a year after his death in 1948, enormously increased his reputation. Over a million copies of his *Sand County Almanac* have been sold since then, turning its author into one of the major heroes of today's environmental movement.

No doubt, Leopold's ideas about what the relationship between people and land should be are the main reason that *A Sand County Almanac* is now included on so many reading lists for high school and college courses exploring environmental issues. Yet the personality shining through his words accounts for at least some of its success, for he was a very likable human being.

Rand Aldo Leopold (named after two friends of his family, but always called Aldo) was born on January 11, 1887, in Burlington, Iowa. He could hardly have had a luckier start in life, for he was the cherished first son of warmhearted and wealthy parents. Both were of German ancestry, and they shared a deep love of nature, too. So their large home on a hill overlooking the Mississippi River had wonderful gardens besides its forty-mile vista up and down the river valley.

Aldo's father, Carl Leopold, operated a factory where about a hundred skilled workmen made big rolltop office desks—and he saw to it that only the most choice wood from cherry or walnut trees was used at his plant. But even while building up a prosperous business, he spent a lot of time enjoying the outdoors with his children.

Aldo's mother, Clara Starker Leopold, was the daughter of one of Burlington's most highly regarded citizens. Charles Starker, after studying engineering in Germany, had left his native land because of political unrest. Then while working with a firm of architects

in Chicago, he was asked to design a new home for a lawyer who soon would be elected Iowa's governor. Starker was so impressed by the "go ahead" atmosphere of the riverside town where this job took him that he decided to settle there.

During the next several decades, all sorts of Starker projects from public schools to an opera house made Burlington a more attractive community than many other small midwestern cities. Aldo's grandfather also refurbished a mansion originally built by a Civil War general, creating a fine home for his own family. It was there that Aldo, along with his younger sister and two younger brothers, grew up so happily.

Elegant as the house was, its parklike surroundings and especially its marvelous view of the river were more important to Aldo. From his earliest years, he would rush outside every spring and autumn at the first sign of the great annual migrations of birds up and down the Mississippi Valley. Thanks to his father's encouragement, soon the boy was keeping a list of all the kinds of birds he spotted—and also making his own maps of the woods or swamps where they went hunting together.

For Carl Leopold loved to shoot wild game, and he carefully trained his son to be an expert hunter, too. In those days, the United States still had so much open space, as well as such an abundance of wildlife, that there was hardly any opposition to this sport that had once been a necessity. Yet Aldo's father realized before most other Americans that many species would surely disappear unless efforts were made to protect them.

So he taught Aldo his own set of rules for voluntarily limiting the number of ducks or deer that he killed. By the time Aldo was twelve and allowed to fire his own gun, he knew that he should never shoot any creature merely to show off his skill as a marksman. He learned, too, that just roaming the outdoors in search of wildlife provided plenty of thrills even if it did not result in bringing home any meat for the family table.

Autumn, winter, and spring, about once a week this father and son would board a local train that chugged across a bridge to the Illinois side of the Mississippi. A hunt club to which Mr. Leopold belonged owned a large marshy area there, providing the habitat for many kinds of birds and animals. However, the family's vacations in northern Michigan every summer gave Aldo even better opportunities for nature study.

Toward the end of July each year, the Leopolds would send off huge trunks filled with clothing and camping equipment. Around daybreak the fol-

lowing morning, the entire family—always accompanied by at least two dogs—boarded a train bound for Chicago. This first lap of their journey took them about five hours.

In Chicago they transferred, with much fuss and excitement, to a big steamship. Then a twenty-four-hour voyage northward on Lake Michigan landed them at the sedate tourist resort of Mackinac Island, noted for its picturesque old fort dating from the era when fur-traders roamed the whole area. After a brief interlude amid souvenir shops, the Leopolds embarked next on a little vessel called the *Islander*.

This brought them to their final destination: a cluster of cottages on an island only six miles long, where members of a select club enjoyed living surrounded by wilderness—although, if they wished to, they could also play golf or tennis.

Aldo much preferred fishing. In addition, he spent many hours just wandering around the island or going out in a canoe to inspect other tiny, uninhabited islands. Most of all, though, he loved the camping trips to more remote places along the shores of Lake Huron that his father conducted during the six or eight weeks they remained out of touch with civilization.

But as Aldo advanced into his teens, he developed an interest in attending the dances held almost every evening at the clubhouse not far from their cottage. Even if this sandy-haired boy with blue-green eyes wasn't particularly tall or handsome, he had little difficulty gaining the admiration of girls his own age.

Also, his enthusiastic curiosity about nature attracted the attention of an adult club member who was the headmaster of a leading boarding school—Lawrenceville, in New Jersey. His interest encouraged Mrs. Leopold to start a crucial campaign. Why, she kept asking her husband, couldn't they give their promising oldest son the advantage of a superior education back East?

Yet Mr. Leopold felt that Aldo would get all he needed at Burlington High School, then Iowa State University, for he hoped to have Aldo helping him in his own business one day and eventually taking over the management of the desk factory. Of course, he thought, the boy should continue being involved with outdoors pursuits, but only as a hobby, so what was the point of sending him such a distance to get special training?

There is no record of what Aldo himself might have contributed to his parents' discussions about his future. But during the summer of 1903, when he was sixteen and had already spent two years at Burlington High, his father took him on a hunting trip to Colorado that

they both enjoyed tremendously. After they returned, Mr. Leopold told his wife that now he agreed with her.

At the earliest possible time for making such a major change—in January of 1904, just before his seventeenth birthday—Aldo entered Lawrenceville Preparatory School, near Princeton, New Jersey. To get there, he traveled over a thousand miles alone by train, vastly relishing this adventure. Still, his first weeks in the East were far from easy.

Besides suffering awful pangs of homesickness, Aldo faced a special problem when it came to making friends. Any newcomer would have had some trouble winning acceptance because his classmates had already spent two and a half years living and learning together. In addition, though, almost all of them had similar backgrounds as the sons of well-off eastern families. Thus, a fellow student from so far away struck them as quite an oddity.

But Aldo soon got used to being asked whether there were many Indians out in "I-o-way." His good-natured reaction when he was teased helped a lot to make the other boys decide that he was all right, after all. By going out for cross-country running, he further proved to them that he wasn't really peculiar.

Then several of them asked to come along on his nature walks to see what interested him so much. A few even turned into bird watchers themselves. Because Aldo not only got to be well liked, but also did well in his classes, the year and a half he spent at Lawrenceville gave him a great deal of satisfaction.

It also gave him a definite plan for his future. Since most of the Lawrenceville students went on to attend one of the prestigious Ivy League colleges, his parents were not surprised to hear him announce that he definitely wanted to go to Yale. Nor did his reason for this decision astonish them.

Just a few years earlier, Yale had set up this country's first program offering a master's degree in a new field called forest management. The new course of study attracted much publicity, thanks to President Theodore Roosevelt's strong support of its aims. Naturally, then, a young man like Aldo Leopold found the possibility of enrolling in it very appealing.

Leopold did enter Yale, in the autumn of 1905. But as a forestry major, he was no ordinary freshman. He was expected to complete the normal amount of undergraduate training, plus an extra year of more specialized learning, all within the same four-year period that most students took to earn just a regular diploma.

What's more, his schedule had been designed specifically to prepare him for a career in the recently established United States Forest Service—somewhat in the same way West Point prepared a cadet to become an army officer. Even if the Yale program was privately operated, its mixture of a solid basic education with technical instruction about trees and timber was supposed to give the new government agency the corps of experts it urgently needed.

While the future foresters were required to take several months of rough field training at various camps, they mostly attended classes—as well as weekend parties—just like any other students on Yale's campus in New Haven, Connecticut. There, early in the spring of 1909, the twenty-two-year-old Leopold received his Master's Degree from the Yale School of Forestry.

Then, with about thirty other new graduates, he went to Texas for a final ten weeks of practical experience. After this, Leopold took and passed a civil service exam. By July he had been formally hired by the U.S. Forest Service, and he was given exactly the sort of assignment he had hoped to receive.

It was to lead a small group of rangers with the mission of exploring the recently created Apache National Forest in the Arizona Territory. On horseback, covering about two square miles of this nearly roadless wilderness every day,

Aldo Leopold as a young forester. *Collection of University of Wisconsin-Madison Archives.*

they gathered data for special maps showing just what kind of trees existed in each section.

Despite all his training, Leopold was still a tenderfoot compared with native westerners. So he sometimes issued foolish orders that first summer, and his first maps were full of errors. But he soon learned better, earning a promotion within two years that made him deputy supervisor of the Carson National Forest in northern New Mexico.

Leopold loved the rugged life he was leading. Outfitted like a cowboy—wear-ing leather chaps over his jeans to pro-tect his legs from thorny cactus and a wide-brimmed hat to shade his eyes— he became intimately acquainted with the spectacular mountains and deserts of America's Southwest. Seeing this area while it still had only a few towns and very few roads, he was constantly amazed by its incredible beauty. From one isolated ranger station, he wrote to his family:

In the early morning a silvery veil hangs over the far away mesas and mountains—

too delicate to be called a mist . . . it isn't describable. And [right outside the door is] a little iris-dotted meadow bordered by the tall orange-colored shafts and dark green foliage of the pines, with a little rippling, bubbling spring, half buried in the new green grass . . . . It's the most beautiful single place I have ever seen in my life.

Possibly part of the reason Leopold felt so enchanted by the Southwest was that by this time he had fallen deeply in love with the dark-haired daughter of one of New Mexico's old Spanish families. Estella Bergere's relatives operated the largest sheep ranch in what was soon to become the nation's forty-seventh state. Although the parents of both of these young people raised objections because of their religious differences—the Bergeres being staunch Roman Catholics, while the Leopolds were much less churchly Protestants—Estella and Aldo managed to convince everybody concerned that they were meant for each other.

They were married in Santa Fe's Spanish-style cathedral on October 9, 1912; he was twenty-five then, and she was three years younger. Despite all the worries beforehand, they proved to be exceptionally happy together. Over the years they had five children, two sons and three daughters, who all would become devoted environmentalists themselves.

But less than a year after his wedding, Leopold went through a terrible siege of illness. Despite feeling unusually tired, he had ridden off to inspect an area miles from any settlement. Caught by a series of torrential rainstorms, he slept three nights in a soaked sleeping bag—and the fourth morning, his body was so swollen that he barely could climb on his horse and ride back to Albuquerque.

The severe kidney infection that almost killed Leopold in 1913 left him so weak that it took eighteen months for him to recuperate. He spent this enforced leisure reading and thinking. When he finally was able to return to work, in many ways he was a different man.

Realizing that he could never again count on having unlimited stamina, he still felt a strong tie with the Southwest. So he decided to stay there, even if he would have to spend more time at a desk than in the saddle. During the next ten years, he concentrated on trying to spur the Forest Service into carrying out some of his new ideas about how to operate the vast tracts of land under its jurisdiction.

As the United States Congress had recently established the framework for a new system of national parks, some people held that a lot of the scenic land within the existing national forests should be transferred over to the new agency. Leopold disagreed, not only because of his loyalty to his own branch of the government, but also because he believed that the Forest Service itself ought to broaden its aims—and offer recreational opportunities within its domain that the parks could not provide.

Already, spectacular sites like Arizona's Grand Canyon and the Yosemite Valley in California were attracting so many tourists, as well as developers, that they could no longer be considered untouched by civilization. Leopold wanted to set aside particularly beautiful national forests where no roads or buildings would ever be allowed. Thus, those Americans who were willing to do without wheels would still be able to have something like the experience of the country's original explorers.

Largely through Leopold's efforts, in 1924 over 700,000 acres of Forest Service land along the Gila River in New Mexico became the first federally owned area to be declared a wilderness forever. But besides being the father of a program that has since preserved millions of acres of wilderness, Leopold also would be called the father of a new profession known as wildlife management.

For although hunting had to be forbidden within national parks, Leopold thought that hunters who abided by certain restrictions should be welcomed within national forests. So he did a great deal of research about wildlife, then wrote a textbook that is still widely used for training game conservation officials.

By the time the book was published, Leopold and his family had moved away from the Southwest. Regretfully, they gave up the wide-open spaces when he was assigned to the Forest Service's research laboratory in Madison, Wisconsin. A few years later, at the age of forty-six, he embarked on a whole new career there.

In 1933, the University of Wisconsin created a new post and appointed Leopold to fill it. At its main campus in Madison, he became the nation's first professor of game management. But as he had grown increasingly absorbed by the developing science of ecology—concerned with studying the relationships between all forms of life and their environment—actually his courses covered a much broader range of topics than his title suggested.

And Leopold proved to be a gifted teacher. Besides inspiring many students, though, he further extended his influence by taking a leading part in dozens of conservationist groups. He even served as a member of Wisconsin's state conservation commission.

To escape the pressures of such a busy schedule—as well as to keep in touch with nature—soon after he began teaching Leopold bought an abandoned farm about fifty miles from Madison.

One of the tiny notebooks in which Aldo Leopold recorded his observations of the natural world. *Jim Brandenburg*.

Its sandy soil had been worn out by poor agricultural practices, but the possibility of returning it to its original prairie and pine-forested beauty appealed to him. Also, its patch of marshy "wasteland" right on the Wisconsin River guaranteed the presence of many birds and other wildlife.

The only surviving building on the 120 acres he purchased very cheaply was a battered shack that had once housed chickens. The whole Leopold family fixed this up just enough to make

it a rude sort of camp where they could spend their weekends planting trees or wildflowers, or practicing their favorite sport of archery, or just enjoying such sights as the astonishing twilight dance of a male woodcock striving to attract a mate.

It was here that Leopold began jotting down notes about the ways that wildflowers and woodcocks enriched his life. Over the years, these personal reflections would be repeatedly polished until they became little jewels of nature

Aldo Leopold examines a tree. *Collection of University of Wisconsin-Madison Archives.*

writing that eventually comprised the main part of *A Sand County Almanac.* But the book would also include several thoughtful essays, which gave it a much greater significance.

For instance, in "Thinking Like a Mountain," Leopold remarkably simplified a very complex and controversial issue. He described how he himself had once shot a wolf, and as its fierce green eyes dimmed he had felt a strange tremor. Yet he had continued to agree with the prevailing idea that the killing off of wolves or coyotes was wise because these predators killed other animals of more value to mankind.

Then many years later, while inspecting a once-beautiful mountainside where almost all predators had been eliminated, he had been struck by many sad changes. Countless small trees that should have been growing sturdily had been gnawed into ugly sticks by the vastly increased population of hungry deer—although horrible piles of bones testified that starvation had, even so, killed far more deer than wolves used to in the old days. Suppose, Leopold suggested, that men could learn to think like a mountain. Might they not decide that killing off the wolves had been a terrible mistake?

Similarly, in about a dozen other essays, Leopold described other human actions that had upset the balance of nature. Concluding with a summary he

called "The Land Ethic," he pointed out that mankind had long ago developed a code setting forth what was right and wrong in people's relationships to each other. Then he said that a similar code regulating man-to-land relationships was badly needed and offered some guidelines for preventing further harm to our natural environment.

In short, Leopold urged that all decisions regarding the use of land should be based on their environmental impact—rather than just on the wishes of the land's owners.

Eventually, these essays of Leopold's would be regarded as something like a bible by growing numbers of environmentalists. Nevertheless, early in the 1940s his manuscript was turned down by several publishers.

At last, during the spring of 1948, Leopold received a telephone call from the Oxford University Press in New York City accepting *A Sand County Almanac and Sketches Here and There,* to give his small book its full title.

Just one week later, however, while Leopold was vacationing at his farm, a fire broke out on a neighbor's property. He was helping to fight it when he suffered a fatal heart attack. He died on April 21, 1948, at the age of sixty-one.

So he never knew what a deep impression his book made after it finally appeared a year later.

Carl Linnaeus

1707–1778   Swedish botanist; classifier of plants and animals

Even as an infant, Carl Linnaeus lived surrounded by flowers. They were his first playthings. His parents often took him out into their garden, putting him on the grass with a flower in his hands to amuse him. When he cried indoors, they gave him a brightly colored blossom—and he stopped.

Carl was born on May 23, 1707, in the village of Råshult in rural Sweden. His parents were Nils Linnaeus, a Lutheran minister, and Christina Brodersonia Linnaeus, whose father had also been a clergyman. She and her husband both hoped that Carl, the eldest of their five children, would be a minister, too.

A farmer's son, Nils Linnaeus loved nature as well as his calling. So he planted a flower garden as soon as he moved to the nearby village of Stenbrohult shortly after Carl's birth. It was a fine garden where, as Carl recalled many years later, not a twig had grown before. One of his first memories was of planting his own small patch of flowers there.

"Thus was born his great love of plants and trees," his brother would write after Carl Linnaeus became world famous.

The foremost naturalist of his own era, Linnaeus developed the method of naming plants and animals that is still used today. As a result, he ranks among the leading scientific figures of all time.

His interest in plant names started at an early age. One summer evening when Carl was only four years old, he went with his father to a picnic. They saw beautiful flowers in full bloom, and his father told him their names. After that, the boy constantly asked the names of plants. Once he forgot a name and his father spoke to him sternly, saying he would not give him any more names if he did not remember them. Carl never forgot again.

When he was ten years old, Carl went off to school in the nearby city of Växjö. There he learned to write and speak Latin, the language used then by educated people all over Europe. For his parents, it was an essential step in preparing him to become a clergyman. But Carl, more interested in the school's garden than in his classroom work, delighted in gathering flowers that he kept showing to his classmates. As a result, he gained the nickname of "the little botanist."

The schoolmaster, Daniel Lannerus, soon found out about Carl's special interest and gave him permission to study plants in the garden, as well as to eat the berries there. Through Lannerus, Carl made the acquaintance of a physician who introduced him to many plants valued in those days as medicines for treating various diseases. That awakened Carl to the idea that being a doctor might provide a practical way for him to earn a living.

Yet his parents were still set on having him enter the ministry. As Carl advanced in his studies, however, his grades clearly showed that he was strongly bent toward a scientific and not a religious career. He rated among the worst of his classmates in subjects like moral philosophy, but among the best in mathematics, physics, and Latin.

The issue came to a head one summer day when Carl's father entertained some friends in the family's garden. After the visitors departed, Carl asked his father to repeat what he had told them concerning men's choice of their careers.

Pastor Linnaeus repeated that he could approve of whatever course a man adopted—"so far as the liking is for that which is good."

"Yes, Father," Carl said, "but do not urge me to be a priest, for I have no inclination that way."

"But what do you want to be?" his father asked.

"I want to apply myself to medicine and botany," Carl replied.

"You know your parents' poor condition," Pastor Linnaeus said, "and the study you wish to choose is very costly."

"If that is correct, God certainly will provide," Carl answered.

With tears in his eyes, his father nodded. "May God grant you success," he said. "I will not compel you to follow that for which you have no liking."

Determined to be a physician and a botanist, Carl Linnaeus enrolled at the university in the Swedish city of Lund in 1727, when he was twenty years old. He lived at the home of a professor who had an interest in natural science, Dr. Kilian Strobaeus. Linnaeus had no books nor money to buy them, so he borrowed books from Dr. Strobaeus's library at night, returning them in the morning so that the professor would not notice. That led to a confrontation.

Strobaeus's mother, noticing candlelight coming from Linnaeus's room each night, told her son that she worried about the danger of fire. Angrily, he entered the room one night after midnight, thinking he would find the student asleep with a candle burning untended. To his surprise, he found Linnaeus awake, still studying. His anger turned to sympathy, and Strobaeus told the young man to go to sleep—that from then on he could use the books in the library by day.

Noting Linnaeus's diligence, Strobaeus invited him to meals and admitted him to lectures free. He even took him to visit patients as he made his rounds.

Linnaeus studied fossils and shells, collected plants, pored over books in the library, and, with other students, made trips to the surrounding countryside to collect plants and to study birds, animals, and minerals. But it became clear that he could not become a physi-

A portrait of Carl Linnaeus. *The Bettmann Archive.*

cian by remaining at Lund, which offered no courses in medicine.

In 1728, at the age of twenty-one, Linnaeus enrolled at the University of Uppsala, one of the great universities of the world. Founded almost three hundred years earlier, it was the oldest university in northern Europe, located in a city that had once been the capital of Sweden. It had a splendid library, a botanical garden, a medical school, and learned professors of medicine and botany.

Linnaeus blossomed in the intellectual climate of Uppsala. With no help from home, though, his funds soon became exhausted. He went into debt for food and had to go almost barefoot, using paper to patch the holes in his shoes. But then, as before, a benefactor appeared.

One day in the spring of 1729, Linnaeus sat in the university's botanical garden, sketching flowers. An elderly gentleman came up to him, apparently astonished at the sight of a student working there. He asked Linnaeus to identify the flowers near them, which he did. The man then asked how many plants Linnaeus had dried and saved. Six hundred, Linnaeus replied.

The elderly man invited Linnaeus home. There, Linnaeus found that his host was Dr. Olof Celsius, one of the most eminent professors at the university. Impressed by the learning of the young student, Celsius began to treat him as a son. Linnaeus ate with the family, roomed at the Celsius house without paying rent, and had free run of the library. His economic position eased further when he received a scholarship and also began to deliver lectures in botany, physiology, and chemistry. Now he was able to buy a new pair of shoes as well as pay off his debts.

That first winter in Uppsala, Linnaeus made a friend—Peter Artedi, a student from northern Sweden near the border of Lapland. Different as they were, the two young men became inseparable. Artedi was tall, silent, deliberate, and earnest, while Linnaeus was small, lively, quick-witted, and much less solemn. Artedi loved chemistry as much as Linnaeus loved plants. At that time, Artedi was studying fish and creatures able to live both in water and on land. Linnaeus concentrated on plants and birds.

Together, the two young students decided to map out a scheme for classifying every animal, vegetable, and mineral—something that the great scientists of the world had attempted, unsuccessfully, ever since the time of Aristotle two thousand years earlier in ancient Greece. Arriving at some workable system was becoming increasingly important in the early 1700s, however, because of the thousands of newly discovered plants flowing to Europe from North America, South America, and the East Indies.

Of course, experts in other nations already had proposed systems. John Ray in England attempted to classify plants by their flowers and fruits. Rudolph Camerarius in Germany and Sébastien Vaillant in France had published preliminary works on the sexual characteristics of plants. But the accepted system at that time—based on flowers, their size, shape, and configuration—was a method evolved by Joseph Pitton de Tournefort of France.

For young Linnaeus, then only twenty-two, none of the schemes of his elders seemed to fit his own observations. He put his thoughts in a paper he presented to his patron, Dr. Celsius, on New Year's Day of 1730. Its title (translated from the Latin in which he wrote it) was "Preliminaries on the Marriage of Plants, in which the Physiology of Them Is Explained, Sex Shown, Method of Generation Disclosed, and the True Analogy of Plants with Animals Concluded."

Linnaeus's treatise was astonishing because of its direct comparison between plants and animals and also because of its poetic language. Here is an example:

The actual petals of the flower contribute nothing to generation, serving only as bridal beds, which the great Creator has so gloriously arranged, adorned with such noble bed curtains and perfumed with so many sweet scents, that the bridegroom there may celebrate his nuptials with the bride with all the great solemnity. When the bed is thus prepared, it is time for the bridegroom to embrace his beloved bride and surrender his gifts to her.

His paper created a sensation among the students and teachers at Uppsala. When it was read at a Royal Society of Science meeting, it gained Linnaeus another powerful patron—Dr. Olaf Rudbeck, the most distinguished professor of medicine and botany at the university. He asked Linnaeus to lecture at the botanical garden, paid him for tutoring his children, got him a royal stipend as a lecturer, and took him into his home to live.

Thus began a most remarkably productive period in Linnaeus's life. By day he continued his botanic and medical studies, as well as teaching and delivering lectures; then at night he worked out his new theories regarding the sexuality of plants. He began to write at least five books in which he catalogued and classified plants. In one of them, *Hortus Uplandicus*, a description of the plants in the Uppsala botanical garden, for the first time he arranged plants according to his new system based on sexuality.

In May 1731, he presented a paper to the Royal Society of Science. As Linnaeus himself put it, "The Society at first thought I was mad, but when I explained my meaning, they ceased laughing and promised to promote my design."

For Linnaeus, the essence of plants was their reproductive organs—the stamens that produced pollen represented the male element while the pistils that received the pollen and carried it to ovaries at their base, where seeds were produced, represented the female. So he classified plants by the number of their stamens and pistils.

In the words of one biographer: "Thus at twenty-four years of age, Linnaeus had completed his sexual system, and by a lucky chance, solved the problem, which hitherto all other botanists had failed to solve . . . [using] a clear and easy scheme by which the many productions of Nature could be arranged and found again."

In the same year of 1731, Linnaeus— with Rudbeck's backing—proposed a scientific expedition to Lapland, the far northern area of the Scandinavian peninsula, then largely unknown territory. His aim was to survey plants, birds, animals, and minerals. It was a most unusual venture because all previous explorations had been undertaken for political or economic reasons, such as determining boundaries or searching for precious metals like gold.

On the morning of May 25, 1732, right after Linnaeus's twenty-fifth birthday, he rode on horseback out of Uppsala heading northward. He returned six months later, his notebooks filled with observations about plants, reindeer, migratory birds, and the strange customs of native Laplanders whose lives seemed primitive by European standards. He also had collected data on insects and minerals, as well as on diseases common among the people he encountered. When his reports were published, they aroused much interest in Sweden and other countries.

For two more years, Linnaeus continued as a medical student at Uppsala while working on his botanical writings. But he faced several problems: he had little money, he could not find publishers for his manuscripts, and he did not get certified as a doctor of medicine because of a belief in Sweden that only a foreign degree was valid. An encounter at a Christmas party in Falun, a town near Uppsala, fixed his determination to go abroad to get the degree.

At the party he met eighteen-year-old Sara Elizabeth Moraea, the daughter of a wealthy physician. After that he called on her frequently, wearing the colorful costume he had brought back from Lapland. Although her father liked Linnaeus, he would not agree to her marrying a man without means or a profession. He consented, however, to an informal engagement—but Linnaeus had to stay away for three years, during which period he was expected to prove himself worthy of Sara.

And so, in April of 1735, Linnaeus set forth from Sweden carrying with him the manuscripts of his works. Arriving in Holland, he enrolled at the university in Harderwijk as many other Swedish students had before him. Within just a week he took examinations, presented a thesis he had prepared in Sweden, and received his degree as a doctor of medicine. He also received a gold ring and a silk hat, attesting to his new status. Then he moved to the university in the Dutch city of Leyden to continue his botanical studies.

There, once again Linnaeus impressed scholars who helped him. First he met Dr. Jan Frederick Gronovius, who after reading one of his manuscripts decided to finance its publication. Another professor offered him a chance to go on a voyage to South Africa and America, which he regretfully refused. Instead, he accepted an offer from the manager of the botanical garden in the neighboring city of Amsterdam to work on classifying plants from Asia.

One day while Linnaeus was wandering through Leyden's collection of medicinal plants, a distinguished-looking gentleman began talking to him. It turned out to be George Clifford, a director of the Dutch East India Company, who had a fantastic garden and zoo on his nearby estate.

"I was astounded when I stepped into the plant houses," Linnaeus wrote later. For he saw orchids, cactus, and spice bushes from many distant lands, as well as menageries containing Asian tigers and apes, North American hawks, and wild pigs from South America.

As other patrons in Sweden had done before, Clifford gave Linnaeus a home. There he lived for the first time as a prince, relieved of worries about money. He had a splendid lodging, grand gardens and greenhouses, and a fine library at his disposal. In return, he prepared a book about the plants in the Clifford garden while also working on his own books.

Linnaeus's accomplishments in Holland were remarkable. Within three years, he published fourteen major works on botany. In them, he set forth a clear and simple system of laws for classifying all sorts of plants, thereby imposing order on an immense multitude of facts. His system spread like wildfire among the scientists of Europe. After a trip to Paris and London, he returned to Sweden as one of that period's most esteemed naturalists.

But he still had to earn a living. So Linnaeus settled in Sweden's capital city of Stockholm in 1738, at the age of thirty-one, and began practicing medicine. During his first year there, he made influential friends who helped him attract patients. Becoming known as a skilled physician, especially in cases involving chest disorders, he was even asked to prescribe for the cough of Sweden's Queen Ulrika.

When her cough disappeared, Linnaeus's career as a doctor started to flourish. He became a royal physician and the royal botanist, besides serving as physician to the Swedish navy and president of the Royal Academy of Science.

At last, he was making sufficient money to get married. Four years after becoming engaged, he and Sara celebrated their wedding on June 26, 1739. But despite the honors and money he earned in Stockholm, Linnaeus still was dissatisfied. He really didn't want to be a doctor—he wanted to work with plants.

In 1741, when Linnaeus was thirty-four, the king of Sweden appointed him Professor of Practical Medicine and Botany at the University of Uppsala. "Through the grace of God, I am now being freed from the wretched practice of medicine," Linnaeus wrote to a friend. "I have obtained the post which I have so long desired."

Linnaeus gave his inaugural lecture at Uppsala on the subject "The Usefulness of Exploratory Expeditions in One's Native Land." From then on, he made many field trips himself besides teaching medicine, botany, zoology, and geology. He also managed the uni-

versity's botanical garden, supervised students, and wrote many scientific papers.

A gifted classroom teacher, Linnaeus illustrated his lectures with many unusual specimens—such as rare flowers, vividly colored parrots from South America, even monkeys and snakes from Africa.

In the summer, he conducted botanic excursions with several hundred students, collecting plants, insects, and birds from seven in the morning until nine o'clock at night. Then they all marched back to Uppsala, Linnaeus at their head, with banners flying high and drums beating as if they were on parade. Arriving at the botanical garden, the students would shout: "Viva Linnaeus!"

During this period of teaching at Uppsala, Linnaeus made his second great contribution to botany. Previously, his method of classifying plants by their stamens and pistils had only touched upon the general principle of naming plants in accordance with some sort of uniform system. It was not until the 1750s that he devised his method known as binomial nomenclature, which uses two words for naming every type of plant—and which, ever since then, has been generally accepted.

Before him, plant names were a jumbled mass lacking any simple pattern that could be recognized by any scientist anywhere. As one example, the common catnip was called *Nepeta floribus interrupte spicatis pedunculatis* by some of Linnaeus's predecessors. He called it *Nepeta cataria*, using only two Latin words to identify both the plant's genus, or family, and also its particular species.

Throughout his life, Linnaeus felt a need to put what he observed into an orderly form. It was a reflection of his deep religious view that God had created the world in an eternal order, from the lowest creatures to the highest. He believed that his own task as a botanist was to put all living things in their proper categories, classify them, and give them names.

"Without the system, chaos would reign," he said.

Linnaeus's method of binomial nomenclature remains "one of the best inventions of man," according to one modern American botanist. "It is effective; it is beautiful in its simplicity. It serves all men and women, it is endlessly extensible. It answered the purposes of Linnaeus and his associates when the number of known plants was few. It is [still effective] when plants are numbered in the hundreds of thousands."

Under the leadership of Linnaeus,

Carl Linnaeus's drawings of a crane fly and an owl. *Council of the Linnaean Society.*

Uppsala became the world capital of botany in the mid-1700s. Students from all over the world flocked to study with him. He sent his best students—he called them his "apostles"—to all parts of the globe to bring back samples of local plants. Among these apostles was Peter Kalm, who around 1750 made some of the first botanical observations in what is now the United States.

In 1758, Linnaeus bought a country estate in Hammarby, about nine miles from Uppsala, where he lived with his wife and their five children. At the height of his fame, he helped Sweden's king and queen to arrange their personal collections of butterflies, insects, and plants. The king awarded him the Knight's Cross of the Order of the Polar Star, an honor no other professor had ever received.

A further token of esteem came in 1762, when Linnaeus was elevated to the Swedish nobility. Thereafter, he called himself Carl von Linné. His new coat of arms bore a drawing of his favorite plant, which had been named after him—the *Linnaea borealis*, producing bell-shaped flowers that grow well in northern climates.

This public recognition helped Linnaeus overcome some of the depression he felt at times because he thought the world had not paid enough attention to his work. For he was not modest about what he had accomplished. In a petition to the Swedish parliament, he once wrote:

"I have built anew the whole science of natural history from the ground up, to the point where it is today. I do not know that anyone can venture forward without being led by my hand."

Despite the boasting, his statement was largely true.

As Linnaeus grew older, he suffered from many ailments, among them rheumatism. He cured it, he said, by eating large quantities of fresh strawberries. Indeed, he recommended wild strawberries as the cure for many sicknesses—so the demand for these delicacies rose rapidly, and their price increased almost tenfold.

But then Linnaeus suffered a series of strokes that left him hardly able to walk. As an old man he liked to sit in his garden, just as he had when he was a child, looking at the flowers. He died on January 10, 1778, four months short of his seventy-first birthday.

More than two hundred years later, Linnaeus remains famous as one of the founders of modern botany, and his method of naming plants is still used all around the globe. Furthermore, he is still honored in many ways in his native land.

Every visitor to Sweden sees his face on the common one-hundred-krona bank note. In Uppsala, the scientific garden that he laid out is still being used by botanical scholars. Facing his house there, which is now a museum, stands a statue of the young Linnaeus studying a flower. In addition, his country home and garden in Hammarby are open to the public as another museum honoring the man who brought order into the previous chaos of the plant world.

John Muir

1838–1914   American crusader for national parks

Many visitors to San Francisco drive across the Golden Gate Bridge, then seventeen miles north to a magnificent grove of redwood trees, some of them towering 250 feet into the air. The giant trees are protected by the United States government as a national monument named Muir Woods in honor of John Muir.

It is a fitting tribute. Although Muir arrived in this country as a poor immigrant, he became one of the leaders of America's first battles to preserve vast areas of western wilderness. Thanks to his pioneering efforts as a conservationist, millions of people today enjoy the scenic beauties of Yosemite National Park and other national parks and forests.

Yet Muir had started life as a city boy in far-off Scotland. He was born on April 21, 1838, in Dunbar on the coast of the stormy North Sea. For his first eleven years, he lived in a narrow brick house where his father sold grain and farm produce from a ground-floor store.

Although the Muirs always had enough to eat, the eight children in the family led a hard life. John's father was a strictly religious man, who considered each meal a sacrament and permitted no laughing, talking, or joking. He beat young John and his brothers with a strap for every infraction of his rules. If John's mother had not hurried him to bed many evenings before his father could catch him, he would have suffered even more than he did.

At the school he attended, the teach-

John Muir, America's first great conservationist. *Courtesy of the Sierra Club*.

ers maintained order with a cat-o'-nine-tails, whipping the students to make them learn their lessons. In this harsh atmosphere, all the boys did a lot of fighting. Boy against boy, group against group, they fought with their fists, rocks, and snowballs, often reenacting Scotland's bloody wars.

"If we did not endure our school punishments and fighting pains without flinching and making faces, we were mocked on the playground," he wrote later.

Such experiences made John wiry, tough, and courageous. From his earliest days, however, he had an escape—his grandfather would often take him to the countryside or down to the sea, teaching him to use his eyes to enjoy the world around him. After he was five years old, John ran away to the seashore every day that he could, despite threats of punishment from his father.

"I loved to wander in the fields to hear the birds sing, and along the seashore to gaze and wonder at the shells, seaweed, eels, and crabs," he remembered long afterward.

His father sought escape, too, from government restrictions on religion. One day in February of 1849, Mr. Muir burst into a room where John and his younger brother David were studying and told them they could put aside their books. The next morning they were going to America!

For John, who had read Audubon's stories about American birds, the news was "the most wonderful, the most glorious that wild boys ever heard."

The following morning, Mr. Muir took John, David, and their elder sister Sarah on a train to the city of Glasgow. Leaving the rest of the family to come later, they boarded a sailing ship bound for the United States.

After about two months at sea, they landed in New York, then transferred to a riverboat that brought them up the Hudson to Albany. Next, they traveled west on an Erie Canal boat, and at Buffalo they began a voyage through the Great Lakes as far as Milwaukee. From there, they carried their belongings by horse-drawn wagon more than a hundred miles into the wilderness—finally settling down on eighty acres of densely forested land near the Fox River.

After clearing the land of trees, Mr. Muir became a farmer growing mostly wheat and corn. It was back-breaking work from sunrise to sunset. He and his sons plowed the fields behind a team of oxen in the spring. They chopped weeds with hoes during the summer. At harvest time, they cut their crops by hand. The boys dared not stop work even for a drink of water because their stern father would beat them if they did.

But John looked upon his tasks as a challenge. Soon he plowed the straightest furrow of them all and became the best rail-splitter in the area. As the oldest boy, John took care of the family's horses and oxen as well as working in the fields.

Still, he somehow found time to observe the larks, woodpeckers, and hawks that abounded in the Wisconsin wilderness. He looked with awe at the windflowers, lilies, and asters that grew along the edges of the plowed land. Even as an old man, he remembered the first time he saw a huge flock of passenger pigeons dropping out of the sky one morning in early spring to feed on acorns where the sun had already melted the past winter's snow.

However, in those days before farmers knew how to conserve their land, it soon became exhausted. So his father bought another farm about six miles away, but the same workload continued for John's mother and all the children. Sometimes they toiled seventeen hours a day, wearily tumbling into bed only to rise before sunrise the next morning to start working again.

When John was fifteen, he was small for his age—but very ambitious. Before going to bed, he managed to spend five minutes reading by candlelight. One winter night his father found him poring over one of the few books the family owned, a church history. "John, go to bed," Mr. Muir called out sternly.

Then, as if deciding he had been too severe on someone reading a religious book, Mr. Muir relented. "If you will read," he said, "get up in the morning and read. You may get up in the morning as early as you like."

The next morning John awoke early and rushed downstairs to see what time it was. He looked at the clock and found it said one o'clock. "Five hours to myself," he murmured. "Five huge, solid hours."

At first, he thought of reading. But that would require a fire, which his father would probably object to. So he went down to the cellar. By the light of a candle he used simple tools during the next few days to make a saw blade, a pair of compasses, and several other things.

His workshop was just below his father's bed. The noise obviously annoyed Mr. Muir, but he kept silent for two weeks, hoping his son would soon tire of the early rising. One morning at breakfast, Mr. Muir could no longer contain himself.

"John, what time is it when you get up in the morning?" he asked.

"About one o'clock."

"And what kind of time is that, getting up in the middle of the night and disturbing the whole family?"

John replied that he had permission to do so.

"I know it," his father said. "I know I gave you that miserable permission, but I never imagined that you would get up in the middle of the night."

John cautiously made no answer. And so his father, a man of his word although a stern taskmaster, permitted him to continue.

John proceeded to build a timekeeping device that would not only tell the hour but also the day of the week and of the month, whittling all the parts out of wood. He also invented an "early-rising" machine by connecting one of his timekeepers to his bed. When the selected hour struck, a rod would tip the whole bed upright, and he would find himself standing up.

Even his father was impressed by John's inventions. His mother hoped he would become a minister, but John thought he would like to be a doctor. He saw his inventions as a possible way to make money to get an education. A neighbor suggested that he take them to the state fair, where he might meet people who could offer him a job.

In 1860, at the age of twenty-two, John left the farm for the fair in Madison. He set up his invention in a building devoted to fine-arts displays. Connecting one of his clocks to an improvised bed, he hired two small boys to demonstrate his early-rising machine —and won a cash prize of ten dollars.

He also got a job in a machine shop but soon tired of its dreary atmosphere. Still determined to get an education, he convinced the dean at the University of Wisconsin in Madison to admit him. To make money for his tuition and books, he worked in farm fields during the summer and taught school in the winter. At college, he made his room into a showplace of inventions and plants.

His professors brought visitors to see his amazing inventions—among them a desk that brought him books to be read. In his own words: "The first book to be studied was pushed up from a rack below the top of the desk, thrown open, and allowed to remain there the number of minutes required. Then the machinery closed the book and allowed it to drop back into its stall, then moved the rack forward, then threw up the next in order."

After three years, Muir left the University of Wisconsin and entered the "University of the Wilderness," as he put it himself. Actually, he fled to Canada to escape the draft during the Civil War. Besides being against all wars, he considered himself still a Scotsman (he did not become an American citizen until he was sixty-five years old). In Canada, he behaved like a fugitive. Staying away from other people, he turned to nature and lost himself in collecting unusual plants.

One of his objectives was to find "the Hider of the North"—a rare orchid that had retreated deep into the wilderness as man advanced. On a late spring day, as he was preparing to camp, he spied two of these gorgeous white flowers growing in a bed of yellow moss. It was, he said later, one of the supreme moments of his life.

"I never before saw a plant so full of life, so perfectly spiritual," he wrote. "It seemed pure enough for the throne of its Creator . . . I sat down beside them and wept for joy."

Muir's concept that God can best be appreciated in nature was reinforced by a series of letters he exchanged with Jeanne Carr, the wife of one of his professors. She encouraged him in his nature studies and suggested that he aim to be a nature writer.

After the war ended, Muir returned to the United States. He got a job running a sawmill in Indianapolis, where he rose rapidly because of his mechanical ability. But the job ended with a tragedy that transformed his life. One day, while working on a machine, he felt a piece of metal fly up and pierce his right eye, leaving it sightless. Then his other eye temporarily went blind.

Lying in darkness for a month, Muir came to the conclusion that he must leave mechanical invention and devote himself to studying "the inventions of God." He decided to take three years off to wander in the wilderness before settling down. At the age of twenty-nine, he became what we would call today a dropout.

As soon as sight returned to his uninjured eye, Muir set out on a thousand-mile walk to the Gulf of Mexico. Everywhere he went, he marveled at nature's beauty. He began to question the generally accepted idea that the world had been made for man's benefit—and rejected it. He wrote in his journal:

Nature's object in making plants and animals might possibly be first of all the happiness of each one of them, not the creation of all for the happiness of man. Why should man value himself as more than a small part of the one great unit of creation?

After a bout of sickness in Florida, Muir took a boat to New York and there paid forty dollars for passage by ship to California. He arrived in 1868 and set out on foot for the Yosemite Valley, enchanted by "the hills so covered with flowers that they seemed to be painted." At the age of thirty, his life as a naturalist began in the mountains and valleys of California.

John Muir's drawing, from his journals, of a cabbage palmetto. *Courtesy of the Sierra Club.*

Yet a practical problem arose: How could he make a living? Muir worked for a time as a sheepherder and in a sawmill. With the encouragement of Mrs. Carr, who had recently moved to Oakland with her husband, he began to write about the wonders of nature that he saw all around him. His magazine articles made an immediate impression on eastern readers.

Muir wrote with a light touch, giving his own personal reactions. Describing nature not as a foe, as many other writers had, he stressed its "essential kindliness," although he also said that it made "no jot of allowance for ignorance or mistakes."

His descriptive words about the beauty of Yosemite had a major impact. When the first railroad trains began to cross the continent in 1869, they brought the first tourists to Yosemite. In the years that followed, thousands more came to the scenic valley, attracted by Muir's articles. The eminent writer Ralph Waldo Emerson came, and so did Asa Gray and Joseph Torrey, two of America's foremost botanists. Muir charmed them all by his enthusiasm and lively conversation.

He became a scientific observer as well. How had giant boulders, as large as twenty to thirty feet in diameter, gotten to Yosemite? When Muir saw deep parallel scratches in nearby gran-

A clearing winter storm in Yosemite National Park, California, 1944. Photograph by Ansel Adams. *Courtesy of the Ansel Adams Publishing Rights Trust.*

ite, he remembered his studies of the Ice Ages in Wisconsin. He surmised that the entire Yosemite area must have been swept by a glacier, even though it was more than seven thousand feet high. At first his conclusions were rejected by the scientific establishment, but he proved his point by placing stakes in existing ice formations and measuring their movement.

As he neared the age of forty, Muir's friend Mrs. Carr decided that it was time he married. She even picked his wife—Louie Wanda Strentzel, the daughter of well-off fruit growers—and arranged for the Strentzels to call at her home on a day when Muir was visiting.

But it took more than a year for this matchmaking effort to succeed. Soon after Muir met Miss Strentzel, he went off to Alaska to study glaciers, on the first of his five trips there.

Traveling in a canoe paddled by Indian guides, Muir entered an area covered with huge glaciers. While the others in his party rested one Sunday, he climbed a 1,500-foot ridge and became the first white man to see a vast outstretch of ice and snow now called Glacier Bay. He also discovered several other glaciers, one of them now named Muir Glacier.

When he returned to California in 1880, the forty-two-year-old Muir married Louie Strentzel. Living on her family's farm, he mastered the art of fruit growing, raising large crops of Bartlett pears and Tokay grapes. In ten years, he made enough money to provide permanently for his wife and their two daughters.

Near the end of that period, Muir's life took a new direction because of a visit in 1889 from Robert Underwood Johnson, an editor at *Century* magazine. Johnson wanted to see Yosemite, especially the beautiful wildflowers there that Muir had written about.

"We don't see them anymore," Muir told him. He blamed their disappearance on the grazing of too many sheep, which he called "hoofed locusts."

Lying beside a campfire, the two men discussed what could be done to save Yosemite. Johnson proposed creating a national preserve modeled on Yellowstone National Park, established by Congress around twenty years earlier as the first protected area in the United States. They decided that while Johnson campaigned in Washington for the establishment of a Yosemite National Park, Muir would write articles on the same topic for the *Century*.

Besides writing these articles, Muir also delivered many lectures in which he vividly described the spoiling of Yosemite by greedy ranchers. Then as now, those concerned about preserving natural beauty faced a bitter struggle against cattlemen, sheep ranchers, and tourist operators who fought to maintain their rights to use government-owned land. But Muir and his associates won in Congress; in 1890, it passed a law creating the Yosemite National Park.

Despite continuing fierce opposition, the movement to preserve the wilderness gained strength. The following year—largely because of Muir's writing—President Benjamin Harrison set aside land in Wyoming, Colorado, and California as the country's first national forests. Muir's effectiveness in arousing public opinion led to his unofficial title as "father of the American national forests."

It also led to an official title for Muir. In 1892, a group of influential men met in San Francisco and organized the Sierra Club to protect the forests and mountains of the nation. John Muir presided over the meeting and became the club's first president.

By then, Muir's reddish hair had turned gray. Although he was still wiry and of only medium height, he made an imposing appearance, with a full beard and piercing blue eyes. He talked easily, displaying a quick sense of humor and a gift for words.

A little amused at his own increasing eminence, he once commented on it to a friend: "Though I never intended to lecture or seek fame in any way, I now write a great deal and am well-known—strange, is it not, a tramp and vagabond without worldly ambition should meet such a fate."

Muir was indeed famous. Thousands of people read his first book *The Mountains of California*, published in 1894, and later *Our National Parks*, published in 1901. Wherever he traveled, in New York, in Washington, and in London, as well as in California, everyone wanted to meet and talk to him.

At home Muir continued to write, as one biographer put it, as if he were working for wages. By the time the sun rose, he was in the kitchen cooking eggs and making coffee before settling down with pen and paper. He wrote beside a window looking out over orchards, in a room cluttered with notes, sketches, pamphlets, and reference books.

Yet he also found time to serve on a national commission to investigate forests as well as to travel to Alaska on an expedition organized by Edward H. Harriman, the millionaire railroad builder. Muir's way with words impressed Harriman so much that he had a stenographer follow him around, taking down everything he said. These notes, in edited form, became Muir's *Story of My Boyhood and Youth*, describing his early life in Scotland and Wisconsin.

When Muir's busy schedule became too hectic, he returned to the wilderness to be refreshed. Also, he delighted in acting as a guide for famous visitors. During the spring of 1903, President Theodore Roosevelt asked Muir to take him through Yosemite.

"I want to drop politics absolutely for four days," the president wrote, "and just be out in the open with you." It was easier said than done because a group of California politicians surrounded Roosevelt, aiming to convince him that the state should continue to control the Yosemite area.

While Muir planned to camp under the stars the first night of their outing, the politicians hoped to lure Roosevelt to a banquet a few miles away. When

Muir was ready to leave for their camp, the president asked for his suitcase but he was told it had been sent to town.

"Get it," the president shouted. Muir reported later, "Never did I hear two words spoken so much like bullets." With the suitcase retrieved, Muir and Roosevelt set out on horseback by themselves.

Both men were good talkers, Muir on rocks and plants, Roosevelt on birds and animals. They camped together by Glacier Point in a grove of firs, awakening under a blanket of snow four inches thick. The next day they rode past spectacular vistas to Bridal Veil Meadow, with the peak of El Capitan looming above them. When Muir, who loved dramatic campfires, lit a dead pine standing safely on rocky terrain, it blazed sensationally in the darkness.

"This is bully," Roosevelt shouted. "Hurrah for Yosemite!"

Muir talked at length to the president about the grim realities of wilderness destruction, which Roosevelt knew about only indirectly. For Muir, protecting the wilderness meant not only preserving watersheds but also providing healing spiritual values. Roosevelt listened. In the remaining years of his presidency, he acted to preserve millions of acres in the West as national forests and parks.

A few years later, America's other outstanding naturalist of the era—John Burroughs, who had met Muir on the Harriman Alaskan expedition—came west to visit him. By that time, Muir was widely known as Johnny of the Mountains while Burroughs was Johnny of the Birds.

Muir took Burroughs first to see the Grand Canyon. "There," Muir cried out, "empty your head of all vanity, and look!"

The two men then went on to visit Yosemite. When they came in sight of El Capitan, Muir, who loved to tease Burroughs, asked him: "How does that compare with Esopus Valley, Johnny?" Burroughs, smiling as he remembered the gentle eastern landscape of his own home, conceded that this western vista was truly magnificent.

As Muir grew older, he received honorary degrees from the University of Wisconsin, Yale, Harvard, and the University of California. But the honor that pleased him most involved a lovely redwood canyon just north of San Francisco.

About thirty million years ago, redwoods had covered wide areas in North America. However, the rising of modern mountain ranges and the Ice Ages eliminated almost all of them. Some of those still remaining had become endangered in the early 1900s, when a California water company announced

Redwood trees in Muir Woods National Monument, California. *George Grant/National Park Service, U.S. Department of the Interior.*

plans to cut them down so the area could be used as a reservoir.

Alarmed at the threat to the mighty trees, the owner of the property gave it to the federal government as a national monument. He insisted that it be named after John Muir, who had been fighting so vigorously to save redwoods and other natural resources. President Roosevelt agreed—in 1908, he named it Muir Woods.

Writing to thank the president, Muir said: "This is the best tree-lovers' monument that could be found. You have done me a great honor and I am proud of it . . . Saving these woods from the axe and the saw, from the money changers and the water changers is in many ways the most notable service to God and man I have heard of since my forest wanderings began."

Six years later, on December 24, 1914, Muir died in California at the age of seventy-six.

Frederick Law Olmsted

1822–1903   American landscape architect; designer of city parks

When Fred Olmsted was fourteen, he went exploring in a swamp one summer afternoon. Unfortunately, he came across some harmless-looking bushes with greenish flowers. From touching them, he got an extremely serious case of poison sumac—like poison ivy, only far more severe.

The poison sumac affected Fred's eyes to the extent that, for several months, he could not see at all. Even after the worst of his misery subsided, his eyes remained very sore. Because he could hardly read, his father regretfully gave up planning to send him to Yale.

Yet, bright as Fred obviously was, he had not shown any signs of turning into an outstanding student even before his terrible bout of suffering. A likable boy, alertly interested in everything around him, he always kept putting off any sort of steady work. Sooner or later, however, he would become more diligent—at least, everybody who knew him expected this to happen.

Still, nobody could possibly have predicted that such an aimless boy would eventually turn out to be the nation's leading figure in a whole new field. By supervising the creation of New York City's Central Park, as well as dozens of other parks from coast to coast, Olmsted improved America's urban environment remarkably during the middle and late 1800s. Even today, although his name has been almost forgotten, millions of people still enjoy the landscapes he designed.

Frederick Law Olmsted was born

on April 26, 1822, into a solidly respectable New England family. One of his ancestors had been among the original founders of Hartford, Connecticut, back in the 1630s. Nearly two centuries later this early settlement had grown into a prosperous trading center with about seven thousand residents, besides being its state's capital city. Fred belonged to Hartford's seventh generation of Olmsteds.

Fred's father, John Olmsted, was a merchant who operated a thriving dry goods store on Main Street. Although his business kept him from taking an active part in community affairs, he regularly supported many charities such as the local orphanage. Fred's mother, born Charlotte Law Hull, also had many relatives with long-standing ties to the area.

But for Fred she was merely a shadowy memory because she died a few months before his fourth birthday. She left a younger son, too, named John after the boys' father. These brothers became very close as the years passed, at least partly owing to the loss they shared—a loss not experienced by the younger members of their family.

For their father remarried a little more than a year after his first wife's death, and the second Mrs. Olmsted had four children. While she was a well-meaning stepmother, she did not have an especially warm nature. So Fred and John could not help feeling somewhat deprived of love.

Still, their father did his best to win the affection of his sensitive oldest son. When Fred was only six, around the time a new baby arrived he was sent on a long visit with relatives in New York State. Lest he feel neglected, after his father came to call for him just the two of them took a wonderful trip together—all the way to Niagara Falls—before returning home.

Although Fred's father retained enough of the Puritan outlook of his forebears to frown on idle pleasures, he believed that viewing grand scenery improved people morally. Any sort of natural beauty, even the peaceful rolling countryside around Hartford, struck him as spiritually rewarding. This feeling of his father's probably influenced Fred more than anything else during his childhood.

For the whole Olmsted family went on frequent outings to observe the hills and farms around Hartford at every season. The young Fred also made several exciting long trips with his father. Traveling by stagecoach, canalboat, or steamboat, one year they went as far as Quebec in Canada. Other times they explored along the Atlantic seacoast or sailed down the Hudson River to West Point and then to New York City. There

Mr. Olmsted took care of some business while his son marveled at America's biggest metropolis, with a population already approaching 250,000 as streams of immigrants kept arriving from Europe.

All of this touring gave Fred a taste for adventure that might at least partly explain why he was not much of a student. Doing barely enough work to avoid being sent home from school in disgrace, he spent a lot of time roaming outdoors by himself or walking long distances to visit relatives scattered around the Hartford area. Years later, he noted: "Such a thing as my running into danger even from bad company seems not to have been thought of."

Another reason for Fred's lack of scholarly zeal could have been the kind of early education his father arranged for him. It was a common practice in those days, when good schools were few and far between, for well-off families to send their sons to live with some clergyman who gave lessons on the side as a means of increasing the small income he earned from his preaching. But the high-minded Mr. Olmsted kept choosing tutors on the basis of their religious principles rather than their teaching ability or their kindness.

So Fred repeatedly found himself in most unhappy situations—sleeping in a room where snow seeped through cracks in the walls, perhaps or, feeling half starved. Since he knew his father would be upset by any protests he made, he tried not to complain.

As he later recalled, though, "once a bigger boy wrote to his own father that a teacher had lifted me up by my ears and had so pinched one of them that it bled." After the other parent sent this letter to Mr. Olmsted, Fred suddenly was summoned home. Then he was allowed to do just as he wished until his father heard of another minister willing to take in a student.

Yet somehow each new set of living conditions proved worse than the previous one. Fred and his brother John spent many months under the rule of one especially harsh, black-bearded tyrant—and it was from this unpleasant teacher-preacher, who was supposed to be preparing both Olmsted boys for Yale, that Fred finally escaped after he came down with such a dreadful case of sumac poisoning.

During the next three years, in the periods when Fred's health seemed sufficiently improved to bear the strain, his father tried to provide him with some practical training as a land surveyor. Even if Yale was now out of the question, he still wanted this son to be able to earn his own living. But soon after Fred started each new series of surveying lessons, his eyes troubled him so much again that he had to stop.

In 1840, when Fred was eighteen, his father decided, after all, to make a merchant of him. So he sent him to New York for an apprenticeship as a clerk in a firm of importers. Mr. Olmsted hoped that, after a few years there, Fred would be ready to become his partner back in Hartford.

This plan failed, too. At the age of nineteen, Fred came home convinced that he was not cut out to be a businessman. By now his brother John had entered Yale, and Fred joined him at college for one semester—attending lectures fairly regularly, even though he lacked the qualifications to enroll as a student himself. Nor did he feel that he would ever be able to do the amount of reading John and his friends did.

What kind of occupation, then, could a barely educated young man aim to succeed at? Idly spending months at a time in Hartford, he made his father worry that he would end up a drifter with no ambition or ability to earn his keep. When Fred at last came up with an outlandish idea, Mr. Olmsted was so relieved to see this son show some enthusiasm about a possible career that he raised no strong objections.

Thus, in April of 1843, two days before his twenty-first birthday, Fred sailed out of New York harbor aboard a ship called the *Ronaldson*—bound for

Canton in China. Convinced not only that the long voyage would greatly benefit his health, but also that life at sea might turn out to suit him permanently, he had managed to be hired as a "green hand" who would live and work with the ship's roughneck crew. At a time when many New England shipowners were making fortunes from the China trade, Fred's father must have hoped that this experience might after all lead his unsettled son into a profitable business career.

Instead, it almost killed him.

Acutely seasick most of the 108 days it took the *Ronaldson* to reach Hong Kong, Fred collapsed there from a fever that made him despair of ever reaching home again. Yet he gradually got back on his feet during the four months the ship remained anchored in the Pearl River just below Canton. He even went ashore several times to walk past rice paddies to a busy warehouse area, where ship captains from the West were dickering to trade the goods they had brought from their own countries in exchange for Chinese tea or silk. This was the only part of China any foreigners were permitted to see, but Fred felt so weak that he hardly minded the restriction.

When he arrived home the following year, he looked pitifully frail. Always thin and not very tall, now his handsome face had such an unhealthy pallor that Fred's father willingly agreed to let him try a new plan because it might build up his strength. The plan was to live the simple life of a farmer.

Fred chose a small and yet very scenic property along the Connecticut shore, which his father bought for him. Immediately, the young Olmsted set out with great enthusiasm to supervise many projects for improving this run-down farm. But once the house and grounds had been fixed up to suit him, he had to admit that growing fruit on such rocky soil could not really be profitable.

From family friends, Fred heard then of a larger, more promising farm—overlooking New York harbor. Again thanks to his father's financial help, he moved there in 1848—and, at the age of twenty-six, he finally started on the path to his future career.

Fred Olmsted's second farm consisted of 120 acres on the still-rural Staten Island, only a short ferry ride from busy Manhattan. With grand ideas for making the best of his property's natural advantages, besides growing outstanding pears and cabbages, he directed a crew of workmen, who soon made the old place exceptionally attractive. Yet merely operating a fine farm did not satisfy the need he felt to make life better for other people, too.

So Olmsted founded a local agricultural society—in his own words "to promote Moral and Intellectual Improvement by instructing us in the language of Nature." But he still craved some wider kind of activity. When his brother and a friend told him about a tour of Europe they were planning, on the spur of the moment he left his farm to be run by a hired hand while he joined them.

This trip proved to be another major step for Fred Olmsted. At the age of twenty-eight, he spent six months during the summer and autumn of 1850 carefully observing the landscapes of England and several other countries. Most particularly, he studied the large parks he was delighted to find in London, Paris, and even many lesser cities.

It struck him that the fast-growing cities of the New World badly needed similar tracts of greenery, where people could relax and raise their spirits. As his wide travels had shown him, many Americans who lived in built-up neighborhoods had no places to enjoy any grassy vistas, except for cemeteries. This was mainly because the kind of huge private parks owned by dukes or princes that, in Europe, had been transformed into public parks simply had not existed on the other side of the Atlantic.

Olmsted was by no means the first American to notice his country's lack of urban parks. Already, a move toward establishing a large park in New York

City had gained wide support among leading citizens. However, the combination of talents that Frederick Law Olmsted proved to possess made him emerge as this movement's most important figure. In effect, he turned out to be the right man in the right place at the right time.

Still, seven more years would elapse before Olmsted actually embarked on his great career as a park builder. During those years he kept further beautifying his Staten Island farm, despite its failure to produce a steady income. Also, he took several more trips around the United States and wrote three books about his travels that won him many literary friendships, even if they failed to bring him much money.

Indeed, his urgent need to earn enough to end his continuing dependence on his father was uppermost in his mind when Olmsted, at the age of thirty-five, had a lucky encounter that changed the rest of his life. In August of 1857, he went to a small hotel on the Connecticut shore, hoping he would find inspiration there for writing something more popular than his newspaper articles and books about his travels. At tea one day, he sat next to a man who was one of the commissioners in charge of the new Central Park that the voters of New York City had recently authorized.

This man confided that his group planned to elect a superintendent for the park at its next meeting. When he added that no candidate who seemed capable of filling the post had yet turned up, Olmsted asked some questions about exactly what the job entailed. His inquiries showed such a grasp of the problems involved in creating and operating a city park that his new acquaintance seemed much impressed.

"I wish we had you on the commission," he said, "but why not take the superintendency yourself?"

"I take it?" Olmsted said. "I'm not sure that I wouldn't if it were offered to me. Nothing interested me in London like the parks, and yet I thought a great deal more might be made of them."

"Well," the commissioner replied, "it will not be offered you. That's not the way we do business. But if you'll go to work, I believe you may get it. Go to New York and file an application. See the commissioners and get your friends to back you."

Olmsted nodded. "If no serious objection occurs to me before morning, I'll do it," he said.

So Olmsted wrote a letter the next day describing his varied experiences in directing landscape improvements on his own farms, and also his careful study of European park operations.

Frederick Law Olmsted in a photograph taken around 1860. *National Park Service, Frederick Law Olmsted National Historic Site.*

Furthermore, he secured letters of recommendation from several well-known newspaper and literary men who had been impressed by his writing.

By a margin of just one vote, Olmsted was elected superintendent of Central Park the following month. Even more importantly, he and a young Englishman with similar interests decided they would enter a crucial contest the city government was sponsoring. Although around 850 acres of far-from-choice land had already been selected as the park's site, the actual plan for the park would be based on the winning design.

Together, Olmsted and his English friend Calvert Vaux submitted an entry that won the prize. Which of them had thought up any specific feature of their plan was a topic they refused to go into. It suited them both to operate as a team, rather than independently.

Nevertheless, since Olmsted had a more decisive personality, people in their own day gave him most of the credit for the partnership's accomplishments—and, because Olmsted kept achieving outstanding results on his own after they went their separate ways about fifteen years later, he is still regarded as the man who practically invented the profession that has come to be known as landscape architecture.

For Central Park, even before the mammoth task of planting thousands of trees and constructing miles of paths had been completed, proved immensely popular. During the late 1850s, when this large rectangle of mostly wasteland was being transformed, the population of New York City had amazingly reached almost a million. Rich and poor alike flocked to see the seemingly natural vistas being created, then quickly formed the habit of taking regular outings there.

But Olmsted did more than just demonstrate a sort of genius as an improver of urban environments. He also showed a strong devotion to the idea that all of his fellow citizens, regardless of their income level, deserved the opportunity to be soothed by nature's wonders. In addition, he displayed a surprising skill at coping with the kind of intense political pressures that the spending of public funds always causes.

Most particularly, Olmsted constantly had to fight against the hiring of incompetent workers who had friends in high places—a waste of public money unhappily very common in New York then. However, frail as he still looked, Central Park's superintendent swiftly convinced every crew of his workmen that they had to put in an honest day's labor or they would be fired, no matter who their friends were.

While Olmsted was just starting to win public notice during the construc-

A drawing of Frederick Law Olmsted's Central Park around 1865, viewed from Fifty-ninth Street. *Museum of the City of New York.*

tion of Central Park, he faced a major personal crisis. His brother John, now a married man with three young children, fell ill with tuberculosis. In Europe, where doctors had sent him to be cured, John realized that instead he was dying.

John's wife was the former Mary Perkins, whose family lived near the Staten Island farm Fred finally sold around this period. For a time, before realizing that his brother loved Mary, Fred himself had thought of marrying this appealingly strong-minded young woman. Now his brother John, in his last letter before his death, wrote to Fred, "Don't let Mary suffer while you are alive."

Hardly more than a year after John's death, on June 13, 1859, Fred Olmsted married his brother's widow. Soon afterward he legally adopted Mary and John's three children. Yet love as well as duty prompted the surviving brother to take this step, and he never regretted it.

Within the next few years, Fred and Mary experienced the great sadness of having two new babies die. But then they had a healthy daughter, Marion, and a son they named Frederick Law, Jr., who would become his father's valued partner at the peak of Olmsted's park-building career. Despite some adventures in other directions, this career kept advancing notably after New

York's Central Park made such an impact on the nation's largest city.

Olmsted's next major project was in neighboring Brooklyn, where he created the impressive Prospect Park. Soon Buffalo sought his help in planning a series of parks, then Boston, Chicago, and even Montreal hired him. Altogether, Olmsted would design extensive parks for seventeen North American cities, besides countless other smaller or more specialized new landscapes.

In between these jobs, Olmsted undertook a startling variety of different occupations. During the Civil War, he spent two years directing a welfare organization called the United States Sanitary Commission, which later turned into the American Red Cross. Then he took his whole family to a remote mountain area of California, where he worked another two years as superintendent of a huge gold-mining operation.

Following a family camping trip to the gloriously scenic Yosemite Valley, Olmsted became one of the leaders in a drive to preserve this matchless area as the country's first national park. A further by-product of his western sojourn was his design of the Berkeley campus for the new University of California.

Among Olmsted's most important other projects, his achievement in

Frederick Law Olmsted's general plan, drawn in the 1870s, for the improvement of the U.S. Capitol grounds. *Architect of the Capitol.*

The U.S. Capitol grounds as they appear today. *Architect of the Capitol.*

Washington, D.C., undoubtedly ranks as one of his most impressive successes. Early in the 1870s, he was asked to improve the setting for the imposing building that housed the halls of Congress—although the huge white structure with its soaring dome was justifiably much admired, its ugly surroundings took away from its majesty. By constructing a large stone terrace, then creating a whole new series of pleasing vistas, he gave the nation's Capitol a lasting grandeur.

Along with all his public projects, Olmsted also designed the grounds of many private estates. He worked so hard that, in a way, he seemed to be trying to make up for his long periods of idleness during his youth. But his health was never too sturdy and, in 1895 when he was seventy-three, his mind began failing. Then he gave over his business to his son Fred, Jr.

Olmsted kept declining both physically and mentally after his retirement until, on August 28, 1903, at the age of eighty-one, he died in a hospital in Massachusetts. By then his reputation as a pioneer park builder had begun to dim and, as the years passed, only specialists remembered him.

But during the 1960s, when a great surge of interest in improving the American environment developed, Frederick Law Olmsted became the subject of renewed attention. In 1972, several museums marked the 150th anniversary of his birth with large exhibits celebrating his achievements. Also, a new book about his life and work called him "one of the lost heroes of American history."

Gifford Pinchot

1865–1946   First professional American forester

One day back in 1889, some students at Yale University were talking about their futures.

"What are you going to do after graduation?" one of them asked Gifford Pinchot.

"I'm going to be a forester."

"What's that?"

"That's why I am going to be a forester," he said.

Pinchot's little joke rested on the fact that, a hundred years ago, forestry was an unknown profession in the United States. Nobody even knew how much timberland the country had, and people generally thought of America's forests as an inexhaustible resource.

Ever since the 1600s, when the earliest European settlers had begun arriving on this continent, the idea that trees were obstacles to be cut down had prevailed. In the late 1800s, trees were still being cleared away to make room for people and their farms. Even worse, lumber companies used a procedure called "chop and run," destroying entire forests for their wood, leaving behind destruction and desolation.

Gifford Pinchot changed that. He became the first American to acquire professional training as a forester in Europe, and then he introduced the principles of scientific forestry to his own country. In addition, he played a leading role in the vigorous new movement, during the early 1900s, aimed at conserving all of the nation's natural resources.

For many Americans, then as now, conservation of trees meant leaving them alone, letting nature take care of our forests and their future. But for Pinchot and other foresters, that was not a wise policy. Pinchot defined his profession this way: "Forestry is tree farming. Forestry is handling trees so that one crop follows another. To grow trees as a crop is forestry."

Good farming of the usual type yielded crops such as apples or wheat, while good forestry produced lumber and firewood. More than that, Pinchot said, it also regulated stream flow, protected soil against erosion, and favorably influenced climate. Arguing against those who believed that forests should be left undisturbed, he held that forests should be used to harvest selected trees for lumber over long periods of time, and thus be preserved.

Forestry was a strange career for a young man like Pinchot. Born into the top level of New York society, on August 11, 1865, he was the son of James Pinchot, a rich merchant, and Mary Jane Eno Pinchot, whose father had been a wealthy real estate investor. His parents named their first son after their friend Sanford Gifford, one of America's most famous landscape painters.

The Pinchots lived a life of luxury. Of French descent, James Pinchot loved France and frequently visited there with his family. Besides serving on the committee that put up the Statue

of Liberty in New York Harbor, he built a country home in the style of a French chateau in Milford, Pennsylvania. His wife built another home in Washington, D.C., where she entertained lavishly. Mrs. Pinchot gave dinner parties so often that once when no guests had been invited, it was unusual enough for her to write in her diary, "No one at dinner."

Gifford and a younger brother and sister grew up mainly in the fashionable Gramercy Park section of New York City. As a small child, he went with his parents every summer to Newport, Rhode Island, a resort for the rich. They also traveled abroad often because of his father's business interests in France. In Paris, Gifford had a French lesson every morning until he learned to speak the language fluently.

Back in the United States, he attended several private schools in New York before being enrolled at a select boarding school, the Phillips Exeter Academy in New Hampshire. On his own for the first time, he found it difficult to adjust "when there is no one to caution me when I go wrong."

But he soon began enjoying the experience. At school, he collected insects and displayed an interest in a scientific career rather than following his father and grandfather into business. At one point, he wrote home that he might have to give up baseball because he wanted to keep his hands "in proper condition for scientific work."

In the summer of 1885, when he was twenty years old and about to enter Yale as a freshman, his father asked him a startling question: "How would you like to be a forester?"

Pinchot's father, concerned about the destruction of forests in the United States, had concluded that the time was ripe for scientific forestry in this country. Having seen the positive impact of forest management in France and other countries of Europe, he believed it would be a suitable career for his son.

To Gifford, however, forestry was a brand-new idea.

"I had no more conception of what it meant to be a forester than the man in the moon," he recalled years later when he wrote his autobiography. "Just what a forester did, since he no longer wore green cap and leather jerkin and shot arrows at the King's deer, was beyond my ken. But at least a forester worked in the woods and with the woods—and I loved the woods and everything about them."

Before that day, Gifford had given some thought on his own about a career. Should he become a minister or a doctor or even a naturalist? But none of these possibilities suited him as well as his father's suggestion. "So," he said later, "my happy adventure started."

Part of the reason for his decision was a commitment, even at that early age, to public service. He once explained: "My own money came from unearned increment on land in New York held by my grandfather, who willed the money, not the land, to me. Having got my wages in advance that way, I am now going to try to [earn] them."

Gifford enjoyed his four years at Yale. He became a halfback and captain of the freshman football team. He joined a fraternity, served on the junior prom committee, and wrote for the Yale literary magazine. But the one activity that gave him the greatest satisfaction was his religious work on the campus. He and two other students conducted daily and Sunday prayer meetings.

In his studies, it was not surprising that he excelled in French. He also won a prize for public speaking. Otherwise, since no forestry courses were available, he concentrated on related subjects such as botany, geology, and the branch of physics concerned with studying the weather.

After graduating in 1889, the twenty-four-year-old Pinchot sailed for Europe to learn more about the forestry profession. His intention was to talk with some foresters, buy books on the subject, and return home. Luckily, several people he met were enthusiastic about the young American's choice of a profession.

So Pinchot received letters of introduction to Sir Dietrich Brandis, considered the world's leading forester. Although German, Brandis had been honored with a knighthood from Queen Victoria of England because of his work in introducing systematic forestry to India and Burma, which were then part of the British Empire.

A formal man, Brandis nevertheless received Pinchot warmly. After talking with him about his education and plans, Brandis recommended that Pinchot enter France's Forest School as soon as possible.

"I don't mind getting up to take an early train," Pinchot said enthusiastically.

"Of course you will take the first train," Brandis replied.

Pinchot did, and went to the city of Nancy in eastern France. Fluent in French since his childhood, he had no trouble with his studies at the Forest School there. The program consisted of lectures every morning, with occasional field trips into the woods, and a great deal of reading on the side. He took courses covering economic and legal aspects of forest management as well as the science of tree growing.

Impatient at the emphasis placed on lectures, Pinchot tried to spend as much time as he could outdoors among working foresters. He watched experienced woodsmen measuring trees, then marking some to be cut down, treating the trees as a crop with an annual yield of wood.

The next summer, Pinchot toured the forests of Germany and Switzerland with Dr. Brandis. Aside from expanding his knowledge of trees, he learned two maxims from his mentor. One he always followed: "Never punish or rebuke a man or defend yourself in anger." The second he found it impossible to obey: "Always be loyal to your superiors no matter what fools they be."

After a year of technical training, Pinchot returned to the United States in 1890 to find his services in demand. He was offered jobs by the United States Department of Agriculture and a large lumbering company, besides being invited to deliver a lecture in Washington about forestry abroad.

But his first real opportunity to put into practice what he had learned abroad came in 1892, on the recommendation of the noted landscape architect Frederick Law Olmsted. Pinchot was asked to make a plan for the management of the Biltmore Forest, a vast tract owned by George W. Vanderbilt near Asheville in western North Carolina.

Covering more than seven thousand acres, it stretched for six miles along the French Broad River.

When Pinchot arrived there, he found the condition of the forest "deplorable in the extreme." First, he compiled detailed data about the existing trees. Then he divided the entire wooded area into ninety-two separate tracts. He began instructing crews to cut down old trees he had marked so that they caused the least damage when they fell, thus permitting younger ones to grow tall and straight.

At the end of his first year, the value of the wood that had been cut totaled $11,324.19. Expenses, including his own salary, amounted to $10,103.63. Pinchot announced a balance of $1,220.56 "on the side of practical forestry"—in short, a successful experiment.

Pinchot's career bloomed. He opened an office as a consulting forester in New York City. Soon he had almost too many commissions—in North Carolina, New Jersey, Michigan, and the Adirondack Mountains of New York. Several universities asked his advice about setting up forestry schools.

But his personal life was not as happy. In North Carolina he had met a young woman, Laura Houghteling, and fallen in love with her. Laura was not well, though, gradually growing weaker until she died in early 1894. Pinchot was crushed. For years after, he wrote notes in his diary about "my lady." One biographer said his memories of her were the reason he did not get married until twenty years later.

During those years, Pinchot rose to national prominence. In 1896, when he was thirty-one, he became secretary of a commission set up to study the creation of national forests on publicly owned land. Based on its reports, the federal government established dozens of national forests in the West.

Pinchot's work with the commission had made him the foremost authority on American forest conditions. This status was recognized when the Department of the Interior—the agency put in charge of the new forests—appointed him as a special forest agent to make a formal survey of the new areas under its jurisdiction.

When Pinchot finished that survey, another opportunity opened up. In 1898, he was asked to become chief of the forestry division at the Department of the Interior. But immediately a hitch arose. The new job came under civil service regulations, which meant that he had to take a test first. However, there was no one in the government qualified to write such an examination.

So an official decided that Pinchot himself should prepare the test. Pinchot conscientiously put down ten difficult questions. One was: "Describe briefly and from personal experience the forests in the Olympic Mountains, the Sierra Nevadas, the Coast Range of California, the Cascades, the Rockies, and the Adirondacks, and the forest conditions of the arid regions."

However, common sense prevailed before he could take his own test. President William McKinley waived the civil service examination in this unique case. And so Pinchot, approaching his thirty-third birthday, began his new job—supervising eleven employees who had to manage nineteen forests covering twenty million acres, with an annual budget of $28,500.

His influence grew after Theodore Roosevelt became president. They had met when Roosevelt, as governor of New York, invited Pinchot to box, one of his favorite forms of exercise. Pinchot obliged. They became firm friends even though Pinchot knocked the future president flat on the floor.

In Washington, Pinchot became one of Roosevelt's most trusted aides. He wrote many of the president's messages to Congress, letters, speeches, and reports. A historian of the period referred to Pinchot as "the unofficial crown prince of the Roosevelt realm."

Pinchot introduced Roosevelt to chopping wood as another form of exer-cise. They also walked together, tossed medicine balls to one another, played tennis (almost always Pinchot beat Roosevelt), hiked, and swam. While they exercised they talked, often about politics and government.

As a man of action, Pinchot suited Roosevelt's taste. Tall, slender, hardy, with a handlebar moustache, Pinchot was a handsome outdoors man, a bachelor very attractive to women. But into his late thirties and early forties, he could not forget Laura and remained unmarried.

With support from the White House, two developments changed American forestry in 1905. The first American Forest Congress was held in Washington, bringing together representatives of the major business and farming interests that shared the common aim of preserving forests. In the same year, Congress enacted a law transferring jurisdiction over all the national forests to the Department of Agriculture, with Pinchot in command.

Now the chief forester of the United States, Pinchot became the protector of a constantly expanding preserve of national forests. It grew to more than two hundred million acres of land—almost as much as the combined area of the entire northeastern part of the country. For many, he was a great public servant protecting America's heritage,

Gifford Pinchot working at his desk in 1908. *Brown Brothers.*

but he was often called a tyrant by others who wanted to use the nation's valuable forest resources for their own gain—lumber companies, water companies, sheep ranchers, and cattle owners.

To help him, Pinchot called upon some of his old friends from Yale who had followed him to the forestry school in France. As his staff expanded to more than 2,500, he proved to be a gifted administrator. But he hated office work.

He left Washington frequently to work in the field with his forest rangers. They admired him because he supported them and because, as one said, he could "outride and outshoot any ranger on the force."

Pinchot also demonstrated talents as a master at politics, tireless in his efforts to awaken public interest in forestry and to gain support for his policies. Before the age of public relations experts, he hired professional writers to bombard newspapers with articles about forestry. More important, he won friends in Congress by his personal charm and by giving many dinner parties.

His message was simple: Practical forestry was the only way the national forests could be saved.

But Pinchot soon discovered that forests were only part of the problem of preserving the natural resources of the nation. He counted the many government agencies dealing with various related issues—three were concerned with minerals, four or five with streams, a half dozen with trees, and at least a dozen with wildlife, soil erosion, and farming.

"Suddenly the idea flashed through my head," he wrote later, "that there was a unity in this complication—that the relation of one resource to another was not the end of the story. Here were no longer a lot of different independent and often antagonistic questions, each on its own separate little island, as we have been in the habit of thinking. In place of them, here was one single question with many parts. Seen in this new light, all these separate questions fitted into and made up the one great central problem of the use of earth for the good of man."

It was an idea whose time had come. Talking to his associates about what it could be called, one of them, Overton Price, suggested the word "conservation." A trio of men—Pinchot, Price, and W. J. McGee, another associate in the forestry division—became the brains of the new conservation movement, born in 1907.

Pinchot took the idea to his friend President Roosevelt, who quickly endorsed it. For Roosevelt, the conservation of natural resources became "the most weighty question before the people of the United States." First, he appointed an Inland Waterways Commission, which recommended a comprehensive plan for the improvement and control of the river systems of the nation. Then, in 1908, he called a governors' conference, which strongly backed conservation measures.

Yet there were also powerful forces opposed to the new conservation movement. They included lumber companies, sheep ranchers, and cattle barons, all of them accustomed to using government land with little or no payment. In addition, many leaders of Congress, opposed to the expansion of the president's power, cut funds for conservation projects. In 1909, Pinchot lost the powerful support of President Roosevelt when his term of office expired.

Looking back at his presidency, Roosevelt later said: "Among all the many able officials who under my administration rendered literally invaluable scr-vice to the people of the United States, Gifford Pinchot on the whole stood first."

The new president, William Howard Taft, had a different philosophy of government. While Roosevelt—and Pinchot—believed that a public official should do whatever was in the public interest and not forbidden by law, Taft followed the policy of doing only what was specifically permitted by law.

That led to one of the most famous feuds in American political history, the Ballinger-Pinchot controversy. Although Taft retained Pinchot as the nation's chief forester, he appointed Richard A. Ballinger as secretary of the interior. Ballinger, who had been a corporation lawyer, opposed Pinchot's program of active government control of resources.

The feud between Ballinger and Pinchot came to a head over the issue of land use in Alaska. Pinchot, acting on information supplied by a federal employee in Alaska, charged that Ballinger had assisted some people in gaining illegal title to valuable coal fields there. President Taft examined the records, then backed Ballinger.

Not satisfied, Pinchot took his case to the public. Taft tried to settle the dispute privately but failed. Then he fired Pinchot, saying: "By your own conduct you have destroyed your use-fulness as a helpful subordinate of government." Pinchot still felt, though, that he was helping the cause of conservation by opposing the Taft-Ballinger policies.

As a private citizen, Pinchot continued to urge the wise use of natural resources. He maintained his close association with Theodore Roosevelt, backing him when T. R. ran unsuccessfully for an unprecedented third term in 1912. During that campaign, Roosevelt introduced Pinchot to Cornelia Bryce—a leader in the increasingly active drive for giving American women the right to vote.

In 1914, the forty-nine-year-old Pinchot married Miss Bryce. They made their home at the Pennsylvania country estate where he had spent happy periods of his childhood, and they later had one son.

A few years after his marriage, Pinchot became Pennsylvania's commissioner of forestry. Then, in 1922, he was elected governor of the state, largely through the support of rural communities—and of women, who had finally gained the vote two years earlier. Although he was defeated when he ran for the United States Senate, at the age of sixty-five he won another term as governor of Pennsylvania in 1930.

Through all those years, and for the rest of his long life, Pinchot remained

Gifford Pinchot going trout fishing. *Brown Brothers.*

a strong advocate of forestry. A few months before his death, he spoke at the fortieth anniversary celebration of the National Forest Service. "I have been a governor now and then," he said, "but I am a forester all the time—have been, and shall be, to my dying day." He died on October 4, 1946, when he was eighty-one.

Three memorials stand today as reminders of Gifford Pinchot's contribution to preserving the forests of the United States.

Most important is Yale University's School of Forestry, established in 1900 with gifts from Pinchot, his parents, and brother. It set professional standards for American forestry education and supplied graduates not only for the faculty of other forestry schools but also for the National Forest Service and scientific forestry everywhere—as it still does.

Two other monuments to Pinchot are open to the public. In 1949, a great forest area along the Columbia River in the state of Washington was named the Gifford Pinchot National Forest. It includes more than a million acres of majestic Douglas fir and yellow pine trees, growing amidst spectacular mountain scenery.

In Pennsylvania, the Pinchot home in the Pocono Mountains is now a national historic landmark administered by the National Forest Service. President John F. Kennedy went there in 1963 to dedicate the Pinchot Institute of Conservation Studies. In his speech then, President Kennedy called Gifford Pinchot "the father of American conservation."

John Wesley Powell

1834–1902   American geologist; pioneer explorer of the Colorado River and expert on western geography

Shortly after high noon on May 24, 1869, ten men climbed into four small wooden boats on the Green River in Wyoming and began a voyage of discovery that made history. Low in the water with heavy loads, the *Emma Dean*, the *Maid of the Canyon, Kitty Clyde's Sister*, and the *No-Name* started downstream.

At the riverside, most of the residents of the tiny hamlet of Green River watched them leave. As the boats disappeared from sight, Major John Wesley Powell, the leader of the expedition, waved his hat with his left hand. On the shore, the people made bets about whether or not they would ever again see Powell and his men alive.

For Powell seemed a most unlikely explorer, a man with only one arm; he had lost the other in the Civil War. How could he manage to survive perils like rock-filled rapids and hostile Indians? What's more, he would have to endure searing heat on this voyage no one had ever tried before—down the entire length of the Colorado River.

Powell's object was to study the geography and rock formations of the great canyons of the Colorado, then an almost completely blank spot on the maps of the United States. In the period right after the Civil War, the whole area from the Mississippi River westward to California was still mostly the home of Indian tribes. Just a few hardy trappers, trailblazers, and scattered settlers had ventured there.

To the north, wagons drawn by oxen and mules rolled across the Oregon

Trail. To the south, traders made their way on horseback and in wagons along the Santa Fe Trail to New Mexico and then through the desert to California. In between, though, a vast mountainous region broken by deep canyons and swift-flowing rivers was largely unexplored.

More than five thousand feet high, the Colorado plateau loomed as a barrier to travel. But its challenge strongly attracted Powell. Despite many tales of other men who had gone into that wilderness never to be heard from again, he felt sure of his own ability to solve its remote mysteries and put them on a map.

At the age of thirty-five, Powell was a naturalist as well as an experienced former Army officer. Before embarking on his military career, he had taught natural history and served as the curator of a small museum—collecting many of its exhibits himself. A man of medium height, with gray eyes and red hair, he could not help realizing after he returned from the war that his empty sleeve made many people pity him. But his injury had in no way reduced his own self-confidence.

Born on March 24, 1834, in the New York village of Mount Morris, John Wesley Powell was the son of a Methodist minister. Because his father, Joseph Powell, had a restless streak, during

the next few years he moved his family repeatedly to other New York communities, then into Ohio. They arrived there in 1841, when feelings about whether slavery should be abolished were growing intense.

At the age of only nine, John got involved in the controversy. As the son of an ardent antislavery man, he fought often with other boys whose fathers were in favor of slavery. So his parents took him out of the town school and sent him to study with a neighbor, George Crookham, who kept a two-room log cabin school.

Crookham was different from most rural schoolteachers. He also kept a small museum in which he collected flowers, plants, birds, and animals. As a result, John received an early introduction to nature study.

Soon he was accompanying his teacher on field trips, seeking additional exhibits for the museum. These outings were the high points of his youth and made him decide that he wanted to be a scientist. As he advanced into his teens, though, his father moved the family again—to Illinois. John had to help with farm work there, attending school only irregularly. While he was still set on studying science, his father hoped he would become a minister.

When John was eighteen, he began teaching in a one-room country school to earn enough money to go to college. His salary was fourteen dollars a month. During the next seven years, he alternated between teaching and absorbing whatever higher education he could at various small colleges. He also made several trips down the Ohio and Mississippi rivers collecting materials for the newly formed Illinois State Natural History Society.

But the Civil War interrupted his career. When Abraham Lincoln became president in 1861, Powell, like many others, realized that a war against the seceding Southern states was inevitable. At the age of twenty-seven he answered Lincoln's call for volunteers, enlisting as a private in the 20th Illinois Infantry. He took his duties as a soldier seriously, studying books on military engineering and fortifications, and rose in rank first to sergeant and then lieutenant.

Thanks to Powell's knowledge of engineering, General Ulysses S. Grant singled him out and put him in charge of some forts along the Mississippi River. Grant also gave him special leave in those early days of the war to go on a hurried trip back to Illinois to marry his cousin, Emma Dean.

Shortly after Powell's return to duty, he took command of a battery of artillery at Pittsburgh Landing on the Tennessee River. In the Battle of Shiloh in 1862,

his cannon stood in the crucial center of the Union line—in a peach orchard called the "Hornet's Nest" because bullets flew so fast and furiously there. Powell helped hold the Confederates off, but a rifle bullet hit his right arm and damaged it so severely that it had to be amputated.

When he recovered from the operation he returned to active duty, an unusual one-armed soldier. During the siege of Vicksburg, he took time to collect fossils in the trenches around the town. Later he commanded the Union artillery in the Battle of Atlanta and marched to the sea at Savannah with General William Tecumseh Sherman. By all accounts, Powell was a good soldier with a natural air of command, and he rose to the rank of major.

After the war, he became professor of natural history at Illinois Wesleyan College. Using the methods he had learned from George Crookham, he took his students into the field as often as possible to collect fossils, animals, rocks, and plants. Not satisfied with teaching, he organized a natural history museum in Bloomington and became its curator.

Powell longed to make a trip westward to the Rocky Mountains to collect more materials for his museum. Before he could do so, though, he needed money and supplies. He solved those problems by using what he had learned in the Army about how to pull the right strings to accomplish his aims. Not only did he secure grants from several institutions, but he also traveled to Washington and got his former commanding officer, General Grant, to authorize rations for his group of explorers at Army outposts in the West.

In May of 1867, Powell made his first major expedition, accompanied by his wife as well as some college students and amateur naturalists. They traveled by train, wagon, and horseback over the grassy Great Plains to Denver and the mountains around it. They climbed Pike's Peak and studied the rivers in the area before returning with their specimens.

A year later Powell, with his wife and about twenty students and naturalists, went back to Colorado. In addition to collecting more specimens, they became the first to climb the fourteen-thousand-foot-high Long's Peak and spent the winter making observations along the White River.

Those trips marked the beginning of Powell's lifelong interest in the American Indians of the West, who were being pushed back and even killed by advancing settlers. He befriended a tribe of Utes and prepared a dictionary of their language. Unlike most frontiersmen, Powell met the Indians without carrying any weapons. By showing them that he meant no harm to them, he found that he could count on friendly treatment from them.

In this period, too, Powell decided that it would be possible to travel down the unexplored Colorado River by boat. Despite gloomy warnings from Army men and others, who insisted that it could not be done, he began making plans for the voyage. Using some contributed funds but mostly his own money, he arranged to have a Chicago shipyard construct four special boats. Three were built of oak, twenty-one feet long, with watertight compartments at either end. The other, of light pine, only sixteen feet long, would serve as the expedition's pilot boat.

On the May afternoon in 1869 when Powell and his nine companions started their great adventure, they used oars at first. They were testing their new craft and equipment as they rowed about seven miles downstream. But soon the oars were used only for steering, with the rapidly running river carrying the boats in the narrow channel between canyons 1,500 feet high.

Despite the spectacular beauty of the scenery it was dangerous, with boulders jutting out of the water everywhere creating hazards for the wooden boats. Sometimes the men had to get out and carry the boats around particularly

John Wesley Powell with Tau-Gu, the Great Chief of the Paiutes. *Hillers/U.S. Geological Survey.*

threatening rocks. At other times they used ropes to nudge the boats gently around protruding boulders.

One evening, the *No-Name* missed a landing point. The swift current carried it over a waterfall into a channel filled with sharp rocks. The boat broke up into small pieces, dropping equipment, food, and clothing into the river. Luckily, the men aboard were washed ashore unhurt. One man, having had enough of the difficult trip, gave up and returned alone to civilization.

As the river twisted and turned, Powell frequently got out to make geological observations. Heedless of his handicap, he was a fearless mountain climber, scrambling out of gorges to the tops of surrounding cliffs. Sometimes he even carried equipment to take readings of the various altitudes.

Powell's fearless climbing almost led to disaster. As he was scaling a tall cliff one morning, he reached a point where he could go neither up nor down. He clung to a crevice in the rock with the fingers of his one hand—and shouted for help from a companion named Bradley. Then, in Powell's own words when he later described what happened:

[Bradley] finds a way by which he can get to the rock over my head, but cannot reach me. Then he looks around for some stick or limb of a tree, but finds none. Then he suggests that he had better help

me with the barometer case; but I fear I cannot hold on to it. The moment is critical. Standing on my toes, my muscles begin to tremble.

It is sixty to eighty feet to the foot of the precipice. If I lose my hold I shall fall to the bottom and then perhaps roll over the bench, and tumble still farther down the cliff.

At this instant, it occurs to Bradley to take off his drawers, which he does, and swings them down to me. I hug close to the rock, let [it] go with my hand, seize the dangling legs, and, with his assistance, I am enabled to gain the top.

Saved by a pair of long underwear, Powell continued his perilous journey. The temperature reached a fierce 115 degrees by day, and there were drenching rains by night. After several weeks of hazardous river running, the explorers entered what Powell called the Grand Canyon, in what is now the state of Arizona. Here is how he described this awesome experience in his diary:

We are now ready to start on our way down the Great Unknown . . . We are three-quarters of a mile in the depths of the earth, and the great river shrinks into insignificance, as it dashes its angry waves against the walls and cliffs that rise to the world above; they are but puny ripples, and we are but pigmies, running up and down the sands, or lost among the boulders. We have an unknown distance yet to run; an unknown river to explore.

Day by day, Powell and his companions made their way down the rapidly flowing river, with canyon walls towering almost a mile above them. They plunged over dangerous waterfalls and barely avoided boulders jutting upward. Finally, they reached a point in the canyon where only impassible rapids, filled with jagged rocks, seemed to be ahead.

With food running short, some members of the expedition said they were ready to quit. They proposed climbing the cliffs and making their way overland back to civilization. But Powell was determined to go on. "To leave the exploration unfinished . . . is more than I am willing to [do]," he wrote in his diary.

Three men departed, but Powell and the five others in their remaining two boats shot into the rapids. Tumbling helter-skelter, they disappeared into foam and waves. Half-submerged, the boats ran the rapids and came out on the other side. Three days later, on August 30, the expedition rounded a bend in the river, the journey completed.

Given up for lost back home, Powell had completed a thousand-mile trip through unknown territory. Soon, though, he learned some bad news. The three men who had left the river trip because it was too dangerous had been killed by Indians. Tragically, the Indi-

An engraving of John Wesley Powell, with unidentified companions, shooting the Colorado River rapids. *North Wind Picture Archives.*

ans had mistaken them for miners who had abused Indian women.

Powell returned to the East a hero. Congress rewarded him by agreeing to support his plan for a geographical and geological survey of the entire Rocky Mountain area. It was the beginning of twenty-five years of work in which Powell laid the basis for government-supported science, for conservation in the arid West, and for understanding the Indian tribes living in that harsh and demanding environment.

Powell's explorations went far beyond mere adventures into the unknown. Out of them came major contributions to our knowledge about Indian languages and customs, about the impact of arid conditions on farming and settlement, and about the way in which rivers and mountains had interacted over long periods of time.

From his trip down the Grand Canyon, where the Colorado River flowed far below the tops of the nearby cliffs, Powell was able to pose a major geologic question: "Why did not the stream pass around this great obstruction, rather than pass through it?"

It was clear to him that if the mountains had suddenly risen, they would obviously have caused the river to change its course. But, he said, the rising of the mountains must have been no faster than the abrasive action of the river cutting its way through its channel.

"The river preserved its level, but the mountains were lifted up," he concluded. "The river was the saw which cut the mountains in two."

Powell extended his studies to the science of man, as well, specifically the Indians of the West. He became fluent in many Indian languages and wrote a book *Introduction to the Study of Indian Languages*. On his trips to the West, he took time to sit and talk with the Indians. One tribe called him Ka-pur-ats, meaning the man with one arm off.

Appointed to government commissions charged with investigating the condition of the Indians, Powell attacked graft and waste among agents responsible for supervising Indian affairs. In 1879 he became head of the federal bureau overseeing such matters, hoping to make things better for the Indians.

But Powell is remembered more today for his recommendations regarding land reform in the West. To easterners, he explained that climate conditions there were really very different. Except along the Pacific's northwest coast, the area got so little rain that it was unsuitable for farming as practiced in the East. He stressed that water, not land, was the key to settlement of the West.

In one of Powell's reports to Congress, he said bluntly: "All of the region of the country west of the 100th or 99th meridian, except a little of California, Oregon, and Washington, is arid and . . . no part can be redeemed for agriculture, except by irrigation." He referred to the half of the United States west of a line drawn from Iowa down to east Texas.

Not content just to state the problem, Powell spelled out his ideas for a scientific and environmental approach to developing the West in a book with a dry but descriptive title, *Report on the Lands of the Arid Regions of the United States,* published in 1878. It was, according to a leading historian, one of the most important books ever to come out of the West.

In it, Powell recognized that the farming practices of the East—with individuals working small, separate farms on land with ample rainfall—would not work in the arid West. Therefore, he proposed a regional approach to solve the basic problem of water resources and who would control them. He outlined a plan of irrigation districts, dams, reservoirs, and mountain catch basins for water.

Powell planted the seeds of conservation, although the word was not in use then. Indeed, his ideas were far in advance of his time. Generally accepted today, they met with little enthusiasm in Washington and even in the West when first presented.

Then as now, science became enmeshed with politics in the nation's capital. Powell had not been alone in exploring the West. Other expeditions, some led by Army officers, also went west to map the area. It was clear to Powell and others that all these western studies should be consolidated. But the question was: Would the effort be under Army or civilian control?

After months of debate, Congress acted on Powell's suggestion, supported by the National Academy of Science. It put land surveys under civilians in a new Geological Survey in the Department of the Interior in 1879. Clarence King, who also had led exploration parties in the West, became the first director of this new agency. Powell was named head of a new division of the Smithsonian Institution—its Bureau of Ethnology, devoted to making scientific studies of different racial groups.

Two years later, in 1881, Powell became director of the U.S. Geological Survey as well, holding both jobs for fifteen years. As head of the Geological Survey, he began a series of detailed maps and reports that to this day form the basis for almost every environmental report. As director of the Bureau of Ethnology, he continued his pioneering work in studying and helping American Indians.

In appearance, Powell was a somewhat rough and striking figure with a full beard and flowing hair. He made friends easily. Just as he could steer a boat around rocks in a river, he maneuvered in the political atmosphere of Washington. A few complained that he sometimes enforced his views as if they

Sitting on a rock ledge, John Wesley Powell overlooks the Grand Canyon at the foot of Toroweap Canyon, North Rim, in 1874. *Hillers/U.S. Geological Survey.*

were military orders, but generally he was well liked by his subordinates as well as politicians.

According to one biographer, Powell had a remarkable gift for leadership, giving every man under him a chance to demonstrate his capacity. As director of two important agencies of government, his door was always open to members of his staff.

Although across the continent from the West, the Geological Survey sat at the heart of controversies about the water resources of the area that continue until this day. Its maps were vital for any development of the land because of the importance of water in every sort of plan.

After the drought of 1887, Congress ordered the Geological Survey to locate water sources and irrigation basins, suspending all settlement in the West until these resources were classified. That gave immense power to Powell, who moved too slowly for those interested in developing the West. Because he

insisted on proceeding in a scientific way, not hurrying for political reasons, western senators gradually began to chip away at Powell's funds to operate his survey agency.

By 1894, Powell had had enough. He had fought and lost a battle to defend the work and the budget of the Geological Survey. So he resigned his post there, although he continued his connection with the Bureau of Ethnology.

After giving up political fighting in Washington, Powell spent much of his time at his summer home in Maine. Although he was not a college graduate, he received honorary degrees from Harvard and the University of Heidelberg in Germany. He died on September 23, 1902, at the age of sixty-eight.

Looking back, one historian said that even if Powell had met with defeat at the end of his career, during his life he had done much to lay the foundation for the American conservation movement.

J. I. Rodale

1898–1971   American popularizer of the organic farming movement

The man who did more than anyone else to make organic farming popular in the United States never even saw a farm during his own boyhood. Jerome Irving Rodale was the son of an immigrant Jewish family from Poland that had settled on the Lower East Side of New York City. His father, Michael Cohen, ran a grocery store where his mother worked behind the counter while raising eight children. They all lived in a small apartment behind the store.

Jerry was born there on August 16, 1898. At the age of six, he went to work helping his father. Early every morning, he delivered breakfast orders of groceries to other families in the crowded neighborhood. The Cohens themselves usually ate crusts of bread left over from the store and whatever

canned fish or meat the customers had not bought.

Outside, after school, Jerry and the other boys played in the streets at a time when horses still pulled trolley cars. Years later, he recalled how much he'd liked watching the horses' tails swish as they galloped over the cobblestones of the pavement. He put bottle caps on the steel trolley rails and waited for the car wheels to flatten them into markers called potsies, which he and his friends used in their games of hopscotch.

Although they were poor, the Cohens had high hopes for Jerry. His father wanted him to become a rabbi because religious leaders were the most respected members of their community. Along with other Jewish boys on his block, Jerry went to Hebrew school after coming home from public school, starting at the age of seven.

He always remembered the Hebrew teacher nicknamed Red Donkey because of his red beard. While the boys chanted from their holy books, Red Donkey would stroke his beard and groom it with a comb and brush. He believed the road to heaven could be achieved only by learning the Old Testament of the Bible by heart. Every Friday, he tested the boys to see how much they had memorized. If they had not learned their lessons well, he punished them.

A boy who failed had to lie down on a bench, his trousers lowered. Red Donkey would beat him with a strap while shouting insults at him. On one occasion, when he had caught a pupil playing with baseball cards instead of studying, Red Donkey outdid himself. "You loafer!" he yelled. "Baseball cards he's got in his pocket. May the cholera get you, and a very bad end to you! May you burn in hell."

Those memories remained vivid for Jerry. Nevertheless, he rejected his father's idea that he should study to become a rabbi. He and his friends were more interested in baseball, trips to the zoo, and their street games. "The old Bible didn't stand a chance," he recalled later.

Jerry wasn't a very good ball player, however, owing to poor health. He had

very little endurance and suffered from constant colds during the winter. His teeth kept getting cavities that—years later—he blamed on all the sugary cookies he couldn't stop eating in the grocery store whenever his father wasn't around. But his eyes were his major problem. Without glasses, he could hardly see the blackboard at school.

Despite his bad eyes, Jerry liked to read. His favorite books were the cheap paperback adventure stories for boys by a writer named Horatio Alger, in which the high-minded young heroes always managed to win fame and fortune. "I had to watch out for two villains," he remembered long afterward, "the one in the book and my father's heavy forewarning footsteps." For his father believed that reading these books was sinful, and he destroyed many of them.

His family always had flowers growing in pots on the windowsills of their apartment. But when Jerry told his mother that he wanted to grow mushrooms under his bed, she put her foot down. "When mushrooms are growing under your bed, you'll be out on the streets," she told him.

Yet somehow in that crowded urban setting Jerry developed a love for nature. He and a friend with the same feeling would travel north to the large parks of the city to walk on the grass and look at the trees. They even went to City Island, connected to the Bronx by a bridge, to go fishing.

At school, Jerry was an average student. In his last year of high school, his grades were: English, 73; history, 88; physics, 78; trigonometry, 65; and public speaking, 75. Later he noted that math was his worst subject "yet I turned out to be an accountant."

He settled on that occupation, he recalled, "for no other reason than a friend of mine, at whose house I used to visit, had a sister whose boyfriend was an accountant and who used to tell fabulous stories about his earnings." So Jerry became a bookkeeper and studied accounting at night. In 1919, at the end of World War I, at the age of twenty-one he got a job in Washington with the Internal Revenue Service.

He traveled around the country checking the financial records of companies in Kentucky, Ohio, and Pennsylvania. Everywhere he went, he took walks in the countryside, delighting in the sight of farm fields and farm families in horse-drawn wagons on their way to town or church. He dreamed of someday living on his own farm.

He had another ambition as well, to run his own business. But before he did so, he faced a problem. In those days when religious prejudice was widespread, someone with a Jewish name like Cohen could have a difficult

time if he tried to enter professions such as finance or publishing. So Jerry decided to change his name.

While working in Washington, he thought about the possibilities. His mother's name before she had married had been Rouda, and he began to say that out loud. Not satisfied by its sound, he added or subtracted a few letters—coming up with Rodale, which he pronounced ROW-dale. At the age of twenty-three, in 1921 he received court permission to change his name legally to J. I. Rodale.

At first, Rodale aimed to go into the business of making cones for ice cream. But his brother Joseph convinced Jerry to join him in manufacturing home electrical devices such as plugs, sockets, and switches. They called their enterprise the Rodale Manufacturing Company and opened a small factory in downtown New York City.

At that time Rodale was a sickly man, suffering from constant colds and headaches. His eyes ached from the pollution of the city air. Of medium height, he weighed only 138 pounds. For recreation, he loved to dance.

At a ballroom, he met his future wife, Anna Andrews, the daughter of immigrants from Lithuania who had settled in Mahonoy City, Pennsylvania. Although she was a Roman Catholic, her grandmother accepted Anna's choice of a Jewish husband because, she said, "he looks like a priest." They were married in 1927.

When the Great Depression started two years later, the Rodale Manufacturing Company moved out of New York to cut expenses. The company and the Rodale family moved to the Pennsylvania town of Emmaus (Ee-MAY-us), just south of Allentown. Emmaus had once been called Macungie, meaning feeding place of the bears, by Indians who had lived in the area.

In these rural surroundings, Rodale's life changed dramatically. Besides actively involving himself with his electrical business, he became a writer in a peculiar way—by collecting and filing clippings. Because he felt an impulse to put down some of his thoughts, he analyzed his own failings when he took pen in hand and decided that his greatest weakness was verbs.

"My words of action lacked action," he later explained. So he began to save examples of verbs he came across in his reading and even hired high school or college students to collect more verbs for him from newspapers and magazines.

After a while, he had hundreds of envelopes and boxes filled with clippings. Rodale decided that these could be the basis of a book to be called *The Verb-Finder*. He published it himself

in 1937, when he was thirty-nine years old, and found that many would-be writers ordered it. In the same way, he put together three other similar books during the next few years.

Rodale liked being a publisher more than he liked making electrical plugs. Using the same system he had used on *The Verb-Finder*, he began to put out magazines that were digests of articles that had appeared elsewhere—the *Health Digest*, *Fact Digest*, and several others.

To find material for his digests, Rodale had to do a lot of reading of other magazines. One day in the late 1930s he found an article in a British publication called *Health for All* written by Sir Albert Howard, an eminent British agriculturalist. Based on his experiences and experiments, Sir Albert advocated farming that did not use chemical fertilizers or poisonous insecticide sprays, but relied on old-fashioned natural practices. He felt that chemical fertilizers did more harm than good.

What interested Rodale the most was a report that students at a New Zealand school who ate food grown without artificial fertilizers had fewer cases of measles, colds, and scarlet fever than before their diet had been changed. To fertilize the fields where their new food was grown, only animal manure and organic refuse such as chopped-up weeds were used. The article said that the harvest from ground that had been treated this way not only seemed to be more healthful, but also tasted better.

"It hit me like a ton of bricks," Rodale recalled later. "It changed my whole way of life. I decided we must get a farm at once and raise as much of our family's food by the organic method as possible."

He bought a worn-out sixty acres not far from Emmaus and began to farm it, using no chemical fertilizers or sprays. The results were remarkable, according to Rodale. At harvest time, wagon load after wagon load of golden ears of corn were picked and stored in his farm's cribs.

Rodale's enthusiasm for his new cause mounted. "I felt I had to share this information with the rest of the country," he said.

So he started to publish *Organic Farming and Gardening,* a magazine that was to become the bible of the organic farming movement in the United States and other countries as well. Its first issue came out in May of 1942, with Sir Albert Howard as associate editor.

The roots of organic farming lie in the use of fertilizers derived from farm animals or vegetable matter. Manure from animals had, of course, been used for centuries by farmers all over the world. But Rodale and his followers also advocated use of vegetable wastes—leaves, weeds, grass clippings—decomposed in piles called compost heaps. In those piles, intense microbiological action breaks organic matter down into a crumbly, dark substance called humus that is rich in many of the elements necessary for growing things.

At first, the rest of the country was not very receptive to Rodale's ideas. Farmers had found that chemical fertilizers were easier to apply than bulky organic matter. Agricultural colleges, chemical manufacturers everywhere, and even the United States Department of Agriculture supported using chemical fertilizers.

Despite attacks on Rodale and the concept of organic farming, he gradually began to build up a following. Home gardeners, in particular, read his magazine and took his advice.

In 1945, his book *Pay Dirt* was published, further spreading the idea of organic farming and gardening. "It more or less made me Mr. Organic," Rodale said in his autobiography. The circulation of his organic gardening magazine increased, too, and he received invitations to speak all over the country.

Rodale became more and more convinced that the way food is grown can be an important factor in preventing disease. His theory was that people

J. I. Rodale in his greenhouse. *Rodale Press, Inc.*

would be healthier if they ate plants grown in soil not contaminated by chemical fertilizers. The plants, too, would be so healthy and strong that they would not need chemical sprays to protect them from insects and disease.

In 1950, Rodale started a new magazine he called *Prevention*, devoted to human health. It became his favorite magazine, perhaps because he himself was not very healthy. "What *Prevention* soon became," he wrote, "was a medical journal for the people, over 90 percent of the material being excerpted from medical journals and other orthodox medical sources. Always the name and date of the source were given, but it was written so that the average person could understand it."

In his speeches as well as in his magazines, Rodale advocated eating less sugar, taking Vitamin C pills, walking daily, eating more fresh fruit and vegetables, and avoiding processed foods. While most of his ideas on diet are widely accepted today, at the time he proposed them he was attacked as a food faddist, someone not in touch with modern times.

From the beginning, the American Medical Association and the whole medical establishment opposed Rodale's concept that one could become healthier by eating organically produced food. The AMA included Rodale's health books in its "quackery" exhibits. It even said, "The belief that organically grown foods are the only reliable foods is characteristic of the nutritionally neurotic."

In 1964, the Federal Trade Commission took action against Rodale's book *The Health Finder*, which was a compilation of articles from *Prevention* magazine. The commission called an advertising brochure false and deceptive because it said the book could "help the average person remain comparatively free of many terrible diseases." The federal action was peculiar because, by then, the book was ten years old and out of print.

After almost a year of hearings, the FTC ordered Rodale to stop advertising that *The Health Finder* would help readers gain energy, prevent colds, and provide other answers to health problems. But when Rodale appealed to the courts, he won on a technicality.

Despite such rebuffs, Rodale and his ideas prospered. Especially among young people, increasing support developed for his program of cutting down on chemical aids to agriculture, rejecting processed foods, and returning to a simpler as well as more natural way of living. His magazines and books gained wide circulation and his publishing empire expanded rapidly. Profits rolled in, making him a millionaire.

Rodale even overcame his own health problems—by taking seventy vitamin and food supplement pills a day, he said. Each morning, he arose at five-thirty and worked in his study till eight o'clock, writing in pen and ink on yellow pads. He breakfasted on stewed prunes, wheat germ, an egg, and, giving in to a nonorganic craving, coffee.

With his wife, he lived in a stone and wood Pennsylvania Dutch house on the edge of the Organic Gardening Experimental Farm, where his ideas on organic farming were tested. There, no chemical fertilizers, pesticides, or herbicides were used. Experiments were conducted trying out various methods of composting, solar greenhouses, insect control by natural means, and other organic farming and gardening ideas. Today, an expanded Rodale

An aerial view of the Rodale farm. *Rodale Press, Inc.*

Research Center is still operating in Emmaus and open to the public.

As Rodale grew older, he remained a compulsive collector of facts and information, filling cardboard boxes and file cabinets with clippings about anything that might make an article or a book. He sent a stream of yellow slips suggesting ideas to staff members of the Rodale Press. But he left the management of the fast-growing business to his son, Robert.

That gave him time for a new occupation—writing plays. To prepare himself for a career as a playwright, Rodale went to every comedy he could see on Broadway, taking notes on what made people laugh. Even so, as other writers before him had found, research does not make an author. Altogether he wrote around forty plays, many about food and nutrition, others adaptations of foreign works, and still others about historical figures such as Benjamin Franklin and John Hancock.

The critics called his plays terrible. One critic said his play "The Goose" should have been called "The Turkey" because it was so bad. But Rodale was not daunted. He even bought a theater in New York City to make sure his plays would be produced. He called it Theater 62, named after Public School 62 that he had attended on the Lower East Side of New York as a boy.

In his old age, Rodale appeared to be a walking proof of his theories that healthy living could overcome many ailments. And he was a happy man because his message about how to lead a healthy life, which he had been spreading for more than thirty years, was obviously gaining wide acceptance. Newspaper articles everywhere praised him as someone who had been ahead of his time.

In June of 1971, Rodale traveled up to New York City to appear on the Dick Cavett television show. Talking to Cavett, he warned against overuse of sugar and urged his audience to eat plenty of raw vegetables besides taking vitamin pills.

After describing his own diet, Rodale added: "I am so healthy that I expect to live on and on. I have no aches or pains. I'm full of energy." Amazingly, those were his last words.

As the show broke for a commercial, Cavett noticed that Rodale had slumped over in his chair, with his head resting on his chest.

"Mr. Rodale, are you all right?" Ca-vett said. There was no reply. Cavett jumped up and asked if there was a doctor in the audience.

The cameras stopped when two doctors began to try to help Rodale. But it was too late. Taken to a nearby hospital, he was pronounced dead at the age of seventy-two from a sudden heart attack.

A few months earlier, Rodale himself had summed up his life in a speech at a dinner in his honor: "Years ago they heaped violence and poured ridicule on my head. I was called a cultist and a crackpot . . . But no longer. Now even the chemical people have suddenly become respectful towards me and my manure philosophy. I am suddenly becoming a prophet here on earth and a prophet with profits."

In Emmaus, the busy headquarters of the Rodale Press continues to give evidence of his achievement. More than a thousand employees each year turn out seven magazines, six newsletters, and about fifty new books devoted to organic farming and healthier living. Around the country, more than a million readers subscribe to *Organic Gardening* and another two million to *Prevention*—the total circulation of all the Rodale magazines is over five million.

Theodore Roosevelt

1858–1919   Twenty-sixth president of the United States; naturalist and powerful supporter of the conservation movement

Anybody who has ever held a teddy bear should remember Theodore Roosevelt, the twenty-sixth president of the United States.

Back in 1902, President Roosevelt went to Mississippi to settle a boundary dispute between that state and Louisiana. As usual, he took time out from his duties to go hunting, one of his favorite sports. No game was found but, on the morning of his departure, a bear cub wandered into his camp and was captured.

Roosevelt's companions urged him to shoot it because he had seen few targets during the trip. He refused, though, because his code of good sportsmanship forbade shooting captured animals. That refusal became the basis for one of the most famous cartoons in American political history.

Under the words "Drawing the Line in Mississippi," Clifford Berryman of the Washington *Post* showed the president holding a rifle—and turning his back on the baby bear. The cartoon caught the imagination of the American people.

Practically overnight, all sorts of souvenirs such as postcards and buttons portrayed the president and the little bear. In New York, a toymaker designed a stuffed bear for his Brooklyn store. Then he wrote to the White House, requesting the president's permission to call the new toy a teddy bear.

The president wrote back: "I doubt if my name will mean much in the bear business, but you may use it if you wish."

Roosevelt was wrong. The teddy bear turned out to be one of the most popular toys ever made, delighting one generation of children after another all over the United States and in many other countries, too.

Today it is a reminder of Theodore Roosevelt's extraordinary career as both a public figure and a naturalist. A bird expert from his boyhood, he later became one of his era's foremost authorities on big game animals—along with all his other claims to fame as a war hero and political leader.

An energetic president, Roosevelt took vigorous steps to preserve the natural resources of the United States. Many programs aimed at protecting the nation's soil, trees, birds, and animals were started while he headed the government. Nearly a century afterward, he still stands out as the most active conservationist ever to occupy the White House.

Roosevelt's interest in wildlife and the outdoors came, strangely enough, from his roots in New York City, where he was born on October 27, 1858. Teedie—the nickname his affectionate family gave him—had two sisters and a younger brother. His parents were Theodore Roosevelt, Sr., a wealthy businessman, and Martha Bulloch Roo-

sevelt, who had spent her girlhood on a large Georgia plantation.

A sickly boy suffering from asthma, Teedie gasped for air constantly. His father often took him driving through the streets and countryside so that he could breathe more easily. As he grew up, the fresh air of the outdoor world became a cherished part of his life.

He always remembered the day he started to take an interest in natural history instead of merely enjoying the outdoors. It was a few months before his eighth birthday, and this is how he told the story years later when he wrote his autobiography:

I was walking up Broadway, and as I passed the market to which I used sometimes to be sent before breakfast to get strawberries, I suddenly saw a dead seal laid out on a slab of wood. That seal filled me with every possible feeling of romance and adventure.

As long as the seal remained there, I haunted the neighborhood of the market day after day. I measured it, and I recall that, not having a tape measure, I had to do my best to get its girth with a folding pocket foot-rule, a difficult undertaking. I carefully made a record of the utterly useless measurements, and at once began to write a natural history of my own.

Somehow, Teedie got the seal's skull when it was sold. With two cousins, he started what they called the Roosevelt Museum of Natural History. During the next two years they accumulated 250 "specimins," Teedie noted in his diary, demonstrating that spelling was not his strongest subject.

His family learned to live with his growing collection of mice, baby frogs, snapping turtles, and other animals gathered during summer vacation trips. At first the museum was located in his bedroom but, after a maid complained, it was moved to an attic room.

When Teedie was eleven, he began studying the very specialized art of taxidermy. He took lessons in how to skin, preserve, and mount birds from John G. Bell, who had accompanied the famous artist John James Audubon on one of his bird-collecting trips to the West.

Not content with maintaining his own display, Teedie also donated specimens to New York's American Museum of Natural History—which his father had recently helped to establish. According to its early records, young Theodore Roosevelt, Jr., gave it: "1 Bat, 12 Mice, 1 Turtle, 1 Red Squirrel, and 4 Birds Eggs."

Teedie's love of nature was also spurred by his reading. He liked to read adventure novels and books about travel in Africa and the West, especially relishing their descriptions of animals. But he had problems when it came to observing anything he couldn't hold right up to his eyes.

He paid no attention to his handicap, however, until the summer he received his first rifle. Taken out for a lesson in using it, he was puzzled as he watched his father shoot birds that he himself could not see at all.

A few days later, he was with a group of other boys who began to read aloud the huge letters on a billboard—and Teedie could not even see the letters. Finally, he understood that something must be wrong with his eyes. When he mentioned the matter to his father, steps were immediately taken to provide Teedie with eyeglasses. They transformed his life.

"I had no idea of how beautiful the world was until I got those spectacles," he said. He was thirteen years old then.

Another event that changed his life occurred that same year. Still a frail, sickly boy suffering from asthma, he was sent off to a lake in Maine for the fresh country air. On his stagecoach ride to the lake, he met two boys of his own age who made fun of his city manners and clothing. He did look odd because he was so skinny, and his glasses gave him an owlish appearance. His voice was squeaky, too.

When Teedie tried to fight back, he found that the bullies beat him easily. He made up his mind that he would never again be put into a helpless position. With the support of his father, he started boxing lessons as soon as he returned to the city—and doggedly kept at them until he won a pewter mug as a prize at the boxing school.

In 1872, when Teedie was fourteen, the whole Roosevelt family went abroad. After traveling all over Europe, they sailed up the Nile River in Egypt on a boat they hired. There, Teedie discovered a new world of birds. Equipped with his glasses and his rifle, he gloried in shooting birds from the sky as rapidly as possible.

But he was not content merely to shoot them. At the end of each day's hunting, he lined up his birds on a table on the boat's deck under a canopy to protect them from the hot sun. As his family and crew members watched, he skinned the birds carefully, cleaning out the insides. He preserved the birds with his taxidermy kit, adding them to his collection.

Back home, he prepared to go off to Harvard College. Because of his love for birds, his aim was to become a naturalist like the great bird painter Audubon. He took as many natural history courses as he could and spent his vacations bird-watching and hunting in the Adirondack Mountains of New York.

To his Harvard classmates, Theodore Roosevelt looked a little comical—and his way of talking also amused them. Arriving there at the age of seventeen, he had reached his full height of five feet eight inches. Behind his thick eyeglasses, his blue-gray eyes squinted brightly. Words tumbled out of his mouth so fast that his fellow students often teased him into an argument just to hear him talk, which he loved to do.

On his own for the first time and now called Teddy instead of his boyhood nickname of Teedie, he blossomed. At college, he showed the traits that would mark the rest of his life— boundless energy, an ability to speak out compellingly, a devotion to sports, especially boxing, and a very good quick mind.

He joined almost every activity: the rifle club, the glee club, the art club, the finance club, and several natural history groups as well as the editorial board of the student magazine. He boxed, he wrestled, he rowed, and he even took dancing lessons. His health improved, too.

With all that, Teddy showed himself to be an outstanding student. Not only was he elected to Phi Beta Kappa, the national scholastic honor society, but he began to write a book, *The Naval War of 1812*. Published a few years later, it became required reading at the United States Naval Academy.

He also fell in love. During his junior year he met Alice Lee, the daughter of a well-to-do Boston family, and he courted her with determination. "See that girl?" he said to a friend. "I am going to marry her. She won't have me, but I am going to have her."

In his last year at Harvard, Roosevelt lost interest in a natural history career for a variety of reasons. He could not see spending three more years of training to earn an advanced degree and he wanted to get married. Also, neither his family nor his teachers had encouraged his original goal. As graduation neared, he wrote to a friend: "I am going to try to help the cause of better government in New York City; I don't know exactly how."

Shortly after receiving his diploma in 1880, at the age of twenty-one he married Alice Lee, who was nineteen then. They moved to New York, where he entered law school and spent his afternoons in libraries doing research for books he planned to write. Evenings, he attended parties with his wife. He also began to take an interest in politics.

In those days, it was unusual for a young man of his social standing to become involved with politics. But Roosevelt joined the Republican party in his district. By attending meetings regularly, he attracted the attention of local party leaders. At the age of only twenty-three, he ran for the New York State Assembly—and was elected.

Although new legislators were expected just to listen and learn, Roosevelt spoke up self-confidently right after arriving in the state capital of Albany. In his high-pitched voice, he repeatedly attacked businessmen who bribed judges or lawmakers. Despite being ridiculed as a "goo-goo," the sarcastic label given to defenders of good government, he quickly won the approval of reform-minded voters and was reelected twice.

But tragedy struck the Roosevelt family in February of 1884. On the same day, his mother and his young wife both died. His wife, only twenty-two years old, had given birth to a baby girl two days earlier.

Grief-stricken, Roosevelt left his infant daughter—named Alice, after her mother—in the care of one of his sisters. He headed west to the wild Dakota Territory, where he owned a ranch. At first, the cowboys there dismissed him as a "tenderfoot." But he gained their respect by riding hard and branding cattle with them as well as hunting cougar, bear, and bison.

On one occasion, while out chasing lost horses, Roosevelt stopped at a primitive, small hotel in the wilderness. In the bar stood a man with a gun in each hand, shooting at the clock. As soon as he saw the bespectacled easterner, he called him "Four-eyes."

"Four-eyes is going to treat," he shouted to the others in the bar room.

Roosevelt tried to avoid trouble, but the bully persisted. Roosevelt said, "Well, if I've got to, I've got to."

With that, he hit the man on the jaw with his right fist, then with his left, and once more with his right. The man fell. Roosevelt took away his guns and calmly sat down for his dinner.

Roosevelt loved the open spaces of the West—the sight of antelope and buffalo, the howling of wolves at night, the soaring of great golden eagles. On his horse, Manitou, he rode out hunting elk, ducks, grouse, deer, and even the dangerous grizzly bears.

Returning to the East refreshed in spirit, Roosevelt carried with him the manuscript of another book he had written, a biography of Senator Thomas Hart Benton of Missouri. In New York, the city's Republican leaders persuaded him to run for the post of mayor. At twenty-eight, the youngest man ever to be a candidate for that office, he did run, but he lost.

In that same year of 1886, his personal life changed for the better. He married Edith Carow, an old childhood friend. They later had five children. They lived in New York City but spent their summers in a house they built overlooking Long Island Sound outside the village of Oyster Bay. With twenty-three rooms, this home they called Sagamore Hill had plenty of space for a large family—as well as eight fireplaces above which Roosevelt could hang his collection of antlers and stuffed animal heads.

Because of his love of hunting, Roosevelt was concerned about the dwindling number of wild animals in the nation. With some friends, he organized an association to press for preserving large game by the passage of protective laws. They called their group the Boone and Crockett Club, after Daniel Boone and Davy Crockett, two famous American hunters. Roosevelt became its first president.

His public life expanded, too. He served as a member of the U.S. Civil Service Commission and as police commissioner of New York City before getting the job he really wanted. In 1897, President William McKinley appointed the thirty-nine-year-old Roosevelt assistant secretary of the navy. That post was particularly appealing because of his fondness for the sea and also because it gave him an opportunity to help build a modern fleet to uphold America's growing stature as a world power.

When war with Spain broke out in 1898, Roosevelt resigned to become second-in-command of a regiment of mounted soldiers. Its official name was the First U.S. Volunteer Cavalry, but it quickly became known as Roosevelt's Rough Riders.

Roosevelt enjoyed the war. Sitting on his horse despite bullets flying everywhere, he led his Rough Riders in a charge up San Juan Hill on the Spanish-owned island of Cuba. His daring helped American forces to win the war quickly. It also made Roosevelt famous.

Returning to the United States a war hero, Roosevelt ran for governor of New York in 1898 and won. As governor, he energetically pressed numerous reforms. He pushed laws for taxing public utilities, forced the adoption of safeguards in the handling of food and drugs, and sponsored measures to shorten the workday of women and children. Yet his program distressed some leaders of his own party, who frequently acted as allies of big business.

In Albany, Roosevelt always found time for boxing and wrestling. One of his wrestling opponents was the middleweight champion of America, who came to the executive mansion several times a week for bouts with the governor. That led to a financial problem.

The watchdog of the state finances refused to approve Roosevelt's purchase of a wrestling mat. If the governor wanted a billiards table, that could be approved as a proper amusement, he said, but a wrestling mat was something unusual and could not be permitted.

More seriously, Roosevelt kept finding himself involved in fights with other prominent Republicans. These conflicts arose because Roosevelt was determined to make his own appointments to various state posts instead of accepting the candidates chosen by party bosses. After one heated dispute, he wrote to one of his friends: "I have always been fond of the West African saying, 'Speak softly and carry a big stick, and you will go far.' "

Roosevelt proved so difficult for the party bosses to deal with that they decided to get rid of him in a strange way—they would nominate him for vice president of the United States. They did so and, in 1900, when McKinley was reelected as president, Roosevelt became vice president.

McKinley was assassinated six months after taking office. On September 14, 1901, Vice President Roosevelt was sworn in to replace him. At the age of forty-two, he became the youngest man ever to hold the country's highest office.

Roosevelt proved to be one of the nation's most vigorous presidents. He started antitrust cases against combinations of businesses. He stepped in to force a settlement of a coal strike. He

An informal photograph of then-president Theodore Roosevelt, 1903. *North Wind Picture Archives.*

pushed through the nation's first pure-food-and-drug law to protect consumers. What he wanted, he said, was "to see that every man has a square deal, no more, no less."

In foreign affairs, Roosevelt took direct action to back a revolution in Panama in 1903 so that a canal connecting the Atlantic and Pacific oceans could be built there. In 1905, he arranged a settlement ending a war between Russia and Japan. For that, he received the Nobel Peace Prize the following year.

"I enjoy being president," Roosevelt said. He also found time for personal enjoyment. He arose at 6:00 A.M. to do push-ups, starting a strenuous day. He boxed frequently in the White House gym, took long walks with his aides, played football on the White House lawn, engaged in pillow fights with his lively children, and went hunting as often as he could.

Stocky in appearance, Roosevelt had bushy eyebrows above his steel-rimmed glasses, a droopy moustache, and prominent teeth. Always full of energy, he was the center of attention wherever he went. One of the most popular of the nation's chief executives, he easily won a second term in the election of 1904.

Throughout his White House years, Roosevelt never forgot his commitment to the cause of conservation. He kept calling his fellow citizens' attention to the way the country's natural resources were being shamefully wasted. Besides writing about the issue in several books and making numerous speeches on the subject, he also took many important actions.

When Roosevelt became president, there were five national parks in the United States. Under his prodding, Congress added five more. By presidential proclamation, he created fifty-one federal wildlife refuges, the first ever. In addition, he established eighteen national natural monuments, protecting unique landscapes such as the Petrified Forest in Arizona, the Devil's Tower in Wyoming, and the Natural Bridges in Utah.

With Gifford Pinchot as his chief adviser, Roosevelt reorganized the country's national forests, putting them under the jurisdiction of the National Forest Service. He added 150 million acres of timberland, an area almost as large as all the Northeast, to the country's forest preserves.

Not content to sit at a desk in Washington, Roosevelt delighted in going to see scenic areas for himself. In 1903, he visited Yellowstone National Park with John Burroughs, the celebrated naturalist. For two weeks they tramped through the park together, watching

Theodore Roosevelt and John Muir ride horseback at Yosemite National Park. *Theodore Roosevelt Collection, Harvard College Library.*

bighorn elk, deer, coyotes, and pine squirrels. Together, they identified birds of many kinds by their song and appearance.

Burroughs later wrote: "The President is a born nature-lover, and he has what does not always go with this passion—remarkable powers of observation."

Leaving Yellowstone, Roosevelt went on to California to explore Yosemite National Park with John Muir, the naturalist who had fought to save the giant sequoia trees there. They talked about conservation as they roamed the beautiful wilderness. Muir spoke out forcefully for speedy action to protect the sequoias from lumbering interests.

But Roosevelt felt less at home with Muir than Burroughs. The explanation came from Burroughs, when he wrote: "I think I could see where the rub was. Both are great talkers, and talkers, you know, seldom get on well together. He finds me an appreciative listener, and that suits him better."

When Roosevelt left office in 1909, he listed his various programs aimed at conserving the country's natural resources as just one of his major achievements. But many historians today believe that his strong support of conservation was his most important lasting contribution.

On leaving the White House, Roosevelt was only fifty-one years old and still vigorous. Accompanied by three other naturalists, he left for Africa the following year on a hunting trip sponsored by the Smithsonian Institution. His expedition sent thousands of animals and birds back to a museum in Washington.

After an unsuccessful effort to return to the political arena, in 1914 Roosevelt revived his spirits by going off to explore the interior of South America. With his son Kermit and a large party, he explored a tributary of the Amazon River in central Brazil, putting a new river on the map. It is called the Rio Roosevelt, or sometimes the Rio Teodoro. As usual, he also collected birds and animals that went into museum exhibits. Unfortunately, though, he fell ill with malaria, which left him a sick man.

When the United States entered World War I in 1917, Roosevelt hoped he would be asked to take on some emergency task. He was very disappointed when his offers to serve were turned down, but kept busy writing new books about birds. He died in his sleep on January 6, 1919, at the age of sixty.

Roosevelt is remembered today in many ways. At the American Museum of Natural History in New York, a display area named for him celebrates his accomplishments, with a statue of him on horseback standing outside. His New York City birthplace and his Oyster Bay home, furnished as they were when he lived in them, are visited by thousands of tourists every year. In addition, his ranch at Medora, North Dakota, is now the Theodore Roosevelt National Park.

Most of all, however, he is remembered as an activist president who took strong measures to preserve the nation's natural environment. Not long ago when the National Wildlife Federation polled its members for nominations to a Conservation Hall of Fame, the name of Theodore Roosevelt led all the rest.

Henry David Thoreau

1817–1862 American naturalist and independent thinker; author of the classic *Walden*

Nearly 150 years ago, Henry David Thoreau built himself a cabin in the woods—overlooking a silvery body of water known as Walden Pond. At the age of twenty-eight, he wanted to test out his idea that he could live happily alone there. But he did welcome some visitors, among them a boy who long afterward remembered being awed by a remarkable demonstration.

Thoreau was talking about wildflowers, the boy recalled, when he suddenly stopped and said: "Keep very still and I will show you my family." Then:

He gave a low curious whistle. Immediately a woodchuck came running towards him from a nearby burrow. With varying note . . . a pair of gray squirrels were summoned and approached him fearlessly. [Then] several birds, including two crows, flew towards him, one of the crows nestling upon his shoulder. I remember it was the crows resting close to his head that made the most vivid impression upon me, knowing how fearful of man this bird is. He fed them all from his hand, taking food from his pocket, and petted them gently before our delighted gaze.

Perhaps this memory of Thoreau may have become somewhat less than completely reliable by the time the former boy published it many years later. Even so, it shows the way a lot of people today picture the author of *Walden*—the book Thoreau himself wrote about why, and how, he chose to live as simply as possible. Over the years, *Walden* has won increasing fame as one of the most outstanding nature books ever written.

Thoreau's underlying theme was that

people have a basic need to refresh their spirits away from towns and cities. Nowadays, when "progress" keeps posing new threats to our natural environment, his message has come to be considered ever more important, especially by those who are battling against all sorts of pollution.

But *Walden* is down-to-earth, too. It tells exactly what Thoreau had to buy in order to build his hut, at a total cost of $28.12. Furthermore, it contains a wealth of his own sharp comments, such as: "I say beware of all enterprises that require new clothes."

Yet most of Thoreau's old-time Yankee neighbors thought of him as just an odd sort of man with some peculiar notions. While he seemed bright enough, wasn't he maybe a little cracked? Only a few perceptive critics predicted that this quirky naturalist would eventually be regarded, all over the world, as one of the greatest men the United States has ever produced—and they were right.

This exceptional man came from the exceptional village of Concord, Massachusetts. About twenty miles northwest of Boston, Concord had been the scene of one of the first battles of the American Revolution. In addition, during Thoreau's lifetime it seemed to be "simmering with ideas" because it was also the home of two already celebrated writ-

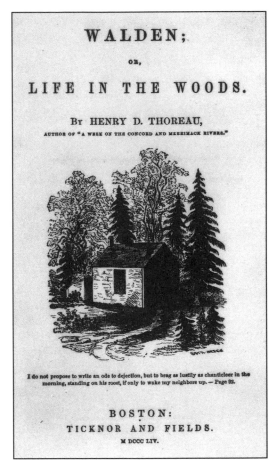

The title page from the original edition of Henry David Thoreau's *Walden. Berg Collection/New York Public Library.*

ers—Ralph Waldo Emerson and Nathaniel Hawthorne.

Of the three, however, only Thoreau could claim the status of a Concord native. He was born there on July 12, 1817, in a plain gray house near the edge of the village. Although a generation earlier his family had been wealthy, a series of business losses had reduced them to having to count their pennies. While most of Concord's two thousand residents were similarly neither rich nor poor, few of them could have been as abundantly blessed with rebellious ancestors as Henry was.

His father, John Thoreau, was descended from Protestants who had left France because of religious persecution by the Catholic majority there. They moved first to an island in the English Channel, and one of them became a not very bloodthirsty sort of pirate whose ship was wrecked near the New England coast. In Boston, this former buccaneer and his relatives turned into prosperous merchants and sea captains.

But John Thoreau, a man who most enjoyed quietly reading his newspaper or playing his flute, had no particular gift for any kind of business. After failing at several ventures, he took up storekeeping in Concord, earning barely enough to support his wife and children during Henry's early years.

That wife—Henry's mother—had grown up in New Hampshire as Cynthia Dunbar. Besides having a grandfather stubbornly in favor of the British during the Revolutionary War, she also had several other relatives known for holding unpopular views or behaving rather strangely. For instance, her brother Charles was said to be the only person

alive with such a lack of ambition as well as common sense that he would fall asleep while shaving himself.

Yet Cynthia Dunbar Thoreau herself struck many of her neighbors as just as much of a character as her always sleepy brother. A large woman, towering a full head taller than her husband, she never hesitated to express her opinions on any subject—so she earned the reputation of being the most talkative woman in Concord. At a time when speaking out against the black slavery system of the American South still seemed extremely radical to most New Englanders, Mrs. Thoreau organized a women's antislavery society and held its meetings in her front parlor.

Nevertheless, nobody could say that she neglected her family. Most of the time, she had several needy relatives living under her roof—along with a few strangers, whose weekly payments supplemented the small income her husband brought home. Since she and her husband had four children, theirs was certainly a crowded household.

Henry, the third of these children, had an older sister and brother, and a younger sister, too. Both of the girls, Helen and Sophia, turned into the sort of independent, spirited women New England was noted for in those days. One became a teacher, the other a not very gifted artist, and neither of them ever married. Remaining closely tied to their childhood home, they were always a source of affectionate support for Henry.

But it was his brother John to whom Henry felt the strongest connection. Just two years apart in age, the Thoreau boys explored the woods around Concord together, fished in nearby rivers together, and attended school together. Much as they enjoyed each other's company, though, their personalities could hardly have been more different.

John was outgoing, carefree, a leader in schoolyard games, while the shy and silent Henry seemed "an odd stick" to most other boys. Also, his appearance was against him. Despite being thin as a rail, he had a surprisingly big nose, and his deep blue-gray eyes had a way of appearing to stare right through whatever he was looking at. Because Henry spent a lot of time reading, he was considered the more scholarly of the brothers, even though his marks on exams were not outstanding.

Only when it came to writing compositions did he really excel. And by the time he was eleven, he had already found that he liked writing about nature. In a small sheaf of papers saved from the Concord Academy of his day, one headed "The Seasons" has his name on it. The young Thoreau had started with a short poem:

Why do the seasons change? and why
Does Winter's stormy brow appear?
Is it the word of him on high
Who rules the changing varied year?

Then, giving up any further attempt to explain the mystery, Henry had proceeded to describe what happens as the seasons change, writing simply but observantly. Although this essay only hinted at the unusual mind he was developing, along with other early efforts it convinced his mother to focus her own ambition on him. Because a few of the men on her side of the family had attended Harvard College, she determined that this literarily inclined son of hers must follow in their footsteps.

The full cost for attending Harvard in those days was $179 a year, according to the college's catalog. By the time Henry finished his final year at the Concord Academy, Mrs. Thoreau had scraped together enough money to promise him a higher education if he passed Harvard's entrance exams. In the summer of 1833, when he was sixteen, he took this series of tests—and even though he came very close to failing Latin, Greek, and mathematics, he was accepted with about forty other young men as a member of the Class of 1837.

Only fifteen miles lay between Concord and Cambridge, where Harvard occupied a small cluster of old brick buildings. Across the Charles River not far away was Boston, but Henry found to his happy surprise that a short walk from his dormitory in practically any direction brought him to open fields. Almost daily during his college years, he went off at least briefly by himself to study the habits of birds and other wildlife in the Cambridge area.

But Henry's main refuge throughout his Harvard career was the institution's fine library. Unwilling to join in any lighthearted extracurricular activities— his fellow students regarded him as very standoffish—he spent long hours poring over poetry and natural science books, copying passages he admired. As far as his classes were concerned, he did just enough work to rank slightly above average.

Perhaps because Thoreau would eventually become famous for protesting against all sorts of established practices, there is a widely believed myth that he refused to accept his Harvard diploma when he graduated. However, the actual certificate still exists among a mass of other papers his relatives saved. It proves that he was awarded a Bachelor of Arts degree at the age of twenty, in the summer of 1837.

Yet his studies had not led him toward any of the three professions—the ministry or law or medicine—that most of his classmates entered. Still, he real-ized that he would have to earn his keep somehow. Like several of his relatives, he decided he might as well try teaching.

Immediately, Thoreau found an opening right in Concord at the grammar school where he had once been a pupil himself. Since the whole country was suffering then from an economic depression, it seemed that he was very lucky. But only two weeks after the term started, a member of the school committee paid a visit to see the new teacher at work.

When this upstanding pillar of the community found the classroom less than totally silent, he called Thoreau into the hall. He told him it was his duty to whip students who made the slightest noise or "the school would spoil." Thoreau stiffly nodded.

As soon as the committee member left, Thoreau picked out several pupils at random. Although he hated the idea of hurting them, he felt that he had to show the absurdity of such punishment. So he grasped the cane traditionally used for keeping discipline and did some whacking—then wrote a letter resigning his post.

All Thoreau accomplished was to make many people shake their heads over his foolishness in quitting a job that paid $500 a year, especially during a period when jobs were hard to find.

While caning might be cruel, couldn't he have administered a few light taps or else merely ignored the busybody's instructions? Thoreau told his family, though, that he just could not teach in any school where he was not allowed to teach his own way.

But another step he took soon afterward probably did even more to convince his neighbors of his oddity. Around twenty years earlier he had been christened David Henry Thoreau, and now he decided to change his legal name himself. Without asking any judge's permission, as law-abiding citizens were supposed to in such cases, he simply announced that henceforth he would be Henry David Thoreau.

Since he had always been called Henry anyhow, what possible difference could the change make? Thoreau never gave his own answer to this question. Yet perhaps he was influenced at least indirectly on this minor matter by the same man who had such a major influence on his whole outlook.

Ralph Waldo Emerson—the mere sound of his name could hardly be more impressive. Among those who analyze such matters, it is clear that the ringing *r*'s at the beginning and near the end create much of the grand resonance. Because a similar effect could be achieved by reversing the order of Thoreau's two given names, might a strong inner desire for a similar grandeur have had something to do with Thoreau's decision to become Henry David?

At any rate, there can be no doubt that right at this same period the young Thoreau came under Emerson's spell. Emerson had just published a masterly essay entitled "Nature," which had a profound impact on Thoreau's own thinking. Also, Emerson became a close neighbor of Thoreau's, as well as the most devoted friend he ever had.

Fourteen years older than Thoreau, Emerson had first attracted attention by preaching notably thoughtful sermons at the Old North Church in Boston. But he found being a minister too restricting. Instead, he began giving lectures open to the public at large, in which he stressed his belief that every person should rely more on the promptings of his or her own inner voice than on any established pattern of rules. Of course, this Emersonian doctrine of self-reliance deeply appealed to an individualist like Thoreau.

At least for the next several years, though, Thoreau's brother remained more important to him than anyone else. When John came home between terms from the school in a nearby town where he was teaching, they roamed the countryside together. They went out rowing on the local rivers together. They also took their small boat up the

Concord River, and the Merrimack, too, for a marvelous trip into New Hampshire.

They even both fell in love with the same young woman, the sister of a pupil at the private school they were by then running together. When Henry realized how John felt about Ellen Sewall, he stepped aside to let his older brother court her. Only after Ellen told John that she could not marry him did Henry try to win her himself. But she turned him down, too—it seems that her strictly religious father did not consider the Thoreau family sufficiently orthodox to suit his daughter.

Following this one disappointment, Henry never again gave any sign of wanting to get married. For two years he and John were very involved in operating their school. More at ease among children than adults, Henry liked teaching without having any committee looking over his shoulder. He especially enjoyed leading weekly nature walks, a new idea of his that helped to make the school gain an increasing number of pupils.

But suddenly, in 1841, his brother developed tuberculosis, the lung disease that was a leading cause of death until a cure for it was discovered around a hundred years later. When John could no longer continue teaching, Henry had no heart for continuing to operate the

school himself and closed it just as it was beginning really to thrive.

Emerson, seeing Henry at loose ends, invited him to come live in his own household, where a handyman was urgently needed. In return for keeping the garden free of weeds and coping with other maintenance jobs that defeated the scholarly Emerson, Thoreau received room and board plus unlimited access to a large collection of books. Besides, he had plenty of time for carrying out his aim of doing some serious writing himself.

So Thoreau was living as practically a member of Emerson's family when an awful blow struck him. John, who seemed to be recovering from his lung condition, cut a finger one morning while he was shaving—and this minor injury brought on the dreaded symptoms of lockjaw. With his face paralyzed, and suffering terrible pain, John died within just a few days.

Henry spent those days tirelessly taking care of John. When John died, Henry sank into a strange silence, and then he horrified his family by showing all the symptoms of lockjaw himself. Even if no cause could be discovered, it seemed that he, too, was doomed.

But gradually Henry began to recover, although he was not strong enough to leave his room for almost a month. Then it took several more

Henry David Thoreau. *Brown Brothers.*

months until he could walk outdoors or even think of working. He was twenty-five when his brother died in 1842, and his drastic reaction to this tragedy might have been at least partly caused by his own deep disappointment over having thus far failed to write anything he was satisfied with himself.

Emerson, from all the hours he had spent listening to Thoreau talk brilliantly on many subjects, still felt convinced that his young friend had a touch of genius. Hoping to bring him out of his depressed mood, he arranged an easy job for him teaching the young sons of a relative of his who lived on Staten Island, just a short ferry ride from New York City. Also, Emerson gave Thoreau letters of introduction to several prominent literary figures there.

Thoreau realized that he was being given a good opportunity to get some poems or magazine articles published, and he tried to take advantage of it. At least one of the men Emerson sent him to—Horace Greeley, the editor of the *New York Herald*—was very impressed by the originality of Thoreau's ideas. From then on he became something like Thoreau's literary agent, seeking writing assignments for him.

Still, Thoreau could not stand the hectic atmosphere of New York. In a letter to his family giving his impressions of the country's largest city, he wrote: "It is a thousand times meaner than I could have imagined. It will give me something to hate . . ." So his relatives were hardly surprised when he returned home after just a few months there.

Back in Concord, Thoreau buckled down to work at a little factory adjoining his family's house. For his Uncle Charles had amazed everybody by doing something sensible—he had acquired the rights, while wandering around New Hampshire, to mine a substance called plumbago, from which the "lead" in lead pencils could be extracted. As a result, Henry's father had begun operating a pencil-making business in what had once been a woodshed.

Yet it was Henry, with his gift for fixing almost anything, who figured out how to make pencils more efficiently than any competitors. He worked hard at improving the procedure so the business would yield a good profit. But was this a reasonable goal for someone who much preferred reading and writing and, above all, communing with nature?

Henry thought not. It struck him with increasing force, during the period he spent at the factory, that work like this left him hardly any energy for the activities he really cared about. Instead of spending six days a week striving to earn money and only one day doing as he liked, why couldn't he turn this ridiculous arrangement around?

Toward that end, early in the spring of 1845 Thoreau embarked on a great experiment. A few months before his twenty-eighth birthday, he started cutting down pine trees in a patch of woods about two miles outside Concord. This land on the edge of Walden Pond was owned by Emerson, who had gladly offered to let his friend clear a space there and then put up a small cabin.

Fittingly, Thoreau moved into his hut on July 4, the anniversary of another famous declaration of independence.

During the two years Thoreau spent in the woods, he finished a book he called *A Week on the Concord and Merrimack Rivers.* Although it has never attracted many readers, at least it satisfied its author's yearning to write something that might serve as his own memorial to his brother. But two other much more important literary works also had their beginnings while he was living in the woods.

One stemmed from a brief but extraordinary adventure during Thoreau's second summer at Walden. For the past several years he had refused as a matter of principle to pay a small tax that Massachusetts levied on every male citizen. Because the state did nothing to oppose black slavery, he reasoned, in effect it

was supporting this hateful system. So he felt a duty to make his own antislavery protest in the only way available to him.

As a result, one day when Thoreau walked into Concord to visit his family, he was arrested by the local constable, then put in jail. He spent just one night behind bars—an aunt of his could not bear this disgrace, and she paid his tax the next morning. Even so, Thoreau wrote an essay entitled "Civil Disobedience"—which would prove to be one of the most influential documents in the world's history.

It was "Civil Disobedience" that Mahatma Gandhi, in India, and Martin Luther King, Jr., in Alabama, both read while they were imprisoned for leading protests against injustice. Later, they both testified that Thoreau's lofty words had given them renewed courage to defy governmental policies their own consciences told them were wrong. Wherever rebellious individuals have been persecuted for their beliefs, very likely they, too, quoted from the same source in their defense.

Of course, the second of Thoreau's lasting contributions that stemmed from his solitary experiment was his classic *Walden.* Ever since his college years, he had kept a journal where he carefully wrote down his daily thoughts. In this, throughout the time he spent

Walden Pond, near Concord, Massachusetts. *Concord Free Public Library.*

alone, he jotted notes that during the next eight years he kept polishing and repolishing.

In 1854, at last he was ready to have his account of his solitary experiment published. By then Thoreau had made several trips up to Maine and to Cape Cod, and he had written magazine articles about these experiences. He had also delivered a few dozen lectures, none of them drawing much attention. With the appearance of *Walden*, he hoped that at last he would achieve recognition as a major literary figure.

But Thoreau was truly ahead of his own time. Although some critics commented favorably on "his habit of original thinking," the majority either ignored him or agreed with a reader who commented: "He is a good-for-nothing, selfish, crab-like sort of chap."

Nevertheless, Thoreau seemed to be contented with his life. For a time he took over running the pencil factory, until larger manufacturers captured the market. Then he became one of the most skilled land surveyors in the Concord area. Yet he still managed to spend many happy hours just roaming the countryside, collecting specimens of rare plants or rocks to add to the bins of his treasures that made his attic room in his family's house practically a museum of local natural history.

Indeed, Thoreau was aiming to write a new book providing a comprehensive picture of nature's amazing variety right in the Concord vicinity. To him, the preserving of unspoiled areas near every settlement was vitally important. As he had put it in *Walden:*

Our village life would stagnate if it were not for the unexplored forests and meadows which surround it. We need the tonic of wildness—to wade sometimes in marshes where the bittern and the meadow-hen lurk, and hear the booming of the snipe. . . . We can never have enough of nature.

But Thoreau was not able to complete his ambitious natural history project. In 1856, when he was only thirty-nine, he showed alarming symptoms of having tuberculosis himself. Till then he had seemed amazingly sturdy, able to walk faster and longer than practically anybody else, besides being a strong swimmer, a good oarsman, an excellent ice skater. Now, however, he tired so easily that he had to limit himself to short strolls in the family garden.

Yet Thoreau did not give up hope. He still kept writing daily entries in his journal and, during periods when he felt a little better, went by railroad to visit supposedly more healthful mountain areas. Even after a difficult trip to the dry climate of Minnesota failed to accomplish the healing miracle that had been predicted, he remained in cheerful spirits.

On May 6, 1862, about two months short of his forty-fifth birthday, Thoreau died peacefully in Concord, surrounded by his family. At his funeral, his friend Emerson said: "The country knows not yet, or in the least part, how great a son it has lost."

As just one sign of how highly Thoreau has come to be valued, in Concord today there is a museum displaying some of his possessions. Also, a nature preserve has been created at the nearby Walden Pond, with a replica of his simple cabin. But the site of his solitary experiment is no longer anything like as isolated as it was during his era—in the 1980s, Thoreau admirers had a hard time preventing the construction of a tall new office building that would have overlooked it.

Alfred Russel Wallace

1823–1913   English collector of plants and animals who, on his own, arrived at the same theory of evolution that made Darwin world famous

When he was fourteen, Alfred Wallace had to give up going to school because of the severe money troubles afflicting his family.

During the next eleven years, however, he learned a lot about plants on his own—looking for wildflowers while he worked as a land surveyor and spending many evenings studying a cheap botany book he had luckily discovered. In addition, a friend he made at a library turned him into an enthusiastic collector of beetles.

Then, when Wallace was twenty-five, he boldly left England to search for rare birds and butterflies and beetles along the Amazon River in Brazil. Nobody sent him on this grand adventure or arranged any of its details. He planned it himself, hoping he would earn enough to pay his expenses by shipping back specimens that museums as well as amateur naturalists were eager to purchase.

Wallace's four years in South America—followed by eight years of roaming the tropical islands between Asia and Australia—established him as one of his era's outstanding natural history collectors. Also, he wrote many articles and books about his findings.

Yet the main reason Wallace continues to interest students today is that he independently arrived at the same theory about the evolution of all living creatures that brought Charles Darwin lasting international fame. Instead of claiming equal credit, though, the unassuming Wallace told his friends: "I really feel thankful that it has *not* been left to me to give the theory to the world."

Many scientists undoubtedly felt thankful, too, for although Wallace always showed very sound judgment as a naturalist, on various other subjects his views were less reliable. As just one instance, he strongly believed that by examining the shape of a person's head it was possible to make predictions about the individual's character. But perhaps the underlying reason why Wallace never won wider acclaim, in a country where ancestry often counted more than achievement, was that he did not come from "the right sort" of family.

Unlike the solidly respectable Darwin—his senior by fourteen years—Alfred Russel Wallace had started life with several disadvantages. He was born on January 8, 1823, in an isolated village called Usk, located in the sparsely populated mountainous western region of the British Isles known as Wales. His parents had moved there from London, aiming to economize by living amid simple rural folk.

Alfred's father, Thomas Vere Wallace, was fond of reading poetry and he assured his children they were descended from a Scottish hero who had won many battles hundreds of years ear-

lier. He also said that a Wallace they were distantly related to had been an admiral in the British Navy. Yet he never spoke about any closer connections, beyond saying that both of his parents had died during his youth.

But, having inherited a small income, Thomas Wallace had been able to live a fairly carefree life in London—until he married Mary Anne Greenell, from the outlying town of Hertford. She, too, was an orphan with a small inheritance. When Mr. and Mrs. Wallace soon began having children, however, the modest sums they both regularly received could no longer pay all of their expenses.

Mr. Wallace tried to earn more money by starting a new literary magazine. Not very prudently, for he had no experience at all with such ventures, he spent a good part of his assets to put out the first issue. And he lost every penny.

Besides pressing financial worries, however, the Wallaces also suffered a series of tragedies involving their children. Their eldest daughter died in infancy while they were still in London and, after they moved all the way to Usk, two other girls were taken from them by lung disease.

Alfred was the seventh of his parents' eight children. But owing to these deaths in the family, he knew only one older sister and two older brothers, as well as a younger brother born two years after him.

When Alfred was five, his parents finally gave up their experiment of living in a stone cottage in Wales and trying to grow their own food. Instead, they went to Hertford, just north of London, where Mrs. Wallace had spent her own girlhood. Even if money woes continued to torment Mr. Wallace—the family rented five different increasingly small houses during the next eight years—at least Alfred had something like a normal childhood there.

It was during these Hertford years that he attended a local grammar school and received a good basic education. Nevertheless, his memories of this period would always be shadowed by private miseries. For he was an unusually tall boy, measuring an inch above six feet by the time he was twelve, so he thought that he stuck out like a sore thumb wherever he went. What's more, he constantly felt disgraced when he had to appear before his classmates wearing ill-fitting, hand-me-down clothing.

In this period, both Mr. and Mrs. Wallace were attempting to earn money by giving various kinds of lessons at home, while Alfred's nearly grown sister Fanny enterprisingly was learning to speak French in the household of a French family so that she would be able to teach that language. As for his older brothers, William had become a land surveyor and John was serving as an apprentice to a London builder who had promised to turn him into a master carpenter. Only Alfred and Herbert, the youngest in the family, remained with their parents in Hertford.

Toward the end of 1836, however, the Wallace fortunes dipped even further. Then a move to a cottage so tiny that there would be no room for Alfred was decided upon. At the turn of the new year, just after his fourteenth birthday, he left the last home he would have until he finally established one of his own almost thirty years later.

Temporarily, Alfred was sent to share his brother John's room in London. There, he waited for word from his brother William, operating a small surveying business in Wales, that he could afford to pay an assistant. Although Alfred stayed only six months with John, that brief London period significantly influenced the shy fourteen-year-old boy.

Six days a week, Alfred accompanied John to the carpentry shop where he worked. Almost without realizing it, Alfred learned so much about using tools that from then on he never doubted his own ability to get along practically anywhere because he felt confident of always being able to fix or make whatever he needed.

In addition, almost every evening the brothers walked to the meeting hall of a workmen's club. At this club, sometimes a visiting speaker gave a lecture. Other times, everybody present participated in a general discussion. All sorts of topics came up, from politics to current excitements like a French doctor's demonstrations of his power to hypnotize people.

Wallace ever after would believe that his whole outlook on life had been expanded remarkably by the "progressive" talk he heard on these London evenings. Still, it was not until he left the city early in the summer of 1837 to join his brother William in Wales that signs pointing toward his own future career began to emerge. Back amid the hills and valleys of his early childhood, he suddenly realized how much he valued the beauties of nature.

Every day as he accompanied William on surveying expeditions, Alfred would catch himself searching for wildflowers instead of concentrating on his measuring chain. Soon he began collecting blossoms and bringing them to the house where they boarded so he could try out different ways of drying them. But it bothered him that he didn't even know the proper scientific name for any of his specimens.

At last, in 1841 when he was eighteen, Alfred started to learn the fundamentals of plant science from a book he bought with one of his hard-earned shillings. During his every spare minute he pored over this botany text, which gave complete descriptions of every family of plants ever found in the British Isles. Many years later, writing his autobiography, Wallace called his discovery of this book "the turning point of my life."

Yet seven more years would elapse until he actually embarked on his career as a plant collector. By then he had managed all by himself to acquire a sound grounding in every aspect of botany, but he also had to keep striving to support himself. After hard times made it impossible for William to continue employing him, Alfred was obliged to undertake some other line of work.

The job he got as assistant to the headmaster of a not very thriving school for boys in the small city of Leicester did not particularly interest him. Nevertheless, the year and a half he spent in Leicester had a crucial effect on his future—because at the public library there Wallace met a fascinating fellow named Henry Bates, whose main goal in life was to collect more kinds of beetles than anybody else ever had.

Thanks to Bates, Wallace took up

insect-collecting himself. Every week-end, the two of them went out searching for rare beetles. They captured hundreds of specimens, which Bates showed Wallace how to preserve. Yet even if England appeared to have an amazing variety of beetles, both young men began to dream of someday going off to a more exotic part of the world where many more types surely could be discovered.

After Wallace got involved with another stint of surveying, and then once more found himself jobless, a spectacular idea occurred to him. Why couldn't he and Bates try right away to support themselves by doing what they most enjoyed? So he set about looking for a London agent who would take charge of selling any rare insects or other natural phenomena they shipped back to England from some distant area.

Wallace quickly found a London businessman who encouraged his plan. After consulting many books, as well as experts at the British Museum, he decided that a good place for inexperienced explorers to seek natural history specimens would be in the Amazon jungles of South America. There, navigable rivers and friendly natives would make the quest easier than in some other tropical regions.

Since Bates proved more than willing to accompany Wallace to South America, the two of them boarded a ship named the *Mischief* in Liverpool on April 20, 1848—bound for Para in Brazil, at the mouth of the Amazon River.

Wallace and Bates landed there a little more than a month later. Both were immediately enchanted by the beauty and strangeness of the butterflies and birds they saw everywhere around them. A few months later, readers of a natural history magazine back in England began to notice a new series of advertisements, starting with:

TO NATURALISTS

Samuel Stevens, Natural History Agent, No. 24 Bloomsbury Street, begs to announce that he has recently received from South America TWO beautiful Consignments of INSECTS of all orders in very fine Condition, collected in the province of Para, containing numbers of very rare and some new species, also a few LAND and FRESHWATER SHELLS, and some BIRD SKINS . . . all of which are for Sale by Private Contract.

Soon, though, Wallace and Bates agreed that they would have a better chance of finding valuable new specimens if they traveled in different directions—thereby doubling the amount of territory they could cover. Throughout their lives they would remain close friends, but from then on they did their collecting separately. After Bates went off on his own, Wallace hired native guides who led him deep into the Amazon interior during the next several years.

In letters to his agent Stevens back in London, Wallace vividly described waterfalls and whirlpools that only a few other Europeans ever had seen. Sailing aboard all sorts of primitive vessels, he found gorgeous butterflies as yet unknown to any scientist. Over the years Stevens published portions of many of these letters along with his advertisements, clearly hoping to arouse more interest on the part of prospective buyers by giving them the story of how the rare tropical specimens he was offering had been obtained.

It is fortunate that this kind of record of Wallace's explorations in Brazil was preserved. During his four years there, he survived many perils—and amassed a matchless personal collection of many thousand specimens, which he expected to sell gradually after he returned to England so he would have money to live on while he pursued further scientific studies. But on his way home, his luck ran out.

The ship *Helen*, carrying Wallace toward London in the summer of 1852, caught fire. Suddenly billows of smoke cut him off from his twenty big boxes of butterflies and beetles packed away in the vessel's hold. He could not even rescue his notebooks in his cabin, containing the full details of his entire adventure that he hoped to use as the basis for writing a book about his South American experience.

Instead, Wallace had to clamber down a rope into a lifeboat supplied with just a few tins of meat, some biscuits, and a cask of drinking water. For ten days and nights he sat wedged into a narrow space, alternately baking under the tropical sun or being doused by salty spray, as sailors from the abandoned *Helen* steered toward Bermuda, about seven hundred miles away. Then on the eleventh morning one of the seamen gave a joyful cry: "Sail ho!"

Wallace and his companions were picked up by a ship bound for London that had barely enough food aboard for its own crew. Following his miraculous rescue, he still had to endure hunger—and three severe storms—before he finally arrived in England eighty days after leaving Brazil. "Oh, glorious day!" Wallace wrote in a letter on the October evening he landed.

Wallace was further elated to find himself the center of attention when he attended meetings of naturalists' groups. The welcome he received encouraged him to write articles for their magazines about some of his South American observations. By using the long letters he had written Stevens to refresh his memory he was even able, after all, to write a book he called *Travels on the Amazon*.

However, Wallace's loss of his twenty

Alfred Russel Wallace in 1853. *Courtesy Department Library Services, American Museum of Natural History.*

boxes of specimens hampered him seriously, for as soon as the money that he had already been paid by Stevens ran out, he would be penniless again. Although he had vowed in the *Helen's* lifeboat that, if his life was somehow saved, he would never again cross an ocean, only shortly after arriving in London he began planning his next plant-collecting expedition.

In later years, Wallace would say that losing all his South American material had perhaps been a blessing in disguise. Otherwise, he explained, he probably would have spent the rest of his days in some rural district of England, living the uneventful life of a devoted amateur naturalist.

Instead, early in 1854 the thirty-one-year-old Wallace sailed halfway around the world to investigate a region said to be richer in plant and animal life than any other part of the globe. During the next eight years, he gathered over 100,000 specimens—including many types that had never before been available for study by European experts. Also, during interludes when heavy rains or attacks of fever prevented him from going out collecting, he did the important thinking and writing that would turn him into a leading figure in a great scientific drama.

The area Wallace had chosen to explore was Malaysia, or the Malay archipelago. This chain of islands stretched over a four-thousand-mile expanse of tropical sea southeast of Asia and included the East Indies (known at an earlier period as the Spice Islands), as well as other lesser groups closer to Australia. Wallace visited every major Malaysian island, besides numerous smaller ones, so he saw an astounding variety of plant and animal life that set his active mind to seeking explanations for some perplexing questions.

Eventually, Wallace would draw a new line on his map of the region, for he had noticed that plants and animals prevalent above his line resembled those found in Asia, while those on nearby islands below it were more like Australian species. Thus, he surmised, there must have been ancient shifts of land masses that would explain the differences—and his "Wallace's Line" opened up a new branch of natural science devoted to studying the geographical distribution of species.

But far more momentously, in February of 1855 when Wallace was confined to a hut on Borneo by heavy rain, he began pondering the basic mystery of how new species originated. The result was a paper he wrote, proposing a theory of evolution remarkably similar to the world-shaking theory that Charles Darwin had been quietly developing in England for almost twenty years.

Wallace's paper appeared in a natural history magazine that autumn, but it did not arouse any stir because Wallace—and Darwin—had not yet arrived at a solution to a crucial problem: What caused the evolutionary changes that had kept occurring down through the centuries?

Then, in February of 1858 Wallace fell ill on an island called Ternate. One afternoon while he was resting during a siege of chills and fever, as he later wrote, "there suddenly flashed upon me the idea of the survival of the fittest . . ." He spent the next few days writing a paper in which he carefully explained his inspiration, then mailed the paper to Darwin who was known to be assembling all available material on the subject of evolution.

By one of the most stunning coincidences ever recorded, the same idea had struck Darwin almost simultaneously—but he had not yet written any report about it. As he read Wallace's paper, an emotion the high-minded Darwin felt ashamed of overcame him.

Having devoted so much time to conceiving a new theory of immense scientific significance, was he now to lose the credit for all his work because of his own delay in publishing anything about it?

However, when Darwin showed Wallace's paper to a pair of friends who were highly respected scientists, they immediately reassured him. They told him to write a brief summary of his own conclusions, along with a pledge that he would complete his book about evolution as soon as possible. At a historic meeting of England's leading naturalists on July 1, 1858, Wallace's paper and also Darwin's summary of his impending book were both read aloud—in effect, the theory of evolution was jointly introduced.

But it was not until the following year, while Wallace was still collecting Malaysian insects, that publication of Darwin's monumental *The Origin of Species* gave evolution much wider publicity. Despite the storm of controversy this book aroused, it also ensured that Charles Darwin rather than Alfred Russel Wallace would go down in history as one of the greatest scientific thinkers who had ever lived.

Still, nobody agreed more strongly with this verdict than Wallace himself. Right after reading *The Origin of Species*, he wrote to a relative: "Mr. Darwin has given the world a *new science*, and his name should, in my opinion, stand above that of every philosopher of ancient or modern times. The force of admiration can no further go!!!"

Wallace also sent a letter to his beetle-collecting friend Bates in which he confessed: "I do honestly believe that with however much patience I had worked and experimented on the subject, I could *never have approached* the completeness of [Darwin's] book, its vast accumulation of evidence, its overwhelming argument, and its admirable tone and spirit."

Yet even if Wallace self-effacingly accepted being overshadowed by Darwin, he still achieved at least a limited renown. After he returned to England in 1862, he much enjoyed visiting and exchanging letters with England's leading scientists—including his hero, Darwin—besides writing numerous papers about rare species he had studied.

In 1866, at the age of forty-three, Wallace married Annie Mitten, the eighteen-year-old daughter of a noted naturalist. With their two children, Will and Violet, they lived happily in various little houses despite recurring money troubles that must have reminded Wallace of his own childhood. Even his 1869 book *The Malay Archipelago*, which attracted more readers than anything else he ever wrote, did not earn enough to make him comfortable financially.

At last, though, in 1881—as the result of behind-the-scenes organizing by Darwin—Wallace was awarded an annual pension from the British government in recognition of his studies concerning the plant and animal life of distant portions of the British Empire.

An illustration plate from Alfred Russel Wallace's *The Malay Archipelago*, 1869.

For the rest of his long life he continued his writing, but he wrote more often about political and social problems than about science as he grew older.

Yet the British scientific establishment gave the aging Wallace several gold medals. No doubt his good sportsmanship in accepting Darwin's superior claim to fame accounted for some of these awards, but his own unusual com-

Alfred Russel Wallace and one of his handwritten letters. *Courtesy Department Library Services, American Museum of Natural History.*

bination of talents also was being recognized. As one writer would sum up Wallace's career: "Not a trained scientist, he lacked the prodigious range of Darwin's knowledge but he was an indefatigable collector both of specimens and facts, and he thought about what he collected with originality and vigor."

At the ripe age of ninety, Wallace collapsed with a heart attack. He died on November 7, 1913, at his Dorset home overlooking the sea in southwestern England.

Gilbert White

1720–1793   English clergyman, naturalist, and writer

Even today, visitors have no easy time finding the old English village of Selborne. It is five miles from any main road, and only winding country lanes connect it with the outside world. Nevertheless, thousands of people drive there every year—because a gifted amateur naturalist named Gilbert White wrote a remarkable book about it two hundred years ago.

The title of White's masterpiece is *The Natural History of Selborne*, which may not sound very fascinating. Yet, according to those who keep track of such matters, among all the books ever written in the English language just the works of Shakespeare and two other great poets have been reprinted more often.

But why should a book devoted to such a narrow topic have achieved such lasting popularity?

Over the years, nature lovers and literary experts have offered a variety of answers. Most of them agree, though, on the main reason for *Selborne*'s great success. It is that this book, supposedly all about birds and trees, somehow gives readers the feeling of having met a truly inspiring human being—Gilbert White himself.

Besides being an exceptionally keen observer of everything around him, White was also a warmhearted man deeply satisfied by the simple life he lived. So the picture of him and his peaceful surroundings that shines through the pages of *Selborne* gives the book a rare sort of charm. Indeed, the noted American poet James Russell Lowell once called it "the journal of Adam in Paradise."

However, adding a little touch of mystery, no actual picture of White has ever been discovered. Nor do we know much about his inner feelings. Even so, it is still possible to piece together his own story from the hints he gave in his writing and the facts his relatives provided after his death.

Gilbert White was born on July 18, 1720—right in the isolated village he would later make famous—at the home of the grandfather for whom he was named. That Gilbert White was serving as the vicar of Selborne's old stone church. While both sides of the future naturalist's family could boast of a few fairly eminent ancestors, such as a lord mayor of the city of Oxford, for the most part his male relatives were respected if not very prosperous clergymen.

But Gil's father had studied law in London. John White lost interest in practicing his profession, however, after he married Anne Holt, the daughter of a well-off country gentleman. Because his wife had inherited some money, he spent most of his time from then on playing his harpsichord or puttering in his garden.

Gil was his parents' first child. Soon after his birth, they brought him to a house of their own in a town not far from London. Although nobody wrote

down any details about this early period of his life, three very sad events did get recorded.

Three times during the next several years, Gil's mother had babies who survived only briefly. But following this series of tragedies, healthy new babies kept arriving every year or two; eventually, Gil would have five younger brothers and two sisters, all warmly fond of one another throughout their lives.

When Gil was nine, his grandfather in Selborne died. His elderly grandmother moved out of the vicarage then, into a house on the other side of the village's only street—and to keep her company, the entire John White family moved there, too. So, after all, Gil grew up living just about a hundred yards from his birthplace.

The Whites' vine-covered brick house was called the Wakes in those days because a family of that name had lived there for a long time. Today, over two hundred years later, the same building is still standing, and it looks almost as it did during the 1700s. But now it is called the Gilbert White Museum.

The building's large garden has also been kept very much as it was two centuries ago. Despite the many changes elsewhere in modern England, even the hilly rural vistas in every direction have remained practically the same. So visitors to Selborne can easily see why the young White became so absorbed by exploring this environment.

If a budding naturalist had searched every part of Britain, he could not have found a better locale in which to pursue his studies. Beyond its unspoiled beauty, the Selborne area provides a surprising variety of plant and animal life owing to its varied soil types—from clay to chalky. Also, its climate is moderated by the hills that surround it.

Yet the very isolation fostered by these hills probably has been the most important factor in keeping Selborne almost like a nature preserve. As the crow flies, the village and its sparsely populated farming environs are only about fifty miles southwest of the vast city of London. But their sheltered setting continues to discourage the kind of development that often makes a landscape less hospitable to birds and wildflowers.

Back in Gilbert White's era, of course, Selborne was much harder to reach than it is today. For the village already had a long history, and the old paths that led to it had gradually been worn down until they had sunk far below the surface of the ground on either side of them. Since some of these tracks were as deep as sixteen or eighteen feet, with the branches of bordering bushes or trees forming practically a roof over

them, they were really more like tunnels than roads.

So travelers often got lost while seeking to find their way through a sort of maze of twisting and turning tunnels. Furthermore, during rainy weather the sunken paths became rivers of mud, and then even the bravest horsemen might hesitate to enter them. In a harsh winter, when snow blocked every approach to the village, it might be completely cut off from the rest of the country.

Although these roads caused many problems, they still were cherished as a symbol of Selborne's great age—it was at least a thousand years old by the time of Gil's birth. Indeed, some of the earliest kings of England had regularly visited the area to hunt game in nearby forests.

During that distant past, a sturdy yew tree had been planted right in front of Selborne's church. Today, the distance around the trunk of this historic tree is an amazing forty-one feet. When Gilbert White himself measured it, the yew was already twenty-three feet in girth.

His description of it, however, along with practically everything else he wrote that has been saved, was set down in his maturity. Only two brief notations remain from his boyhood. On March 31, 1736, when he was sixteen, Gil jot-

A view of Selborne, England. *North Wind Picture Archives*.

ted: "A flock of wild Geese flew North." Then, that April 6: "The cuckoo heard."

So we know that, even as a youth, White liked to keep track of birds. From these two clues, later admirers of his writing have deduced that he must have been the sort of boy who loved roaming outdoors more than anything else. Still, all we can be sure of is that he began his formal education around the age of fourteen.

Probably Gil had been given lessons by his father up until then. At any rate, for the better part of the next several years he boarded at the home of a clergyman who kept a boys' school—in the town of Basingstoke, about fifteen miles from Selborne. With other sons of moderately well-off families, he was prepared there to enter one of Britain's leading universities.

White was admitted to Oxford in 1739, at the age of nineteen. But on the very date he received word that he had been accepted, his mother died. We can guess that, beyond his sorrow, Gil may have felt hesitant about leaving his home, because he delayed going to college for a full semester.

Yet it seems to have been assumed by all concerned that he should aim to be ordained as a member of the Church of England clergy. Toward that end, four years of undergraduate training were necessary—and then several additional years of religious studies.

Still, the Oxford of Gil's time had a far-from-strict atmosphere. While he was living there he devoted many hours to lighthearted amusements, such as boating and hosting wine-drinking parties. In addition, though, he won a prize for being an outstanding student at the 1743 ceremony at which he received his Bachelor of Arts degree.

From the standpoint of White's future readers, however, the most important part of his entire Oxford experience was the lifelong friendship he formed with a fellow student named John Mulso. Mulso delighted in writing letters. Since dozens of the cheerful, chatty letters he addressed to "Dear Gil" over the next several decades somehow did get saved, these provide a mine of information about the daily life and even the appearance of the celebrated naturalist.

Mulso himself was richer and also better connected than White, being the nephew of a bishop. Nevertheless, he felt lucky to have become Gil's friend— and he constantly marveled at Gil's serene outlook on life as well as his gentle wit and his keen powers of observation. Apparently, Mulso perceived before anybody else that Gilbert White was a very special person.

Outwardly, White did not look at all impressive. Besides being a small man, slender and only about five feet three inches tall, he was quiet and unassuming. Also, even though he most fortunately recovered from a siege of smallpox soon after he earned his bachelor's degree, the disease left a few scars on his face. Perhaps these were the reason he never sat for any artist to draw his portrait, as most of his relatives did in those days long before cameras and snapshots.

White was not so shy, though, that he avoided the society of young women. On the contrary, it seemed for a time that he and Mulso's lively sister Hester—"Hecky" to her whole family— might be on the verge of becoming engaged. Other romantic rumors linked him with the daughter of an Oxford merchant and various female visitors to Selborne.

But until White finally was ordained in 1749, when he was twenty-nine, he could not seriously think of marrying because he did not have enough money to support a wife. By the time he completed his studies, though, another compelling interest kept him from taking on any new responsibilities.

This overwhelming interest was the garden at his family's home in Selborne—as well as all the varied birds and other natural wonders in the Selborne vicinity.

If White could have looked forward to securing the position his grandfather had held as vicar of the village's church, his personal life might have turned out

very differently. However, he could never be given this post. Under the prevailing system for making clerical appointments, only men who had taken their religious training at a specific branch of Oxford were eligible for it.

Why, then, had White not followed precisely in his grandfather's footsteps and enrolled in that branch? The answer must be that he simply had not realized ten years earlier how much Selborne meant to him. Indeed, during the years while he was studying at Oxford, he often paid lengthy visits to friends or relatives in other parts of England— and relished these opportunities for inspecting different kinds of landscapes.

Yet White could not bear the prospect of living elsewhere for the rest of his life, as he would have to if he were to become the vicar in some distant parish. Instead, he made a sort of compromise. In order to stay in Selborne, over a period of more than forty years he filled a lowly post that prevented him from ever marrying.

For White did not, after all, seek the comfortable income and the prestige that came with being the clergyman in charge of a parish. Ordinarily, Church of England priests spent only a few years right after being ordained serving as a vicar's assistant, or curate. White, however, remained a curate throughout his entire career.

Even so, he had a wonderfully happy if uneventful life. Beloved by his brothers and sisters, he kept in close touch with all of them after they married and set up homes of their own. When he was thirty-eight the death of his father, who had been ailing for many years, left him alone in the house Selborne still called the Wakes. But regular visits from his relatives kept him from feeling lonely.

While performing his not-very-time-consuming churchly duties, White had plenty of leisure for making his garden a showplace. He planted melons and apricot trees, he designed new beds of flowers, he laid out inviting paths including a picturesque zigzag trail climbing the steep hill behind his home, and at its top, he built a thatched-roof hut where he often held tea parties for his young nieces and nephews.

Also, despite the fact that White rarely left his native village during the next forty years, he developed into a great naturalist.

In his garden and in his daily walks around Selborne, Gilbert White identified thousands of different specimens of plant and animal life that he carefully studied. Among them were a few types of birds or mice never before noticed by specialists. Still, these comparatively minor additions to the sum total of scientific knowledge would hardly have

spread his name beyond the footnotes of an occasional heavy book.

But White's many years of observing accomplished something far more significant. At the time he began keeping detailed jottings of what he actually saw outdoors, natural scientists were mostly occupied with indoor activity like classifying plants or animals into families of related types. In effect, White proved that nature itself was the best possible laboratory.

Besides demonstrating the importance of field studies, though, he also showed that dedicated amateurs can make a real contribution to science by recording their own data about the habits of particular birds or about the unexpected locations of particular plants. Indeed, White's example would inspire countless other amateur observers to collect similar information—after they read *The Natural History of Selborne*, which he finally began working on when he was around sixty years old.

Modest as White was, he might merely have continued jotting down private notes about his findings if two scientists he met on a visit to London had not urged him to publish a book. They convinced him that a full description of his own area's plant and animal life would surely be welcomed by the country's scientific community. What's more, since the study of nature had lately become a favorite hobby among rural English landowners, wouldn't such a book interest them, too?

Because White still hesitated to put himself forward in any way, he wrote his small volume as a series of impersonal letters to the two men who had prodded him into embarking on the project. Nevertheless, he could not really disguise the special flavor of his own personality. And his ability to write very clearly made even rather complicated matters easy to understand.

For instance, here is a part of his detailed account of how a particular bird built its nest:

About the middle of May, if the weather be fine, the martin begins to think in earnest of providing a mansion for its family. The crust or shell of this nest seems to be formed of such dirt or loam as comes most readily to hand, and is tempered and wrought together with little bits of broken straws to render it tough and tenacious. As this bird often builds against a perpendicular wall without any projecting ledge under, it requires its utmost efforts to get the first foundation firmly fixed, so that it may safely carry the superstructure. On this occasion the bird not only clings with its claws, but partly supports itself by strongly inclining its tail against the wall, making that a fulcrum; and, thus steadied, it works and plasters the materials into the face of the brick or stone.

The frontispiece engraving, "Queen Anne Viewing the Red Deer in Wolmer Forest," from an 1853 edition of White's *The Natural History of Selborne*.

And, in another passage, this time about the feeding habits of bats, White wrote:

I was much entertained last summer with a tame bat, which would take flies out of a person's hand. If you gave it anything to eat, it brought its wings round before the mouth, hovering and hiding its head in the manner of birds of prey when they feed. The adroitness it showed in shearing off the wings of the flies, which were always rejected, was worthy of observation, and pleased me much. Insects seem to be most acceptable, though it did not refuse raw flesh when offered; so that, the notion that bats go down chimneys and gnaw men's bacon, seems no improbable story.

White had no difficulty arranging for his manuscript to be published because one of his brothers was a London book dealer who issued it himself. Right from its first printing in 1789, this obscure clergyman's little volume received high praise. "A more delightful, or more original work than Mr. White's History of Selborne has seldom been published," one early reviewer wrote.

However, White was sixty-nine years old when his book began diverting readers—in the same year that, across the Atlantic, George Washington became the first president of the new United States. White was so set in his own habits by then that his emergence as an admired author made little difference in his daily routine.

He still rose early for his daily walk around Selborne. In between assisting at weddings and funerals or Sunday church services, he continued to inspect his fruit trees and to supervise improvements along his favorite zigzag path up the hill behind his house. Also, he joyously welcomed visits from his many nieces and nephews as well as their children. Altogether, there were sixty-two offspring of his seven brothers and sisters who brightened the old age of their dear Uncle Gil.

While officiating at a funeral one rainy day only four years after his celebrated book was published, Gilbert White caught a severe cold. A few days later, on June 26, 1793, less than a month before he would have turned seventy-three, he died peacefully at his home in Selborne.

Further Reading

Titles marked by an asterisk are most suitable for young readers.

GENERAL

*Bailey, Liberty Hyde. *How Plants Got Their Names*. New York: Dover, 1963.

Comstock, Anna Botsford. *Handbook of Nature Study*. Ithaca, N.Y.: Cornell University Press, 1967.

Dictionary of Scientific Biography. 16 vols. New York: Charles Scribner's Sons, 1973.

*Lampton, Christopher. *Endangered Species*. New York: Franklin Watts, 1988.

*Leopold, Aldo. *A Sand County Almanac and Sketches Here and There*. New York: Oxford University Press, 1987.

*Meadows, Jack. *The Great Scientists*. New York: Oxford University Press, 1987.

**The New Book of Popular Science*. 6 vols. New York: Grolier, 1984.

*Nickelsburg, Janet. *Ecology: Habitats, Niches and Food Chains*. Philadelphia: J. B. Lippincott, 1969.

Peattie, Donald Culross. *Green Laurels*. Garden City, N.Y.: Garden City Publishing Co., 1938.

*Rossbacher, Lisa A. *Recent Revolutions in Geology*. New York: Franklin Watts, 1986.

*Strong, Douglas H. *Defenders and Dreamers: American Conservationists*. Lincoln: University of Nebraska Press, 1988.

*Wayne, Bennett, ed. *They Loved the Land*. Champaign, Ill.: Garrard, 1974.

AGASSIZ

Agassiz, Louis. *My Life and Correspondence*. Elizabeth C. Agassiz, ed. 2 vols. Boston, 1885.

Lurie, Edward. *Louis Agassiz: A Life in Science*. Chicago: University of Chicago Press, 1960.

*Robinson, Mabel L. *Runner of the Mountain Tops: The Life of Louis Agassiz*. New York: Random House, 1939.

ANDREWS

Andrews, Roy Chapman. *An Explorer Comes Home*. Garden City: Doubleday, 1947.

*Archer, Jules. *From Whales to Dinosaurs: The Story of Roy Chapman Andrews*. New York: St. Martin's Press, 1976.

AUDUBON

Adams, Alexander B. *John James Audubon*. New York: G. P. Putnam's Sons, 1966.

*Ford, Alice, ed. *Audubon By Himself*. Garden City: Natural History Press, 1969.

Herrick, Francis. *Audubon the Naturalist*. 2 vols. New York: D. Appleton and Co., 1917.

*McDermott, John Francis, ed. *Up the Missouri with Audubon*. Norman: University of Oklahoma Press, 1951.

BAILEY

*Bailey, Liberty Hyde. *How Plants Got Their Names*. New York: Dover, 1963.

Dorf, Philip. *Liberty Hyde Bailey*. Ithaca: Cornell University Press, 1956.

BARTRAM

Benson, Adolph B., ed. *Peter Kalm's Travels in North America*. New York: Dover, 1987.

Berkeley, Edmund, and Dorothy Smith Berkeley. *The Life and Travels of John Bartram*. Tallahassee: University of Florida Press, 1982.

*Sanger, Marjory S. *Billy Bartram and His Green World*. New York: Farrar, Straus & Giroux, 1972.

Van Doren, Mark, ed. *The Travels of William Bartram*. New York: Facsimile Library, 1940.

BENNETT

Brink, Wellington. *Big Hugh*. New York: Macmillan, 1951.

BURBANK

Burbank, Luther, with Wilbur Hall. *The Harvest of Years*. Boston: Houghton Mifflin, 1927.

Dreyer, Peter. *A Gardener Touched with Genius*. Berkeley: University of California Press, 1985.

BURROUGHS

Barrus, Clara. *The Life and Letters of John Burroughs*. 2 vols. Boston: Houghton Mifflin, 1924.

———. *Our Friend John Burroughs*. Boston: Houghton Mifflin, 1914.

Burroughs, John. *In the Catskills*. Boston: Houghton Mifflin, 1910.

———. *Under the Apple Tree*. Boston: Houghton Mifflin, 1916.

Westbrook, Perry O. *John Burroughs*. New York: Twayne, 1974.

*Wiley, Farida A., ed. *John Burroughs' America: Selections from His Writings*. New York: Devin-Adair, 1951.

CARSON

Brooks, Paul. *The House of Life: Rachel Carson at Work*. Boston: G. K. Hall, 1985.

*Carson, Rachel. *The Edge of the Sea*. Boston: Houghton Mifflin, 1955.

*———. *The Sea Around Us*. New York: Oxford University Press, 1954.

*———. With photographs by Charles Pratt and others. *The Sense of Wonder*. New York: Harper & Row, 1965.

*———. *Silent Spring*. Boston: Houghton Mifflin, 1962.

*———. *Under the Sea Wind*. New York: Oxford University Press, 1941.

Gartner, Carol. *Rachel Carson*. New York: Frederick Ungar, 1983.

Graham, Frank. *Since Silent Spring*. Boston: Houghton Mifflin, 1970.

CARVER

Eliot, Lawrence. *George Washington Carver*. Englewood Cliffs: Prentice-Hall, 1967.

Holt, Rackham. *George Washington Carver*. New York: Doubleday, Doran, 1944.

*Means, Florence. *Carver's George*. Cambridge: Riverside Press, 1952.

COUSTEAU

*Cousteau, Jacques, with James Dugan. *The Living Sea*. New York: Harper & Row, 1962.

*Cousteau, Jacques, with Frederic Dumas. *The Silent World*. New York: Harper & Row, 1953.

Dugan, James. *Undersea Explorer: The Life of Captain Cousteau*. New York: Harper & Row, 1957.

Madsen, Axel. *Cousteau*. New York: Beaufort, 1986.

DARWIN

*Barlow, Nora, ed. *The Autobiography of Charles Darwin*. New York: W. W. Norton, 1958.

Clark, Ronald W. *The Survival of Charles Darwin*. New York: Random House, 1984.

*Cole, Sonia. *Animal Ancestors*. New York: E. P. Dutton, 1964.

Darwin, Charles. *The Origin of Species and the Descent of Man*. New York: Modern Library, n.d.

Darwin, Francis, ed. *The Autobiography of Charles Darwin and Selected Letters*. New York: Dover, 1958.

De Beer, Gavin. *Charles Darwin*. Garden City: Doubleday, 1964.

Irvine, William. *Apes, Angels & Victorians: Darwin, Huxley & Evolution*. New York: McGraw-Hill, 1955.

*Moorehead, Alan. *Darwin and the* Beagle. New York: Harper & Row, 1969.

FABRE

Bucknell, Percy F. *The Human Side of Fabre*. New York: Century, 1923.

Fabre, Augustin. *The Life of Jean Henri Fabre*. New York: Dodd, Mead, 1921.

*Fabre, Jean Henri. *The Life of the Fly*. New York: Dodd, Mead, 1920.

HUMBOLDT

De Terra, Helmut. *The Life and Times of Alexander von Humboldt*. New York: Knopf, 1955.

*Meadows, Jack. *The Great Scientists*. New York: Oxford University Press, 1987.

LEOPOLD

Flader, Susan. *Thinking Like a Mountain*. Columbia: University of Missouri Press, 1974.

*Leopold, Aldo. *A Sand County Almanac and Sketches Here and There*. New York: Oxford University Press, 1987.

Meine, Curt. *Aldo Leopold: His Life and His Work*. Madison: University of Wisconsin Press, 1988.

Tanner, Thomas, ed. *Aldo Leopold: The Man and His Legacy*. Ankery, Iowa: Soil Conservation Society of America, 1987.

LINNAEUS

*Dickinson, Alice. *Carl Linnaeus*. New York: Franklin Watts, 1967.

Jackson, Benjamin D. *Linnaeus*. London: Witherby, 1923.

Peattie, Donald Culross. *Green Laurels*. Garden City: Garden City Publishing Co., 1938.

MUIR

*Clark, Margaret Goff. *John Muir*. Champaign: Garrard, 1974.

Clarke, James M. *The Life and Adventures of John Muir*. San Francisco: Sierra Club, 1980.

Muir, John. *The Story of My Boyhood and Youth*. Boston: Houghton Mifflin, 1913.

OLMSTED

Roper, Laura Wood. *FLO: A Biography of Frederick Law Olmsted*. Baltimore: Johns Hopkins University Press, 1973.

Stevenson, Elizabeth. *Park Maker: A Life of Frederick Law Olmsted*. New York: Macmillan, 1977.

Todd, John Emerson. *Frederick Law Olmsted*. Boston: Twayne, 1982.

PINCHOT

Pinchot, Gifford. *Breaking New Ground*. Seattle: University of Washington Press, 1947.

Pinkett, Harold T. *Gifford Pinchot: Public and Private Forester*. Urbana: University of Illinois Press, 1970.

POWELL

Rabbitt, Mary C. *John Wesley Powell: Soldier, Explorer, Scientist*. Washington: U.S. Geological Survey, 1969.

Terrell, John U. *The Man Who Rediscovered America: A Biography of John Wesley Powell*. New York: Weybright and Talley, 1969.

Watson, Elmo Scott. *The Professor Goes West*. Bloomington: Illinois Wesleyan Press, 1959.

RODALE

Jackson, Carlton. *J. I. Rodale: Apostle of Non-Conformity*. New York: Pyramid, 1974.

Rodale, J. I. *Autobiography*. Emmaus, Pa.: Rodale Press, 1965.

ROOSEVELT

Cutright, Paul Russell. *Theodore Roosevelt: The Making of a Naturalist*. Urbana: University of Illinois Press, 1985.

Morris, Edmund. *The Rise of Theodore Roosevelt*. New York: Coward, McCann & Geoghegan, 1979.

Roosevelt, Theodore. *Theodore Roosevelt: An Autobiography*. New York: Charles Scribner's Sons, 1920.

THOREAU

*Boda, Carl, ed. *The Portable Thoreau*. New York: Viking, 1947.

Harding, Walter. *The Days of Henry Thoreau*. New York: Knopf, 1967.

Krutch, Joseph Wood. *Henry David Thoreau*. New York: William Sloan Associates, 1948.

Schneider, Richard J. *Henry David Thoreau*. Boston: Twayne, 1987.

Thomas, Owen, ed. *Thoreau's Walden*. New York: W. W. Norton, 1966.

WALLACE

Brooks, John Langdon. *Just Before the Origin: Alfred Russel Wallace's Theory of Evolution*. New York: Columbia University Press, 1984.

Fichman, Martin. *Alfred Russel Wallace*. Boston: Twayne, 1981.

George, Wilma. *Biologist Philosopher*. New York: Abelard-Schuman, 1964.

Marchant, James, ed. *Alfred Russel Wallace: Letters and Reminiscences*. London: Cassell, 1916.

Wallace, Alfred Russel. *My Life*. 2 vols. London: Chapman and Hall, 1916.

WHITE

Emden, Cecil S. *Gilbert White in His Village*. New York: Oxford University Press, 1956.

Mabey, Richard. *Gilbert White*. London: Century, 1986.

Massingham, H. J., ed. *The Essential Gilbert White of Selborne*. Boston: David R. Godine, 1985.

White, Gilbert. *The Natural History of Selborne*. New York: Dutton, 1976.

Index